The Doctor Calling

Meredith Appleyard lives in the Clare Valley wine-growing region of South Australia. As a registered nurse and midwife, she has worked in a wide range of country health practice settings, including the Royal Flying Doctor Service. When she isn't writing, Meredith is reading, helping organise the annual Clare Readers and Writers Festival, or at home with her husband and her border collie, Lily. *The Doctor Calling* is her second novel.

meredithappleyard.com.au

ALSO BY MEREDITH APPLEYARD

The Country Practice

Meredith Appleyard

The Doctor Calling

MICHAEL JOSEPH
an imprint of
PENGUIN BOOKS

MICHAEL JOSEPH

UK | USA | Canada | Ireland | Australia
India | New Zealand | South Africa | China

Penguin Books is part of the Penguin Random House group of companies
whose addresses can be found at global.penguinrandomhouse.com.

Penguin
Random House
Australia

First published by Penguin Group (Australia), 2016

1 3 5 7 9 10 8 6 4 2

Text copyright © Meredith Appleyard 2016

The moral right of the author has been asserted.

Design by Grace West © Penguin Group (Australia)
Cover photographs: female by Roger Richter/Corbis; hospital background by lenetstan/
Shutterstock; rural landscape by robertharding/Corbis; male by Dean Pictures/Corbis;
sky by vichie81/Shutterstock; stethescope by piotr_pabijan/Shutterstock.
Typeset in 11pt/18pt Sabon by Grace West, Penguin Group (Australia)
Colour separation by Splitting Image Colour Studio, Clayton, Victoria
Printed and bound in Australia by Griffin Press, an accredited
ISO AS/NZS 14001 Environmental Management Systems printer.

National Library of Australia
Cataloguing-in-Publication data:

Appleyard, Meredith, author.
Doctor at heart / Meredith Appleyard.
9780143797173 (paperback)
Love stories, Australian.
Medical fiction.

A823.4

penguin.com.au

To have joy, one must share it.

Lord Byron

Chapter 1

The blind went up with a snap. Laura peered through the blurry glass into the narrow strip of blue sky between the verandah and the tangled native hibiscus. The morning was clear. No excuse to go back to bed and renege on the day's exercise. Ten minutes later she was dressed and stretched, and letting herself quietly through the galvanised-iron gate that connected her yard with her neighbour's.

As usual the sleek black-and-tan dog was straining on his chain, tail wagging. Freed at last, he danced around her like she was a maypole and then took off down the driveway to wait by the rusty front gate. Together they stepped out onto the deserted street. Wheelie bins were lined up alongside the kerb, beads of dew sparkling on their lids. In the distance she heard the discordant morning song of the galahs, the rumble of the garbage truck and the grumble of a road train on the highway.

Laura walked towards the end of the street, gradually increasing her speed until she was jogging past the aging fibro houses and the occasional stone cottage so much like her own. The spring air was sweet and damp, the gardens ranged from manicured lawns and precision-pruned roses to unkempt messes of weeds and straggly geranium bushes. The houses petered out and, just past the Potters Junction area school, the bitumen ended and gave way to gravel. Here, paddocks dotted with low scrub and saltbush stretched to the horizon, fading into the bruised shadows of the Flinders Ranges. Laura settled into the six-kilometre run and let her mind wander, the kelpie loping along beside her.

Usually the running helped ground her, helped her start the day on a positive note. She found the vast emptiness, the silence and the stillness, soothing to her soul. The vibration of each footfall reassured her, the rhythmic slap of her thick braid against her back comforted her. She smiled, reflecting on that first morning a couple of months back when she'd barely made it past the school before her lungs had felt about to burst. Every breath had burned like fire, and her legs had been jelly. She had come a long way from the physical and emotional wreck she'd been then. There was a way to go yet, but the worst was behind her.

After about fifteen minutes Laura reached up to adjust the sweatband. The dog, tongue lolling, didn't miss a beat. He knew better than to show more than a passing interest in the few sheep grazing amongst the saltbush. Within her sights, Laura made out the clump of scrubby vegetation that bordered a tight bend in the road. The outside sweep of the bend dropped away into a rocky ditch. Her halfway mark, three kilometres from home, where she turned to retrace her steps back along the gravel road.

'Come on, boy,' she challenged, increasing her speed as they neared the bend. She fumbled in her pocket for her phone, nodded with satisfaction at the time. Feeling alive, and glad that she was, she focussed on the beat of her feet hitting the ground, the morning air fresh and cool against her skin.

And then with a shriek she was lunging for the verge, sliding feet-first down the embankment and screaming for the dog as a massive black motorbike thundered past in a spray of dust and gravel.

The dust settled with the silence. Shaken, Laura clambered to her feet, testing each limb. A breeze fizzed across her skin. She shivered, brushed at the dirt and scrambled back up onto the road, calling for the dog. He'd vanished. She limped along the middle of the road, spitting out grit and trying to keep the rising panic from her voice as she called for the dog.

Her head jerked around when she heard a low growl. The motorbike had done a U-turn and was moving slowly back towards her. The bike was almost alongside her when something burst from the saltbush, a glistening streak in motion. With a startled yelp, Laura jumped back as a rabbit, ears flat, followed closely by the dog, raced past her.

'You come here, Skip,' she cried, but the dog was sliding under a fence on his belly and into the paddock, the gap widening between him and his prey.

The rider pulled onto the verge and stopped. Angry colour surged into Laura's cheeks. She spun around to glare at him, frustrated when she couldn't penetrate the visor of the tinted full-face helmet. He was covered from neck to toe in black leather riding gear.

'Have you got a death wish or something?' She gave a sweep of her arm in the direction the dog had taken. 'You could have killed us, as well as yourself! This early there are roos along here, emus, stray stock – humans and dogs, even.'

She planted her hands on her hips, waiting while he kicked down the side stand, swung a leg over the bike. Finger by finger he worked off his leather gloves and dropped them onto the petrol tank, and then eased off the helmet, resting it on the seat. He raked tanned fingers through straight, black hair matted to his forehead. At least a day's worth of stubble shadowed his jaw. His eyes were red-rimmed and road-weary.

'Are you hurt?' he said, his voice as gravelly as the road.

'No, I'm not.' She took a step back and stared at him. He was tall, over six feet, and filled out the leathers with solid, hard muscle.

'I really am sorry. I didn't expect anyone to be out here at this hour.' He frowned, moved towards her. 'You *are* hurt,' he said, gesturing towards her left leg.

She glanced down and sucked in a quick breath when she saw the oozing mess on the outside of her thigh. Preoccupied with finding the dog, she hadn't noticed the scrape.

'Ouch,' she muttered, as with tentative fingers she brushed away some of the loose particles of dirt and felt the sting of the wound for the first time.

'I've got a rudimentary first-aid kit in my gear pack if you need.'

She swallowed, pushing through an unexpected wave of nausea and light-headedness. He stepped closer, stopped when she held up her hand. 'I'm all right. It's only gravel rash. I can clean it up and put a dressing on it when I get home.'

'You don't look all right. You're white as a sheet. Do you want to come and sit on the bike, put your head down for a minute?'

'No, thanks. And trust me, I'd know if I wasn't okay. The tumble just shook me up a bit.' The words came out croakily and she cleared her throat.

'Do you want some water?' He went to the gear pack on his bike, unzipped it and proffered a bottle of water.

'Thank you.' She cracked the lid's seal and took a long swallow. 'That's better,' she said and swiped the back of her hand across her mouth.

'I can give you a ride home if you like.'

She looked from him to the bike with its bulky luggage. 'Thanks, but there's the dog.'

He watched her, his expression inscrutable, and then lifted his broad shoulders. 'Suit yourself.'

The dog came back, contrite, panting, and pressed himself against Laura's shins. She leaned into him, her legs still wobbly.

'We're out here every morning, so please do watch out next time you're passing through,' she said, reaching down to scratch the dog behind his ears.

Skip licked her hand and, forgiven, trotted over to the rider to sniff at his boots, and then the bike's tyres. Laura straightened up. Her skin bristled with goose bumps as the wind picked up and she rubbed at her arms.

'Are you sure there's nothing I can do?' He glanced at the bike. 'Can I phone for someone to come and pick you up?'

'It's all right. I have a phone.' Her hands plunged into the pockets of her shorts, came out empty. 'I *did* have a phone . . . it must have fallen out of my pocket when I fell.' She hurried back along the road to where she'd gone over the edge.

The rider followed her. The dog trotted along beside him, looked up at him, grinned. Laura was about to clamber down the short but steep incline when he touched her on the shoulder. 'You stay put. I'll look,' he said. In two sliding strides he was down the embankment and picking through the rubble.

From her vantage point, Laura decided his hair was a russet brown, not black as she'd first thought. He was more rugged than classically handsome. Deep grooves bracketed a wide mouth, the firm set of his chin suggesting stubbornness, and she suspected he didn't smile easily, or often.

He dropped to his haunches and moments later called, 'Found it.' Next thing he was beside her, wiping the dust off the phone with his hand and passing it back. 'Couple of scratches but otherwise intact,' he said and raised his eyebrows. 'See if it still works.'

She turned it on, reassured when the screen burst into life. Laura keyed in her code and tapped the screen several times. 'It works,' she said, and slipped the phone into her pocket. Relieved, she reached up to tuck a few wayward strands of hair under the sweatband.

'Anyway, thanks for pulling over to help, and for finding my phone,' she said, squinting into the sunshine. 'Not everyone would have bothered to stop.'

'Make sure you get something onto that gravel rash,' he said. He looked like he was going to say something more but then, thinking better of it, he turned and walked back to the bike.

She hurried to keep up. His leathers creaked as he moved and she wrinkled her nose at the intrinsic animal smell. His profile was unyielding and the flicker of attraction she felt for the stranger caught her off guard. But then he eased on his helmet, and slipped into anonymity behind the darkened visor. Strong fingers slid into the leather gloves and he swung onto the bike. The engine roared to life and he tipped his hand to the helmet in a brief salute before easing the powerful machine onto the road and pulling away.

From where she stood she watched him until all she could see was a smudge of dust. They hadn't even exchanged names. She sighed and raised her arms, rolled her head from side to side, fighting the stiffness rapidly settling into her back and limbs. The gravel rash on her thigh bit as she flexed.

'Skip?' she called, and the dog appeared. 'Let's go home,' she said, and he took off in the direction of Potters Junction. She followed, walking slowly and stiffly at first. As she warmed up, her legs loosened and the bite from the gravel rash receded with each step.

Chapter 2

Jake Finlay knew his father was expecting him, sometime. Ever since that day twenty years ago, Jake made a point of being hard to pin down. His sister Jess always knew where he was, but that was because she kept in touch, not because he did. So his showing up unannounced before eight in the morning wasn't likely to surprise his father.

'Dad.' Jake shook the outstretched hand, hoped his shock didn't show as he took in the gaunt face, the almost hairless pate, the dressing-gown hanging like a loose sack from the wasted frame. Neill Finlay looked old, tired and very, very sick.

'It's been nearly four years, boy,' Neill said and Jake winced at the reproach in his voice.

'That long?' he muttered, and stepped across the threshold, bag slung over one shoulder. 'Town still looks the same.'

He hadn't been able to resist a lap of the main drag on his way in. There'd been no-one about. He'd seen the daily newspapers stacked outside the newsagency, a lonesome car and a shopping trolley marooned in the middle of the hotel car park and, when he'd lifted his visor, he'd smelled the aroma of baking bread. No, nothing had changed. It could have been four days, not four years, since he'd been home.

Neill grunted. 'The town has seen some hard times. There're only two banks left and there's talk one of them will go. The Commercial Hotel closed a couple of years back, the hardware shop hangs on by a thread. If you get sick you're pretty much buggered. The hospital's still open, but you can't have an operation or a baby there anymore. Milt Burns is the only GP in town.'

'Right,' Jake said. All good reasons not to live here. He followed Neill down the passage to the kitchen. The carpet runner was threadbare, the framed prints on the walls faded. In the kitchen there was an open newspaper, a cup, a teapot and a crumb-strewn plate on the small, laminex table. The air smelled of burned toast.

'How are you?' Jake asked, dropping his gear pack onto the floor and shoving it into the corner with one booted foot.

Neill lifted bony shoulders. 'As well as can be expected. I suppose Jess has filled you in?'

'She emails me from time to time. She said you were sick.'

Guilt hollowed his gut as he tried to recall the exact details of Jess's earlier emails, but couldn't. In her recent messages the urgency behind her insistence that he come home to visit had finally penetrated. It was the reason he was here now.

'What does the doctor say?'

'Not much more he can say,' Neill said. He busied himself filling the electric kettle and getting out another mug. 'Now then, son, tea or coffee?'

Jake's lips thinned. From the clipped tone of his father's voice the subject of his health wasn't open for discussion. 'Coffee's good, thanks. Black, strong, two sugars.'

'Toast?'

'Maybe later. Coffee first.'

Neill spooned coffee into a drab ceramic mug Jake recognised from a lifetime ago.

'Surely you didn't ride all the way from Melbourne overnight?'

He shook his head, unzipped his jacket and slipped it off. Throwing it on top of the bag, he sat down at the kitchen table. 'I stayed with a mate in Adelaide and got up early this morning.'

'It must have been an early rise.' Neill freshened his tea from the pot and sat down opposite his son, pushing aside the newspaper. Jake picked up the coffee and took a sip. He screwed up his face, reached across the table and grabbed the coffee jar from the counter, spooning in another heaped teaspoon of instant coffee. Neill raised his eyebrows. Jake shrugged and took another sip.

'So,' Neill said, sweeping the toast crumbs on his plate into a neat pile with his finger. 'How are *you*?'

'Good.'

Silence hovered. Like it always did. Another uncomfortable silence to add to the preceding twenty years' worth of uncomfortable silences. Jake felt the old man's assessing gaze. He shifted in his seat.

'You look thinner,' Neill said, ignoring the irony of the comment, how thin he was himself.

'I might have lost a couple of kilos. Work has been hectic. I was careless and got a dose of gastro before I left Istanbul.'

'Istanbul, so that's where you've been.'

'Yeah. We're working on a documentary about the refugee crisis.'

Neill nodded but Jake knew he probably wouldn't have a clue. Neill Finlay's life had consisted of Potters Junction and farming.

A gate slammed, metal on metal, and there was the sound of a dog's playful yip followed by the husky murmur of a vaguely familiar female voice. Jake's body tensed. It couldn't be *her*. He glanced at the old man, who rose awkwardly to his feet and shuffled across the kitchen.

'That'll be Laura, my neighbour. She takes the dog for a run.'

It was her. Jake sat back and folded his arms. Laura. So that was her name.

'Hello, Neill! Are you up and about?'

'In the kitchen,' Neill called and Jake heard the back door open and seconds later the dog bounded into the kitchen.

Neill smoothed his hand over the dog's velvety black head, mumbled a few gentle words and the animal plonked itself down on the floor with its tail thumping. The back door snapped shut. From where he was sitting Jake had a clear view to the kitchen door and he held his breath as she came into the kitchen. She handed Neill a bulging paper bag, the chemist's logo emblazoned on the front. She was lean, taller than average, wearing short shorts from which emerged legs that went on forever, and then some. He'd noticed that out on the road earlier.

She'd taken off the sweatband, and wispy curls of chestnut-coloured hair framed her face. He knew if she turned around there'd be a thick braid of hair hanging down her back. That was another fact he hadn't missed out there on the road. That and the reality that he could have killed her. Breath hissed out through his nose. After months of driving in developing countries, he'd let himself become complacent on the quiet South Australian country roads. His gaze flicked briefly to the open wound on her thigh, and then back to her face. Jake knew the moment she saw him, and recognised him. Her blue eyes widened when they latched on to his. Colour flared across her cheekbones. She was distracted but only for seconds. She blinked, turned to Neill.

'I won't stay,' she said. 'I haven't even changed yet but I wanted to bring you the scripts I picked up yesterday afternoon. I thought you might need them this morning.' Jake suspected she'd had every intention of staying until she'd clapped eyes on him.

'Thanks, lass.' Neill opened the bag and peered in and then dropped it onto the kitchen bench.

Jake cleared his throat and his father started, as if he'd forgotten his recently returned son.

'Oh, Laura, before you go you must meet my son, Jake Finlay. He's ridden across from Melbourne.' He turned to Jake. 'Jake, this is Laura O'Connor, my neighbour.'

Jake stepped out from the table and leaned towards her, extended his hand. 'Hello, Laura O'Connor, nice to meet you.' He grasped the cool, slim hand. Her grip was firm.

'Hello,' she said.

Laura glanced from son to father. Jake felt his muscles tighten. He was ready for her to condemn him for what had happened barely an hour earlier. How his reckless inattention could have killed her. But it didn't come.

'Neill, I didn't know you had a son,' she said, tugging her fingers to release them from his grip.

'Sorry,' he mumbled, letting go.

'He doesn't come home very often,' Neill said. The words held no censure and Jake felt suddenly worse for his long absences. He could feel Laura watching him and he quelled the sudden and irrational desire to explain to her why he'd stayed away.

'Sure you won't have a cuppa? It's no trouble,' Neill said, reaching for an extra cup.

'No, really, I'd better go.' Laura was already backing out of the room. 'I'll let you visit with your son. Shall I take Skip outside?' she said. 'The gates are shut.'

'Thanks, lass.'

She was gone, the dog at her heels and the door slamming in her wake.

Jake squared his shoulders and stared at the spot where she'd been standing seconds before. He could have sworn some of the light left the room with her.

Neill, clean cup still in his hand, had a bemused expression on his face. 'Laura brings the dog back from their run and generally stays for a cup of tea.'

'She probably had other things to do today, Dad. Maybe I will have some toast now.'

Neill put the cup away and dropped two slices of bread into the toaster.

Laura closed Neill's back door with more force than she realised, wincing when it slammed. As if pursued, she hurried across his barren yard and through the gate, stopping only when she reached the sanctuary of her own home.

Neill Finlay had a son. An attractive son. All six-foot-plus of him, who had her heart pounding in a way she'd forgotten. Braced against the kitchen sink she looked out onto the verandah where the pots were lined up, freshly filled with potting mix ready for the parsley, coriander and basil to be planted. Taking steady, deep breaths, she imagined the full-grown herbs, lush and fragrant, while she waited for her heart rate to settle.

Since she'd moved into her great-aunt's rundown house in

Potters Junction two months earlier, a tentative friendship had blossomed between Laura and her elderly neighbour. Neill was dying. Slowly, painfully, metastatic cancer cells were overwhelming his liver and his lungs. He'd been diagnosed two years ago. Not only had the surgery to remove the primary tumours in his bowel failed, but the chemotherapy that followed had done little to slow the progression of the disease. It had left him frail but resolutely clinging on to life.

Laura, on the other hand, was coming back to life after loss and grief had left her bruised and bewildered. She was getting her appetite back, putting on weight, beginning to look forward, finding pleasure again in simple things.

Because of his failing health Neill hadn't been able to exercise his dog. Skip's incessant barking had the neighbours talking, making all kinds of threats, and when Laura had heard them she'd offered to take him along on her runs. Having the dog waiting gave added impetus to get out of bed on the mornings when it would have been easier to pull the covers over her head and let the world go by without her. But, over the weeks, she'd grown fond of the dying man and his dog. And now, here was his son. She frowned at her reflection in the kitchen window.

Laura had met Jess, Neill's daughter, several times. Jess, with her two young sons, visited her father regularly and Laura had first met them on one such visit. She was married to a farmer and they lived on the Finlay family property about fifteen kilometres south of the town, on the road to Magpie Creek. When Neill spoke about the farm, as he often did, it was with despondency. Reading between the lines Laura suspected the son-in-law fell short of Neill's expectations as a farmer, and Jess probably bore the brunt of disappointment from both sides.

But Neill had never spoken of a son so meeting Jake Finlay had been a surprise. Jake's resemblance to his sister was unquestionable. The same hazel-coloured eyes, the shape of their noses, the stubborn tilt of their chins. His resemblance to his father? Not so much, but then Jake's features were firm where his father's had been ravaged by time and disease. Laura's frown deepened as she remembered the feel of Jake's palm against hers. The warm, strong fingers that had gripped her hand for longer than necessary when they'd been formally introduced. She shivered, rubbed at the skin on her bare arms. She was cold, that was all.

After a hot shower and a change of clothes, Laura was warm again. She cleaned and dressed the gravel rash with a non-adherent dressing, feeling infinitely better for it.

She filled the kettle and dragged out the prehistoric toaster. It wasn't long before the yeasty smell of toasting bread filled the kitchen and made her mouth water. She spread the thick slices of fruit toast with a generous layer of butter, grateful her appetite had returned. The bathroom scales told her she was on the way back to a healthy weight, even if she could still count her ribs in the mirror.

As she ate, Laura pondered the day ahead, mentally planning her relentless schedule. She would start with more work in the garden, then pull up the carpet in the front room in readiness to sand and seal the floorboards below. Then, if she had the time and energy, she'd start sorting through the junk in the back sheds. When she fell into bed physically exhausted each night, Laura found that she slept, rather than lying awake, staring into the darkness and thinking, remembering . . . It was a solution to the sleeplessness and it worked, most nights.

★

When they'd typically run out of things to say, and Jake's jaw was aching from yawning so much, Neill showed him to the spare bedroom. They walked down the hallway of the two-bedroom fibro house, floorboards creaking underfoot. Jake's memory of the house had been vague – he'd stayed there for a single night on a whirlwind stopover four years before. It had been another visit his sister Jess had talked him into, for the occasion of Neill's seventieth birthday.

'There's a spare pillow and blanket in the wardrobe. Shower if you want to. You remember where the bathroom is.'

Jake muttered his thanks, tucked the proffered towel and scratchy face washer under his arm.

'Good to have you home, boy,' Neill said, pulling the bedroom door closed as he left.

Jake dropped his gear onto the floor beside the single bed and sighed. He was shattered, every muscle ached. He'd spent over three hours on the road this morning, on top of yesterday's ride from Melbourne. Breaking the trip with an overnight stay at a mate's place had been a sensible idea, but after a beer turned into a few beers he'd been lucky to get four hours' sleep.

Too tired to shower, he shucked off his boots, pulled off the leather trousers and dropped onto the thin mattress, rubbing at his gritty eyes with the back of a hand. He told himself he'd feel more positive about being there after some shut-eye.

But sleep wouldn't come although his body screamed with exhaustion. The orange chenille bedspread smelled of dust and mothballs, and looked and felt a lot like the one he'd had at the farm all those years ago. He ran his fingertips back and forth across the nubbly surface, remembered doing the same as a child. He threw an arm over his eyes, pressed them shut. White spots danced behind his eyelids, his heart thundered.

All that caffeine . . . and the fact he was back in his home town after vowing to himself he'd never return.

He forced himself to lie there for an hour but tossed and turned, his mind buzzing with memories. He relived the day he'd come home from school to find his mother gone, his father silent, stoic. No explanation had been given. Jess had cried, refused to go to school for the rest of the week. Jake had been hurt and angry. He'd tried to understand why, but couldn't. Until the day came when he'd realised he had to get out of Potters Junction. He had, and he'd left behind two hurt and angry people, and no explanation. He groaned out loud, couldn't believe he was in Potters Junction *again*. But Jess's email had said that this might be their final opportunity to be together as a family. Neill's sallow skin, the gaunt cheeks and the line of pills and potions on the kitchen windowsill all hinted at the same conclusion. Jake'd have to be blind as well as stupid to miss that something serious was going on with the old man. His sister had probably been right to pressure him.

For a moment he wished he'd returned of his own volition, that, for once in his life, he'd done the right thing without being prompted. But he'd be lying. His single-minded sister was the only reason he was there.

He rolled onto his side and punched at the musty pillow. Skip barked, a car door slammed, he heard a woman's voice.

Laura O'Connor. The name flitted through his consciousness. He punched at the pillow again and wondered what her story was. Neill hadn't said much, only that she had moved into the stone cottage next door in the middle of winter, and she lived alone. He couldn't imagine why she would have *willingly* exiled herself in a place like Potters Junction.

Jake gave up all pretence of sleep, lifted his legs over the edge of the bed and sat up. Rasping fingers across a day-old beard, he pondered Laura O'Connor's legs. She looked good in running gear. They were nice legs, the kind he wouldn't mind getting between, in another time and another place. He stood up and yawned, ran both hands through his hair.

Nice legs or not, he wouldn't be around long enough to do anything other than admire them and wonder.

Chapter 3

Jess Phillips waved her sons Sam and Mikey off on the school bus and trudged back along the pothole-ridden driveway. The brilliant morning sunshine highlighted everything that was wrong with the shabby farmhouse, which had been her home since the day she was born. The little paint that remained was peeling, the gutters sagged and the roof was pocked with rust. On the plus side, her rose bushes were bursting with blooms and the tomato seedlings she'd planted the week before were looking perky in their bed of pea straw.

The dogs barked. They were still in their pen. Jess's pace quickened on a spurt of anger. It was her husband Darren's job to see to the dogs first thing. He'd been up before her; the smell of bacon lingered in the kitchen when she'd risen to get the boys up and off to school. Now a quick scan of the farmyard confirmed his vehicle wasn't there. When she'd asked the night before what he had on his schedule for the next day, he'd given her a sullen look and stalked off to bed. She had no idea where he was or what he was doing.

Hungry and manic after a night of confinement, the two dogs nearly knocked her off her feet in their rush to get through the gate. She threw several scoops of dry food into their tray and topped up the water bucket.

Sam had already let the chooks out and collected the eggs. Jess's eldest son was dark-haired, serious and studious. He reminded Jess so much of herself at that age.

She'd come to rely on Sam more than she sometimes felt was fair. She had to remind herself he was only ten. Mikey was six, blond and blue-eyed, the spitting image of Darren. Mikey worshipped his father, followed him around like a shadow, and dreamed of being a farmer when he grew up. It was a bittersweet thought.

Being a farmer had been a dream come true for her childhood sweetheart Darren Phillips and, when they were first married, Jess had been optimistic that his enthusiasm would go some way to make up for his ineptitude. But over the years his enthusiasm had waned, his proficiency hadn't improved and her optimism had dwindled.

While her father had been fit enough to keep a handle on the farm all things had run relatively smoothly. But then Neill had lost weight, had started complaining of feeling fatigued all the time. When he kept losing weight and started feeling short of breath Jess forced him into seeing Milt Burns, and the rest was history. Now her father was dying. Each time Jess visited him she noticed he was doing less around the house. He'd given up on the pitiful garden weeks ago, and his ute sat silently in the garage.

While Jess was struggling to keep the household in order and her father comfortable, her husband did the barest minimum around the property. Darren spent more and more time away from the place, a big chunk of it at the pub in town. The farm, the product of a lifetime of her father's commitment, was dying alongside Neill.

And where had Jake been when all this had been going down?

Somewhere else, that's where. Long ago Jess had realised that the anger she felt towards him for always leaving everything to her – his younger sister, for crying out loud! – was a waste of energy. If he hadn't left, she and the boys would never have had those holidays to Darwin and Bali, paid for by Jake. The trips were his way of seeing his sister and his nephews without returning to South Australia. Why he'd stayed away she'd never understood, and no matter how often she asked, he always fobbed her off. It still hurt that he'd rather be risking his life in some strife-ridden country than living here with his family.

But he *was* coming home, sometime this week. Jess felt no remorse for using emotional blackmail to get him back to town. Even if he only stayed for a few days there were decisions that needed to be made – most pressingly, they needed to talk about the farm. The land was freehold, which was how she'd been able to hang on as long as she had. They would never have managed had there been a mortgage. When Neill's secondary cancer had been diagnosed, he had updated his will. Jess knew what was in it. Regardless of her anxieties about her family's future, she was glad Neill hadn't written Jake out altogether. Her brother didn't deserve that, no matter what had happened to make Jake hate the place so much. Throughout their childhood, he'd worked hard on the farm on weekends and school holidays. As soon as he'd been tall enough to reach the pedals in the ute, strong enough to heft the bales of hay for the sheep, old enough to realise he had no real choice, Jake had been there beside his father.

Part of her envied him for escaping all those years ago, and some days she tried to imagine what her life would have been if she'd packed her bags and walked away like Jake had. But until her father died, she would pretend everything was all right. And the failing farm would continue to be a noose around her neck, slowly strangling the life out of her.

Jess scraped the bottom of the pellet bin and topped up the feeder, the chooks milling about her feet, a sea of brown and white. They'd have to survive on grain screenings and scraps when the pellet bin was empty. There was no more credit at the fodder place until they paid their bill. Oblivious now to the clear, blue sky, the singing birds, the perfect spring morning, Jess traipsed back to the house and tried not to let herself be swamped by despair.

By lunchtime when there was still no sign of her errant husband, Jess put the dogs back in the pen and drove into Potters Junction. There was grocery shopping to do and the mail to pick up, plus she needed to check in on her father. Some days were harder for him than others. If that took her until school was out, she'd fetch the boys and take them to say hello to their poppa.

The Foodland supermarket was almost deserted and Jess whipped around the aisles, grateful not to meet anyone she knew who'd look at her with a dozen questions on their lips and pity in their eyes. In a town the size of Potters Junction people knew everyone else's business. Everyone would have noticed that Darren's ute was parked way too often in the hotel car park. It was probably parked there now. Jess flexed her fingers on the handle of the shopping trolley. She tried to swallow around the ache in her throat, forced herself to focus on what was left on her shopping list.

'How goes it, Jess?' Melanie asked at the checkout as she packed Jess's meagre groceries into bags. There was no avoiding old school mates. 'How are those boys? How's your dad?'

'All good. Dad's still managing on his own.'

'Such a shame about his illness, the poor old bugger. Cancer, there's a lot of it about. Why, only the other day —'

'Thanks, Melanie,' Jess said, stretching the smile wider. She shoved her credit card into her purse and picked up the bags of groceries. 'See you next time.'

'Give my regards to your father,' Melanie called, just as the automatic doors closed behind Jess.

'Yeah, sure,' she muttered. There was nothing stopping Melanie, or anyone else for that matter, dropping in to see Neill and giving him their regards face to face. But did they? It irked Jess that her father had lived all his life in the district and, now that he was sick and dying, no-one could be bothered to visit him and say hello. Where was everyone's sense of community? Wasn't that what small towns were supposed to be good at?

Unable to stop herself, Jess did a lap of the town on her way to her father's place. She drove at a crawl past the hotel but didn't see Darren's ute. She wasn't sure if she was relieved or more worried. If he wasn't at the pub, where was he?

She pushed down her dread. Minutes later she was parking her clapped-out Honda Civic at the kerb of her father's place when she saw Jake's motorbike in the carport. Her heart gave a little tattoo of joy. He was here. The band around her chest shifted, eased. Jess leaped out of the car, slammed the door and jumped the gate in one long-legged stride. Her big brother was home.

Chapter 4

The next morning, when Laura let herself through the gate to pick up the dog, the chain was hooked over Skip's empty kennel. The house was silent, the backyard cast in shadow. She crept through the carport to the front gate, making her way slowly past Jake Finlay's motorcycle, a black behemoth crouching against the wall. The first rays of sunshine struck the chrome of the exhaust and the flash of brightness caught her in the eyes.

Neill's front lawn was overgrown, all tangled weeds and kikuyu grass, and spindly lavender and rosemary bushes clung to life in a neglected garden bed. Neill never claimed to be a gardener, quite the contrary, and Jess had enough to do in her own backyard to be tending to her father's. Stepping over the front gate, Laura took off in her usual direction.

The sun was inching over the horizon, the trees along the street throwing long shadows. Laura jogged past the deserted school and out onto the dirt road. The only sound in the sweet-scented stillness were the stones crunching underfoot. Today's run was going to be a tough one. Her limbs were sluggish and the wound on her thigh burned with each step. When the dog hadn't been waiting for her, she'd contemplated going back to bed.

And it was lonely without the dog. Laura kept looking down, missing him. The road stretched out in front. Laura was starting to loosen up a kilometre or so into the run when she heard the pounding of feet and Skip's familiar yip. Moments later Jake-bloody-Finlay breezed past her. He gave her a brief nod. Sweat was running down his face and his t-shirt was streaked with it, but he ran effortlessly. The dog threw her an apologetic grin and a quick flick of his tail, and continued alongside Jake. *Traitor.* She sped up and each breath became a short, fiery burst. But the gap between them widened anyway, so she slowed down to her usual speed and watched as they disappeared into the distance.

When Laura arrived home there was no sign of either man or dog and the blinds remained drawn at Neill's place. She didn't dwell on the rush of irritation she felt. Best not to analyse why the change in routine annoyed her so much. The answer might not be the one she wanted. She let herself into the house, focussing on the day ahead – another fourteen hours or so to work herself to the point of exhaustion before collapsing into bed. The upside was that the backyard was taking shape, and if the hardware shop's garden section had any seedlings left, she was ready to put them into the plot of freshly turned soil. The spring days were mild and rain was forecast the following week – no better time to get the summer vegies in.

Taking a coffee into the backyard, she paced out the prepared patch, imagining where she'd put what. Her mum had had a green thumb, and so had her husband, Brett. Laura hoped she'd gained enough knowledge from watching and listening to them, and all the reruns of *Burke's Backyard* they'd watched over the years, to start her own productive garden. Never before in her life had she found the time to try her hand. Carefully perched on a bale of pea straw, with the sun warm on her back and the dry stalks scratching her legs, Laura sipped the coffee and envisaged her future vegetable garden – lush, green and laden.

The gate squealed on its hinges, dragging Laura from her reverie. The dog raced towards her. Her welcoming smile dimmed when Jake Finlay followed moments later. Careful not to scrape her gravel rash, Laura brushed the straw from her backside and sank to her haunches to return Skip's greeting, conscious of Jake standing watching them.

'Hello again.' She pushed herself to her feet and the dog padded off towards the shed, snout pressed to the ground. She pulled at the hem of her shorts, wishing she'd changed out of her running gear before being sidetracked by coffee and the garden. She didn't usually feel uncomfortable in her sports clothes, but she was suddenly self-conscious.

'Good run? How's the leg?'

'It's okay. Is Neill all right?'

He kicked at a weed growing through a crack in the cement. 'Yeah, far as I know.'

She raised her eyebrows, edged past him on the narrow path. 'What's up then? You didn't come over just to ask how my leg was.'

'Coffee would be good.'

That stopped her in her tracks.

'I bet you've got something better than that forty-three-bean crap Neill drinks,' he said.

To Laura's total bemusement he followed her up the path, across the verandah and inside. He stood in the kitchen doorway and looked around, his expression curious. Since his run he'd showered and changed. His hair was still damp. She hadn't noticed it yesterday but he had a shallow cleft in his chin – almost a dimple, but not quite.

'How do you have your coffee?' she stammered, suddenly conscious she'd been staring at him. Laura hoped he'd think her flushed cheeks were a result of sitting in the sun. She quickly turned her back and plugged in the Nespresso machine, one of the few possessions she hadn't left back in Adelaide with everything else.

If she'd still been looking at him she would have seen the gold flecks in his eyes glint and his mouth twitch with amusement.

'Short black, two sugars.' He folded his arms and leaned against the doorframe and Laura felt him watching her.

'Let's sit out back,' she said minutes later, handing him a fine bone china cup.

'Mmm,' he said. 'What about yours?'

'I've just had one.'

'Have another. I don't like to drink alone.'

'Are you always this bossy?' she snapped and he threw back his head and laughed. Laura's eyes widened. In their short acquaintance he'd struck her as serious; she hadn't taken him for the belly-laughing type. It did amazing things to his face – crinkles appeared at the corners of his eyes, his teeth gleamed, stark white against the shadow of his beard.

'Yes, I am always this bossy,' he said.

They moved out to the back where two ancient, mismatched cane chairs sat side by side. Tubs of plants bordered the northern end of the wide verandah. This time of the year they still caught the morning sun. A galvanised-iron water tank stood on a chest-high stand adjacent to the house, moss growing around the base.

Laura sat down. This spot was one of her favourite places and since arriving in Potters Junction she'd only shared it with her sister Alice, the one time she'd visited. The other chair creaked when Jake eased down beside her, kicking long legs out in front and crossing them at the ankles. The dog came and sat down on the cement beside them.

'What are you going to plant?' Jake tilted his chin in the direction of the freshly turned plot.

She shrugged, blew on her drink. 'Tomatoes, cucumbers, zucchinis, capsicum, and maybe beetroot and spring onions, if I can get a hold of the seedlings. I've got herbs and lettuce in the tubs.'

He scanned the work-in-progress that was her garden. In two swallows he'd finished his coffee. He rested the mug on his knee, bounced it up and down several times. Neither of them spoke. The dog looked up then dropped his head and went back to sleep.

'Mind if I get another coffee?' Jake said eventually.

She opened her mouth, closed it again, felt a bit like a guppy. 'Sure. Why not? Help yourself.'

'Do you want one?'

'No, thanks,' she said, covering the cup with her hand.

He came back a few minutes later and leaned against a verandah post, gulping the coffee down like it was medicine and gazing out towards the neighbour's fruit trees. She nursed her empty cup.

'You've got your work cut out for you,' he said at length.

'Yeah, there is a lot to do. But I guess I can see what's been done.' She stepped up beside him. 'You should have seen it before. It hadn't been touched in years.'

'What are you going to do with the dead tree? And all the junk by the shed?'

'It's a quince tree; I'll eventually get rid of it. And the junk, well, I'll get around to sorting through it and dump what we don't want.'

'We?'

'My sister Alice and I. Great-aunt Dorothy left the place to both of us.'

He straightened up, handed her his empty mug. 'Tomorrow morning,' he said, 'I'll bring Dad's chainsaw and cut the tree down for you.'

'You don't —'

'Nine o'clock. Have the coffee on.' He whistled and Skip sprang to his feet, looking up at him with adoring eyes. When he got to the gate he stopped. 'Damn.'

She folded her arms across her chest. 'What?'

'The reason I came over in the first place. Neill wants to know if you'll take him to a seventieth birthday bash on Saturday night. He wants to go but reckons he's not up to it alone.'

'No, he's not,' she said, walking to the corner of the verandah. 'He doesn't drive at all anymore. He has little stamina for anything.'

'What shall I tell him? Can you take him or not?'

'Why can't you take him?'

'Won't be around.'

'You're leaving already?' The brief twist she felt in her stomach wasn't disappointment, it couldn't possibly be.

He looked away. Bored, the dog wandered off towards the shed again.

'What about Jess? She'll be going, won't she?'

He shook his head. 'We talked yesterday, and she can't go.'

Two children and neither of them would take their dying father to a community event. She had thought better of both of them. Who knew? Laura chewed on her bottom lip. What she *did* know was whose birthday party it was; she'd seen the invitation on Neill's fridge and the announcement in the local paper. The whole community was invited. Just because she'd kept to herself didn't mean she hadn't taken notice of what went on around her. And she hadn't missed the furtive glances, either. She'd seen the unspoken questions in the eyes of the girls at the supermarket checkout, the woman in the post office, and the men at the hardware store when they realised she'd been around too long to be a visitor.

She coughed against the sudden full feeling in the back of her throat. A large community gathering was not on her immediate agenda. A large community gathering to celebrate the local GP's birthday was *definitely* not on her immediate agenda.

Ease back into your life, her psychologist had told her. *You'll know when you're ready but don't put it off for too long. The longer you leave it, the harder it'll be to return to everyday life.* If the thought of a large crowd and the local GP had her pulse racing and her mouth going dry, Laura suspected she'd already put certain things off for too long.

'All right, I'll take him.'

With the words out, she tugged at the neckline of her t-shirt, rubbed at her lips with her fingertips. Feeling as if she was losing her balance, Laura put a hand out to the verandah post to steady herself. Then Jake was standing so close she could see the way his thick, black lashes curled at the ends. He was peering into her face.

'What's wrong?'

He stepped up beside her and they were no longer eye to eye. He took her arm and began to propel her back towards the cane chairs.

'What are you doing?' she said, and tried to shake his arm off.

'I thought you were going to pass out. Are you sure you didn't hit your head yesterday morning?' He let go of her arm, his gaze moving to the raw wound on her thigh.

'I'm all right, thanks. And no, I didn't hit my head yesterday. It's nothing. Don't let me hold you up.'

'If you say so.' He dropped down onto the path and the dog materialised beside him. 'I'll tell the old man you'll take him. He'll be pleased. I'll leave you to make the arrangements.'

When he was almost to the gate he turned back. 'You're sure you're all right?'

'Yes, I'm sure. Too much coffee and no breakfast.'

Not anxiety.

His gaze bored into her like a laser, and then he said, 'Thanks.'

'Thanks? For what?'

'For taking him to the birthday party.' From where she sat she noticed his mouth flatten. 'And for not telling him that I'd run you off the road.'

'Oh,' was all she managed before the gate closed. She heard him talking to the dog and moments later the slam of Neill's back door. Shaking her head, she went inside to make breakfast.

Chapter 5

'How long can you stay?'

The question was expected. Jake was surprised it had taken Neill over twenty-four hours to ask it. He'd told Jess he'd be gone again by the weekend. Today was Wednesday. She hadn't said anything in response but her mouth had tightened and her hazel eyes, so much like his own, had hardened.

'I need to be back in Melbourne by Monday. We're nailing down the funding for another documentary about the Syrian refugee crisis. I have to be there.'

He didn't really, that wasn't his role, he just needed to be ready to roll when the funding was secured. But already, after only a day and a bit, he was restless. The house felt claustrophobic, the smell of death and decay was permeating every corner. The old man's gaze followed him everywhere and the atmosphere was thick with all the things not said.

'Is there anything you want me to do while I'm here?'

Neill scraped a hand across the crown of his head. 'There's a lot of rubbish in the garage that could go. We could sort through it, load up the ute and the trailer. Dump's open this arvo and then again Friday.'

'Are the ute and trailer registered?'

'Of course,' Neill said indignantly. 'I was driving the damn thing a few weeks ago.'

'All right. Let's do it.'

Neill clambered stiffly to his feet and piled the lunch dishes into the sink. 'I can do them later,' he said, taking the garage key from the hook by the kitchen door and handing it to Jake.

The short walk across the yard had left Neill puffing and Jake grabbed a dilapidated folding chair and plonked him down in it. 'You give the orders, I'll do the manual labour.'

'I'm sorry,' Neill said and Jake couldn't ignore the anguish on the old man's face. 'You probably think that's all I ever did – give the orders and expect you to do the work.'

Jake rolled his eyes. He'd never thought that, way back when. He'd been proud to work alongside his father, to learn whatever he could teach him. 'You don't know what I think,' he said and Neill lifted what was left of his eyebrows.

'No, you never would tell me.'

Jake pushed back the familiar burn of rage, of hurt, of disappointment. *No, you never would tell me anything, either.* 'Where do you want to start?'

Neill recoiled at the hard tone.

Jake took a long breath, let it out slowly and rephrased his question. 'What do you want to do first, Dad?'

Neill shifted in the seat; it squealed in protest. 'Probably best to move the ute out of here first. That'll give more room to load the trailer. What do you think?'

'Keys?'

'Hanging up by the kitchen door, son, same place as the shed key.'

Jake was being a prick and he knew it. This place always gave him the shits, brought out his ugly side. He snatched the keys off the hook. Minutes later the ute coughed to life and in a cloud of diesel fumes he drove it into the yard. By the time the trailer was loaded with rusty drums, wire, bent star droppers and other junk, he was filthy.

'I can't believe you brought all this back from the farm,' Jake said. He wiped his hands on a piece of rag. 'What were you going to do with it?'

After the rocky start, they'd worked together amiably enough and Neill looked almost happy.

'You know me, never throw anything away.'

'Yeah, I know. The day after you get rid of it you always need it and then you have to go buy a new one.'

Neill grinned and Jake's lips twitched as he held back a smile. The number of times he'd heard the old man say that.

'How about I go and put the kettle on?'

Jake screwed up his face. 'You wouldn't have a beer in the fridge?'

'Reckon there might be a couple of stubbies on the bottom shelf. They'll only be light, though. Doctor's orders.'

Jake shrugged, threw the rag onto the bench. 'Better than nothing,' he said and they went into the house.

Later that afternoon Jake knocked on Laura's back door and waited. Skip stood beside him looking up at the door and wagging his tail.

'You like her, don't you, boy,' he muttered, giving the dog a nudge with his knee. 'I don't blame you. There's something about her, especially the legs.'

He knocked again, louder this time, and then pounded with a closed fist when there was no answer.

'We both know she's in there.' He winked at the dog and opened the screen door to try the tarnished brass doorknob. It twisted easily in his hand and before he could change his mind he pushed the door open. He called out. Silence. He stepped inside and into the small utility area that led into the kitchen. Skip bounded past him, through the kitchen and up the passage, obviously more sure of his welcome.

As he'd imagined when he'd been there earlier that day, the floor plan of the house was simple – kitchen and wet areas along the back, four symmetrical rooms at the front separated by a passageway. It was obvious the kitchen, laundry and bathroom had been added on years after the original four-roomed stone dwelling had been built. The musty smell of salt damp brought back memories of the farmhouse Jake had grown up in.

Jake walked up the passage, the floorboards creaking beneath the carpet. He glanced into a room where a queen-sized bed was covered with a latte-coloured doona, a white cotton robe flung carelessly across the foot. Laura's bedroom. Feeling like a voyeur he stepped into the doorway of the room opposite. It had been stripped of furniture and it wouldn't be long before the carpet went the same way. Laura was on her knees patting the dog.

'So, you really are renovating. Neill said so. I'm impressed,' he said. She leaned back onto her haunches. Skip looked from Jake to Laura and back again, tail flicking from side to side, and grinning like a fool.

'Who invited you in?' she said. 'I thought it was Neill.' He flinched at her bluntness. Not that he could blame her.

'I knocked several times, then I tried the door. You shouldn't leave it unlocked.' He quirked an eyebrow. 'Anyone could wander in.' He walked into the room, looked around. 'What are you going to do?' He scuffed at the bare floorboards with a booted toe. 'Leave them exposed?'

'Yes.'

'Have you done this kind of thing before? Don't you need a sander or something?' he asked. He wasn't going to be put off by her curtness.

'Yes, and yes.' She stood up, surveyed her handiwork. 'I'll paint the ceiling, walls and woodwork before I sand the floor.'

When she turned to him he searched her face. There was no welcome in her steady blue gaze, but nothing to say he should get lost.

'So, what do you want?' she said.

'I wanted to make sure you were all right.' It was partly true. Mainly, he'd needed to get out of the old man's house for a while. He stepped over the rolled-up carpet to peer out of the single sash-window. 'You were as white as a sheet on the verandah this morning. I thought you were going to pass out.'

'I'm good. There was no need for you to bother checking up on me,' she said. And then, with a wry quirk of her lips, she added, 'But thanks anyway.'

He felt inordinately gratified. 'You're welcome.' Right now she looked anything but pale, her face flushed with exertion, dirt streaked down one cheek. He couldn't stop his gaze dropping briefly to the front of her grubby, washed-out t-shirt, and then right on down to the denim jeans that clung lovingly to those gorgeous legs. 'Do you want a hand to drag the carpet out?'

She pursed her lips, glancing at him and then at the carpet, and then back at him. He could see wariness in her expression.

'Thanks, that would be terrific.' Practicality won.

Together they finished rolling it up, then dragged it out into the passage and through the front door, dropping it onto the verandah in a cloud of dust. Laura sneezed.

'Bless you.'

'Thanks. I'll get Gavin to pick it up and take it to the dump.'

'Gavin?'

'Gavin O'Driscoll, local handyman, jack-of-all-trades. I couldn't have got this far without him,' she said and pulled off her gloves. 'He used to look in on the place while it was empty, after Great-aunt Dorrie died.'

Jake's mouth turned down at the corners. 'Name sounds familiar. I reckon I was at school with him.'

'Mmm,' she said, her eyes sweeping him from head to toe. 'You look about the same age.'

The dog sniffed up and down the carpet, tail arced upwards. He started to lift his leg and then scuttled off when Jake told him to git.

'You need a hand with anything else?' He could be handy when the mood took him. Just ask Neill.

Her eyes took in the front yard. 'No, I'm okay for now,' she said. Her face brightened and he was glad his need for a distraction had taken him to her doorstep.

'Come on then, Skip,' he said. The dog reappeared. 'We might as well head off to the pub for a real beer.'

'Okay,' was all she said and he was halfway down the path when he paused. She was standing on the shadowed verandah watching him. She cut a sad, even lonely, figure. When he'd asked, his old man hadn't known how old she was, but he'd figured she was well over thirty. He'd noticed the fine lines in the corners of her eyes and reckoned he'd spotted a grey hair or two when he'd been standing close to her that morning. And he'd smelled her spicy, cinnamon scent which, with surprise, he realised he'd liked a lot.

'You're welcome to come with us,' he said. 'You look as if you could use a break and a cold beer.'

She straightened, threw a quick sideways look at the open front door and he held his breath, hoping she'd say yes and pull it shut and come with him.

'Thanks, but no, thanks,' she said, and he let out his breath, disappointed. Was it regret he'd heard in her voice?

'Suit yourself.' He whistled up the dog and unlatched the gate. 'But remember, all work and no play makes Laura a very dull girl.'

His words sent anger coursing through her. If she'd had something in her hand she would have thrown it after him. But as quick as it came, the anger evaporated and she went inside and closed the door, plunging the passage into musty gloom.

Had she been caught up in her own misery for so long she'd forgotten how to have fun? Had she become a very dull girl? She shook away the uncomfortable thought. What did it matter, anyway?

Pushing Jake Finlay out of her mind, Laura scanned the empty room and imagined the walls with a fresh lick of paint. She would make them brighter, lighter, and would restore the Baltic pine floorboards to their honey-gold richness. It would transform the room. Just removing the dark and dingy carpet had already lightened the space.

She straightened her spine. She could do it, she *would* do it, room by room, until the whole house was transformed. The years of neglect would disappear under layers of fresh paint and varnish.

But as quickly as her positivity came, the warm feeling dissipated. If she kept up the extreme pace she'd set herself, the renovation would be finished in a few months. What then? What would she do to keep herself busy and keep the demons at bay?

As she dragged her great-aunt's vintage vacuum cleaner into the room, Jake Finlay's parting words wormed their way back into her consciousness. She bit her bottom lip until it hurt. Damn the man. She couldn't remember the last time she'd gone out and had fun. She pictured herself walking to the Junction Hotel with Jake, pulling up a stool at the bar and having a drink, just because she could. *Yeah, right, dream on.* She plugged the vacuum flex into the power outlet. So she'd never been the life of the party – that was her sister, Alice – but she'd certainly never thought of herself as dull. Diligent, disciplined, dedicated to her work, devoted to her family, maybe . . . but that didn't make her *dull*.

She flicked the switch. What life had dealt her in the last two years *had* changed her. There was no point pretending otherwise. She wasn't the same person she'd been before. She felt older, sadder, like an essential part of her had been ripped away, leaving her hollow and unsure of who or what she was. And although she kept reminding herself that what happened would have changed anyone, she missed the person she'd been before.

The roar of the vacuum cleaner did nothing to drown out her thoughts; they just got louder. Would she ever get back to the place where she'd be able to drop everything and go to the pub for a beer with someone, an attractive male no less, who she barely knew, and without giving it a second thought? She snorted. Get real. She'd *never* been the type to drop everything and rush off on a whim, attractive male or not. Who was she trying to kid? Her relationship with Brett had been a slow burn; there was nothing impulsive or reckless there. What had started as a business acquaintance had developed into a tentative friendship, and then they'd fallen in love and been married, and she thought it was for life.

How wrong you could be. How cruel fate could be.

Down on her hands and knees vacuuming along the skirting boards, with her thoughts a cacophony in her head, things started to blur. Laura felt as if her heart were being squeezed by a giant hand. She stopped, concentrated on her breathing. She turned off the vacuum cleaner. With precise movements she removed her gloves, climbed to her feet and went to the kitchen and filled a large glass with water, sipping slowly and staring sightlessly out the kitchen window.

It had been weeks, almost months, since she'd had an anxiety attack, and she wasn't going to have one now. No matter what Jake Finlay said, or implied, about her, and where she'd let her thoughts take her as a consequence. She tilted her chin forward and stood tall. Each day she *did* feel better, stronger, and more like the self she remembered. Some days she even felt normal, whatever that was, and she wasn't about to let Jake Finlay, or anyone, barge in uninvited and undermine her painstaking attempt to reclaim her life. She just could not let that happen.

She finished the water, focussing on its coolness on her tongue, the slide of it down her throat, the fullness in her stomach. She thought about paint colours and brushes and where she was going to hire a sander. Then she rinsed the glass and went back to the front room. She flicked on the vacuum cleaner, let the roar of the motor fill her head, smother everything else. Without another thought she snatched up the hose and set about sucking up the decades' worth of dust and dander.

When she emptied the vacuum cleaner bag into the wheelie bin, the last of the day's sunshine was slanting across the verandah and into the kitchen window. She filled the kettle and lit a gas jet on the green enamel stove. The stove had been there as long as she could remember, squatting in the corner on its stumpy, curved legs. Waiting for the kettle to boil, Laura took in the cluttered, homely kitchen, which was almost uncomfortably warm in the late-afternoon sun. It was a special space, the atmosphere was so steeped in memories it was almost tangible.

It was the room she best remembered from their holidays with Gran and Great-aunt Dorothy; she recalled the smell of Anzac biscuits baking, the clink of teaspoons against fine china teacups, and the love and the laughter. The same ivory lace cottage curtains, frayed from years of washing, hung at the windows, and the same large, rustic dresser stacked with crockery and odd-looking knickknacks stood against the wall. The scrubbed pine kitchen table was, as ever, adorned simply with a bunch of colourful flowers in a chipped stone jug. The only difference being these flowers had come from the supermarket, wrapped in plastic, not picked fresh from a carefully tended garden. A Westinghouse refrigerator, circa 1960, rattled away, fitting in with the ambience of the room. With summer on its way she'd need to do something about the afternoon sun beating in on the back of the house. Perhaps a blind on the verandah would do the trick . . .

It hit her as the boiling water swirled onto the tea bag that few of the things in the house were her own personal belongings. They'd all belonged to her great-aunt. With an unexpected pang of longing, Laura realised for the first time since moving there that she missed being surrounded by her own things. Most were in storage because she'd leased her house in Adelaide to a schoolteacher. But there were half-a-dozen striped Cheap as Chips bags crammed with clothes and shoes languishing in her sister's spare room. Laura paused, the tea bag suspended above the cup. She couldn't remember the last time she'd thought about the accoutrements of her previous life. Or missed them. A slow warmth filled her. She *was* healing.

She sat at the kitchen table, sipped tea and watched the shadows lengthen in the backyard. Her eyes drifted shut, she concentrated on the rhythmic movement of each breath . . . and then she was watching the shadows lengthen from the deck of their home in the suburbs, a home that she and Brett had lovingly renovated. She was sipping wine, Brett had a beer in his hand and they were watching the sun sink over the sea. Brett's arm was slung around her shoulders and her head was resting against him . . . Her Brett. Tired and dusty, still in his work clothes and teasing her about something she'd said to a patient she'd seen that day.

She jumped, jolted back to the present by the screech of her mobile phone. Hot tea splashed onto her hand. Laura blinked and let the door shut on the memories, promising herself as she picked up the phone that she'd go back to them again soon. It *was* getting easier. Time was a slow and stealthy healer.

Chapter 6

The yip of a dog and a scraping sound on the front verandah had Laura throwing off the bedclothes and grabbing her robe. It was after eight. What had happened to the alarm? She flicked back the lace scrim at the window and peered around the edge of the blind. Jake was dragging the roll of carpet down the path, Skip was digging a hole under the native hibiscus, and Neill was leaning against an early model white 4WD ute. His washed-out flannelette shirt was tucked into stiff denim jeans that gathered at the waist. His belt was pulled to the last notch. He watched his son.

'What are you doing?' She stepped outside barefoot, hurriedly knotting the tie of her robe.

The carpet hit the footpath with a dull thud and a cloud of dust.

'Getting rid of your carpet,' said Jake. 'The dump's open tomorrow morning. We're cleaning out Neill's shed, and with your dead tree we'll have a load, or two. Thought I'd put the carpet on the back of the ute first.'

'Right,' she said, blinking into the sunshine. 'Do you want me to help?'

She lifted her arms and swept her hair into a bunch, twisting it into a knot at her nape. He was watching her and her face flooded with colour when his gaze suddenly dropped to the gaping lapels of her robe. She hastily pulled the edges together.

'Nice,' he murmured, and she would have had to have been dead from the neck down to miss the meaning in his challenging stare. Her cheeks burned and then he winked at her, slow and sexy, and she felt as if all the air had been sucked out of her lungs.

'Good morning, Laura,' Neill called, cutting through the moment. He wheezed his way to the gate. 'I hope we didn't wake you.'

'No, you didn't,' she stammered, folding her arms tightly across her chest. 'It's good to see you up and about. My alarm, I don't know what happened . . .'

He pushed open the gate and stood back as Jake manhandled the carpet through.

'Don't worry, the dog didn't miss out on his run. He went with Jake.'

She walked down the path, the cement cool and gritty underfoot. 'How are you?'

'Oh, fair,' he said, leaning heavily on the fence post. 'I'm afraid I can't do much, don't reckon I ever will again.' He gave a self-deprecating laugh that segued into a rattling cough, then he spat into a wad of tissues dragged from his pocket. He caught his breath before going on. 'Good thing Jake turned up when he did – we're clearing out the garage, taking the rubbish to the dump, tidying up the yard.' He paused, his breath coming short and sharp. 'Can't do it myself and, well, the son-in-law . . .'

'Sounds like you're keeping Jake busy while he's here.'

'He won't be around for long and I'm not one to miss an oppor-tunity.' He looked over at his son. 'And a rare opportunity it is.'

'Then there's no need for him to worry about my tree. He said he'd cut it down this morning. I'll get Gavin to do it sometime. There's no hurry.'

Jake finished loading the carpet and came to stand beside his father, dusting off his hands. 'I'll be back in an hour and we can do that tree,' he said, ignoring their conversation. He whistled and the dog appeared and jumped up onto the back of the ute. 'Come on, let's get more of that junk loaded.'

He was already walking away and swinging into the cab of the vehicle before Laura could open her mouth to protest.

Neill rolled his eyes and followed, waving away her offer of help and heaving himself into the passenger seat. He slammed the door. The window rolled down. 'Don't worry, lass, it'll burn off some of that caffeine and sugar he's got running about in his system. It's all the coffee he drinks. Sorry we woke you.'

She lifted a hand to shade her eyes from the sun. 'Don't worry, and thanks,' she said, peering past Neill to Jake just as the engine rattled to life and the vehicle moved away from the kerb.

Jake, a man of his word, was back in an hour. After he'd reversed the ute into the backyard, as near to the dead quince tree as he could get, he lifted an old but well-maintained chainsaw out of the cab.

'Tree comes down and then I get coffee. They're my terms and conditions,' he said with a brief lopsided grin.

'Okay. Sounds fair.' Laura pulled on leather work gloves.

He slipped on safety glasses and twisted earplugs into his ears and, with one almighty heave, brought the chainsaw to life. He was chuffed that it started on the first pull. He'd spent an hour that morning fuelling it and sharpening the blades. Funny how the things you learned as a teenager never left you. That was one thing about the old man, he'd been a patient and thorough teacher.

It wasn't a huge tree, just a load of dead limbs, and when he suggested she stand back, Laura watched from beneath the Hills Hoist until the stump was the only thing left sticking out of the ground.

'You'll have to get Gavin to grub the stump out for you,' he said as he pulled the plugs out of his ears and stowed the chainsaw. 'You could probably do it yourself, it wouldn't be too hard. It's riddled with borers, which is probably what killed it.'

'I'll see how I go,' she said, and together they began piling the branches onto the ute, on top of the carpet.

Out of the corner of his eye he observed the way she worked, steadily and methodically. She was taller than average and, although slim, the muscles in her upper arms were well formed and he figured it was from all the manual labour. She didn't come across as a gym junkie.

'What brought you to this godforsaken place?' he said when they'd almost finished.

She looked up and their eyes met. 'I suppose I needed a break,' she said, picking up the last branch. With a grunt she threw it up onto the tray.

He grabbed a rusted rake that was propped against the shed and began dragging the remaining twigs and dead leaves into a pile.

'So, where are you and what are you doing when you're not having a break?'

She stopped, planted her gloved hands on her hips and gave him a narrow-eyed look. 'What is this, twenty questions?'

'Only two. Just making conversation.' He leaned on the rake.

He was curious, that was all, and she wasn't getting away until she'd answered some of his questions. He waited, making like he had all the time in the world.

'Well, let's say for the sake of conversation that I'm between jobs and homes at the moment, and taking a break in Potters Junction.'

She scooped up an armful of debris to dump on the trailer and he saw the flash of something in her eyes. It could have been anger.

'Helluva place to have a break,' he said with a shake of his head. She stared at him and he went back to the raking, feeling strangely satisfied. Anger had to be better than the haunted sadness he'd seen lurking below the surface.

When they'd filled the tray, she pulled off her gloves and helped him secure the load using a small tarp and a stiff nylon rope he'd found in his father's shed. 'Two half-hitches. Awesome,' he said, taken aback by her speed and dexterity.

'Dull I might be, but I have certain skills,' she said as she reached up to refasten her hair.

'So I see,' he said.

'And I'm not always dull.'

He chuckled at her truculent tone. 'I bet you're not,' he answered, his voice low, and his amusement intensified when her blue eyes widened. On impulse he reached out and with his thumb wiped a smudge of dirt from her chin.

She jumped back as if she'd been burned.

'You had dirt on your chin,' he said slowly, gently, taking his cue and backing off. He wouldn't let on that her jumpiness had startled him.

'Oh.' She swiped at it with the back of her hand.

He took the rake and propped it against the shed where he'd found it. When he turned around she was still standing beside the ute and his gut gave a surprising twist when he saw the perplexed look on her face. 'Laura? What's the matter? Is it something I did?'

She held up a hand as if to ward him off, shook her head. 'I'm sorry.'

It was his turn to look perplexed. 'For what?'

'It's just —' She paused, fiddling with the gloves, her eyes darting all over the place, looking everywhere but at him. She moistened her lips, closed her eyes and swallowed hard.

He'd obviously upset her. And to make matters worse he couldn't tear his gaze away from her glistening mouth, the way she was biting at the fleshy part of her bottom lip. He'd never taken much notice of her mouth before. He'd noticed plenty of other things about her. But here was her mouth, delicious, rosy pink and plump, the bottom lip full without being pouty. His mouth went dry and his blood rushed south. He blinked and ripped his gaze away when she opened her eyes.

When he looked back she'd drawn herself up to her full height, all cool and composed, and he could have been forgiven for thinking he'd imagined the flustered woman of moments before.

'Come inside and I'll show you where you can wash your hands, and I'll make you a coffee. That was the deal.'

He dragged his hand through his hair, shook his head in bemusement and followed her in, not even trying to stop himself from watching her firm but curvy backside, and the graceful sway of her hips, as she preceded him up the path.

This cannot be happening. Laura's cheeks flamed as she filled the water container on the coffee machine. She could hear him in the bathroom, washing his hands. He'd be back in the kitchen any minute. When he'd swiped at the dirt on her chin and her mouth had gone dry and her heart had begun to race, she hadn't tried to fool herself. What she felt wasn't anxiety. She was attracted to him. She slammed a coffee pod into the machine, pressed the back of her hand to her burning cheeks.

'Your toilet needs a new washer, and so does the cold-water tap on the handbasin.'

She spun around at the sound of his voice. His hair looked as if he'd wet it and finger-combed it, and there were splashes of water down the front of his t-shirt. He almost took up the whole doorway.

'I know.' The words came out like a croak. 'I've never changed tap washers before, or fixed a toilet cistern. And it's not easy getting a plumber. I've tried.'

He pulled out a chair and sat down at the table. 'Maybe Gavin could do it for you. You know you'd be wasting litres of water every day.'

'I do realise that.'

'I was just saying. I've been in a lot of places where water is very scarce, and I have a thing about it being wasted.'

Laura gritted her teeth, her fingers tightening around the mug in her hand. 'For your information, Gavin's away for a month. He's gone to Roxby Downs to work. I've phoned the local plumber *three* times and left messages, but he hasn't had the courtesy to call me back.'

She put his coffee in front of him and the mug hit the tabletop with a crack.

'Sorry,' she said. Damn. She could have broken one of her aunt's treasured mugs. Taking a tin of biscuits off the dresser, Laura carefully sat it down beside his coffee.

'They look homemade,' he said.

'They are. Peanut butter and chocolate chip.'

He bit one in half and chewed slowly. 'This is good. You bake as well as renovate houses – *and* you can tie knots. I am impressed.'

She sat down at the opposite end of the table, as far away from him as she could. 'My mother, my grandmother and my great-aunt were persistent teachers,' she said. 'Alice and I left home with a repertoire of home-making skills.'

'Any brothers?'

'No brothers and no other sisters.' She reached for a biscuit and looked down at it in her hands. 'I've put on three kilos in the last month. It's the first time in my life I've had to eat to gain weight.'

'What happened?' he blurted.

She crumbled the edge of the biscuit, and then scraped the crumbs into a tiny heap. When she raised her head his eyes caught and held hers.

'Two years ago my mother died of cancer, and a few weeks later my husband, Brett, was killed in a workplace accident. He was electrocuted.' She hesitated, suddenly beset by misgivings. She could count on one hand the number of people she'd shared her story with.

'And?' Jake said quietly.

'I thought I was coping, focussing on my work, and then, well, let's just say about six months ago things started coming apart at the seams. I realised I wasn't doing so well at all.'

'Hence the break, in Potters Junction, of all places.'

'Yes, the break. Surely this place isn't that bad.'

Jake frowned.

'Well, I can't complain so far,' she said.

'That would have been tough. Losing your mum and then your husband.' Jake was stilled by the news.

'It was tough.' Her eyes flicked to his. 'But my break is doing me the world of good. The lifestyle and pace of this place seem to suit me. I'm doing okay. I'm better each day, I think.'

'I'm sure you are, Laura. Neill does nothing but sing your praises.'

'That's very kind of him,' she said. 'He has become a good friend.'

When they'd finished their coffees, Jake snapped the lid on the biscuit tin and stood up. He stacked his mug in the sink with her breakfast dishes. 'Thanks for the morning tea. I'd better get on with it. Haven't really made a dent in the junk he's got in that shed and we're out to Jess's for dinner tonight.'

'It'll be a big day for Neill but I bet he's loving having all of you together. With your dad the way he is I imagine you'd all want as much family time together as you can get.'

'Something like that,' Jake muttered. His response was just loud enough for Laura to hear but clearly not intended for her ears, and it had her wondering if all was well in the Finlay family. With a small frown creasing her brow she followed him out.

'Jake,' she said and he stopped, turning to face her. 'Thanks for your help, I really have appreciated it. I can do most things myself but sometimes . . .'

'All in a day's work,' he said.

Moments later the gate closed behind him and Laura sent up a silent prayer of thanks that he was only around for a couple more days. The effect he had on her equilibrium was disconcerting.

Jess was in a panic. Jake and her father were coming to dinner in eight hours' time and the house was a mess. The only meat she had in the freezers was lamb and she'd forgotten to take a leg out to thaw. The night before when she'd told Darren they were coming and could he please be home, he'd just grunted and gone out. Her dad hadn't been out for a meal in God-knew-how-long and Jake hadn't been near the place in years. She wanted everything to be perfect and the fact that everything was far from perfect had bitter tears burning in the back of her throat.

Nine-fifty a.m. Jess would drink her coffee and let her pity-fest run another ten minutes, and then she'd get on and do the best with what she had. It was a skill she'd honed over the last couple of years.

After all, the boys would be rapt to see their Uncle Jake again, and their excitement would help counteract the family animosities that always bubbled just below the surface. She'd given up hoping Darren and her father would ever have anything civil to say to each other, or that she'd ever understand what had caused the bad blood between Jake and Neill. Roll on six o'clock, she thought.

In the end it wasn't the complete disaster she'd imagined. Darren showed up at five and showered and changed without being prompted. He had only one beer and helped the boys with their homework while she put the finishing touches on the meal – lamb chops with vegetables, and a rhubarb crumble and custard for dessert.

At the dinner table Sam peppered Jake with questions about his travels while Mikey sat wide-eyed. Darren barely said a word, and made up for the beers he hadn't had before the meal.

'Where do you go next?' Sam asked, sitting on the edge of his seat, eyes bright. 'And did you bring all your cameras with you to Poppa's?'

'Sorry, Sam, they don't fit on the back of the bike. I left them in Melbourne, and some of my gear is still in Istanbul.'

'Wow! That's in Turkey, isn't it? Is that where you're going after you leave Poppa's?'

'Sure is. If we get the funding to do the second documentary. If not, I'm not sure where I'll be next.'

'But what about your gear? Don't you have to go and get it?'

'Isn't it kind of dangerous over there now?' Jess said and felt everyone's eyes turn to her. 'We're always hearing about journalists and cameramen in the region being taken hostage, or thrown into gaol on trumped-up charges.'

Jake wiped his mouth with a paper napkin, pushed back his empty dinner plate. 'I don't know that it's any more dangerous than it has been in the last couple of years,' he said and Jess snorted in disbelief.

'You don't really believe that, do you?' Neill said from the other end of the table. 'If what you say is true, it makes a mockery of all the stuff we hear and read in the media day after day.'

Jess's attention shifted from her father to her brother. Jake's mouth tightened, and then Mikey piped up. 'When can I go for a ride on your motorbike, Uncle Jake?'

'I dunno, mate. It's a pretty big bike, takes a lot of muscle to hold it up.'

Mikey held out his arm, flexed it. 'I've got muscles,' he said and the tension in the room dissipated as quickly as it had built.

'Even if you were big enough to ride it there won't be time, Mikey. We've got school tomorrow and Uncle Jake goes again on Saturday,' said Sam.

Mikey pouted, poking the peas around his plate with his finger.

'Stop that and eat the damn things, or you won't get any dessert,' Darren said, glaring at his son. Mikey picked up his fork and stabbed at the peas.

'You're definitely leaving on the weekend,' Jess confirmed.

'Yep,' Jake said. The clipped syllable didn't invite discussion or negotiation.

She stood up and started collecting the empty plates. When she came to her father, his food had barely been touched.

'Sorry, love. Thanks for going to all that trouble but I just don't have the appetite I used to.'

She touched his shoulder. 'That's okay, Dad. I shouldn't have given you so much. Would you like a small serve of dessert? It's rhubarb crumble, one of your favourites.'

Neill reached for her hand and gave it a squeeze. 'Just a very small serve,' he said.

When she looked up she found Jake staring at them both. The desolation she saw in his eyes stunned her. He looked away quickly.

Turning her back to stack the crockery on the sink, Jess frowned. What on earth was going on with Jake? That was *real* pain she'd seen in his eyes. Whatever the cause, he needed to make peace with his father before it was too late. He hadn't given himself much time to do it, and if the palpable tension between the two men was anything to go by, he hadn't made any inroads yet. Jess chewed on her bottom lip as she laid out the bowls and began spooning in the rhubarb crumble.

Chapter 7

Jake heard a door slam, then the crunch of footsteps across gravel and moments later the tinny clink of Laura's front gate. Noise carried in the stillness of early morning. He'd been awake for hours, lying in the narrow single bed, both thinking and trying not to think, while watching the first light seep in through the curtains.

Last night's family dinner hadn't exactly been a roaring success. However, it could have been worse. There'd been no overt bickering and the meal was good. Jess had always been a top cook. She'd had to learn fast in the days after their mother had left. By age twelve she could knock up a decent roast dinner with all the trimmings. And apple pie for dessert.

The only people who'd seemed to really enjoy themselves had been the boys. Sam was a thinker and you never knew what he was going to come out with next, and Mikey was a pocket rocket. But typically Darren had barely said boo all night, and had steadily worked his way through a six-pack of beer. Jake hadn't missed the anxious looks thrown Darren's way by Jess.

He'd never connected with Darren. On the few occasions they'd been together over the years they'd always been civil to each other, but Jake had no interest in the farm and Darren had shown no interest in Jake's life. If there were problems in the marriage, well, Jake wasn't sure he needed to know. He didn't want to see his sister unhappy . . . But there wasn't much he could do from the other side of the world, was there?

He stretched, propped his hands behind his head and stared at the ceiling. It always felt strange going back to the farm. It had felt even weirder driving back there in the ute with the old man sitting beside him, particularly given the neglected state of the place. In their monthly phone calls, Jess had never given any indication the place had deteriorated the way it had. Jake had been taken aback by the bare paddocks where crops should have been and he knew by the old man's grim expression that he hadn't missed anything either. Neill said he'd enjoyed himself but he'd been so depleted when they arrived home that Jake had practically had to carry him in from the ute.

With a sigh he tossed back the bedclothes and got up, dragging on shorts and t-shirt before pulling on socks and running shoes. Laura had left the dog for him and Skip barked when Jake crept out the back door.

'Shut up, Skip,' he whispered, not wanting to wake Neill. He unchained the dog and didn't bother with stretches. Laura had had a good head start already and he was going to enjoy coming up behind her again, admiring her backside as he pounded along the dirt road towards her. Nice legs and a nice backside . . . and then there was her mouth. But damn, she was way out of his league. She'd been married, still would be if her husband hadn't been killed.

There was nothing to stop a man from looking, though, was there?

She was definitely not a woman a man could love and leave . . . He frowned. A bit early in the day for serious thoughts like that. And he'd only be in Potters Junction another day, hardly enough time to get serious about anything. He stepped over the front gate and Skip bounded over the fence after him. *Bugger.* He probably shouldn't be teaching the dog bad habits.

When he caught up with her, Laura was halfway to the spot where he'd run her off the road. She shot a quick look over her shoulder when the dog raced past and he fell into step beside her.

He could hear Laura's steady, even breathing. Casting his eyes sideways, he saw sweat beginning to trickle down her temple, missed by her sweatband. It wasn't much of a mind stretch to imagine sweat trickling down between her breasts – breasts he'd had a tantalising glimpse of the morning before when her robe had fallen open. Slim she might be but she sure had curves in all the right places. Bloody hell . . . Now was definitely not the time. He needed his blood supply elsewhere. He focussed on the road in front of them.

As they neared the bend Laura broke the silence. 'I always turn around up here and go back.'

'Okay,' he answered. 'I'll keep going for a bit. Catch you on the way back.' She nodded. He powered off and, after taking a nano-second to decide, the dog bounded off in front of him.

She'd just hit the bitumen on the outskirts of town when he fell into step beside her again. She'd really been pushing it. Her face was flushed now, sweat beaded above her top lip. He imagined licking it off. When they turned onto the home stretch, instead of peeling off at Neill's place, he followed her around the corner into her back-yard.

'Don't want to wake him,' he said between gulps of air. 'I reckon I heard him up a couple of times in the night.'

She began her cool-down routine. He kept his eyes forward so he wouldn't be tempted to eyeball her backside when she leaned forward to stretch. With a curl of self-disgust, he decided he was nothing but a pervert. It wasn't as if he really *liked* her, she was way more uptight than the women he usually went for, but for whatever reason he couldn't seem to stay away from her.

He dropped into one of the cane chairs and slicked back his sweat-soaked hair. Skip slurped noisily from the bucket of rainwater near the tank stand and then paddled his front paws, which left little puddles when he padded over the verandah to drop down beside Jake.

Laura disappeared inside, returning with a towel and two large glasses of water. He took the towel and a glass of water. 'Thanks,' he said, taken by her thoughtfulness. She sat down, slowly sipping the cool drink, then put the half-empty glass on the cement beside her. Jake swallowed the water down in a few gulps, mopped his face and hair with the towel.

'Your leg looks a lot better.'

She angled her thigh so she could see it better. 'It is. It doesn't hurt much anymore. It was only superficial, though. It looked worse than it was.'

'You sound like you know.'

'I do.'

He waited but she didn't elaborate.

'So,' he said. 'What home renovations and garden makeovers are planned for today? Or is there a baking challenge brewing?'

'Not sure,' she answered seriously, ignoring his mocking tone. 'Yesterday afternoon I started prepping the front room for painting.

But . . .' She paused, pulled at her bottom lip. 'I might see if I can buy those vegetable seedlings and set them.' She waved a hand at the cloud front moving in. 'If rain's on its way I might be better off in the garden today.' She picked up her glass and drained it.

'What happens when Laura gets bored with baking and gardening and home renovating? Laura must have a life to go back to.'

'Who says Laura will get bored?'

'Just a thought.'

'What about you? Packing up today? What time do you hit the road tomorrow?'

He was but it sounded like she couldn't wait for him to leave Potters Junction and that irritated him. And then he was annoyed with himself for being irritated, because, damnit, he was heading to Istanbul any day now and he'd never see her again. He shifted in the seat, purposefully avoiding looking at her bare legs.

'I'm heading to the tip first.' He shook his head. 'I can't for the life of me understand why Neill brought the crap in from the farm when he moved.'

'When did he move in from the farm?'

Jake pursed his lips. 'I dunno, ten, eleven years ago, I reckon. Around the time Jess and Darren got married.'

'You never wanted to take up the farming life?'

'Nope. I enjoy what I do.'

'Just a thought.'

'Touché,' he said.

He stared out at the backyard, his high from the run evaporating fast. The truth was, Jake probably would have kept farming if things had gone differently back then. The place wouldn't look as damned rundown as it did if he had. The old man was right – Darren Phillips wasn't a farmer's bootstrap. He never had been and never would be.

Any wonder Jess looked anxious.

Jake jumped to his feet, startling her. 'We all have our what-ifs, Laura, and our demons.' That would be the understatement of the year. 'I'm sure you have yours.'

Woken by the sudden movement the dog was on his feet and already waiting by the gate.

'Thanks for the water.' Jake draped the towel over the back of the chair and strode across the verandah. He slammed the gate shut behind him on his way out. So much for not waking the old man.

The rain came at dusk, without any fanfare, and Laura was pleased she'd made the effort to go buy vegetable seedlings and set them. Potters Junction wasn't a big town, it had a population of about 1500, but there was a hardware shop with a reasonably sized gardening section. Clearly there were some keen gardeners in town.

It rained into the night, soft and steady, and she drifted to sleep listening to it gurgle in the gutters. The only evidence of the rain on Saturday morning was found in the potholes she dodged as she ran off the bitumen onto the gravel. There was no sign of Jake or the dog and she was relieved. Maybe he'd left already, although she hadn't heard his bike, and in the quiet before dawn she would have heard it; the whole town would have heard it.

Laura caught the unmistakable sound mid-morning, when she was staking the tomato seedlings. She stopped what she was doing and listened, ear cocked to the movement next door, miffed that he hadn't said goodbye. He wasn't a bit like Brett. In fact to look at they were polar opposites – Brett's smiling blondness and Jake's brooding darkness. Good heavens! Why on earth was she comparing him to Brett? She gave her head a shake, picked up the hammer and started pounding in the next stake.

She'd arranged to pick Neill up at eight p.m. for the seventieth birthday party at the town hall. It was unfair of her to hope, but after the exertion of his farm outing on Thursday night, she was optimistic that he'd change his mind about going. Laura kept her phone close by all day. By late Saturday afternoon there'd been no call and she'd resigned herself to the event. There was no doubt in her mind that Neill Finlay wouldn't be around to celebrate the good doctor's seventy-first birthday.

Showered, hair washed and dried, she closed the wardrobe door with a frustrated howl. All of her dressy clothes were in bags in Alice's spare room back in Adelaide. Up until now it hadn't bothered her but for a moment, while rummaging through her limited options, she wished she'd visited Potters Junction's clothing boutique to buy something fitting for the occasion. Maybe she could talk Alice into visiting sometime soon and bringing along the clothes.

In desperation she slipped on the only skirt she had, teamed it with a silk shirt that matched her eyes and dressed the outfit up with a colourful scarf. Her reflection in the spotty mirror of the old wardrobe told her there were a few kilos to go before she'd fill out the linen skirt like she used to. With practised fingers she swept her hair into a knot, not bothering with any makeup except a dusting of face powder and a smear of lipstick. She didn't stop to check her reflection again on the way out.

Neill was waiting when she drove into the driveway at eight. The front light was on and Jake's bike was gone from the carport. It was done, he was gone.

'You look nice,' Neill said. She held the car door open for him. 'I don't think I've ever seen you in a skirt before.'

'You don't look too bad yourself,' she said, taking in the

precision-pressed slacks and jacket, ignoring the fact they looked about three sizes too big for him.

'Don't fill 'em out like I used to,' he said, reading her mind.

The Potters Junction town hall was bursting with light and music, people spilling out onto the footpath.

'Look at that,' Laura said with a bubble of incredulous laughter as a car pulled out of a parking space just past the main entrance. 'Couldn't have done better if I'd planned it.'

Helping Neill out of the car she laid a hand on his arm and said, 'When you're ready to go, please tell me. Remember I'm here for you and I don't care if we only stay half an hour.'

'Don't worry, I'll let you know when I've had enough.'

They found their way in through the press of partygoers and Laura looked around. So many people. They stood shoulder to shoulder, the sound of live music competing with a hundred conversations. There were several familiar faces – the man from the hardware shop acknowledged her, one of the checkout girls from the supermarket gave her a little wave and the woman from the post office who looked a bit like a horse seemed surprised to see her there. But there was no-one she actually *knew* and it wasn't long before Neill was pulled into the crowd, leaving her hanging on the fringes like a wallflower. She stood on tiptoes, craning her neck to locate him, and swallowed her rising anxiety, telling herself not to be ridiculous. He'd be okay. He knew these people, they were his community, and they'd look out for him if anything happened. Besides, there was a doctor in the house. Two doctors, actually.

She made her way to the bar and took the proffered glass of bubbly from a man in a snowy white shirt and a bowtie. He bobbed his head in recognition and she remembered him as another employee from the hardware shop.

Glass in hand, she skirted around groups of people talking animatedly. Snatches of conversation gave her the impression the townsfolk thought Doctor Milt Burns was looking to retire, that he would have cut back already if they'd found another GP to take his place. She overheard someone say they thought Doctor Burns was unwell, and another conversation snippet revealed that his wife Linda wanted to move to Adelaide to be closer to their grandchildren.

The bubbly tickled her nose and fizzed across her tongue. Not at all unpleasant. It had been months since she'd had a glass of champagne. Or anything alcoholic, for that matter. When people peered at her with curiosity she smiled and moved along, silently cursing Jake and Jess and wishing she were someplace else. Home, preferably.

'You all right, love? You look lost,' a gravelly voice asked in her ear and she spun around in surprise. A short barrel of a man thrust out his hand. 'Stan Wiley, local Landmark agent,' he said and Laura's hand was swallowed by a large, sweaty paw. He tipped one of his chins at her empty glass. 'Need a refill?'

'Er, no, thanks.' She fanned her face with her hand, searching the crowd again for Neill's familiar face. 'There's my friend,' she said when she spotted him sitting at a table with several other men, all with the sunburned, grizzled look of old farmers. 'I'd better see if he's okay. He has been unwell.' She gave the man called Stan what she hoped was an apologetic smile before squeezing through the partygoers to where Neill sat.

'Only trying to be friendly, darl,' she heard Stan say as she left him in her wake.

She hadn't gone far when someone grabbed her arm and pulled her to a stop. What now? Surely Stan had got the message. But the hand gripping her arm was slim, cool and definitely belonging to a female. When the owner of the hand spoke, Laura felt the blood drain from her face.

'Laura O'Connor, as I live and breathe! What on earth are you doing here?'

Laura squeezed her eyes shut. Damn Milton Burns for turning seventy. Damn Jess for being too busy and damn Jake for being too irresponsible to bring his father.

'Meghan Kimble – what a lovely surprise,' she said, stretching her mouth wide in the facsimile of a smile. 'Meghan Kimble!' she repeated in an attempt to convince herself this wasn't a dream.

Meghan gathered her into an awkward embrace around a very pregnant belly, and Laura knew it was no dream.

'After all these years, Meghan, and in Potters Junction of all places. Someone from the old crowd told me you'd come back from the UK and gone bush.'

'Yeah, I've gone bush, all right.' Shaking her head with disbelief she added, 'Wow! I can't believe it's you. Of all the people to run into.'

Of all the people, all right. Even in her most paranoid moments, never had Laura imagined that out here she'd run into someone from her old life. Someone who'd known her *before*.

When she'd been considering her move to Potters Junction, Laura knew there was a slim chance a local might remember her from her visits to Great-aunt Dorothy's as a teenager. It had been a lifetime ago, though, and Dorothy had been dead for years. Laura certainly hadn't anticipated bumping into an Adelaide friend.

'So, Meghan, what have you been up to?' Laura looked from the glowing woman she'd known since medical school to the handsome, taciturn man standing behind her. A toddler with coppery red curls the same colour as Meghan's was perched high on his hip.

Laura's tinkle of laughter sounded hollow even to her own ears, like she was in a tunnel. She took a slow breath in through her nose, coaching herself to calm down, and tried not to stare at Meghan's abdomen. 'Silly question, when it's quite obvious what you've been up to.'

Meghan proudly smoothed a hand over her belly, looking over her shoulder to the man behind her. 'Meet my husband, Sean Ashby, and our daughter, Lucy.'

Laura shook Sean's warm, work-hardened hand. Sean said something she didn't quite catch and when she said hello to Lucy the little girl pushed her face into her father's chest and he tightened his grip on her.

'Lovely to meet you both,' she said, and felt as if her face would crack if she kept this up for much longer.

Meghan with a husband and a child. And another one on the way. Laura tried to step back, away from her friend, and melt into the people pressed around her. Her heart was hammering and her hands were clammy against the linen of her skirt.

While Meghan was making her first foray into marriage and motherhood, Laura had been grieving for the family she'd lost. A sudden, vicious punch of raw grief winded her and she steeled herself not to visibly recoil from it. She had to get out of there.

Meghan opened her mouth to speak but suddenly, miraculously, Neill was beside her. 'I'm ready to go whenever you are, lass.' He grasped her arm, his fingers digging into the skin, almost making her wince. But it took her mind off her own distress and gave Laura the excuse she needed to leave. Neill's face was ashen, his breaths coming in short, wheezy bursts. For a moment she wasn't sure who was holding who up.

Relief washed over Laura as Meghan turned her attention to Neill. But the relief was short-lived.

'How are you, Mr Finlay?' said Meghan. 'And how on earth do you know Laura?'

'I'm so-so, Doctor Kimble,' he said. 'I have my good days and my bad days. Laura is my neighbour and she kindly offered to bring me tonight when Jess couldn't come.'

'I hear Jake's home again,' said Sean, from behind his wife.

'Was. Only for a few days,' Neill replied.

'And now it's time to take you home, Neill.'

Making her goodbyes, Laura began to inch towards the door with Neill on her arm but Meghan was insistent.

'Are you around for long? We must catch up. We have *so* much to talk about.'

Laura tried to think up an excuse but her mind had stopped functioning. 'That would be lovely.' It felt as if everyone was watching her, waiting for her answer. 'I'm here for a while.'

'That's great news, isn't it, Sean? Laura, ring Magpie Creek medical centre and ask Julia to give you my mobile number if I'm not there. Last place I ever thought I'd run into you, or anyone from the old crowd, really. And are you here on your own, or is —'

'Give the poor woman some air,' Sean said.

Laura could have grabbed Meghan's husband and kissed him. He'd sensed her discomfort, stepped forward – hitching the toddler up on his hip – and wrapped his free arm around his wife's shoulders, pulling her against him. 'Neill's just about ready to drop.'

Meghan flushed. 'Oh, I'm so sorry! It's just that it's been so long.'

'I'll phone,' Laura said and when Meghan looked sceptical she added, 'I promise.'

'If I don't hear from you soon, I'll track you down.' She winked at Neill. 'I know where you live!'

Neill leaned heavily on her arm as they made their way out into the slap of the cold night air. He looked exhausted.

'I reckon I probably should have stayed home,' he said between breaths, as Laura helped him into the passenger seat of the car.

'Did you enjoy yourself?'

He hesitated. 'Yes, I did.'

'It was worth it then.'

'I suppose.' He leaned back against the headrest and closed his eyes.

She slid behind the wheel and started the car. 'Are you all right?'

'Pooped, lass, but okay. Are you okay?' He tilted his head sideways to peer at her.

'I'm all right,' she said lightly, certain he wouldn't be able to see her expression in the eerie glow of the dash lights.

'I watched you coming towards me. You went as white as a sheet when Doc Kimble recognised you.'

She didn't answer him. She couldn't. She heard him sigh.

'It's all right, lass, we all have things that are private, and I'm sure if you'd wanted me to know, you'd have told me.' He coughed and it rattled through his whole body. He held up a bony finger. 'But you remember, I knew Dorothy. We were neighbours for five years before she died. I saw lots of photos.' He coughed again and Laura chewed on the inside of her cheek, not sure if she wanted to hear any more. Neill cleared his throat and when he spoke again his voice sounded rougher, raspier, as if it were almost worn out. 'And her house was never sold. That handyman bloke used to check on everything. I put two and two together. Dorothy was very proud of her great-nieces, the doctor and the lawyer. I know you're not the lawyer.'

She could feel his gimlet gaze boring into her through the

darkness, daring her to contradict him. She had nothing to say to him and so kept her mouth closed for the rest of the drive home. The carport was empty when they arrived but Neill had left a light on inside.

'I wasn't hiding anything, Neill,' she said quietly. 'I just needed some anonymity while I sorted myself out.'

'It's out of the closet now, lass. Everyone saw the exchange tonight, the town was all ears.'

'Never mind. Like I said, I wasn't hiding anything.'

'Well,' he said and unclipped his seatbelt and fumbled with the doorhandle. 'I hope it doesn't cause you any difficulties.'

'Why would it cause me any difficulty here? No-one knows me.'

'You'd be surprised.' He paused and Laura waited for him to catch his breath. 'My bet is when they find out you're a doctor, and a GP no less, they'll be camping out on your doorstep, trying to sweet-talk you into hanging up your shingle here. The word is that Milt wants to retire.'

Laura felt her insides drop. 'I hadn't thought of that.'

'But it's not your problem,' he said and gave her arm a pat. 'Thanks for taking me.'

'I'm glad you had a good time. Do you need a hand? Do you want me to help you inside?'

'No,' Neill said, as the verandah light flicked on and, much to Laura's amazement, the door opened and Jake appeared on the doorstep. He was barefoot, his hair was tousled and he appeared as though he'd been asleep. She climbed out, gaping at him across the roof of the car. The dog barked.

'I thought you'd gone?'

'Minor change of plans. I went out to the farm to see Jess again.' He shoved his hands into his pockets. 'Good crowd?'

'Yes, the hall was packed.'

'I thought you'd be longer than this.'

'Neill wanted to come home, he's exhausted.'

'Right.'

'You could have taken Neill after all,' she said and he looked away. Then she wouldn't have run into Meghan Kimble.

'Shit happens,' he said and swung down the steps.

'Yeah, doesn't it. I'll leave you to it.' She slid back into the car.

'Dad, let me give you a hand inside,' Jake said and effortlessly helped him out of the car.

'Goodnight, Neill,' Laura said. When Jake slammed the car door she reversed out of the drive and drove around the corner and home, her thoughts in turmoil.

Chapter 8

Laura sank down onto the side of the bed, dropped her phone onto the bedside cupboard and toed off her shoes. All this time Neill had known who she was and he'd said nothing. Of course Dorothy would have bragged about her and Alice. A dog-eared photo album of the two sisters still collected dust on the kitchen dresser, bulging with snaps of their summer holidays spent in Potters Junction. Framed graduation photos sat on the mantelpiece in the sitting room.

Dorothy had never married and had no children of her own, so she'd always taken an interest in her older sister's grandchildren. She'd always been proud of their achievements. Pressing the heels of her hands into her eyes, Laura chastised herself for being deluded enough to think Neill wouldn't have worked out who she was. He'd never probed, had always been polite and respected her privacy. Of course he would have known who she was. But then again, did it matter?

With a frustrated snort she flopped back on the bed, staring at the ceiling until the patterns in the pressed tin began to undulate. She rolled onto her side, dragged a pillow down and buried her face in it. Her safe little bolthole had been discovered.

Throwing off the pillow she lunged for her phone and tapped in a familiar number.

'You'll never guess who I ran into tonight,' she said before her sister Alice had a chance to speak.

'No, probably not.'

'Meghan Kimble.'

'And?'

'Well, you know, Meghan Kimble.' Laura heard her voice go up an octave. She took a steadying breath.

'Where were you to run into her? Have you given up living like a hermit? Anyway, what's the big deal? I thought you were friends from way back.'

'Alice, she's the GP in the next town, she's married with a toddler and another one about to drop.'

'That's good news, isn't it?'

'Yes, I suppose so, but what if . . .' Laura took the phone away from her ear and glared at it. Sometimes Alice was too pragmatic for her own good. She'd been hoping for understanding and sympathy from her sibling and all she got was practicality and common sense. She pressed the phone back to her ear.

'Look, Laura, from what I remember Meghan was pretty cool. I can't imagine her gossiping about you. And what is there to gossip about anyway? It's not as if you did anything wrong. You just took some time out. You're worrying about nothing.'

'Yeah, you're probably right. Meghan was a good friend.' She felt silly now, panicking and phoning her sister. Back when Laura had first come to Potters Junction she'd talked to Alice every day, sometimes more than once. Since Laura's life had spun out of control, months prior to the move, Alice had been her rock. But Laura was back in control again and it was almost ten on a Saturday night. She mightn't have a social life but her sister did. 'God, I'm sorry, Alice, hope I didn't interrupt anything important.'

'Nope. I'm watching a crappy movie on SBS on my own,' she said and yawned. 'Sure you're okay?'

'Yeah, I'm fine, now. I just had one of those moments —'

'Moments? Do you need to see your shrink again?'

Laura almost heard Alice sit up in her seat. 'No, I don't, I really am okay.' She pulled at a loose thread on the hem of her shirt. 'I guess I've been in a bit of a bubble, ignoring the rest of the world while I fiddle around here painting and gardening . . . And then I run into someone from the past.'

'Laura, maybe it was a good thing, running into Meghan like that. I know you're holed up at Dorrie's because you had to take time out, but you can't put your life on hold forever.'

'I know, it's just —' She halted, closed her eyes, dismayed to feel tears not far away.

'Laura,' Alice said, her voice gentle. 'I know life will never go back to the way it was. But you know you can't hide away up there forever.'

A tear pushed through, trickled out the corner of her eye and onto the doona.

'Mmm,' she said, not wanting to give her sister any idea she was crying, that she still had moments when she felt like such a failure. She *should* have been able to cope with what happened – she had the training, the skills to know what to do – and instead she'd gone down in a screaming heap. Literally.

'Everyone grieves in their own way, sweetie, and I know there's no time limit, but it's been over two years since Mum and Brett died. If you were one of your patients, you'd be telling yourself to start thinking about the future, I know you would. You've been off work for six months. You need to get on with it before you forget how.'

Work. Wasn't that what she did here every day until she almost dropped with exhaustion?

She held the phone hard against her ear as the cold, familiar fingers of dread squeezed at her insides. She knew it wasn't the grief that was holding her back anymore, it was the fear – the fear of going back to medicine, the fear of folding the moment the going got tough. The fear of letting her patients down, her colleagues down, herself down.

Laura pressed her fingers to her mouth. It wasn't easy to admit she was afraid to go back to what she'd always believed had been her calling. She hadn't told anyone about the numbing fear, not her sister or her psychologist. Most of the time she managed to keep it buried deep away from everyone, especially herself. But now her sister was telling her it was time to think about going back to work, and she knew Alice was right and she couldn't ignore the fear any longer.

'Laura? Talk to me!'

Alice's voice intruded on her thoughts and she moved the phone to the other ear.

'Laura?'

'I'm here and I'm fine,' she said, surprised at how normal she sounded. Her stomach was churning and her heart was pounding as she wiped one clammy palm across the doona, but she sounded fine.

'Do you need me to drive up tomorrow? I can,' Alice said. 'We can talk, drink wine in the middle of the day.'

She swiped a hand across her eyes. 'Thanks, Alice, but you don't need to do that.' *But can't I put off making the hard decisions for a bit longer? I like my safe little bubble.* 'It was a bit of a shock, you know, running into Meghan like that. She's a blast from the past. My whole career, my whole life flashed before my eyes.'

'I'll look at my schedule, plan a weekend, and drive up there soon. Unless you decide to come home before I get around to it?'

'I doubt it. Too much to do here,' Laura said, knowing full well that deciding where home would be was another decision waiting to be made. She said goodbye to her sister and they disconnected. The phone plopped onto the bed beside her. She felt drained, hollowed out by her conscious admission it was fear, not grief, that was holding her back now.

She was afraid of picking up her stethoscope and stepping behind a consulting desk again. She was terrified she wouldn't be able to cope with whoever sat down on the opposite side of the desk; then the anxiety attacks would come back and she'd be exposed for the fraud that she was.

When her vision began to blur from staring at the ceiling, she lifted herself off the bed and opened the wardrobe, wrinkling her nose at the smell of camphor. Like an automaton she slipped off her clothes and slung the skirt over a coathanger. Face washed and teeth cleaned, she piled up the pillows and settled herself into bed with a book and a cup of camomile tea.

But the tea was tasteless and the book was boring. The words ran into each other and, as hard as she tried to stop them, her thoughts kept going back over her conversation with Alice.

With a sigh the novel went back onto the bedside cupboard with the half-drunk tea and she sank back onto the pillows. She had a lot of thinking to do. If practising medicine wasn't her work anymore, she needed to make a conscious decision about that, and she needed to act on it, instead of drifting to some other destination because she didn't have the guts to make the tough decisions.

And being a doctor was more than just *work*. As corny as it sounded, it was a calling. Why else had she studied until she went cross-eyed, worked appalling hours for very little, and forfeited a social life and any kind of meaningful relationships while she was at it?

And what would she do if it wasn't medicine? Her gut twisted. Climbing out of bed, she dragged on her robe and went to the kitchen to make herself another cup of camomile tea, this time adding a generous spoonful of honey. It was past midnight when she went back to bed. Her feet were frozen and her backside numb from sitting at the kitchen table too long, contemplating her life and searching for answers. None of it was easy, she decided, flicking off the bedside light and promising herself she'd think about it more tomorrow. Sleep came eventually.

At first Laura thought she was dreaming. Was it her heart or was someone pounding on her front door? When she heard her name shouted she threw back the covers, fumbled for the lamp on the bed-side cupboard. She grabbed her robe off the end of the bed.

Switching on the outside light, she opened the door a crack. Jake Finlay stood on the verandah, t-shirt inside out and jeans zipped but not buttoned. His feet were bare.

'You'd better come. Neill's fallen over. I'm not sure what happened. I heard a crash and found him on the floor. He's cracked his head and it looks like it might need stitches.'

She pulled the lapels of her robe closed, gripping the edges with one hand. 'Is he conscious? Have you called the ambulance?'

'Why would I call the ambulance when you're right next door? The old man said you're a doctor.'

She stepped back, gripped the lapels of her robe even tighter. 'Technically yes, but I'm not practising.' She swallowed. She wasn't practising but that was her choice. There were no legal or professional reasons why she shouldn't or couldn't help Neill.

'Well?' he demanded. 'Are you coming?'

Neill was a friend. Health professionals should never treat friends. It had been drummed into her.

'Maybe you should call an ambulance,' she said.

Jake swore and spun on his heel.

What was she thinking?

'Wait! I'll come. I'll get some clothes on.' She could at least have a look. Render first aid. Any friend would do that.

She donned trackpants and a sweatshirt, and grabbed the soft black medical bag that she always used to carry with her. Her knuckles were white around its handles. It was a fluke she had the bag in Potters Junction at all. After that awful day six months ago, she'd left the bag right where she'd dropped it when a concerned colleague had driven her home from the practice. Alice must have collected it because when she'd helped her pack for Potters Junction, she'd given Laura an exasperated look and shoved it in the car with her, saying, 'You can pretend for now you're not a doctor, but you are, and you always will be.'

When she went back to the front door, Jake had gone. She let herself out and, seeing the insipid yellow glow of Neill's back light, Laura made her way down the side of the house. She stumbled in the dark, shivering despite the warm clothes. Jake had left the gate open. Clutching the bag, she hurried across the backyard. It was three in the morning and she was wide awake. She could do this. She would do this. It was a simple bump on the head, probably not even a concussion.

She heard a whimper and the scrape of Skip's chain. 'It's all right, fella,' she murmured as she went past, unconsciously crossing her fingers.

She found them in the bathroom. Neill was propped up against the bathtub, pale and bloody, his pyjama jacket gaping. Jake was hunkered on the floor beside him.

'What happened?'

Jake stood up and eased past her to make room, and she dropped to the floor beside Neill.

'I don't know what happened. He said he went to the toilet and came in to wash his hands and then he was on the floor,' Jake said, shoving his hands into the waistband of his jeans. 'I was awake and heard him get up. I heard the toilet flush and then the thud. I reckon I was in here in seconds.'

'Was he unconscious?'

'No. I don't think so.'

'Neill,' she said and gently touched his shoulder. 'Did you pass out?'

He shook his head without opening his eyes. She unzipped the bag and reached in. Even after six months, her fingers knew exactly where to find what she needed.

'Neill, I'm going to shine a bright light in your eyes for a second.'

He opened his eyes and she shone a penlight into each one. He blinked and, satisfied, she slipped the torch back into her bag, took his wrist and felt for his pulse. She searched for the stethoscope, her fingers going straight to the pocket where it was stowed. There was a smear of blood on the vanity and more splashed down the front of his pyjamas. Scalp wounds always bled profusely. The blood was clotted in a mess with what little hair he had.

Shifting her focus to why he'd fallen, she warmed the end of the stethoscope in her hand and pressed it to his bared chest. As she listened to his heart, she observed his ribs through the wrinkled, translucent skin. About ninety beats per minute, regular, nothing overtly cardiac going on. She pulled the stethoscope out of her ears.

'Do you remember what happened, Neill? Did you have any chest pain before the fall?'

'No. I felt a bit woozy . . . It's all the painkillers, I reckon. And I was tired after all the outings. I must have slipped, lost my balance.'

'Does it hurt anywhere else?'

He flexed his arms and moved his legs, shifted his backside on the hard floor. 'Everywhere,' he said. 'But no new pains.'

Laura let herself relax slightly. She heard Jake's relieved sigh.

'We'll help you up and I'll clean that head wound, see if it needs stitches.'

Together they lifted Neill to his feet and helped him into the kitchen. She sat him on one of the vinyl chairs and Jake filled a bowl with warm water and collected several clean face washers from the linen press. He draped a towel around his father's shoulders.

Without hesitating, Laura lined up the things she'd need on the kitchen table and pulled on disposable gloves. She cleaned away the caked and clotted blood to expose a jagged laceration. It had started oozing again.

'It does need a few stitches.'

She peeled off the gloves and went to the kitchen sink to wash her hands, grateful that as a GP she'd insisted on doing her own skin excisions. A lot of GPs didn't. She confidently tore open the disposable suture kit, setting it up on the kitchen table. When she took a needle and syringe from their packets, Jake visibly paled.

'Local anaesthetic,' she said, as she checked the labelling and twisted the top off a plastic ampoule. Her hands were steady. Jake pulled out a kitchen chair and sat down.

Neill sat with his eyes closed.

'You okay?' Jake said and the old man grunted.

After cleaning the wound with antiseptic wipes, Laura injected the local. She listened to his heart and checked his pupils while the anaesthetic took effect, aware of Jake watching her every move. Washing her hands again, she pulled on another pair of sterile surgical gloves and carefully sutured the laceration, covering it with an adhesive dressing. The room was still, Laura's focus on her patient, the only sounds his ragged breathing and the snip of the scissors after each stitch.

'Stitches out in a week to ten days,' she said and began repacking her bag, dropping the used needles into a small sharps container. Jake scooped up the rubbish and threw it into the bin.

'You might want to make an appointment to see your own GP as soon as you can,' Laura said and put the back of her hand over her mouth to stifle a yawn. The adrenaline had dissipated and she was coming down fast. 'Maybe your pain medication needs reviewing.'

Neill stood up, wobbled a bit, leaned on the kitchen table. Laura and Jake watched, both ready to reach out if he needed support.

'Cup of tea?' Jake washed his hands, picked up the electric kettle to fill it.

'Thanks, son. With a couple of sugars.'

'I'll leave you to it,' Laura said. She zipped up the bag and lifted it off the table. 'Neill, I'm sure there's no concussion. You know my mobile number, and if anything changes, please ring me. Or the hospital.' She paused, and then turned to Jake. 'Yes, ring the hospital if he vomits, or if his headache gets worse, or there's anything else you're worried about.'

'You won't stay for a cup of tea, lass?'

She yawned. It was after four. 'No, but thanks anyway.' Stifling another yawn, she added, 'I'll see my own way out.'

The gate clanged shut, the sound echoing in the early morning silence.

It took her a moment of panic, groping around in the dark at the back door, to remember that Jake had come to the front door and she'd followed him out that way.

The sky was open but there was no moon and she cautiously felt her way around the side of the house, and swore when she got to the front door and discovered she'd locked herself out. She dropped the bag onto the ground and had to bite her bottom lip to stop herself from crying out in frustration.

The fly-spotted lightbulb cast a feeble wash of light across the cracked cement of the front verandah. A sliver of brighter light shone below her bedroom blind. She'd left the light on and she remembered opening the window a few inches before she went to bed.

'Ah-huh,' she said. If she could get the flyscreen off, she'd be able to push the window up and climb through. Grinning, she set to work on the bedroom flyscreen. The potted aspidistra rustled in the shadows.

Chapter 9

One torn fingernail and a bruised thumb later, Laura gave up. All she had to do was get the screen off and she could push the window up and climb in. But the damn thing wouldn't budge. If it hadn't been a security screen, by now she would have put her fist through the wire and got in that way. Where was a pair of tinsnips, or a hammer and a chisel, when you needed it?

With an angry curse, she made her way out her front gate, along the footpath, through Neill's gate and up his driveway. As she'd hoped, there was light coming from the side window under the carport. The spare room. Jake's room. Her pulse thudded as she tiptoed through the carport to the window.

'Jake,' she hissed, leaning forward, her face close to the flyscreen. The window was open about six inches and the gauzy curtain billowed inwards on a puff of breeze. No response. She spoke louder and rapped on the window frame, jumping back when the curtain was wrenched aside and she found herself at eye-level with a bare navel.

'Laura?'

'I've locked myself out.'

He pushed the window up as far as it would go. 'What?'

'I've locked myself out,' she said, the words coming out louder than expected, bouncing around the empty carport.

He grinned and she could have smacked him.

'Wait right there,' he said and the curtain dropped.

She folded her arms and waited, looked for the hulking shape of his bike in the carport. It wasn't there.

'Where's your motorbike?' she said when he appeared out of the darkness, pulling on a t-shirt. 'I thought you'd gone.'

'In the morning,' he said, and took a torch out of the back pocket of his jeans. 'And it's in the shed.'

'Right,' she muttered and followed him down the driveway, leaping the gate behind him, almost running to keep up.

'What took you so long to come over?' he said, the torchlight bouncing along in front of them on the walk.

'I tried getting the screen off myself but it wouldn't budge. All the tools are locked in the back shed and the key's inside.'

'You haven't got a house key hidden anywhere outside.'

'Well, duh,' she snapped. 'Do you think I'd be here now if I had a key hidden outside?'

'It was more of an observation than a question.'

'Oh, sorry.'

He stopped abruptly, and she put out a hand to prevent herself from slamming into his back. He turned around, pointed the torch at their feet.

'Don't be sorry, Laura,' he said, his voice a low rumble. 'I'm not. I'm more than happy to rescue a damsel in distress.'

She followed him through the front gate and up the path. Going

THE DOCTOR CALLING 83

to the bedroom window, he shone the torch around the edges of the screen. He passed the torch to her, gripped both sides of the screen and with one powerful jerk it was out in his hands.

'Brute force,' he said smiling. 'Works every time.'

He leaned the screen on the verandah. With a screech the window flew up on its sash, the Holland blind followed and he was folding himself through into her bedroom. Seconds later, the front door opened.

'Voila,' he said and with a flourish stood back to let her pass. He stepped out onto the verandah and retrieved her bag, pulling the door closed as he came in.

Laura went into her bedroom and shut the window, pulled down the blind.

'The screen and the window frame might need a bit of maintenance in the morning,' he said.

'Thanks,' she said.

He leaned in the doorway and she felt him watching her. Unconsciously her hand went to her hair, which she'd pulled into a hasty knot on the top of her head. Heat blossomed on her cheeks as she realised how shabby her trackpants and sweatshirt were. Her face burned when she remembered her underwear was hanging on a hook on the back of the bathroom door.

He shifted his survey from her to the bed, the doona tossed back, her robe in a tangle at the foot. She shivered although she wasn't cold. When his eyes lifted to her face again she bit her bottom lip and he sucked in a quick breath, pushed himself upright.

'A coffee wouldn't go astray,' he said, and rubbed an unsteady hand across his whiskery jaw.

'At this hour? You have to be joking.'

'Sleep's out of the question now,' he said.

'You could still get a couple of hours.'

'No point. I've got a long trip ahead of me.' He stood back, barely giving her enough room to pass, and followed her down the passage. Laura flicked on the light as she went into the kitchen.

'How was Neill?' she said as she turned on the coffee machine and took two mugs from the draining rack on the sink.

'All right. He had a cup of tea and went back to bed. The dressing looked okay. I'd just checked on him when you came creeping up to my bedroom window.'

'I wasn't creeping,' she retaliated.

'Whatever,' he said and sat down at the kitchen table.

'Do you want anything to eat?' She put his coffee and the sugar bowl down on the table in front of him.

'No, thanks,' he said and spooned sugar into the coffee.

She sat down beside him with her decaf.

'Why didn't you tell me you were a doctor? What's with keeping it a secret?'

'It wasn't a secret. Like I said to Neill, I just needed to be anonymous for a while. I haven't told anyone – your dad worked it out for himself, with what Great-aunt Dorothy had shared before she died. They were neighbours for years. And the house was never sold, and then I show up out of the blue.'

'When are you going back to your medical practice? I suppose it's in Adelaide.'

'Yes, it is, and I'm on leave for the time being.' Laura pressed her lips together, her grip tightening on the mug handle. It seemed as if everyone was taking a sudden interest in her career.

Jake finished stirring his coffee. He scanned the kitchen. 'You look like you're settling in here. You should hang up your shingle in Potters Junction, give the good Doctor Burns a run for his money.'

'I get the impression you don't like Milton Burns.'

'You catch on quickly,' he said with a sardonic curl of his lips. 'You could say there's no love lost between me and the man.'

'I'm yet to meet him.'

Jake leaned back in his chair, drummed his fingers on the pine tabletop. 'So, Doctor Laura, tell me about Neill. How long has he got left?' He deflated, the hubris of seconds before disappearing. 'I'll be honest, I didn't realise just how bad he was. Jess said he'd had cancer, but I thought the surgery and the chem—'

'You need to talk to his GP, Jake.'

He snorted. 'Don't bullshit me, Laura. You might be pretending you're not a doctor for whatever reason, but I watched you earlier and I'm sure you know full well what's going on with him. And you went through it with your mother. You must have some idea.'

'I'm not his doctor, Jake. I don't know the intricacies of his condition or of his treatment, and I wouldn't even hazard a guess at how much longer he has. What I can tell you is he refused more chemotherapy because it wasn't slowing the spread of the metastases, and I believe that was several months ago.'

'So how do you know that, then?'

'He relayed the conversation that he'd had with his oncologist, Jake. Nothing underhand is going on here. One morning he wanted to talk and he shared it with me as a friend,' she said. 'I'm not his GP. I'm his friend so I'm not breaching any patient confidentiality telling you that.'

'I suppose Jess knows everything.'

'I'm sure she does. She's been here throughout Neill's illness. They seem very close.'

Jake's frown deepened. The silence stretched. Jake stared into his drink; Laura took another sip of hers and shuddered. Camomile tea would have been far more appropriate.

'Look,' Laura said gently. 'Many people find death and dying difficult to talk about and by your own admission you haven't been around much.'

'No, I don't suppose I have. But I've always kept in touch with Jess. We see each other every couple of years. I haven't completely neglected her, or my nephews.'

'Jake, I don't think anyone's been keeping secrets from you. I don't know anything about your relationship with your father or why you stay away, but you're his son and I'm sure he loves you.'

'That's the thing,' he said bitterly. 'I'm not his son.'

'What?' Laura's mug hit the tabletop with a crack. 'What do you mean you're not his son? But Jess is your sister, you have the same colouring, your eyes —'

'Yes,' he interjected. 'She's my sister. My half-sister. We have the same mother. Neill's her father. I have no idea who my father is.'

Laura regarded him for a moment. 'Don't you mean you don't know who your *biological* father is? Didn't Neill bring you up, provide for you, love you? The same as he did for Jess?'

Jake sat there scowling.

Laura stood up, reached for his empty cup. 'Another one?' He nodded. She went to the coffee machine on the bench and dropped in another coffee pod. 'Does Jess know?'

'I don't think so. She's never said anything. I wouldn't know either if I hadn't overheard a conversation between the old man and the good Doctor Burns.'

'Oh.'

'I'd just had my nineteenth birthday. Jess was sick with tonsillitis or something. We were shearing, flat out. Milt Burns made a house call for Jess and he was talking to Dad in the kitchen afterwards, having a proper catch-up. They were good mates, used to play golf together. They had no idea I was there, I was meant to be cleaning up in the shearing shed. I overheard the conversation, I don't even know how it came up. I was so angry that I'd never been told, never given a choice about knowing who my real father was. I saw red. As soon as the shearers had finished I packed my bags and left. Twenty years ago, almost to the day.'

'That must have been a shock for him and Jess. Did you say why you were going?'

'Nope. I was a bit of a hothead back then. I thought I knew everything. And I'd been eavesdropping. You're the first person I've ever told.' He gave her a bemused look. 'I'm not sure why I'm telling you now.'

'Why haven't you ever talked to him about it?'

The wooden chair creaked as Jake moved. 'I dunno. The longer it went the harder it was to bring it up. I don't come back here very often.'

'Did you ever ask your mother who your biological father was?'

He lurched to his feet and began pacing around the kitchen. 'When I finally tracked her down in Perth years ago she wouldn't talk about it. All she said was that Neill married her because she was pregnant, and for all intents and purposes he was my father.'

Laura's impression of Jake's mother went up a notch. It sounded like she'd recognised the role Neill had played in Jake's life, his generosity in taking on another man's child. 'How long ago did your parents split?'

'I was fifteen. Jess was eleven. I don't think Mum was ever happy. She hated being a farmer's wife. She never would have married him if she hadn't been pregnant, if her bible-bashing parents hadn't pushed her into it.'

'How do you know that?'

'Milt Burns talked about that as well, that day in the kitchen. I guess he knew all the gory details. After all, he'd delivered me at the local hospital. He kept saying to Neill he was glad he'd told him about Mum, that he was better off without her. That she eventually would have left, no matter what, and if it hadn't been the stock and station agent it would have been some other bloke. And Neill should be grateful he'd ended up with two bright kids.'

'You must have been eavesdropping for a while.'

'Yep. I remember I got pins and needles in my feet.'

Laura put the coffee on the table, placing the biscuit tin beside it. 'I can make some toast if you like,' she said.

'No, thanks,' he said and sat down again, dropped his head into his hands. She leaned against the sink and folded her arms.

'There are always secrets. There always have been,' he said in a low voice.

Laura's shoulders lifted in a slight, tight shrug. 'It's what parents do, Jake, they can't help themselves. They keep secrets. They want to protect their children. And it doesn't matter how old we are, what we do, we're still their children and they always want to protect us. Sometimes it all backfires.'

Laura couldn't control the edge of pain in her voice.

'Laura?' he said, his eyes widening with concern.

'Jake, I have a bit of an idea what you might be going through. Not all the paternity stuff, of course, but Mum died of cancer. She – they – whoever – didn't tell me until it was too late to do anything. And I had a good relationship with her.' She uncrossed her arms, shoved her hands into the pockets of her trackpants. 'I'd noticed she was losing weight and was always tired. Her GP put the symptoms down to menopause. At the time it all seemed reasonable, quite plausible, in fact. If she'd been my patient I might have come to the same conclusion.' She paused and he waited intently.

'But she was my mother, for god's sake. I'm a doctor. I should have taken more notice, *made* her go and get a second opinion. If only I hadn't been so busy with my own life.' Her eyes were glassy with unshed tears. 'Ah, the *if onlys*. If only Mum had done something earlier and got a second opinion, if only I'd been looking out for her, if only Brett had been more careful, if only I'd taken better care of myself, if only . . .'

'Laura,' Jake said gently and came to her. 'You have had a bugger of a time, haven't you.'

She gave him a shaky smile. 'Yeah, but this isn't about me. We were talking about you and your dad.'

'Enough's been said about that.'

Her answering expression was sceptical but the warmth and strength of the hands cupping her shoulders sent a shudder of yearning right through her. It had been so long. She could feel the heat from his body. So close. When the pressure on her shoulders intensified she didn't draw back. She heard the sigh of her own breath as she pressed her cheek into the hollow of his shoulder, let her hands slide around his waist. So good.

Chapter 10

'You have to go,' she murmured. Laura lifted her head from his shoulder, could still feel the imprint of his lips on her temple. She imagined tipping her head back so he could kiss her lips. A fierce longing coursed through her. Sunrise was a heartbeat away.

'I do.'

Jake stepped away from their embrace. Laura shivered.

'Thanks for breaking into the house for me. I'd still be out there trying to get in.'

Jake's smile had Laura melting all over again. 'I wish,' she started. 'No . . .' The word whispered out on a sigh. 'Forget that. I'm too old to wish. I know it's nothing to do with me, but what are you going to do about the father business?'

'You're right, it's nothing to do with you.' There was no edge to his words.

'He's dying, Jake. You might not get another chance to sort things out.'

He scraped his hand across his jaw, the sound loud in the silent kitchen. 'I have to go. I need to be back in Melbourne tomorrow.'

She didn't want to feel disappointed, but she did.

'Okay, I'll see you around then?'

Jake didn't attempt to answer the question she knew was written all over her face. 'Will you look in on the old man later?' was all he said.

'Of course I will.'

'Thanks. I'll talk to Jess before I leave, tell her about the fall.'

'Travel safely.'

He nodded, a brusque incline of his head, and Laura was left standing in an empty kitchen.

An hour later she was lying in bed trying to sleep when she heard the angry roar of his motorcycle. She rolled over, put her hands over her ears. She wouldn't think about Jake anymore. She couldn't pretend he hadn't been there. Couldn't pretend she hadn't thought What if? for a moment when his arms had folded around her and her body had clenched with anticipation. But he was gone. And he'd made no promises, false or otherwise, about coming back.

She'd been numb since Brett's accident, dead from the neck down. The ache filling her pelvis told her that her body had woken up, with a vengeance. But although her body was ready Laura wasn't sure she was. She rolled onto her side, drew her knees up towards her stomach and thought about sleep. It would be silly to fill her head with foolish *what ifs*.

When she woke again it was almost midday. Her phone had started ringing from somewhere else in the house. She threw back the doona, dashed down the passage to the kitchen, scooped it up off the dresser.

'Laura. You are there. I hope you don't mind me ringing, and I hope I didn't disturb you.'

'Neill, hello. No, I don't mind you calling at all. You didn't disturb me. How's your head?'

'It's all right. I just wanted to say thank you for last night, well, early this morning really. It was a relief not to have to go up to the hospital.'

'No nausea or vomiting? Headache?'

'Nausea, ha. These days I feel sick all the time. I've had a bit of a headache, but that's par for the course as well. So, really, nothing out of the ordinary except a lump on my head and your stitches.'

'I'll come and check the dressing later.'

'Yes . . .' he said, his voice trailing off.

'Neill, are you there?'

'My son's gone,' Neill said at length. 'I don't know when Jess will visit next. Jake said he'd stay for a few days, and I suppose he did. The time went so fast.'

Laura closed her eyes. 'Is he coming back?' she asked, already knowing the answer.

'He didn't say he was. He will have convinced himself he's done his duty. Jess will be disappointed.' Laura heard the painful resignation in his voice.

Jess wasn't the only one who was disappointed.

'I'm sorry,' Laura said. How inadequate those two words were.

'Yes, so am I. I hardly know or understand him anymore. He's like a stranger. I was hoping —' He drew in an uneven breath. 'I thought —' he started again.

'Go on,' she said.

'I thought we seemed to be getting on better this time. He seemed different, somehow. I saw glimpses of the sensitive, thoughtful boy he was until —' He broke off.

'What a shame,' she said, forcing her voice around the lump in her throat. 'If there's anything I can do, Neill, please ask me.'

'All right, lass,' he said. She heard defeat in his voice. 'See you tomorrow when you come back with the dog. We'll have a cuppa and you can check the dressing then.'

The phone went dead in her ear. She put it back on the dresser, rubbed her hands over her face.

Neill was desperate to reconcile with his son. It would be awful to know there was something wrong, but to not know what, to experience a relationship's demise, and to have no idea why. Couldn't Jake see that?

Laura tried to imagine how she'd feel if her sister Alice walked out of her life tomorrow with no explanation. To imagine what it'd be like if over the next twenty years she only saw her a handful of times, and that those times were stilted, stifled and without a shadow of the rich relationship they'd shared. She couldn't imagine it. If Jake were here she'd shake him until he saw sense.

Monday morning dawned fresh and clear with the promise of a perfect spring day. The streets were still deserted when Laura returned from her run, the dog disgruntled when she chained him up again because it was early and there was no sign of life at Neill's place.

She sat on the back verandah and ate breakfast, trying hard to concentrate on the paint colour charts spread out on her lap. At eight-thirty when the hardware shop opened she wanted to be there to buy paint for the bedroom, and to get another key cut for the front door. Being locked out would never happen again.

When she'd inspected the window flyscreen before breakfast, she discovered the lugs that held it in place had been ripped out of the wooden frame. *Brute strength,* he'd said . . . They'd have to be replaced.

She began making a list of other things to buy at the hardware shop. A swirl of wind rattled the gate and her head snapped up. Damn it, she was jittery. She threw down the pencil in frustration and shifted uncomfortably in the cane chair. Barely a week ago she hadn't even heard of Jake Finlay. In a handful of days he'd managed to disrupt her carefully reconstructed life, and had her wanting things from him she'd never imagined she'd desire again. And now he was gone and she despaired of herself for listening out for his motorbike, for the clank of the gate, for his tread on the gravel path.

Neill was at the Hills Hoist pegging out washing when she let herself into his yard. It was mid-morning and before she opened the tins of paint she was keen to see with her own eyes that he was okay.

'Good morning,' she called. 'Skip and I were out early this morning. Your blinds were all drawn.'

Neill turned at the sound of her voice. Laura could see the simple task of hanging washing was almost too much for him now. Was it possible he'd lost *more* weight since Saturday? He looked grey and gaunt, and there was a yellowish tinge to the greyness.

'Hello, lass, I slept in a bit.'

She bent to pick the last items from the basket, taking a handful of weathered plastic pegs from a small tin bucket.

'How are you?' The dressing she'd applied to his head was gone and the black sutures were caked with dry blood. She guessed he hadn't shaved since Milton Burns's party.

His breath was coming in short, shallow bursts. 'Can't complain,' he said.

'Is there any more washing to hang out?' She picked up the empty basket, followed him slowly into the house. She sat the basket on the washing machine and saw the open bag of dry dog food and what looked like mouse droppings by the laundry trough.

'No,' he said. 'Heather comes this week to do my cleaning and she'll do the sheets and towels for me.'

Heather Bailey was employed by a local community service organisation and came in once a fortnight to clean and do other chores. Laura stepped into the kitchen and realised Heather probably needed to come more often. While there were no dirty dishes in the sink, the floor needed sweeping and washing, and the bench was covered in toast crumbs.

'Can I make you a cup of tea, Neill?'

He eased himself down onto one of the kitchen chairs, puffing like he'd just run a marathon.

'I should be making you one, lass,' he said when he caught his breath.

She filled the kettle at the tap and wiped down the benches while she waited for it to boil, anger building inside. How could Jake just walk out and leave his father to it? Jess had her own home and family to care for, and by the sounds of things, it was tough going at the farm. Couldn't he see before he left that his father wasn't managing by himself anymore? And yes, as far as Laura was concerned, Neill was absolutely Jake's father. The man had reared him as his own, all Jake's biological father had done was donate the sperm.

She tied the bulging rubbish bag, putting it beside the door to drop in the wheelie bin on her way out. There was a roll of new rubbish bags in the cupboard under the sink.

'Have you made an appointment to see your GP since you fell?'

He shook his head. 'My regular appointment is next Monday.

And you're not doing a bad job as my GP for the time being. I don't mind at all having a lovely doctor make house calls.'

Laura opened her mouth to protest but the words died on her lips. She didn't mind being the doctor calling if it cheered him up a bit. She found tea bags and sugar. When she opened the fridge for the milk, she was dismayed to find an almost-empty carton right on its use-by date, a six-pack of beer and very little else. It rekindled her anger at Neill's absent son.

She made the tea and put it down in front of him. 'Can I get you anything else? Have you had breakfast?' She was beginning to sound like her mother.

He reached for a battered-looking biscuit tin sitting on the table, dragged it towards him and opened the lid.

'There's a biscuit here.' He dipped an arrowroot biscuit into the tea and caught it just before it fell in. He slurped it loudly. 'Don't seem to have much appetite anyway. Biscuits and the odd bit of toast will do me.'

She sat down at the table opposite him. 'Would you like me to get you a few groceries when I do my shopping?'

He looked at her over the rim of his cup. 'I can ring the super-market and they'll deliver,' he said. 'Anyway, Jess'll pick up a few things for me later in the week. She's a good kid.'

'Yes, I know she is, but there's nothing in the fridge now. I know you most likely won't phone the supermarket, and I don't mind get-ting groceries for you.'

He slowly put down the cup, smoothed a gnarled hand across his bald head. 'You wouldn't mind?'

'Of course I don't mind, Neill. I'm going to the supermarket any-way.' Today, tomorrow, it made no difference when she went.

'All right then. Thank you.'

'I'll make a list,' she said. Today was the day for it. Laura picked up a notepad and pencil from the bench by the telephone and there, on the top page in bold, black script was Jake's name and mobile phone number.

She quickly scribbled it down on the next page before tearing that page off for the list. For whatever reason, and she wasn't going to try and analyse it just now, she felt relieved to have his number, to have some way of contacting him. She sat down again, pencil poised.

Who was she kidding? The moment she'd clapped eyes on Jake Finlay out there on the road, clad in black leather, she'd had his number.

'Okay,' she said. 'What do you need, besides milk?' and she started writing.

When she returned an hour later with several bags of groceries, he didn't refuse her offer to unpack them.

'Is there anything else I can do before I go?' she said, folding up the green recyclable shopping bags. 'Shall I make you a sandwich for lunch?'

He leaned both forearms on the kitchen table; the flannelette shirt and trackpants he'd dragged on sagged on his bony frame. He still hadn't shaved.

'Thanks, lass, but I'll manage. You've helped enough.'

'I don't mind,' she said, and meant it.

He shuffled to the fridge and took out the cheese slices and butter she'd just loaded in. She watched while he spread two slices of fresh bread and made himself a sandwich. 'You see, I am going to eat something,' he said.

'Good.' She picked up the empty shopping bags and her car keys. 'Well, if that's all for now —'

'Oh,' he said and held up his hand. 'Before you go, would you mind stripping the sheets off the spare bed? It's just a bit much for me today and I'd like to have them ready for Heather, when she comes.'

'Not a problem at all.' Laura put down her things.

'You know which room?'

'Yes, the one opposite the bathroom.'

The bedroom was small and smelled stuffy when she opened the door. She slowly inhaled through her nose, unconsciously searching for a hint of the previous occupant. The bed was made, the faded orange chenille bedspread skimming the floor. She pulled it back to expose stiff, matted woollen blankets with pastel-coloured checks, identical to the ones in Dorrie's linen press.

The bedhead was a dirty white, the paint scratched and chipped, with a discoloured plastic reading lamp clamped to the top. She dragged off the threadbare flannelette sheets, thinking she wouldn't be at all surprised if this was the same bed Jake had slept in when he was a boy growing up at the farm. Now, only a hint of his aftershave remained, and when the sheets were laundered, even that would be gone.

She bundled up the sheets and carried them to the laundry, wrangling the tangle of emotions she felt whenever she thought about Jake. He seemed to shove Brett right out of her mind. Brett had been her husband, she'd loved him, and he'd been unfairly taken from her. She dropped the sheets into the laundry hamper, vowing to herself for the umpteenth time that she would *not* think about Jake Finlay again.

Neill was on the second half of his sandwich when she went

back into the kitchen to say goodbye.

'I'll take the dog for our usual run in the morning. If you're not up, I'll come by again mid-morning.'

'Thanks, Laura, I'm sure I'll feel better tomorrow,' he said. 'Shut the front gate on your way out, will you, and I'll let Skip off.'

'Ring me if you need anything and Jess can't do it. And make sure you take your painkillers.'

'You even sound like my GP,' Neill said, the words choking into a cough.

As she went back to her car, she couldn't help but think like his GP. It would be all downhill for him from now on. Professionally, she doubted if he had more than three months left in him, if that, although you could never predict. And his needs would escalate as his health deteriorated. Had the family thought this through? Had they talked about it? Did he want to die at home, or was he happy to go into hospital? Was there a plan for his care during the final days? Had anyone asked the questions?

She put the key in the ignition and reversed the car out of his driveway. Without warning an image of her mother's skeletal frame popped into her head, barely a bump under the sheet, and her vision blurred. Laura felt the familiar prickle at the back of her throat.

Neill's family would have to step up to the plate soon – Jake with all his baggage, Jess with all her problems. But Laura wasn't Neill's GP or even his confidante. She was his neighbour. She sighed, climbed out of the car to close the gate. Becoming embroiled in this family's grief, their anger, their secrets, wasn't safe, or clever. She'd end up pouring too much of herself into the mix. She usually did. And they weren't her problems to resolve. She had enough of her own problems on her plate.

The thought of the empty house, the silence and the unopened paint tins had her driving down the street instead of turning the corner and into her driveway. She didn't have a destination in mind, she just knew she didn't want to go home. She turned right onto the main road and headed south, past the fodder place, past the turn-off to the health centre and hospital, past the silos and the roadhouse. When the *Magpie Creek* signpost flashed by, she wondered if, subconsciously, it was where she'd been heading all day.

Chapter 11

'Laura! Come in, sit down. What a stroke of luck – I'm just about to have a late lunch.' Doctor Meghan Kimble smoothed a hand across her belly. 'Will you join me for a coffee? We've got this flashy new machine and the coffee is good. Plus, this chair is comfortable, and the toilet is close by.'

'Coffee would be lovely. You look well, but tired,' Laura said, noting the bluish-purple smudges underneath Meghan's eyes. 'Country practice and motherhood suit you.'

'Six weeks to go, thank God. I feel like a whale. And I have been well, but it's always busy. Working, running after Lucy and Sean, cooking for the shearers – it's never-ending.'

'I can sort of imagine how it would be,' Laura replied. She drew in her breath in an attempt to control the punch of grief that, as ever, had caught her unaware. If things had been different . . .

'But Laura, it is *so* good to see you. To have someone I can talk to without having to watch everything I say. Small towns are great,

but they can also be your worst nightmare.' She sat down, swivelled
the chair towards Laura. 'Everything is everyone's business, what
they don't know they make up and, trust me, not everything is as
wholesome in the country as the pundits would have you believe.'

'But you look like you've found your niche. All you ever wanted
was to be a GP in the country.' She scanned the neat, functional consulting room.

'It only took me ten years but I finally got there.' Meghan shifted
in her chair. 'Tell me what you've been up to, Laura. How on earth
have you ended up in Potters Junction of all places?'

Laura crossed her legs and smoothed the worn denim of her
jeans while she considered what to say.

'My sister and I inherited an old stone cottage there, years ago
now. I needed a bit of a break from Adelaide and the house needed
some work. If we'd left it much longer, all we'd have had left was a
pile of rubble.'

'I remember Alice. She's younger than you. She studied law.'
Meghan tilted her head to the side, studying Laura's face. 'You're
much thinner than I remember. Are you well?'

'And you're definitely much bigger than I remember.'

Meghan looked down at her belly and then back at Laura, her
expression sobering.

'You seem —' she paused, her eyes narrowing. Laura could
almost feel her assessing, clinical gaze — 'sad,' she said. 'That's it.
You seem sad. I noticed it the other night. Are you up here on your
own? I'd heard on the grapevine you'd married.'

Laura shifted in her seat, fidgeted with the hem of her t-shirt.

'Oh, damn! There I go again.' Meghan slapped her forehead
with the heel of her hand. 'This is a social call and here's me making
it like it's a consult.'

'Probably something to do with the setting,' she said. There was a knock on the door. The stout woman with the thick-lensed glasses who'd greeted Laura at reception came in bearing a tray with two mugs of coffee and a plate with two finger buns on it, gooey with icing.

'Julia, you've brought buns!' Meghan threw her hands up in dismay. 'Did I mention not bringing me buns anymore? Have you seen the size of my bottom?'

Julia put the tray on the desk and grinned.

'Yes, you have told me, many times. No more buns or you'll be the size of a house. But I thought, seeing as this was such a special occasion, I'd bring buns.' She winked at Laura. 'It's not every day she has an old friend visit.'

Laura reached forward and took a bun from the plate. 'Thank you, I will have a bun – I'm not watching my weight at the minute.'

'Lucky you! You'd be pretty much on your own around here.' Julia turned to Meghan. 'Your next patient is in twenty minutes.'

'Okay, thanks.'

When the door had closed, Meghan picked up her coffee. 'Laura, I'm relying on you to eat both of them because I really mustn't eat any at all. Doctor's orders.'

Laura licked icing off her fingers. 'I'll do my best.'

'Now, where were we? We might have let the friendship lapse but surely we can pick up where we left off. You haven't been sick, have you?'

'No, not really.'

'What do you mean, not really? Not *really* sick, or not really *sick*?'

'Not really *sick*, I guess.'

Laura concentrated on a blob of icing at her knuckle. For a time, all those years ago, she and Meghan had been close friends. They'd met when Meghan was on placement in Accident and Emergency. It was one of those intense friendships that develop quickly when people are thrown together in complex and traumatic situations. The working hours meant they were usually exhausted, and they often felt out of their depth. When Meghan had moved on to another placement and Laura had been accepted into the general practice training program, the two had drifted apart.

'Laura, I know it's been a long time but if you want to talk, you know you can trust me.'

Laura put down the half-eaten bun and slowly wiped her fingers with a paper serviette.

'Two years ago my mother died of ovarian cancer, Meghan. You know the story, no specific symptoms, her GP said it was all to do with menopause until it was too late and there were metastases everywhere . . . and Mum kept it all to herself until she was so sick she couldn't hide it anymore.' She took a sip of coffee. 'She stayed at home almost to the very end and Alice and I took turns caring for her.'

'I'm so sorry,' Meghan murmured. 'I remember your mum. She was such a gentle, loving woman. I could never understand why she didn't remarry after your father died.'

Laura swallowed, carefully blotted her lips before putting the napkin on the plate with the uneaten piece of bun. She was surprised that Meghan had remembered. Laura's father had died suddenly when Laura was a teenager.

'I think she enjoyed being on her own. She had her fair share of suitors. Alice and I probably scared them off.'

'Ya think? I can't imagine you getting in the way of someone who made your mum happy.'

'Perhaps, but you know what teenage girls can be like. It's all about them.' Laura paused, told herself she could do this. 'Anyway, you might as well know the rest. A few weeks after Mum died, my husband Brett was killed in a workplace accident.' She blinked, waited a beat to steady her heart. 'It was beyond awful.'

'And you couldn't save either of them,' Meghan said quietly.

'No,' she whispered. 'I couldn't save either of them. Afterwards I threw myself back into work. I took on more work, in fact. I kept busy, thought I'd be able to manage better that way, you know what I mean. I avoided being in an empty house, I avoided having any spare time to feel sorry for myself.'

'Wouldn't we all,' Meghan said gently.

'Yeah, wouldn't we,' Laura said. 'And I thought I'd done so well. Friends and colleagues, even my own family, congratulated me on how I'd managed to get through it. But really, I'd put the grief on hold, and then, about six months ago, when Mum's little dog died, I fell apart completely.'

Unchecked, silent tears ran down Laura's cheeks. Meghan reached for the box of tissues on her desk and scooted her chair closer, passing over a handful and watching while Laura mopped at her eyes and blew her nose.

'I am so *over* crying.' Laura pinched the bridge of her nose. 'Just when I think I've got it all under control.'

'It sounds to me like you've had plenty to cry about.'

'Ah, but I haven't finished yet. I'm saving the best for last.'

Meghan leaned back in her chair, lifted her eyebrows.

'The first anxiety attack came right in the middle of a consult with a woman about Mum's age, who'd just been diagnosed with breast cancer.' She shook her head. 'At first I thought I was having a heart attack, but after ECGs and every test under the sun, just to be sure, they decided I was overtired, working too hard, the textbook stuff.'

Laura focussed on her hands in her lap, fingers busily shredding the soggy tissues. Meghan reached out and took one of her hands.

'And . . .'

'Well, it happened again, and again, and, as if the anxiety attacks weren't bad enough, I'd have these awful crying jags where the tears just wouldn't stop.'

With her spare hand, Meghan passed her more tissues.

'The other GPs in the practice were terrific, very supportive. But it's a busy practice and they needed someone they could rely on, not some flake who burst into tears or tachycardia when the going got tough. So I took a leave of absence, dragged myself to a GP and then to some intensive counselling, and here I am.' She gave a watery sniff and released her hand from Meghan's to blow her nose.

Meghan reached around for the wastepaper basket and Laura dumped the tissues. 'I can understand why you needed some time out, but Potters Junction? Isn't it an unusual choice to come to heal? You're so far away from your network of support, for starters.'

Laura picked up her lukewarm coffee and took another sip. The sticky bun sat like a lump in her stomach.

'Not really. It's quiet, peaceful and away from everyday reminders. I'd finished up with my psychologist and I didn't think I'd run into anyone I knew, which was what I was looking for.'

'Oops,' Meghan said.

'No, no, please don't take that the wrong way. Alice came up with the idea that a complete change of scenery was what I needed and suggested I stay up here for a while. Friends have used the house as a holiday getaway but it sits empty for most of the year, and was desperately in need of repairs. Feeling how I did then, I would have agreed to anything.'

'How did Alice cope with your mother's death, and then her brother-in-law's . . . and the dog?'

'How you'd expect a normal person to behave – she grieved openly and loudly at the time, in true Alice style, and then got on with her life. I was busy soldiering on by myself, bottling it up, trying not to let anyone down.'

The look she gave Meghan was bleak and Meghan reached out and pulled her into an awkward, sideways hug. When they came apart there were tears in Meghan's eyes.

'You poor thing, Laura. You really have had a shit of a time. I wish I could have been there for you.'

Laura wiped her eyes, blew her nose again. 'I'm good now, every day I get better, stronger. I don't wake up anymore wishing I hadn't. I just get up and get on with it. And I haven't cried like this for ages.'

She reached to the floor beside her for her shoulder bag. 'My twenty minutes must be up. When do you want my Medicare card, now or later? And I don't need a prescription for happy pills, I already have one. Haven't had it made up, but have it just in case.'

'Don't be daft, we're friends. And this afternoon I'll live up to the GP's reputation of always being late.' Meghan lumbered to her feet. 'How long were you married?'

'Thirteen months and twenty-two days. We'd been together two years before we were married.'

'It only took a year and an unplanned pregnancy to get Sean down the aisle. What did Brett do?'

'He was a carpenter. I was renovating an old bungalow and needed help with the bigger jobs. I didn't have the time, expertise or muscle, and Brett was looking for after-hours cash work. We met, he turned out to be everything I'd ever dreamed of, and the rest is history. It just isn't fair,' she added quietly. 'It's like we never had a chance to really know each other.' She closed her eyes. 'Sometimes I have to think to remember how his voice sounded, how he liked his coffee . . . And you know what? Sometimes I wonder if it *was* a dream after all.'

'How about the anxiety attacks?'

'Haven't had one since I came up here, and I've been here almost three months. I still get a few symptoms but I'm managing them, mainly with self-talk and exercise.'

'There's not much counselling on offer around here.'

'I'm managing well. Keeping myself busy, and I can ring the psychologist in Adelaide anytime I need to. So far I haven't needed to.'

'So what's your plan?'

Laura lifted her shoulders. 'I don't really have a plan other than to get through each day.' She examined her work-roughened hands, the nails short and blunt. 'I'm still doing some tidying up and renovation work on the cottage. The garden was as much of a mess as the house.'

'When are you going to go back to medicine?'

Laura's heart lurched. She ran two fingers around the neckline of her t-shirt. When Meghan stepped towards her, concern on her freckled face, Laura held up a hand. 'I'm okay. Really.'

Meghan stepped back, perched on the edge of the desk supporting her belly with her hands.

'The reason I ask is because Milt Burns could do with some help. Linda, his wife, is keen for him to cut down his hours. It might be just what you need, Laura. Ease back into it.'

Laura clutched the handle of her bag tightly, her knuckles blanching. 'I'm not sure,' she murmured. 'To be honest I haven't thought that far ahead.'

'Consider it a sort of return-to-work plan. You're an experienced GP but you need to get back into it. Milt Burns needs a break. He's seventy —'

'Yes, I know that.' Laura's chin jutted. 'I was at his birthday party, remember. I'm just not sure if that's what I want to be doing just yet.'

Meghan pushed herself to her feet and stretched. 'Forgive me, Laura, for poking my nose in where it probably doesn't belong. You'll know when you're ready, and I'm sure when that time comes, you'll want to go back to your practice in Adelaide.' She broke off a corner of the second bun and popped it into her mouth, chewing slowly.

'I worry about Milt, about this place. He can't go on for much longer at the pace he's going, and soon I'll be out of action, too. We have locums booked to cover here for three months after I have the baby, and then I'll come back part-time. In the meantime, Milt'll be expected to pick up the slack, and I'm not sure he has the capacity anymore. We're always trying to recruit.'

Laura stood up. 'I'd better go or Julia will be dragging me out by the scruff of the neck. Thanks for the coffee, and the Clayton's consult.'

'Not a problem. Like I said, we're old friends. I'm so glad I ran into you. Don't be a stranger, Laura. Come for dinner sometime. Meet Sean and Lucy properly.'

'That would be terrific.' Laura slung her bag over her shoulder.

'You know I've seen your neighbour Neill Finlay a couple of times when Milt's been away. How has he been since Saturday? He didn't look so crash hot.'

'He's not travelling very well at all. He had a fall on the weekend. His son was home for a few days.' Her heart gave an extra beat. 'But he left yesterday and Neill is on his own again.'

'His daughter Jess isn't far away.'

'Yes, I've met Jess several times when she's visited Neill. She seems nice.'

Meghan's lips thinned, her expression thoughtful. 'Mmm. I don't know anything about the son. Sean said he's been gone for years, that he fell out with his father. The mother ran off with the stock and station bloke. Jess has always been good to her dad. She's a lovely person. We play netball together.'

'She'd have her hands full with two boys and a farm,' Laura said as she walked towards the door.

'Just between you and me, I reckon the husband, Darren, is more of a handful. Sean says he's clueless, that he'd rather be anywhere but the farm and that since Neill's been sick, he's just about bankrupted the place. They struggle.'

Laura stopped and turned back to Meghan. 'I had no idea.'

'Yeah, they have some problems. It's a pity the brother didn't stay around for a bit longer.'

'I'd give Neill a week or two more. After that he won't be able to cope at home on his own. I don't know if they've talked about what comes next. If they haven't, they need to very soon.'

'I haven't got a clue what the plan is for his terminal care. But if he's deteriorating as rapidly as you say, they'll need to sort things out sooner rather than later. You know you're starting to sound like his GP.'

'Hmph,' Laura said and opened the door to a disgruntled-looking Julia.

'My fault,' Laura said. 'I couldn't stop talking.'

'Don't worry, Laura. I would have left you to talk all afternoon but they're getting a bit restless out in the waiting room.'

'Think about what I suggested, Laura. Julia, I'll get the first patient. Can you please give Laura a quick tour before she leaves?'

'Sure, come with me,' Julia said and Laura followed.

Although she'd never been to Magpie Creek medical centre, it felt familiar. There was that same smell of disinfectant hand gel. The music piped into the waiting room and there was a hobby box of toys stacked neatly in the corner. The paintwork looked fresh, the blinds pristine. When she'd arrived, Laura had noticed the chairs lined up against the walls were new. She sniffed the air and detected paint. Laura didn't miss the curious looks of the waiting patients, either.

'The place has recently had a facelift,' Julia said. 'Meghan had to fight tooth and nail with the hospital board to get it done. The CEO —' She threw her hands up. 'Well, anyone would think the money came out of his own pocket.'

'It looks terrific.'

The medical centre was small and it was obvious Julia was proud of every inch of it. There were two consulting rooms, a primary health-care room and toilets, a utility area and a poky little kitchenette.

'Potters Junction health centre is much bigger and flasher than this. They had a plan for the Junction to become the regional centre for health services, but they forgot about needing to recruit doctors and allied health staff for it to work,' Julia said. 'We would have been in pretty dire straits if Meghan hadn't come along to do a four-week locum and fallen for a local farmer.'

'You didn't have a doctor at the time?'

'No. Our long-term GP left and the board hadn't been able to recruit another one. Potters Junction will be in exactly the same situation when Milt falls off his perch. The man is seventy.'

'So everyone keeps telling me,' Laura muttered.

Lying in her bed later that night, wide awake, Laura smoothed her hands across her bare stomach. Talking to Meghan had been good, had helped bring some things into focus. Meghan had known her 'before', had met her mother, and somehow that was comforting. Talking things through out loud had helped her move another step closer towards making the important decisions she needed to make. As for the tears, well, they were valid and there was probably a bit of PMS mixed in there with everything else. Laura made a mental note to take Meghan a box of tissues next time she visited.

The week had been an emotional roller-coaster. Laura shifted onto her side and curled into a ball, dragging the doona up under her chin. In the darkness of night-time she thought about the one thing she hadn't revealed to another living soul. Not even Alice, and she told her sister most things. Brett had known, of course, but he was dead.

Three lives had been lost during those awful weeks two years ago. She lost two of the people she loved the most in the world. And she also lost a child. A tiny foetus had been forming in the lush warmth of her womb and she had flushed it away after an agonising cramp and a gush of blood in the days after Brett was killed. The bleeding only lasted a week and her period was back a month later, so there'd never been any need to tell anyone. It was her and Brett's secret.

So overwhelmed with the loss of her mother and her husband, Laura had tucked the memory of the miscarriage away in a mental box. And thinking about it now she felt sad, but dry-eyed. Had she finally run out of tears?

Anticipating the birth of their first child had been daunting. Brett had been so excited. They'd agreed to start a family soon after the wedding – she was almost thirty-five and, knowing the risks,

Laura hadn't wanted to leave it any longer. They'd discovered she was pregnant in the days after her mother died. The miracle of that still left her gobsmacked.

Then, in a moment, Laura's foreseeable future had been snatched away.

Suddenly she was a widow and had a glimpse of what her mother went through when Laura's father dropped dead of a ruptured cerebral aneurysm when Laura had been seventeen. He hadn't even known about it.

Still numb from her mother's death, Laura was on autopilot those first days – weeks even – after Brett died. She couldn't remember when, or if, she'd stopped feeling pregnant. Thinking back, she'd probably started to miscarry that horrific afternoon she'd identified his body. He'd lain there, in that harsh, sterile room, looking as perfect as ever. It was a cliché but he looked like he was asleep. But when she'd placed her cheek against his, the skin was cold, clammy and stiff, and the grief had paralysed her, then made her physically sick. It was the only time she'd come close to losing it completely – that is, until she did actually lose it. How she'd managed to make the funeral arrangements, stand beside the grave and watch while Brett was lowered into the dank earth, she didn't know.

With the benefit of hindsight, Laura could see her response to the loss of that tiny foetus had been clinical, almost mechanical. She felt the pain, saw the blood, knew what had happened and what she had to do. But in her heart of hearts she could admit that after the rush of blood there'd also been a rush of relief. It had been *their* baby, *their* dream. She accepted that motherhood wasn't something she'd always craved, not now, not then. It had seemed a most natural thing to do after she'd married Brett – he had been so keen to start a family – but with him gone she didn't burn to be a mother.

But maybe, she wondered, lying in her lonely bed, so far from the life she thought she'd have, maybe she wouldn't have come apart at the seams if there'd been a baby to care for and to love. She sighed, long and deep, into the dark. As she'd told herself time and time again, there were too many things that were facts to spend time worrying about the *what ifs*.

Chapter 12

Mikey woke up Wednesday morning with a sore throat. His temperature wasn't up but Jess kept him home from school. Her youngest son was like she'd been as a child, prone to tonsillitis and middle ear infections. If his temperature went up, she'd take him to the health centre.

By lunchtime it was pretty clear to Jess there was nothing wrong with her son except a case of not wanting to go to school. After lunch – another meal Darren ate in surly silence, the atmosphere so tense that even Mikey noticed – Jess drove in to Potters Junction to get the mail and pick up a repaired tyre from the mechanic.

'I'll take Mikey and call in to see Dad,' she said and her husband grunted.

During the twenty-minute drive, Jess let Mikey play with her tablet so she could stew on what she was going to do about the deteriorating situation with Darren. It didn't matter how many times she asked, he just wouldn't talk about what was wrong. And there was definitely something wrong. He'd never been the most communicative of men but in the eleven years they'd been married he'd never shut down like this. Jess's hands tightened on the steering wheel and her head felt as if it were being squeezed in a vice. If only she could keep everything together until her father died. After that it wouldn't matter so much if everything fell apart. For her dad's sake she just needed to keep it all together until then.

Much to Jess's surprise, Doctor Burns's early model Holden Statesman De Ville was parked in front of her father's place, one wheel on the kerb, the other in the gutter. She'd always thought that if there were two car years to every human year, the early model petrol guzzler would be about as old as the doctor. Heart thumping, Jess pulled in behind it, told Mikey to wait in the car, leaped over the fence and sprinted up the drive and through the front door.

Relief rushed through her when she found the two men in the kitchen chatting. It had only been five days since Jess had seen her father and she couldn't believe the change in him in that short time. Jake had told her about the fall but Jess wasn't expecting the lump and scabby wound on his head, and as he moved about the kitchen making them tea she was shocked to see how doddery he was on his feet.

'Jess,' Neill said, when he noticed her standing in the doorway between the passage and the kitchen.

'Dad, are you okay?' she said, breathless from her dash from the car. She zeroed in on Doctor Burns.

'He's all right, Jess, no need to worry. I had to see a patient in the next street so I thought I'd drop in, see how my old mate was.'

'Jake didn't tell me you had stitches, Dad. When did you go to the hospital?'

'I didn't. Laura from next door stitched me up. She's a doctor, as it turns out, and has been checking up on me each day.'

'Mum?' came a plaintive voice. 'Can I come in now?'

'Mikey!' Jess rushed up the passage to find her son's freckled nose pressed to the screen door. She opened the door and he came in, his eyes wide.

'Is Poppa okay?'

'He is, mate, for now. Doctor Burns just dropped in to say hello.' Mikey took off down the passage and Jess followed at a more respectable pace. When she stepped into the kitchen Milt Burns was firing off a volley of questions at her father.

'Why didn't you tell me you had a doctor living next door? One of Dorothy Handley's great-nieces, you say? What's her story? Do you reckon she'd come and work for me? If I don't cut back soon, Linda will probably divorce me.'

'You'd have to ask Laura,' Neill said, turning to hug his grandson. 'Althouh I will say, she looks a helluva lot healthier than she did when she first arrived. She's been doing up the old place: painting, pulling up carpet.'

Jess noticed how her father's breathing had deteriorated – he could only say a few words between each rasping gasp and the doctor's concern was palpable. She tried to hold back the ever-present panic lurking just below the surface.

'Mum, can I go play with Skip?' Mikey pulled on her hand. When she nodded, he bolted out the back.

'What did you say her last name was?'

'I didn't. It's O'Connor. Laura O'Connor.'

'She's planning on staying a while, then?' Milt said.

Neill shrugged. 'Like I said, you'd have to ask her.'

Milt scratched his head, dislodging his comb-over. 'I might just ask around,' he said. 'It's a small world in our business. One of my colleagues is bound to know something about her and why she's in Potters Junction.'

'That's not very fair,' Jess blurted. 'Surely the woman is entitled to her privacy? Why don't you just ask her directly, and if she wants you to know, she'll tell you.'

Doctor Burns had the good grace to look guilty.

'Jess is right,' Neill said. 'It's probably not fair to go snooping around behind her back. You risk getting her offside before you start.'

Milt scowled. 'I'd better get going,' he said gruffly and picked up his battered black doctor's bag. 'The girls at the surgery will send out a search party if I don't show up soon. When is your next appointment with me?'

'This coming Monday.'

'I'll see you then, old boy. Jess, walk me out, will you.'

Jess swallowed. Milt followed her to the front door.

'He's a lot worse, isn't he?' she said when they reached the verandah, out of earshot. 'He's trying to pretend he's not, but I can see that he is.'

Milt scraped at his chin. 'Jess, you need to talk to him about what he wants.'

'How much longer has he got?' Jess said, her voice a hollow croak. This was happening way too fast, faster than she'd ever imagined. She felt hot and cold at the same time, tears at the ready.

'I don't know, Jess, and that's the honest truth. But, given the speed of his deterioration, he might make his birthday but I doubt he'll make Christmas.'

'Shit,' she said, doing a quick calculation in her head. It was barely two months to his birthday and Christmas wasn't long after. Shit, shit, shit. A tear scalded its way down her cheek. Milt reached out and squeezed her rigid shoulder.

'Jess, you must talk to him, soon, find out what he wants for his last days – whether he wants to stay at home or go into the hospital; who will care for him if he chooses to stay at home; what he wants for his funeral. I'm sure you aren't in a position to drop everything and look after him twenty-four seven, even if you wanted to. Get onto that damned brother of yours. Tell him to get his arse back here and sort out whatever it is that's going on with his father, before it's too late. You're all going to need to support each other more than ever in the coming weeks.'

Jess was too choked up to speak.

'Will I see you on Monday, will you bring him in for his appointment?'

Jess's head bobbed up and down. She pressed her fingers tightly to her lips to hold back the hysterical sob waiting there. She'd known her dad was sick, that he was going to die, eventually, but she'd been sure they'd have one last Christmas together on the farm. She'd been sure that Jake would eventually come to his senses and come back. But time was running out.

'And Jess,' Milt said quietly. 'If you have anything you need to sort out with your dad, now's the time. Better to do it now than not and then regret it for the rest of your days.'

'We're fine,' she said.

'Good.' He left her standing on the verandah feeling like the bottom had dropped out of her world.

Laura tipped paint out of the tray and back into the tin. After two solid days of painting the front bedroom, she was exhausted. Everything ached – from the top of her head to the tips of her toes – and she had paint spray all over her clothes and face. Using the hammer she tapped the lid firmly back onto the paint tin. The colour would do for the hall, as well.

The window was up to let the paint fumes escape so she heard the metallic clink of the latch on her front gate, the scrape of footsteps on cement, then the brusque rap on the screen door.

'Yes?' she said, wiping her hands on a rag. 'What can I do for you?'

'Laura O'Connor? Or should I say, *Doctor* Laura O'Connor?'

She squinted through the flyscreen. Whoever was there was a silhouette against the afternoon light.

'Yes?' she repeated, feeling her heart rate accelerate. The screen door didn't lock but Laura reached out to hold it shut. She had the uncanny feeling that if she opened the door now, her life would never be the same again.

Too late.

The handle slipped from her fingers and she was standing face to face with Doctor Milton Burns.

'Hello,' she said. 'How can I help you, *Doctor* Burns?'

'You know who I am?'

'I took Neill Finlay to your birthday party.'

'Hello,' he said, his sharp brown eyes taking her in. 'You do look like Dorothy. It's the eyes. And your voice is similar.' He extended his hand and if he was surprised by the strength of her grip he didn't show it.

'You knew her?'

'Oh yes, I knew her. Like almost everyone else in this town, I was her GP. And I considered her a friend. I signed her death certificate, went to her funeral.' He frowned, bushy eyebrows meeting in the middle. 'That must've been, what, five years ago?'

'Six years next month,' she said, and his eyebrows headed towards his hairline.

'Bloody hell,' he said. 'Where does the time go?'

They stood staring at each other until Milt Burns broke the silence. 'Well, aren't you going to ask me in?'

Laura tucked an errant strand of hair behind her ear. 'Mmm, I'm not sure if I should.' She thought of her earlier feeling of foreboding.

He threw back his head and laughed, sending his jowls into a frenzy. 'I think we're going to get on just fine.'

'Why would we need to?'

'Because I'm going to ask you to come and work for me, with me – whichever option floats your boat.'

'I don't have a boat.'

'Laura.' His voice softened. 'Ask me in, hear me out. That's all I ask.'

She regarded him for several long seconds. 'All right,' she said. 'Come in. But I have to rinse the paint tray and put the brushes in to soak before I do anything.'

She offered him a chair in the kitchen, and carried the painting paraphernalia to the outside tap. When she came back in he was looking perfectly at home, leafing through the dusty photo album he'd picked up off the dresser.

'You do look a lot like Dorothy,' he said and chuckled. 'She had one hell of a temper. It took a bit to get her going, but when she did! And stubborn . . .'

'You sound as if you knew her quite well.' Laura couldn't say for sure, because her eyes hadn't adjusted to the dimmer kitchen after the sun, but she thought Doctor Burns blushed.

'I was her GP,' he said, his face almost buried in the photo album. Then he closed it with a thud and cleared his throat. 'I was visiting your neighbour earlier today and he happened to mention it was you who'd stitched him up on the weekend.'

Laura gave a cynical snort. 'And now he's stitched me up, by the sounds of things.'

Milt rested his arms on the table and sighed deeply. 'As a matter of fact he didn't. When I heard you were a doctor I was going to ask around to find out what I could about you. Neill and Jess told me to pull my head in and ask you what it was I wanted to know.'

'And what is it you wanted to know?'

'I'll be frank with you. As you know I'm getting on and my health is —' He wobbled his hand from side to side. 'And my wife, Linda, is keen for me to retire. Me? I'm not so keen. Wouldn't know what to do with myself. But I would like to cut down some, work maybe three days a week instead of five or six.'

'And?'

'And? Well, I don't know what brought you here to Potters Junction, I don't know what plans you have, when you plan to go back to wherever you came from, but . . .' He flapped a hand at her paint-splattered self. 'If you're doing the place up I thought you might be around for a while and might be interested in some work.'

'Have you been talking to Meghan Kimble?'

'Nope.'

He hadn't hesitated and Laura gave herself a mental slap for not trusting her friend. She leaned against the sink, folded her arms.

'I suppose the least I can do is be frank right back. I'm not willing to share the reasons why I'm here, they are very personal. I have taken twelve months' leave from the practice I work at in Adelaide. Six months of that time have passed already. Up until recently I'd avoided thinking about my career at all.'

'I see.'

Laura toed at the mat underfoot. Milt Burns's quiet acceptance of her answer had her feeling unsettled. She'd half-expected him to rant and rave about GP shortages and wasted skills. But he hadn't. He stood up and placed the photo album back on the dresser.

'I'll think about what you've suggested,' she said. 'At this stage I can't offer any more than that. And I know what a small world GP medicine is, but I would ask you to please respect my privacy.'

'I'd appreciate if you would think about it. Any help I can get would be a bonus. In six months we might be able to recruit some-one permanent. Who knows?' He sighed wearily. 'And pigs might fly as well.'

As Laura closed the screen door after him he said, 'And I prom-ise not to snoop.'

'Bloody hell.' Laura counted on her fingers the days since Saturday. 'Four days, that's all it took,' she muttered, angrily unfurling the hose so she could water the herb pots on the back verandah. Preoccupied with Milt Burns's conversation, she turned on the tap before she had the end of the hose in her hand. Water burst through and the hose spat and hissed across the verandah like a snake with its head blown off.

With a howl of frustration she dived for the end and shut off the tap. She didn't know whether to laugh or cry. Looking down at her sodden feet, laughter won and she toed off her wet sneakers and socks and propped them up against a pot plant to dry in the late afternoon sun.

The days were lengthening, warming up. Summer was on its way. The seedling vegetables were doing well. A couple of the let-tuces looked like they wouldn't make it, but everything else looked perky. And so did the weeds. She swore she could see them growing in this warmer weather.

She slipped on her flip-flops, watered the pots and got stuck into the weeding. There was plenty of daylight left. After inhaling paint fumes for two days, the fresh air was wonderful. As the pile of weeds on the cement path got bigger, the dirt under her fingernails more ingrained, her thoughts kept circling back to her conversation with Milt Burns.

She could understand that from where he and Meghan sat, it would look like she was wasting her skills and training. But from where she sat, well, things looked a little bit different. With a hefty sigh she stabbed the hand fork into the ground, rooting out the last weed without dislodging the seedlings. The sun had almost set and she was thirsty and hungry, and her muscles were screaming. She loaded the weeds into the wheelbarrow and dumped them on the growing compost pile, surveyed the garden beds with satisfaction.

Her mobile phone rang just as she was debating whether to have a glass of wine with dinner. She didn't recognise the number but took the call anyway. Somewhere, at the back of her mind, she was hoping Jake would call.

'Laura?' a tentative voice said. 'It's Jess, Neill's daughter.'

'Jess, hello. Is he all right?'

'Not really, but then you would have noticed how quickly he's going downhill. You've been so good to check in on him each day.'

'Yes, he has deteriorated over the last few days, especially since Jake left.'

'I know, and that's what I'm ringing you about. Doctor Burns says I should get Jake home because Dad hasn't got long to go. I'm just worried that Jake won't come, even when I tell him how serious it is and that I need his help. I'm always on at him to come home and see Dad. I know I'll get really upset with him, and that won't be helpful.'

'What do you want me to do?'

'I thought maybe if you could ring him, seeing you're a doctor and all and you understand how serious things are and what needs to be done so Dad can die in peace. Jake might listen to you. Dad's too stubborn to do it.'

Laura's chest rose and fell. 'What makes you think he'll listen to me? Maybe Milt Burns could talk to him. He knows more about your father than I do.'

'Doctor Burns! Jake won't listen him. He hates his guts, blames him for encouraging Mum to leave. Personally, I don't think Doctor Burns did encourage her. I might have only been eleven but I remember how unhappy Mum was. She hated the farm. Towards the end I sometimes think she hated Dad – and us.'

'Oh, Jess.' Laura sank down onto one of the kitchen chairs. She closed her eyes. 'All right, I'll ring him. But I can't promise anything.'

'I know that, Laura. Thank you. Please let me know what he says.'

Chapter 13

Heart racing, and before she could talk herself out of it, Laura scrolled through her contacts. She knew Jake's number would come up because she'd put it there days before. Without giving herself a chance to think, she pressed connect. It rang, and rang. She felt hot and then cold, and relieved and then disappointed when it went to message bank, and then nearly dropped the phone when his voice said, 'Jake Finlay. Name and number and I'll get back to you.'

She stabbed disconnect and was disgusted to notice her hand was shaking. What was the matter with her? He'd never ring back if she left a message. Maybe if he saw a missed call from a number he didn't recognise, curiosity would get the better of him. But before she'd even put the phone down it rang. Jake Finlay flashed on the screen. Her stomach dropped into her pelvis. She pressed accept and put it to her ear.

'Laura?'

So much for not recognising her phone number.

'Jake?'

'Are you all right?'

She felt her fingers loosen on the phone. 'Yes, yes, I'm fine. You?'

'Good.'

'Good, that's great.' She gave a nervous giggle, felt ridiculous. 'Where are you?'

'Singapore, waiting for a connection to Istanbul, then on to the Syrian border. We've secured the money to keep going with the second documentary.'

Her heart sank. 'Oh, great. So we won't see you back here anytime soon.'

She heard him clear his throat. 'Wasn't planning on it.'

'What about your dad?'

'Ah,' he said, dragging the single syllable out. 'So that's what this is about.'

'He's dying.'

'So you told me once before, remember?'

She closed her eyes. 'Yes,' she said. 'And you told me he wasn't your father, but I beg to differ, Jake. He thinks he is and he's hurting because you've left him high and dry.'

She could hear him breathing, noise and voices in the background.

'Did he put you up to this?'

'No, he did not! He might not be your biological father but you both carry the same stubborn gene.'

'I can't just up and leave. I'm one of the cameramen. We've been planning this for months. Raising the money, visas, all that shit. I really shouldn't have spent time back there at all.'

In her mind's eye she could see him drag his fingers through his hair.

'Jake, your sister shouldn't have to do this on her own. And you need to say your own goodbye. You can't run away forever.'

'Ha!' The sound was harsh. 'Look who's talking.'

'How long?' she said between gritted teeth.

'Six, maybe eight weeks, who knows? Could even be three months. Too many variables to know for sure. The place is so bloody unstable.'

Anger came, fast and furious, stabbing like a red-hot poker. 'Well, I hope you'll be able to live with yourself for the rest of your life because you won't get another chance to put things right. Goodbye.' She disconnected, slammed the phone down on the table. It bounced off onto the floor with a crack. She fought against the first sting of tears, and won. She was heartbroken for Neill and Jess, but buggered if she'd let herself shed a tear over Neill's son.

He said her name and then realised he was talking into an empty space. He stood up, resisted the urge to fling the phone across the transit lounge. He closed his eyes, told himself to get a grip. Was it only four days ago that he'd walked out of her kitchen, and out of her life, like the coward he was? For such a brief acquaintance she'd been on his mind an awful lot.

He'd put over 6000 kilometres between himself and Potters Junction and Laura but whenever he thought about their conversation early that Sunday morning, how he'd wrapped her in his arms, he wished, yes, damnit, he wished their platonic hug had been something much more. Whenever he remembered the silky warmth of her skin, the scent of her hair, the way her lips turned up at the corners when she was amused, it left him with a hollow feeling deep inside.

He paced back and forth, ignoring the curious stares of his fellow travellers. For a minute there he'd thought, hoped, she was calling to ask how he was. But no, it was all about Neill. Of course he'd said goodbye to the old man when he'd left last Sunday. He stuffed the phone back into his pocket, sat back into the uncomfortable plastic seat and dropped his head into his hands.

She was right, damn her, he'd said goodbye but he hadn't said his *goodbyes*. He was running away again. But how long would it take for him to make good on a lifetime of hurts and things unsaid? Longer than Neill had left, so did it really matter? He slapped his thigh. Why couldn't people just mind their own fucking business?

And then there was Jess.

'Fuck,' he spat. For a moment guilt and self-loathing threatened to suffocate him. The woman on the seat beside him gave him a filthy look, stood up and walked away.

But then the boarding call came over the public address and, with a skill born of many years of experience, he pushed everything but the immediate to the back of his mind. Concentrate on the here and now, he told himself. And really, they were all a lot better off because he'd left; they probably just didn't realise it yet.

It seemed only minutes since she'd hung up on Jake, and Jess was calling again. Laura scooped her phone up off the floor, grateful she hadn't broken it.

'He's not coming back.'

'Shit.'

'He's in Singapore, on his way to Istanbul, as we speak.'

'Bugger.'

'Jess, we've done what we can. We've asked. He is a grown man.'

Of that she was certain. 'And he's capable of making his own decisions.'

'How was he?'

'Angry. I pretty much hung up on him.'

'Go girl,' Jess said. 'He probably deserved it. I love him but he can be a stubborn sod. I just wish I had some idea what happened between him and Dad. I've asked him and I've asked Dad. Jake clams up and Dad says he doesn't know for sure, that's what makes it so hard on him. At least if he knew, he could try to talk to Jake.'

'It's a pity, Jess, all round. He's not coming back, but I promise I'll help you with your dad. We can talk about exactly what your dad wants during his last months. I can find out about what palliative care services are available, and things like delivered meals.'

Jess's relief was almost palpable. 'You are a doll. I don't know what we did to deserve you, but I sure am glad you're living next door to Dad.'

After Jess disconnected she sat at the kitchen table, staring at nothing in particular. In for a penny, in for a pound, she thought. It was well and truly dark outside, she was exhausted, beyond hungry, and felt as if her emotions had taken a flogging since Milt Burns turned up on her doorstep late that afternoon. She yawned, ignored her grumbling stomach and went to bed.

Neill was up and at the door the following morning when Laura came back with Skip.

'Gorgeous day,' she called as she chained up the dog and refilled his water bucket. 'I slept in. How are you?'

'So-so.'

'Did you sleep?'

'Not much.'

'Pain?' She peered at him through the screen door. He pushed it open and she followed him inside.

'Plenty of that,' he said. 'It's like toothache, only in your whole body.'

'Your medications aren't doing their job. Are you taking enough painkillers?'

'They make me woozy. After that fall I worry I'll fall again.'

'I can understand that.' Laura washed her hands at the kitchen sink, dried them on the towel hanging on the handle of the oven door. The kettle was hot, just needed to be brought to the boil again, and Neill had cups sitting side by side on the table. When she lifted the lid on the teapot the tea had already been spooned in.

Laura went to the fridge for the milk. 'I'll look at those stitches while I'm here.'

The water sizzled when it hit the tea-leaves. 'They're starting to itch like hell, so it must be healing.' He carried the teapot to the table, poured the tea, pushed a steaming cup and saucer across the table towards her. 'Jess rang last night and said Jake's definitely not coming back.'

Laura stirred the brew and murmured, 'It's a shame.'

'Yep, that about sums it up. But there's no need for you to worry.' He blew on his tea, took a tentative sip, the cup rattling in the saucer when he put it down.

'Is there anything I can do?'

'No, thanks, lass. The boy was never the same after his mother ran off with that bloke.' He gave a phlegmy cough. 'Don't suppose any of us were. But Jake was a teenager, restless, resentful, always looking for an argument. Then he eventually took off.' He reached for the biscuit tin, grappled with the lid. 'Don't know for sure what made him bolt. I don't like to think the need to get away from his family was the only reason he left.'

She silently cursed Jake for leaving her in this position. 'What happened to her, to Jake's mother?'

'As far as I know she married the bloke. She could have more kids for all I know, lives in WA. Never bothered with Jake or Jess. Broke Jess's heart. Jake got angry.' He stabbed a biscuit into the milky tea.

'What about you, how did you cope?'

'Just got on with it. Had two kids to raise. A farm to run, bills to pay. Jess was only eleven, Jake fifteen.'

'Did you ever see her again?'

He plucked out another biscuit and pushed the tin towards Laura. 'Funny thing, that. She walked out the door with two suitcases and I've never clapped eyes on her since. We talked on the phone a couple of times, but I haven't seen her. Strange. Sixteen years of marriage, two kids, and poof.' He snapped his fingers. 'She was gone. She didn't want anything in the way of money, either. She just wanted out at any cost.'

Laura watched as he dunked the biscuit, wondered if he'd ever thought he'd paid enough – raising a boy that wasn't his. 'Do you want me to make you some toast, an omelette?'

'Jess ask you to look out for me, did she? Make sure I was eating, sleeping?'

Laura glanced down at her hands, a slow smile lighting up her face. 'What if she did,' she said, and he laughed, and then coughed, his face a rictus of pain.

She fetched him a glass of water, pushed the box of tissues closer. There were splotches of blood on the wadded tissues in his hands.

'Does Milt know about that?'

He nodded. 'You know,' he gasped when he finally caught his elusive breath, 'as much as he's a good doctor, and a good friend, Milt Burns can be an interfering old bugger.'

Laura's eyes widened in surprise.

'He sometimes pokes his nose in where it doesn't belong.'

She gulped her tea and burned her tongue. That's exactly what Jess had said Jake thought.

When they'd finished Laura took away their empty cups, washed up and wiped down the table.

'I'll look at those stitches now.' She was satisfied the wound was healing. 'They'll be ready to come out on Saturday. Jess said she'd be in this afternoon but you ring if you need me.'

Laura left without another word but she worried about leaving him on his own, and in her mind she rehearsed again what she'd say to his son if she ever got the opportunity.

Chapter 14

On Saturday morning Laura made her decision.

She would take up Milt Burns's offer and go back to work part-time. It was the right thing to do. It was time. Since her conversation with Alice last weekend, with Meghan Kimble on Monday and Doctor Burns on Wednesday afternoon, Laura had thought of little else. In her mind she'd envisaged the pros and cons and then on a sheet of paper she'd drawn up two columns and written them down.

The pro side was considerably longer. Two days' work a week would leave her time to work on the house and garden; she would be utilising her skills; it was better to ease back into her chosen profession where no-one knew her; she missed working; and the money would be helpful.

The first dot-point in the cons column read, *Not being able to cope and having another meltdown*, and it had her heart rate picking up every time she glanced at it.

The only one other dot-point in the cons column, *Hospital*

emergency and after-hours cover, had her mouth going dry.

It wasn't because she wouldn't be able to manage it. Until six months ago she had been diligent with her continuing medical education and refreshers. Since Brett's death she'd picked up a week-end a month in A&E at one of the large private hospitals. It'd kept her busy and allowed her to re-hone her A&E skills.

But it had been a while since she'd crawled out of bed at three in the morning to see a sick kid, a drug overdose or a road trauma victim. And here in Potters Junction, if Milt Burns was out of town she'd be on her own, apart from the nurses and a voice at the other end of the phone. That was where country and metro general practice really differed.

Decision made, Laura was bursting to tell someone, so she rang Alice. She knew her sister would be sitting on the deck reading the paper and drinking green tea at this time of day.

'I've been offered a job and I've decided to take it,' she said without preamble.

'Okay.' *Unflappable Alice.* 'What would this job be?'

'Medicine, of course, what else would it be?' Silence. 'Alice? Speak to me.'

'Yes, I'm still here. I'm just a bit choked up, that's all. I've been so hoping to hear you say that, I'm so pleased, Laura! Tell me more.'

'I don't know much more yet but the local GP heard about me on the grapevine and he called in last Wednesday and offered me some work while I'm here.'

'What's your plan?'

'I'll contact him on Monday and take it from there. He said he wants to cut back and I thought maybe I could do two days a week.'

'You must have about half of your leave left. Will you come back to Adelaide then?'

Laura contemplated her paint-encrusted fingernails. 'I haven't thought that far ahead. I do know I want to stay here until my neighbour dies. He's a nice man and he's in the terminal phase. I like his daughter, she's a real battler, and —' She paused, thinking how to put her feelings into words.

'You want to be there for him, the way you couldn't be for Mum because it all happened so fast with her.'

Laura's grip on the phone relaxed. 'You were always good at summing up. No wonder you're the lawyer.'

'And you're always good at the caring stuff, that's why you're the doctor. Now listen to me, Laura, before you go back to work you need a complete makeover. You need to do something with that hair. And I bet you haven't had your legs or your eyebrows waxed in six months.'

'I'm not cutting my hair! But I will do something about the other stuff. Promise. And I'll need more clothes —'

'The ones in my spare room. That would be terrific. I could have my spare room back.'

They agreed to meet in the Clare Valley the following weekend. It was about halfway for both of them. Alice would load her car with Laura's clothes, shoes and whatever else she could fit in. They'd find a dinky little B&B to say in on Saturday night and do the clothing swap there. They'd go somewhere nice for dinner, share a bottle of wine, and catch up in person.

'Yes!' Laura said when they disconnected. She had the promise of a job she was looking forward to, and it felt wonderful. How did that saying go? Something about everyone needing something to do, someone to love, and something to look forward to. Two out of three was a good start.

The next two weeks flew by and the butterflies in Laura's stomach felt more like a flock of corellas when, on a bright and warm Monday morning in late October, she sat down at the desk in consulting room two at Potters Junction Health Centre. She checked her lipstick in the mirror above the handbasin and rearranged the things on the desk, for the third time.

Wiping clammy palms on her linen trousers, she tried to ignore the sound of her rushing pulse as she prepared to see her first patient in almost seven months. She wriggled back in the chair. It felt different, but the same. The gyprock walls, melamine desk and fresh but simple appointments of the room were far removed from the stone walls and wood-and-leather furnishings of her consulting room in Adelaide; her current view of an asphalt car park and native shrubbery no competition for her leafy green vista in Glenelg. But this felt good, right, and the only word she could think of to describe the way she felt was excited.

'So, you're all set? Ready to go, Doctor O'Connor?'

Kaylene Curtis, the practice manager, stood in the open doorway of the consulting room. She was a tall, slim woman, her short, stylish hair glossy with highlights. The tailored navy blue blouse had *Potters Junction Health Centre* embroidered in gold lettering above the pocket.

Kaylene had shown Laura through the health centre ten days previously, after her meeting with Milt Burns where they'd worked out the terms and conditions of her employment. The health centre was a brick veneer building about five years old. There were four consulting rooms, a meeting room, a huge lunch room, a treatment room and the usual utility areas. The reception and waiting room were large, light and airy with colourful prints lining the walls.

They'd agreed she'd work Mondays and Tuesdays. Milt Burns

would be there the first week but after that he'd take those days off, and they'd alternate the weekends on call. They had discussed the on-call at length, Laura voicing her concerns.

'I can see that a country GP needs to be prepared for anything. I'm a city GP and, okay, I did weekends in A&E and I've kept my skills up as much as I could, but I haven't worked at all for over six months.'

Milt Burns pulled at his jowls and reiterated that support for country GPs from a major metro teaching hospital was only a phone call away.

'And the nurses know what they're doing. Well, most of them.'

'But I'm the doctor on the spot,' she'd said, 'and a phone call can only offer so much support.'

'Call me if you're worried or you ever need a second pair of hands. And I know Meghan Kimble wouldn't mind at all if you called her if I wasn't around. No doubt she'll be busting to get back to work.'

His comments had allayed her anxiety a little. But Laura knew she wouldn't sleep much the nights she was on call.

'We are *so* pleased to have you, Doctor O'Connor,' Kaylene said as she walked into the room. 'Doctor Burns isn't getting any younger.'

'My pleasure, Kaylene. I'm all ready to go.' The practice manager had given her a brief orientation to the computer software and medical centre routine. Everything was stocked and the first patients waiting.

'Any questions, remember I'm just down the corridor. Our other receptionist, Susan, starts at ten and goes through until six. She's part-time. There aren't any visiting specialists today and I'm sure Doctor Burns won't mind being interrupted if you need anything.'

'Thank you. I'm sure it won't take me long to settle in.' She

mirrored Kaylene's bright smile, forced the rising bubble of appre-
hension back down her throat. 'I guess we'd better get on with it so
I'm not behind before I start.'

Laura followed Kaylene out to reception to collect the first
patient, an unwell young mum with two toddlers in tow, and with
what turned out to be a urinary tract infection.

From there, the day progressed like any day in general practice. After her third patient, an older man with a chest infection,
Laura felt like she'd never been away from it. When five-thirty
came around and there'd been no emergency call-outs to the hospital Laura mouthed a silent *thank you*. In fact, apart from the
surprised, and then curious looks on the patients' faces when Laura
collected them, nothing unexpected had happened. As she packed
her things into her bag she couldn't help but feel satisfied. It had
been a momentous day. In her lowest moments Laura had wondered
if she'd sit this side of a consulting desk again.

Laura let herself out the back door of the health centre and
stepped into a wall of late-afternoon heat. It'd been in the mid-
thirties, hot for a spring day, the smudge of smoky-grey clouds on
the horizon the only indicator of the forecast change. Throwing her
bag onto the passenger seat she started the car and the phone rang
before the air conditioner had begun blowing cool air.

'How'd it go?' Alice asked.

'Good. The practice staff are terrific. No emergencies at the hospital, thank God, but there were a couple of frustrating things.'

'Like what?'

'No podiatrist at all, and the dietician only comes once a week,
and there's a two-month waiting list for outpatients. They've been
trying to recruit a podiatrist for three years. Would you believe it!'

'No visiting podiatrist?'

'Nope. The practice manager said there was one for a while, but he got fed up with all the travel. Patients have to drive to Port Augusta, two hours away.'

'Four-hour round trip to have your toenails cut?'

'That about sums it up. And it's only the tip of the iceberg. Because people have to travel for health services, they wind up doing their grocery shopping, going to the hardware shop and wherever else they have to go while they're there. Local businesses miss out all round.'

'Wow. You're all fired up after one day on the job.'

Laura gave a dry chuckle. 'Sorry, but I can't help thinking these people do it tough. Today was the first day for years that people have had a choice of GP at the health centre.'

'Yeah, we take all those things for granted. Anyway, I still have work to do before I go home. I just wanted to make sure your first day went okay.'

'It was all good. Thanks for giving me the nudge I needed to get back to work. Love ya.'

They disconnected and Laura made the short drive home. If it wasn't for the hospital emergency work, she could have walked to the health centre, but the hospital was on the outskirts of town, a fifteen-minute walk from the health centre.

When she turned into her street, her heart missed a beat at the unmistakable shape of an ambulance parked in Neill's driveway. The rear door of the vehicle was open, the stretcher missing. Neill's house was open, the unlatched screen door banging against the wall. Braking hard she pulled into the kerb, jumped out of the car and flew up the drive, heart pounding, and then was almost light-headed with relief when she heard voices followed by a burst of laughter. Neill lived, at least.

'What's going on?' she asked, as two volunteer ambulance paramedics manoeuvred a laden stretcher into the hall.

Neill was strapped into place and as white as the sheet drawn up under his chin. He lifted a hand in greeting, voice muffled by the oxygen mask covering his mouth and nose. 'Milt reckons I need a blood transfusion,' he said, breath wheezing between each word.

It was a booked admission, not an emergency. Laura looked from one paramedic to the other. 'I'm his neighbour,' she said. 'When did all this happen?'

The person who seemed to be in charge was an older woman. She was thin, haggard and enveloped in green overalls a size too big. Her lank grey hair was pulled into a tight ponytail.

'I dunno. We was booked to pick him up and take him to the hospital this arvo. We're late because we had to transfer a patient to Port Augusta. Dunno anything else, darl. Sorry.'

She frowned. Jess or Neill hadn't mentioned it . . . or perhaps they had and she'd been too preoccupied over the weekend to take it in. Neill lay on the stretcher, his eyes closed, life seeping out of him with each laboured breath. She put her hand on his arm and he opened his eyes.

'Do you want me to come to the hospital with you?'

'No need, lass. Will you see to the dog?'

'Of course I will.'

'There's a spare house key on the hook in the kitchen, but I should be home tomorrow.'

Laura glanced at the paramedic and the woman raised her eyebrows. 'You might be in a day or two longer than that, Mr Finlay,' she said, and with a nod to the other ambo they began to wheel the stretcher towards the front door.

'Is Jess coming into the hospital later?' Laura said, squeezing around furniture to stay beside the trolley.

'Yes,' he said, his voice a hoarse whisper above the hiss of the
oxygen.

The paramedics eased the stretcher out of the house, manoeuv-
ring it down the verandah steps. When they'd loaded him into the
back of the waiting ambulance, she stood by as the thin woman
climbed in and fiddled with his mask and the oxygen tubing. The
other ambo, a short barrel of a man with a head like a hard-boiled
egg, slammed the rear door and heaved himself into the driver's seat.

'I'll come up and see you later,' Laura called as the ambulance
pulled out of the driveway, knowing he wouldn't hear her.

She walked back to the car. Two weeks ago, when she'd had the
meeting with Milt Burns, she'd suggested Neill might benefit from
a blood transfusion. Milt had scowled, pulled at an earlobe and not
said a word. But he'd obviously heard her, and with a unit or two
of blood in him, Neill would feel a lot better . . . until he needed the
next unit or two. The ambulance was out of sight when she turned
the corner into her own driveway.

Although she'd spent the day sitting at a desk Laura was beat,
worse than after a day spent painting, gardening and sanding floors.
Without dwelling on it, she changed her clothes, laced her running
shoes and picked up the dog. She hadn't run that morning and if she
didn't do it straight away she'd be tempted to pour herself a glass of
wine and put her feet up.

When she let herself into Neill's backyard Skip strained on his
chain and wagged his tail so hard the kennel moved. She kept him
on the lead until they'd passed the outskirts of town and he took off
like a rocket when she let him go. The run was hard work. It was hot
and humid and halfway through the wind came up, swirling dust.

After their run she collected Skip's bowl and dry food and

took the dog home with her. She checked Neill's house was secure, nothing left turned on, and locked up after herself. In the growing gloom of evening she looked around his deserted backyard and wished for the umpteenth time that Jake Finlay would come to his stubborn senses and return home to finish saying goodbye to his father. He was fast running out of time.

Chapter 15

The outreach nurse brought Neill home from hospital on Thursday, his respirations were less laboured and he had a hint of colour in his sunken, sallow cheeks. It was almost seven when Laura let herself through the gate into his backyard that night, laden with Skip's bowl and dry food. The daylight savings sun was still hot on her bare arms.

'How was it?' Neill said, meeting her at the back door, his rheumy hazel eyes gleaming with curiosity.

She knew full well he was talking about her first days consulting at Potters Junction Health Centre. They hadn't had a chance to talk about it.

'It was good.'

'And?' He stood back and held the door open for her.

'Just a tick.'

She filled Skip's bowl before stowing the bag of dry dog food in the laundry, took the food out to the dog, checked his water bucket was clean and full.

'Come on, tell me all about it,' Neill said the moment she stepped back in the door.

She washed her hands at the laundry trough. 'The health centre is really nice,' she said and followed him into the kitchen. 'It's modern, there's plenty of room and up-to-date computers. You could hold a party in the lunch room.'

Neill flicked on the kettle, it took only seconds to re-boil, then he poured water over the leaves waiting in the teapot.

'It was busy. Milt Burns and I were both consulting. Kaylene Curtis keeps everything under control, runs the place with military-like precision, and I like the practice nurse.' Laura went to the fridge for the milk. She stood back to appreciate the fact that it had been restocked with fresh food.

'Jess did the shopping,' he said.

'How is she? I haven't seen her since Monday night when we were visiting you at the hospital.'

He took the teapot to the kitchen table and sat down. 'I dunno,' he said and took a moment to catch his breath. 'She seems flat.' When Laura opened her mouth to speak he held up his hand. 'I know she's upset because of how things are with me, but this is something different. And I think she's lost weight.'

'How are things at home? That's the first question I'd ask a patient.'

Neill raised his eyebrows. 'You might be right. That Darren . . .' His mouth turned down at the corners. 'The girl could have done better for herself.'

'She fell in love. When that happens we tend not to take much else into consideration. Especially when we're young.'

'I wouldn't know about any of that,' Neill mumbled.

'What, you've never fallen in love?'

He shrugged and she watched as he stirred sugar into his tea, thought how fond of him she'd become in a such a short time. She fervently hoped she'd never have to treat him. She should have added that to the cons column when she'd been making the list of the pros and cons of working at the Potters Junction Health Centre. A few stitches in his scalp was one thing, managing his terminal care was an entirely different thing. The Australian Medical Association didn't have protocols about treating close friends and relatives for nothing.

'Do you reckon you'll stay?' he said.

'What?' she spluttered, almost spilling her tea. 'Stay where?'

'Here. In Potters Junction.'

She ran her fingers through her hair, caught unawares, yet again, by the short, soft curls. She never should have listened to Alice. Every time she looked in the mirror it took a second to recognise who it was looking back at her.

'I'm not making any big decisions yet,' she said. Top of the list for now was rebuilding the confidence she'd lost. Although everything had gone smoothly, two days back at it was hardly long enough to know. She'd think about making long-term plans when she was a bit further down the track.

'I suppose when the time's right you'll be off back to that practice in the city.'

'Who knows what the future holds? I'm taking it a day at a time. And I know you understand all about taking things a day at a time.'

'I do. And I like your hair like that. It suits you.'

'I'm getting used to it. My sister —' She stopped, fluffed her hair again. 'The *new* me.'

'There was nothing wrong with the old you,' he said.

'Try telling Alice that.'

Neill laughed and that made him cough until he turned an unhealthy shade of puce. Laura passed him a glass of water.

'Can I make you something for your evening meal?'

'Toast is all I feel like tonight.'

'Are you sure?'

'They fed me pretty well in that hospital, you know.'

'All right, I'll let you off this time.' She stood up, began collecting their empty tea cups.

He reached out, put his hand on her arm, his grip surprisingly firm. 'I can do that,' he said. 'You go on home, you look tired. Thanks for looking after the dog.'

The weekend passed in a haze of heat. No matter how much water she poured onto them, the tomato bushes were slumping listlessly by Saturday afternoon and the leaves on the zucchini plants curled and crisped around the edges. Having observed what other local vegetable gardeners had done, on Sunday morning Laura tied an old queen-size bed sheet onto dropper stakes as a makeshift shelter for the vegetables. She threw on another layer of pea straw mulch, and the plants looked quite perky by the end of the day. Next week she'd visit the hardware shop again to buy shade cloth and make a more robust shelter for the vegie garden.

On Sunday evening she cut up a fresh fruit salad and took Neill a bowl.

'It's bloody hot for this time of the year,' he said even though he wore his usual flannel pyjamas and thick dressing-gown. 'I reckon we're in for a stinking hot summer.'

'Have you got the air conditioner on in the sitting room?'

'Yes,' he said and she put the fruit salad in the fridge. He peered at her, concern deepening the lines in his face.

'Are you all right? You look a bit peaky.'

'A bit too much sun, I think. I spent too long in the garden.'

'Are you sure that's all it is?'

'Yeah,' she said. 'Positive. A cool shower and an early night is all I need.'

The shower refreshed her, but she'd barely had a chance to slip off her robe and slide between the sheets when her mobile phone rang.

'I damn well knew this would happen. She wouldn't bloody well listen to me. She should have given up work weeks ago —'

'Who is this?' she said, elbowing herself up in bed.

A moment's silence and then a mumbled, 'Sorry. It's Sean Ashby, Meghan's husband.' He cleared his throat. 'Her waters have broken. She asked me to ring you and tell you to get your arse, I mean backside, down here ASAP.'

There was a scratching sound, a clunk like the phone had been dropped, and then Meghan was on the other end, her breathing ragged.

'Laura, thank God you're there. Believe it or not I'm in labour, contractions every three minutes. Can you come? This isn't meant to happen. I'm barely thirty-seven weeks! I was going to Adelaide for the birthing.'

'I'll be there as soon as I can.' Her voice was calm but her hands were trembling, her mind racing – it had been aeons since she'd been in a labour ward, delivering a baby. There wasn't much call for that in city general practice.

'Bless you,' Meghan said, and Laura could hear the relief in her friend's voice. She crossed her fingers and hoped Meghan's confidence wasn't misplaced.

'Do you need an ambulance? I'll phone the hospital now, meet you there. Or would you rather come to Potters Junction? Milt Burns is around.'

Meghan snorted. 'No, I do not need an ambulance. And thanks, but the last thing I need is Milt Burns scowling at my private parts and telling me how to have my baby. I'll go to Magpie Creek, I know Jayne's on and she's a midwife from way back when they delivered babies there. Sean can drive me in and I'll —' She stopped, groaned as a contraction took hold. 'Hurry.' The phone went dead.

'Shit,' Laura muttered, thoughts whirling. She pulled on underwear, capris and a t-shirt, forced her feet into sandals, phone pressed to her ear. Jayne, the RN at Magpie Creek hospital, answered and Laura identified herself.

'Meghan's in labour. Her waters have broken. Contractions are three minutes apart. Sean is bringing her to you now. I'll be there as fast as I can.'

'You're kidding! She only left here a few hours ago after seeing outpatients. Said she had backache and what she thought were Braxton Hicks contractions. Sean must be beside himself.'

'Something like that,' Laura said, grabbing her bag and keys. 'See you soon.' She slammed the back door and was on the road.

Twenty-nine minutes later, she tore across the deserted car park to the front entrance of the Magpie Creek hospital. There wasn't a breath of breeze. Moths and insects spun around the entrance light, a smattering of corpses on the step. The door was unlocked and an enrolled nurse was waiting at the nurses' station ready to escort Laura to the makeshift delivery suite.

'We're set up in the palliative-care room,' the nurse said as Laura followed her down the corridor. She'd never been to Magpie Creek hospital before. Milt had suggested she visit the place, get her bearings in case she ever had to cover call there. Well, she was visiting it now and quickly getting her bearings.

'It used to be a two-bed ward but we took one bed out and added a recliner. Sean can stay afterwards if he wants to.'

'When did they arrive?'

The nurse glanced at her watch. 'Ten minutes max. We'd barely got all the gear into the room. Doctor Kimble was wanting to push in the car. I reckon Sean must have broken every speed limit.'

'What about their little girl, Lucy, where's she?'

'With friends. Meghan's parents are on their way from Adelaide.'

The nurse pushed open the door to the palliative-care room and Laura was assailed by the long-forgotten raw, metallic smells of a labour ward. Her heart leaped into the back of her throat and nearly choked her. Obstetrics had never been her favourite – too many things could go wrong.

Jayne had one gloved hand resting on Meghan's raised knee and was peering between her splayed legs.

'Nearly there, sweetie, time to give it your all . . . You know the drum, push with the next contraction.'

Meghan's eyes were tightly shut, freckles harsh against the pallor of her skin, sweaty copper-coloured curls plastered to her forehead. Her hand was gripped firmly by a pale-looking Sean perched on a chair beside the bed. An emergency delivery bundle was open on a trolley beside Jayne and a rudimentary infant resus trolley had been pushed into the corner.

Jayne looked up when Laura entered the room. 'You must be Doctor O'Connor. Everything's okay so far. Foetal heart rate was one fifty.'

Meghan opened her eyes. 'Hi, Laura,' she croaked. 'Thanks so much for coming. I'm sure we would have managed but I'm glad you came.' Sean acknowledged her with a nod. He didn't loosen his grip on his wife's hand and, noting the terror in his eyes, Laura wondered who was holding whose hand.

'Do you want to take over?' Jayne said and Laura shook her head, held up her hand.

'No, no, please, you keep doing what you're doing. I'll take the baby.' She dropped her shoulder bag and car keys onto the floor and went to the handbasin to wash up. She took a white cotton hospital gown and slipped it on over her clothes and mentally catalogued the equipment on the trolley, praying she wouldn't have to use any of it.

Meghan screamed, swore, her face purple as she pushed. Sean glanced at his wife, eyebrows lifting, holding on tightly when she tried to push him away. Jayne quietly coached and Laura stood by, ready to help, pulse thrumming in her ears as she watched the baby's head crown, watched Jayne feel around its neck for the cord. In her mind she went over and over what she'd do if the baby was flat when it delivered. *Airway, breathing, circulation . . . Apgars at one and five . . . keep baby warm . . .* Should she have rung the Women's and Children's? Should she have let Doctor Burns know?

'Doctor O'Connor, can you please give the oxytocic?'

'Sure.' Laura checked the drug with Jayne and drew it up into a syringe as the midwife delivered the baby's shoulders. Meghan didn't flinch when Laura swiped her thigh with an Alcowipe and jabbed in the needle.

And then Jayne was holding the newborn up and it took one gasping, gurgling breath and let out a gutsy wail.

'Thank God,' Laura said softly, light-headed with relief. As Jayne gently put the baby into Meghan's waiting arms and prepared to cut the cord, Laura felt the first prickle of tears. Happy tears, sad tears. Meghan was smiling, her eyes glistening, and Sean looked stunned.

'It's a boy,' Meghan said, her voice cracking. 'Sean, we have a son.' She beamed up at her husband. He leaned down and put his arms around his wife, kissing her firmly on the lips.

'Well done,' Laura said, smiling at the proud parents and the midwife. 'No episiotomy or tears or anything.'

Meghan wasn't listening, staring blissfully at the slippery, squirming body in her arms. Together they wrapped him and Laura quickly assessed him while he rooted around for his mother's nipple.

'Are you sure you had your dates right?' Laura asked.

Jayne looked up from where she was busy delivering the placenta. 'Bigger baby than I expected, not much vernix,' she said. 'I wondered about that myself.'

Meghan lifted her shoulders off the bed in a tired shrug. 'Could have been a week or so out, I suppose . . . Who knows? I missed one of the earlier scans.' She gasped as a hungry, seeking mouth tried to latch on to her breast.

Laura glanced at Jayne. 'I'll check with the Women's and Children's first but I'm sure they'll say it's okay to keep him here.'

Meghan yelped with surprise when the baby successfully attached and started to suck. Sean watched in awe. Jayne murmured with satisfaction when the placenta plopped into the waiting kidney dish, and Laura noted the neonate's Apgar scores on the delivery sheet.

Two hours later, exhausted, her emotions mixed, Laura left mother and baby sleeping under the watchful eye of one very proud dad. After the emergency delivery, the hospital routine had quickly settled back to normal. Jayne, still there hours after the end of her shift, gave Laura a quick hug on her way out.

'Thanks for coming. I'm so glad everything went smoothly. I've done a couple of mini refreshers but it's at least seven years since I've delivered a baby. When Meghan rang after you had, I suggested she'd be better off at Potters Junction. It's only a few years since they stopped obstetrics and Milt Burns would have delivered a lot of babies.' Jayne gave her head a shake. 'But no, she was adamant about coming here.'

A cool change was blustering through when Laura drove out of the hospital car park. Roly-polies skittered across the road, starkly white in the headlights. The drive home took forty-five minutes and, in the dusty darkness, Laura realised in less than six hours she'd be up and getting ready for work again.

Meghan had asked if she'd fill in at the Magpie Creek medical centre for a couple of days, cover call until the booked locum arrived the following week. Laura had promised she'd talk to Milt the next morning about doing Thursday and Friday at the medical centre. While the thought of covering emergency call for the weekend had her mouth going dry, she hoped Doctor Burns was agreeable to her helping Meghan.

Although it was his day off, Milt Burns was at the health centre when Laura arrived Monday morning, and he already knew about Meghan's baby.

'Congratulations,' he said. 'Meghan phoned me early this morning. Said you'd risen to the occasion. They're calling him James. No second name, just James Ashby.'

'Meghan and the midwife did all the work. I suggested she come here, but she preferred to go to Magpie Creek.'

'Don't blame her either. If the baby had taken one good look at me it probably would have crawled right back up there.'

Laura chuckled, remembering what Meghan had said about having Milt deliver her child.

'I talked to the paediatric registrar at the Women's and Children's and the baby will stay in Magpie Creek if all goes well. At 3.6 kilograms Meghan might have had her dates out a bit. I'll drive down again this evening and check on them. Unless of course you want to?'

'I might just do that this afternoon. I'll take Linda. She likes to goo and gah over new babies. And I don't see there'd be any problems with you doing Thursday and Friday in Magpie Creek this week, if you're happy to do it.'

They chatted for a few more minutes, and then Milt disappeared to finish off his paperwork and Laura detoured past the lunch room to make herself a strong coffee before she started the day's list. She was tired. Her eyes felt like sandpaper. Witnessing the birth of Sean and Meghan's baby had been *very* special, but sleep had proven elusive afterwards. Wide-eyed and dry-eyed, she'd lain awake until the first hint of dawn lightened the sky, bombarded by her own memories and what might have been, if only things had happened differently.

Chapter 16

Doctor Burns's car was taking up two spaces in the car park when Laura pulled in to the Potters Junction Health Centre the following morning. Another day he wasn't having off! He must have a lot of paperwork to catch up on. Laura collected her bag, locked the car and went in to find the place abuzz with staff.

'I thought Milt was having today off?'

'Doesn't like to miss the cardiologist's visit,' said Kaylene.

'Oh, that's today.'

'And it's the dietician's day as well,' she said, rushing off.

By eleven a.m. all four consulting rooms were in use and the usually unflappable Kaylene sounded harassed when she rang Laura between patients.

'Hospital is on the line. They say it's urgent. Come back as soon as you can, please, Laura, the waiting room is packed and Milt's on a go-slow.'

'Okay, I'll do my best.'

Kaylene put the hospital through.

'I have a man here in A&E, thirty-five, history of kidney stones,' said the RN on duty. 'He has a temp of thirty-eight, lower back and right-flank pain radiating into his groin and blood in his urine. BP is okay.'

'How bad's the pain?'

'Eight, nine out of ten.'

'I'll be there in about ten minutes,' she said. 'And please get a urine sample to send off.'

Laura took a minute to psych herself up, grabbed her car keys and shoulder bag and, with a wave to Kaylene, she flew out the back door of the health centre. This was her first emergency call-out to the Potters Junction hospital and anxiety fluttered in her stomach.

Paul Kennedy, the director of nursing, had given her a brief tour of the hospital the week before. It was bigger and busier than Magpie Creek hospital, with more acute-care beds and about the same number of residential aged-care beds.

When she arrived in A&E the patient was writhing around on the bed, eyes tightly shut. His name was Jason Coombes and he took up every square centimetre of the mattress, his sock-clad feet hanging over the end. He wore jeans, stiff with dirt and grease, and an orange high-vis work shirt. His large, paw-like hands were black with grime. The RN said he'd vomited minutes before. Laura checked for drug allergies and ordered him pain relief and an anti-emetic, and then looked through the RN's notes and at the patient's vital signs.

Thirty minutes later Jason's pain had eased, she'd examined him, explained the treatment, written up blood test requests and completed the hospital admission paperwork.

'I'll come and see him again after I finish at the health centre this evening,' she said. 'Let's hope a stone passes spontaneously like it has other times.'

With a disdainful look at Laura, the RN picked up the wad of paperwork. 'I hope so too. Jason's one of the few mechanics in town and now is his busiest time, with haymaking and harvest on the go.'

'With any luck he will be out of here in the morning.'

'If he passes a stone Doctor Burns would let him go tonight.' The RN clutched the paperwork to her chest, her eyes cool.

Laura didn't falter. 'I'm not Doctor Burns. I'll see Jason later today and make a decision then. He is febrile and that's worth following up.'

The RN's mouth thinned to a tight line. She spun on her heel and returned to A&E. Laura watched her retreating. So, that's how it was going to be.

Jess threaded her fingers through Mikey's silky blond hair. Resting on her lap, his face was flushed and hot to touch, his breathing faster than it should have been.

'Michael Phillips?'

Jess nudged her dozing son awake, gave a grunt as she lifted him into her arms. He really was too big for her to be carrying him but he was so miserable. She followed the doctor down the corridor to the consulting room.

She had only ever seen Laura in daggy paint-splattered work clothes and she was taken aback by the transition. Laura wore tailored linen slacks and a cobalt-blue blouse that matched her eyes perfectly. Diamond studs sparkled in her ears and Jess could see no traces of paint in her hair or underneath her short, clipped fingernails. She took the proffered chair, wondering if she should call her Doctor O'Connor.

'Call me Laura,' she said as if reading Jess's mind. 'Mikey, you don't look well at all, mate.' Laura gently took his hand and Mikey watched her from his fever-glazed eyes.

'I think he has tonsillitis again. He said he had a sore throat a few weeks ago but that seemed to pass, and then yesterday morning he woke complaining of it again, and his temperature was up this time.'

'You said *again*. Is it something he suffers from regularly?'

Jess nodded. 'Poor little bugger. I did too, until Doctor Burns took my tonsils out.'

'Has he been to see a paediatrician, or an ENT specialist?'

'No, he hasn't.'

Laura took out a digital thermometer and carefully put it in Mikey's ear and began her examination. Mikey stayed on Jess's lap throughout and when Laura had finished she washed her hands and said, 'Let's get him over this bout and then we can think about what to do next.'

'Okay, that works.'

Laura handed Jess a script for Mikey's antibiotics. 'I haven't seen you since your dad was in hospital a week ago. You look worn out.'

'I was awake a bit in the night with Mikey,' she said. Awake thinking about the rip-roaring argument she'd had with Darren, too. The bed in the sleep-out they used as a spare room was hard as a rock, and the space was hot and stuffy even with the louvres jammed open.

She shifted in the seat. With Mikey on her lap for so long her legs were going to sleep, and Laura's all-seeing gaze was beginning to make her feel uncomfortable.

'I know you pop in to see your dad nearly every day now. Why don't you take a break while Mikey's sick? I can keep looking out for him and call you if the need arises. What do you think? I'm off tomorrow and then in Magpie Creek for Thursday and Friday, but I'll be home each evening.'

Jess fought to hold back the tears, which these days were always there, waiting, just behind her eyes. 'That would be brilliant. And Dad does seem better since the blood transfusion.'

'He is. But you know it won't last, that he's still coughing up blood . . .'

'Yes, I do understand that,' she said, relieved when her voice didn't come out as shaky as it felt. 'I think he only agreed to have the transfusion in the hope it'd give him more time, enough time for Jake to come home again.'

'Have you heard from him?'

'No.' She eased Mikey off her lap and onto his feet. 'I can't carry you anymore, mate. You're getting too heavy. Let's get to the chemist and get some of this medicine into you.'

They walked together out to the waiting area.

'I'll ring you tomorrow, let you know how Neill is.'

'Okay, and thanks, Laura.' With Mikey hanging on to her hand, Jess went to the reception desk to sort out the paperwork, conscious that Laura was still watching her.

Laura thought about Jess on and off for the remainder of the afternoon, right up to the end of the day, whenever her mind wasn't occupied with another patient. There was a woman on the edge, if ever she'd seen one. What could she do to help take the pressure off? Because Laura wouldn't dream of prying into her personal life, she resolved that helping Neill was the only way she could help. If Jake was here . . . Shoving the stethoscope into her bag she closed her eyes. He wasn't here. They'd have to manage. End of story.

What she discovered when she stopped by the hospital on her way home was a different story altogether, and it distracted her from worrying about the Phillips and Finlay families. Jason Coombes had been discharged about twenty minutes earlier – by Doctor Burns, no less.

The RN on the afternoon shift was an older woman with tight, iron-grey curls, bright pink lipstick, her blouse gaping over a generous bosom. *Elaine* read her name badge.

'Elaine, did Jason pass a stone? Had his temperature gone down before he left?'

The woman rooted around in a pile of case notes on the desk until she found Jason's. She flicked through the file, scanned the clinical notes, and Laura watched her face turn a mottled shade of crimson.

'It doesn't look like he passed anything and I don't think anyone took his temperature again,' she said and Laura nodded, determined to keep her expression blank.

'Was a follow-up appointment made with his GP?'

'That's not up to us,' Elaine said.

Laura took the case notes from her and looked at Doctor Burns's brief discharge note. There was no mention of follow-up care or further investigations. She put the file back on the nurses' station desk. Elaine wouldn't meet Laura's eyes.

'I'm covering call tonight,' Laura said. 'You have my mobile phone number.'

Elaine started tidying the desk. Laura picked up her bag and had to dodge the meal trolley on her way out. When she got to her car she threw her bag onto the passenger seat and sat there for a few minutes, seething. What was going on here? She'd written in her earlier entry she'd be back to review the patient that evening. It was supposed to be Milt's day off, and she was covering the after hours on-call. She drummed her fingers on the steering wheel. There was no way she could let this slide. If Milt Burns didn't trust her to manage one of his patients in an emergency, they'd better have it out, sooner rather than later. Before she could change her mind she scrolled through her contacts until she came to his name and tapped the green button.

Milt Burns answered on the third ring, his voice gruff.

'Why did you discharge Jason Coombes?' She was so incensed she didn't bother with pleasantries. 'I wrote in my clinical note that I'd be back to check him.'

He gave a surprised grunt. Laura suspected no-one had challenged him in a long time.

'He said he felt all right and needed to get back to work. He's the only mechanic in town this week.'

'When I admitted him his temperature was thirty-nine five. There was macroscopic blood in his urine. He hadn't passed anything when he was discharged. There are no blood results yet. I checked.'

She heard her colleague's sharp intake of breath. 'I didn't realise he was febrile.'

And you didn't look?

'I'll ring him,' Milt said and disconnected.

Laura let herself sink into the seat. Even with the window down, the car was a hotbox. She had pulled into the shed at home when the phone rang.

'He refused to go back, said he had too much to do. I couldn't force him,' Milt said.

Laura didn't speak. She didn't know what to say.

'I interfered. It won't happen again,' he said and rang off.

Laura stared at the phone. It was as close to an apology as she'd ever get, she suspected. She climbed out of the car and wondered how long it'd be before Jason showed up in A&E again.

✦

Mikey willingly crawled into bed as soon as they got home. Since seeing Laura, Jess had picked up Sam from school, dropped him off at a mate's for a sleepover, and visited her dad. She'd made macaroni cheese for Neill's dinner while Mikey half-heartedly watched television.

'Dad, Laura will be around tomorrow.'

'I'll be fine. You take that boy home and get those antibiotics into him. If he's anything like you were, he'll be on the improve in twenty-four hours.'

Now at home in his own bed, Jess looked down at her sleeping son and hoped her father was right. She wandered into the kitchen and thought about dinner. There'd been no sign of Darren or his ute all day but on the way home she'd noticed the windmill was working again and there were sheep in that paddock, so he must have been around.

After bringing in the washing and shutting up the chooks, she thawed sausages in the microwave. Staring mindlessly out the kitchen window into the growing gloom she started peeling potatoes. The dogs . . .

'Shit!' She dropped the vegetable peeler onto the chopping board and wiped her hands. The dogs had been shut in their pen when she'd put the chooks away. She'd noticed but it hadn't registered. She frowned, pushed a hand through her hair. Why were the dogs in so early? Where was Darren? He'd taken the dogs this morning and he usually didn't put them away until last thing. She glanced at the clock. It was almost seven.

With a quick look in on Mikey, she flew outside. The farmyard was empty, no sign of Darren's ute in any of the sheds. Everything there looked remarkably neat. The gates to the home paddock were shut. Dread began to gnaw at her insides. The pub, she'd ring the pub first.

Nobody had seen him. The neighbours, his drinking mates, the bloke at the servo all said they hadn't seen him for a couple of days. When Jess put down the phone she shuddered, like someone had walked over her grave.

It was dark now, a sliver of lighter sky along the western horizon the only remnant of the day. Flicking on the lights, Jess paced from room to room, her mind buzzing, her stomach hollow with worry. What should she do next? Take her car and look around the property? Instinct told her she wouldn't find him. Everything pointed to him not being there: the closed gates, the dogs penned. Her pulse roared in her ears.

Their argument the night before had been ferocious. Darren had never raised a hand to her but his vitriol had cut deep. They'd covered a lot of ground and, like every argument they'd ever had, it ended with all her faults, and what was wrong with the effing farm and her effing family.

Jess had never spent a night in the sleep-out before, but after their fight she couldn't face the prospect of lying beside Darren all night. She'd known she wouldn't sleep a wink. This morning when she'd emerged from the opposite side of the house, yawning, her eyes red-rimmed from crying, Sam, ever the early riser, had given her an unreadable look. He'd been more reserved that usual and the thought that Sam and Mikey had heard their parents arguing had made her feel sick.

'Dad's already gone out in the ute,' Sam had said. She'd nodded and asked him to check if Mikey was up, and she'd set about her usual morning routine.

Jess went to their bedroom last. The room they'd shared for eleven years. The room in which they'd conceived both of their children. The room that had been her parents' room before it became theirs. Jess paused on the threshold.

Chapter 17

And there it was, propped on the bedside cupboard, an envelope with *Jess* scrawled across the front. The sight of it made her feel light-headed; tiny white spots danced in front of her eyes. She dropped onto the bed, her insides in freefall. Fingers to her mouth she pressed against the rising nausea. The only other times there'd been envelopes with her name written in Darren's unmistakable hand had been her birthday, Mother's Day or Christmas. Today was none of those.

Jess stared at the envelope. Her heart thudded. She felt like her whole body was beating a steady beat, a timer ticking off the minutes, a countdown to something that she was desperate to know and fearful she already knew.

'Mum?'

She twisted her head around. Mikey stood in the doorway in his shorty pyjamas. The pair with the tractors on them, his favourites.

'Mikey.' Jess blinked. 'What's up, mate?'

'What are you doing? Where's Dad? I'm thirsty.'

She carefully stood up. The white spots had gone. 'Come to the kitchen. I'll get you a drink.'

Mikey settled back into bed after a cold lemonade, another dose of paracetamol and his evening antibiotics. The half-peeled potatoes had browned on the sink, the sausages sat in a puddle of condensation on the microwave plate. Jess shoved the lot in the fridge and the peels in the compost bucket. When she was sure Mikey was asleep again she went back to the bedroom to check under the bed but all she found were dust bunnies. The suitcases were gone.

She looked at the envelope propped against the lamp, felt her heart accelerate, her mouth go dry.

I'm sorry, Jess, it began and so did her tears.

He'd gone.

After our argument last night I knew I had to do something. This place is falling down around our ears and I don't know how to stop it. It's got so as I don't care anymore because nothing I do makes a difference. I've grown to hate the place. Your old man was right – I'll never make even a half-decent farmer. When Neill dies you should sell the lot, use the money to make a better life.

Tell Sam and Mikey I love them. And Jess, I want you to know there's never been anyone else but you. I'll be in touch when I sort myself out. I'm so sorry. You married a loser. I know you'll manage. You always do.

Darren

With a fist hard against her mouth she smothered a cry. Her teeth cut into her lip, the metallic taste of blood filled her mouth. She let the letter flutter to the floor. Away. She had to get away. She walked out of the bedroom, out of the house, across the farm-yard, behind the shed. When she was far enough away that she wouldn't wake Mikey, she collapsed onto her knees in the dirt and let the cry escape, like a dam bursting, the sound rending the still night air.

★

Jake couldn't believe he was back. Dog-tired from what felt like an eternity in transit, and with a feeling of déjà vu, he opened the screen door and knocked on the glass-panelled front door. It was twilight. A liminal time. How many weeks since he'd been in Potters Junction? He listened for the shuffle of feet as Neill slogged his way to the door. The porch light came on and the door opened.

'Son.'

The single syllable sighed out on a breath, and the old man's eyes glistened.

Jake swallowed, conscious of the lump that had formed in his throat.

'I'm back,' he said.

For as long as it took for moths to appear and spin with no dis-cernible purpose around the forty-watt bulb, the two men stood on either side of the threshold.

Jake hadn't considered that he wouldn't be welcomed home, but as he watched a range of emotions flit across Neill's face, the thought now sprang to mind. And with the thought came the reali-sation that he wouldn't blame the old man if he turned him away.

And then came a surge of emotions that left him feeling a bit like he'd been poleaxed. Jake took a small step back, tightening his grip on the gear pack in his hand, ready to turn.

'Well,' said Neill, after what seemed like an age. 'Don't just stand there, come on in.' The old man held the glass door wide.

And now, almost twenty-four long hours later, Jake swiped a sweaty palm down the front of his t-shirt and with the same sense of déjà vu knocked on another door, a wooden back door with a loose brass doorknob.

It was almost dark and light blazed through the kitchen window. When his knuckles hit the timber panel, the door inched open of its own accord, tired old hinges squealing. No answer. He pushed the door wider and walked in, past the bathroom and laundry, pausing in the kitchen doorway.

'Laura?'

A black-clad backside and two feet protruded from under the kitchen table. The backside was decidedly female. A dull thud, followed by a curse and the backside reversed carefully out from under the table.

It wasn't Laura. This backside was curvier, wasn't denim-clad. After the backside came the back, not a thick, chestnut braid in sight. So Laura had left town.

The stranger finally cleared the table and sank back onto her haunches, looking up.

'Jake?'

Laura. He sucked in a broken breath.

'Christ. Laura? What have you done to your hair?'

Her fingers skimmed the short curls.

'What are you doing here?'

'I've warned you before about leaving the back door unlocked,' he said as he stepped into the room, watching her, updating his memory banks.

'It's barely dark. I've been in and out . . .'

Her face was a little fuller, her lips glistened as she spoke, and the sometimes sad look in her blue eyes had gone. The emerald-coloured knit she wore over black linen pants hugged her curves like a second skin. He could have been looking at a different woman. But it wasn't a different woman, it was Laura. He was pleased to see her, and the intensity of just how delighted he was unnerved him.

'When did you get back?'

'Last night.'

'Oh. I didn't hear your bike. I was probably at the hospital. One of the oldies fell out of bed, hit their head.'

'Jess said you were back doctoring.'

'This is my second week. I've been in Magpie Creek today, and again tomorrow. Meghan Kimble had her baby early. I'm filling in until the locum arrives.'

'So Jess said.'

'I bet your dad was pleased to see you.'

'I thought for a minute he wasn't going to let me in. Wouldn't have blamed him.' He closed his eyes, remembered how he'd felt. When he opened them she was watching him.

'Laura, I —'

'Do you want a coffee?'

What she'd saved him from saying, he wasn't sure. A smile tugged at his lips. 'Ever known me to knock back an offer of a decent cup of coffee?'

She lifted two cups from the draining rack on the sink.

'No,' she said, and turned towards the coffee machine, but not before he saw something flare in her eyes and he knew, like him, she was remembering what almost happened the last time she'd made him coffee.

She fumbled with the coffee machine, dropped the pod onto the floor. He'd come back. The words chased each other around and around in her head as she bent to retrieve the pod.

'Floor's clean,' she mumbled, and jammed the thing into place. The machine coughed and rattled; the aroma of brewing coffee filled the room. She heard him clear his throat, then the scrape of a chair as he sat down.

'You've seen Jess already?'

'I went out to the farm this afternoon.'

'How's Mikey?'

'Better. Jess said his temperature is right down.'

She put the coffee in front of him, took the sugar bowl off the dresser and placed it alongside. This felt surreal – she'd never expected to see him again.

'Sorry, but I don't have any biscuits.'

'Darren's gone.'

'What?' Laura said.

'He's left her. He didn't come home Tuesday night, he'd cleared out. She found a note.'

Laura heard the contempt in his voice. 'I *knew* something was wrong,' she said.

'She doesn't want the old man to know. Doesn't want to upset him, but she said things with Darren had been difficult for a while.'

'He already suspects something's going on. But I won't say anything to him, if that's what Jess wants.' She looked into her drink, swirled the cup and watched the creamy layer on top lick at the white porcelain.

'No matter how bad things got between them, I don't think she thought he'd leave the boys.'

'She must be devastated.'

Abruptly, Laura jumped to her feet.

'I'll go out and see her. She probably isn't sleeping. I can give her something.' She made for the dresser to grab her things but Jake caught her arm. She paused, her eyes drawn to his fingers encircling her wrist.

'She doesn't know I'm telling you, Laura, so maybe not tonight. I don't think she's ready to talk to anyone about it yet. I'm going back tonight so I can listen out for the boys and she'll try to get some sleep. She's exhausted. Sam's hardly said a word since she told him, and Mikey keeps asking when his dad's coming back.'

'Why didn't she ring me? I could have helped.'

'She already feels bad enough about all you've been doing for Neill.'

'That's ridiculous! I don't mind at all.' She pulled her hand out of Jake's grasp, opened the dresser drawer. 'Here,' she said and handed him a white plastic bottle. 'They're sleeping pills. Ones I haven't used. Tell her to follow the instructions on the bottle.'

'But —'

'But nothing. Tell her I gave them to you because you said you couldn't sleep. Make something up!'

'Thanks.' He wrapped his long, strong fingers around the bottle and dropped them into the pocket of his shirt. He finished his coffee and stood up. 'I'd better get going,' he said but didn't move.

'Okay, I'll see you out,' she answered but stayed where she was.

'Laura,' he said. 'I was a bit of a prick to you on the phone. You didn't deserve any of it.'

She held up her hand. 'Don't apologise. I practically hung up on you and you didn't deserve that.'

'I did, and you know it.'

Their gazes snapped together. He was the first to break away, taking his cup to the sink to rinse.

'How long are you here for this time?' she said and hoped she didn't sound desperate. Heat flashed through her at the very sight of him, at the very realness of him standing in her kitchen.

'For as long as it takes,' he said, his voice low, and they both knew he meant until Neill died. He jammed his hands into his pockets, focussed on his feet. He kicked at the mat with a booted toe.

'I wasn't coming back again, ever. But then you phoned. I had a twelve-hour flight to think. When I landed in Istanbul I called in some favours,' he said. 'It took a while to sort out, but here I am.'

'Neill and Jess would have been so happy to see you.'

'What about you, Laura, are you pleased to see me?'

'This isn't about me.'

'You reckon?' he said quietly.

No words would come but she felt every cell in her body come alive. He smiled. 'What were you doing under the table when I came in?'

'Salt damp,' she rushed. 'The place is riddled with it. I was checking out how far up it went on that wall.'

'Oh, right,' he said, nodding as if he understood. 'I'll see you soon.'

Seconds later the back door slammed. She realised her hands were shaking. With a frustrated moan she clasped her fingers together tightly until the shaking stopped. He'd come back when she was sure he wouldn't. But Neill would be lucky to make Christmas, and Jake wouldn't hang around for long after that. The wisest thing would be to have as little to do with him as possible, because he *would* leave again. And then there was Jess, and the bottom dropping out of her world. Her father was dying and now her life partner and the father of her children had walked out on her, right when she needed him the most.

Laura emptied the remains of her lukewarm coffee, washed the cup and put it on the draining rack next to Jake's. Bracing her hands on the edge of the kitchen sink she chewed on the inside of her cheek and stared out into the near darkness. It was only weeks ago she'd told herself it wasn't smart, or safe, to become involved with this family. But here she was up to her armpits in it and if her body's tingling response to Jake was any indication, she was ready and willing to go even further.

But who knew what the future held? Jess would eventually move on, Jake would leave and, honestly, Laura didn't know how long she herself would stay put in Potters Junction either. One day at a time, she thought. After all she'd had firsthand experience of what it was like to plan and anticipate a future, and then have it snatched away in a second.

With a sigh she trudged to the bedroom and changed her clothes, trying to work up some enthusiasm for dinner. She opened the fridge. There was one lonely egg, a paper bag containing a handful of shrivelled mushrooms, half a punnet of cherry tomatoes and a few limp vegetables in the crisper. Damn. She'd forgotten to do the shopping.

One thing was certain, she thought as she closed the fridge door and fossicked for the servo's takeaway menu. She wouldn't be going anywhere until Neill Finlay had taken his last painful breath.

Chapter 18

'I'd say keep it,' said the beaming man at the counter, 'but there's another bloke who wants it. I hadn't hired it out for weeks, and now suddenly everyone wants it.'

Laura had hired the sander from the hardware shop the weekend before and it had sat in the front bedroom unused, its very presence an accusation. On Saturday morning she took it back to the shop, bemused by the shop assistant's sudden transition from Mr Morose to Mr Chatty.

She'd been a regular customer at the shop since her move to Potters Junction and a grunt was the most she'd ever got out of him. Must have been something to do with her treating him at the health centre and reassuring him it wasn't a brain tumour that was causing his deafness. His ears were clogged with wax and probably had been for years. After a few doses of softening drops she'd successfully syringed them and, voila, hearing restored.

She loaded her new tins of paint into the back of the car. They were for the passageway. The cracks had all been filled, the walls were just waiting to be painted. That job was on her afternoon agenda. But for now she'd take half an hour off and wander down the main street, look in the windows.

Potters Junction was bustling with Saturday morning traffic and shoppers, several people acknowledged her with a wave, and the footpath was an obstacle course of A-frames advertising everything from preservative-free mincemeat and lamb-and-rosemary sausages to tissues and toilet rolls. The car park alongside the supermarket was packed. The pharmacy's front window was crammed with Christmas decorations and gift ideas. Laura hadn't given Christmas more than a passing thought – it'd really sneaked up on her this year.

It was just before ten and already heat was shimmering off the bitumen. The cool change had been short-lived and the locals were grumbling that they'd missed spring again this year and slipped straight into summer. Farmers were mumbling about the lack of spring rains, and what there was to harvest would hardly be worth the fuel it cost to get the crop off. She'd already learned the land to the north and east of Potters Junction was marginal, on the wrong side of Goyder's Line, and seasons like this were the rule rather than the exception.

On impulse she stopped in at the Potters Junction Cafe, ordered a chocolate milkshake and sat down in one of the retro booths. She hadn't had a milkshake in years but it seemed the right thing to do on a hot Saturday morning. The town was beginning to grow on her. When she couldn't come up with a reason to linger any longer she went home and got started on the painting.

In the cool of the evening, Laura relaxed on the back verandah and rubbed moisturiser into her hands and arms. She'd showered and scrubbed the paint off her hands, leaving them dry and wrinkled. She was pretending she wasn't straining to hear the conversation in the yard next door, when her mobile phone rang.

'Doctor O'Connor, it's the RN on duty at the hospital. I apologise for bothering you, I know you're not on call. I've tried several times to raise Doctor Burns and he's not answering his phone, and in this patient's case notes, I noticed that you'd admitted him briefly last Tuesday.'

'Jason Coombes,' Laura said with a sense of foreboding.

'That's right. His wife brought him earlier with similar symptoms, his temp's thirty-nine eight, his BP is one hundred on sixty, his urine has large blood and protein in it and he looks *really* unwell.'

'Give me ten minutes and I'll be there.'

'Should I keep trying Doctor Burns?'

Laura hesitated. This was new territory for her. Officially Doctor Burns was on call. 'Yes, I think you should keep trying his mobile. See you in ten.'

Two hours later Laura was sitting at the nurses' station desk finishing her paperwork when Milt Burns came blustering in through the front door. The nurses were down in A&E cleaning up after the patient had gone – transferred via ambulance to the regional hospital in Port Augusta.

Laura felt her whole body tense. She signed her entry in the patient's clinical record, closed the case notes and stood up.

'What are you doing here?' Milt Burns's words came out like an accusation and Laura steeled herself.

'I've been seeing Jason Coombes. He's sick and septic and I've transferred him to Port Augusta. You didn't answer your phone.'

She watched his Adam's apple bob up and down as he swallowed. Bright spots of colour formed on his cheeks giving him a flushed look.

'Phone was on silent. Damn thing,' he grouched, pulling the offending device out of his pocket and glaring at it. 'Linda was looking after the kids from next door and they must have been playing with it.'

'Well, everything I've done is written in his notes.'

'I'll ring Port Augusta hospital tomorrow.'

'Okay, but I'm happy to follow up on him.'

'I'll do it, I'm on call.'

Voices drifted down the corridor and the two nurses appeared.

'Doctor Burns, you're here,' the RN said, and Laura could see she was embarrassed. 'I'm sorry but when I couldn't raise you, I called Doctor O'Connor and she came straight away. The patient was very sick. I assessed him and concluded he needed to be seen as soon as possible.'

Milt Burns gave the RN an implacable look and said, 'Well, then, I'm obviously not required so I'll go home again. Call me if you need me.' He spun on his heel and stalked out.

'Oops. I hope I didn't drop you in it, but I did try to contact him. If there's any fallout, blame me. I'm from the agency and can plead ignorance.'

'You did the right thing. The patient needed to be seen.' Laura slung her bag over her shoulder. 'If I hadn't been here, would you have called the Magpie Creek GP?'

'No. Unless it'd been arranged for them to cover, I would have rung A&E at the Royal Adelaide, taken it from there.'

'I see.' Laura thanked the nurses and left, vowing to have a conversation with Milt Burns about on-call protocols.

On Sunday morning Laura drove to Magpie Creek to see the handful of outpatients needing urgent attention. 'That's my usual weekend routine,' Meghan had said. 'If there aren't any outpatients, I don't go in. The community's gradually learning what a *real emergency* is.'

Laura saw no reason to change what the community was used to; needless to say the majority of the outpatients that day could've waited until Monday. When she arrived, the RN briefed her about the outpatients then followed with a sheepish apology. 'Sorry, Doctor O'Connor, they know Meghan's not here. Believe it or not this is only half of the ones who tried.'

The only outpatient who couldn't have waited was a middle-aged man on his way to the Flinders Ranges to go camping. 'Sorry, Doc, but I forgot my blood pressure pills,' he said.

'For medications you can't miss, it's a good idea to carry a spare prescription in your wallet. Somewhere you won't forget it,' she said. She took his blood pressure, twice, wrote him a script and the RN provided a few tablets from the hospital pharmacy cupboard to tide him over. He left a happy man.

Laura was finished by midday and, following the directions Meghan had given her over the phone, she stopped off at *Ashdale* on her way back to Potters Junction. It was a green oasis in a brown-and-gold landscape, the farmhouse a handsome double-fronted stone villa with simple lines and several verandahs. Meghan met her with a hug. There were dark shadows under her eyes but she was smiling. Laura followed her into a cavernous country kitchen.

'How's James?' she said, as Meghan put the kettle on.

'Perfect. He's steadily putting on weight and only woke me once last night. Sean is besotted.' Meghan turned to Laura. 'What is it about men having to have a son? I know Dad always wished one of us had been a boy.'

'Beats me. Is your mother still staying?'

'No. Much as I love her I'm glad she only stayed a few days. Sean's out in the paddock doing God knows what. And Lucy's in bed with a tummy ache. I reckon she feels a bit left out, so I've been lavishing her with attention.'

They chatted and drank tea and Meghan fed James. When she'd finished she put him down to sleep.

'Thanks for covering Magpie Creek. The locum arrives in the morning.' Meghan said when she came back into the kitchen. 'So Laura, how are you? How's everything going?'

'Magpie Creek was a breeze. The nurses were terrific and, of course, Julia is wonderful. More to the point, how are you? I can see the baby's thriving, but are you doing okay? No baby blues?'

'No. I feel great.' Meghan rubbed a hand across her flabby stomach and wrinkled her nose. 'I'll be even better when I get rid of this and can get back into normal clothes again.'

'No worries about anything else? Vaginal loss settling down? No problems with breastfeeding?'

'Is this a home visit, or what? Don't worry, I have an appointment with my obstetrician later this week and I've a friend who's a paediatrician and he'll run his eye over James.' Meghan looked at the kitchen clock and jumped to her feet. 'Bloody hell, is that the time? Have you eaten? I'll call Sean. Stay for lunch.'

'Thanks, but no. If I stay for lunch I'll never get anything done at home. I'm back at Potters Junction Health Centre in the morning.'

'You know I really appreciate you helping out, Laura, more than you know.'

'I realise that, and it's okay. I'm glad to help.' Laura shouldered her bag and Meghan followed her out to the car. She threw her bag onto the seat, turning to say goodbye. Meghan was watching her, her gaze bright, assessing.

'What?'

'I didn't miss how you so cleverly changed the subject, giving Magpie Creek a rave review and not a word about how you are. What's happening in your neck of the woods? How's Milt, the grumpy old sod? Has he been giving you a hard time?'

'No —' She paused when Meghan raised her eyebrows.

'You don't need to fib to me, I know what a pain in the bum he can be. He was fantastic when I first started here and didn't have much of a clue – I couldn't have made it without him. That's not to say we haven't had our moments.'

'Potters Junction is good. The health centre staff are lovely, and the hospital staff, well, I guess they're gradually coming around. They've obviously become so used to dealing with Milt Burns for all these years that some of them have been downright hostile towards me.' She leaned against the side of the car, folded her arms. 'And Milt, what can I say? So far he's shown up at the health centre on every one of his days off. He always has a good reason, but I thought he wanted to cut down.' She sighed. 'I know it's early days, but there have been a few issues with the hospital routines – who's responsible for particular patients, after hours call, that kind of thing.'

'Mmm, I'm not surprised. It's been a long time since he's had to consider another doctor. I was a complete novice when it came to general practice and I was dependent on him to a certain extent until

I got the hang of it. You're an experienced GP. He probably feels threatened.'

Laura's mouth dropped open. 'Noo!'

'Yeah, I wouldn't be at all surprised,' Meghan insisted. 'There was a female GP who joined the practice years ago, and she ended up telling him where to stick it. He told me she couldn't cope and left because of that, but Linda implied that Milt had made it so difficult and uncomfortable for the poor woman that she eventually left.'

Laura shook her head in disbelief.

'And I know he has the staff curled around his little finger. But I said to him if he's serious about retirement, he's eventually going to have to let go. Have you met Linda?'

Laura leaned back against the car. 'Not yet. Kaylene says she's in Adelaide. New grandchildren or something. Twins.'

'No wonder he's in such a stinking mood. He says he loves it when she goes away, but he's lying. He hates her being away. He's okay for a day a two, but then he really starts to get grumpy. And the dirty dishes begin to pile up.'

'For this to work – with me now, and then when they recruit someone permanent – there are a few things that need to be sorted out.'

'I would love to be a fly on the wall when you talk to him.'

Laura slid into the driver's seat.

'I'm glad you're okay, Laura. I was worried maybe I'd bullied you into going back to work when you weren't totally ready.'

'You didn't bully me, Meghan. You gave me a little nudge and it came at the right time.' She met Meghan's keen gaze. 'I wouldn't have said yes to Milt if I wasn't ready.'

Meghan gave a thoughtful nod and then her face brightened. 'I know – why don't you ask Milt over for dinner while Linda's away? He is a sucker for a home-cooked meal. Ply him with good food and a bottle of red and he'll be putty in your hands.'

With a hoot of laughter, Laura started the car, waved and bumped her way down the rutted driveway to the road, and then out onto the highway. Dinner with Milt Burns? Not going to happen. Laura doubted they'd ever have that kind of friendship, but she hoped that, over time, they'd develop a mutual respect for each other.

Chapter 19

'I hope you haven't been staying away on my account,' Jake said, holding open the screen door for her.

'Of course not. Why would you think that?'

He shrugged.

'I've been working. I was called out last night, and today I've done an outpatient clinic at Magpie Creek, amongst other things.' Laura managed not to brush against him as she went through the door, but she felt the warmth from his body and she breathed in his scent. She couldn't help herself.

It was late on Sunday afternoon and heat rippled off the galv rooftops. The air was still, heavy, hard to breathe. Fluorescent, purple-tinged cumulonimbus clouds billowed on the horizon.

'Storm's coming,' Neill confirmed. 'Feel it in my bones,' he said. 'Or perhaps that's just the cancer.'

Laura glanced at Jake; the lift of his shoulders was almost imperceptible.

'How are you, Neill?' she said, scanning his face. The pallor was back, shadowed with a bluey-grey. The flush of colour he'd had since the blood transfusion had leached away.

'How am I? As well as can be expected for a dying man,' he said with no hint of bitterness. 'Tea?' He levered himself up from the kitchen chair.

'No, thanks, I've not long had one. I only came to say a hello and to see how you were,' she said. Jake sighed. She cast a brief look to where he leaned against the kitchen sink.

'I'm going to feed the dog,' he said.

Moments later the screen door snapped shut and she could hear the low rumble of Jake talking to the dog.

'God knows what's got into him,' Neill said. 'He spent most of the weekend out at the farm with Jess and the boys. He's been like a bear with a sore head ever since.'

'I guess he hasn't seen them for a while.'

Neill half-heartedly lifted his bony shoulders. 'They've been thick as thieves since he returned.'

She slid into her usual spot opposite Neill at the kitchen table. 'Is there anything I can do for you?'

'No, thanks, lass.'

'How's your pain? Better, worse, the same?'

'About the same.' He laboured to get the words out.

'Sleep?'

Neill responded with the same half-hearted lift of his shoulders. Even in the heat he had on a thick shirt and trackpants. 'My sleep is broken. I just doze, really.' he said. 'You're sure you're not my GP?'

'I'm just asking as a friend. Has Doctor Burns talked to you about the next step in pain relief?'

'Yeah.' He coughed and spat into tissues and, with a sinking feeling, Laura saw blotches of bright blood. 'I'm not quite ready for the needle,' he said.

'You'll know when it is time.'

He inclined his head and clasped his hands together on the table in front of him. 'Would you do something for me?'

'Of course, Neill. Whatever you want, you just have to ask me and if I can do it, I will. As long as it's legal.'

Understanding flashed across his face. 'Nothing illegal, lass. I would never ask that, of anyone.' He lifted his chin towards the back door. 'I know there's something going on. Jake won't say anything but I haven't seen Jess or the boys for days . . .'

Laura couldn't look at him. She hated not telling him what she knew. His daughter, in an effort not to upset him by pretending everything was normal, was causing Neill more pain. They would have to tell him about Darren.

'So, will you try to find out what's going on?' he said. There was hope and despair in his voice.

She reached for his arm across the pockmarked laminex table-top. 'I'll see what I can find out.'

The back door banged and Jake looked up from where he was watering a straggly lemon tree. He had no idea why he was bothering for the dozen or so wizened-looking lemons. Skip stood up, pulling on his chain and wagging his tail. Laura detoured to pat him and murmured something that made his tail wag faster. Christ, if she gave him as much attention as she did the dog, his tail would wag as well.

'Neill's not travelling so well, is he.' It wasn't a question.

'No,' he said. He dropped the end of the hose on the ground

under the tree and went to turn off the tap.

What was she brewing? He could feel her steady gaze on his back and she'd been talking to the old man for a while. He turned to her, not in the mood for a lecture.

She folded her arms and scuffed the ground with her foot.

'Where's your bike?' she said, peering into the carport at Neill's battered 4WD ute.

'Out at the farm.'

'Oh.'

'Laura,' he snapped when he couldn't bear her standing staring at him any longer, 'was there something you wanted?'

Bearing the brunt of his abruptness, she seemed to have made up her mind about something and her expression visibly changed. She exhaled slowly.

'No, not really,' she said simply. She spun around and in four strides was at the gate fumbling with the latch. Seconds later it slammed shut behind her.

Why the bloody hell there was a gate there in the first place he had no idea.

He scratched his head. As pissed off as he was with everyone and everything right at that moment, he could still admire the way her shorts covered her backside like a second skin, the smooth, golden length of her legs. He wasn't sure about the short hair, though. It looked good on her but there was something about that thick braid, the silky feel and fragrance of her hair that one and only time he'd been close enough. He growled, swore again and went back into the house.

The dog retreated to his kennel, ears flat, tail between his legs.

★

Sorry, Neill. She mouthed the words as she closed the gate. Jake wasn't in the right space to talk to her, or to anyone, by the looks of things. While Laura really felt for Neill, Jess's secret was hers to tell. Laura had called Jess the day before on the pretext of seeing how Mikey was doing. Although she'd given ample opportunity, Jess hadn't uttered a word about Darren.

After stowing the ironing board in the dining room, now officially her storage room, she hung the carefully pressed blouses back in the wardrobe. And then, feeling sick to the stomach because she'd let Neill down, she rooted around in the pocket of her shorts for the phone. She knew what was going on with Jess, and by default Jake, and she needed to persuade them to tell their father. Before she could change her mind she rang Jake.

He picked up on the second ring.

'Coffee?' she said.

Silence. She opened her mouth to fill the void, to take back her offer.

'Give me five minutes,' he said.

It was more like fifteen minutes before she heard the clank of the gate, the not-so-gentle rap on the back door, and by then she'd tied herself up in knots. She squeezed her eyes shut and when she opened them he was standing there, taking up the whole kitchen doorway, hands firmly planted on his hips. *You can do this.* Blood thrummed in her veins.

'Hi,' she said.

His eyes narrowed. 'What's the old man put you up to this time, Laura?'

She stiffened her spine. 'Your *father* wants to know what's going on with Jess, and someone needs to tell him. You're worrying him more by not telling him. You know how it feels when other people keep secrets from you.'

'Let's go to the pub, discuss this over a beer.'

'Okay,' she said, momentarily disarmed. 'But mine will have to be a soft drink. I'm on call for Magpie Creek until the locum arrives tomorrow morning.' She pocketed her phone, reached for her purse and car keys.

'Let's walk,' he said, then, 'No, I don't suppose you can. You'd need your transport close by in case you get a call.'

'You've got it in one.'

Fifteen minutes later Jake sat hunched over a schooner of beer, forearms resting on the rickety table. There were only a few punters in the front bar. The barman was polishing glasses while he watched the widescreen television blast out a soccer game. He'd looked put out when Jake had ordered their drinks.

Laura sipped her bitters, lime and soda and looked around. 'I've never been in here before.'

'You definitely don't strike me as a front bar kind of a girl.'

She pulled a face at him. 'I've been in front bars before! I've just never been in *this* front bar.'

He took a long swallow of beer, licked the foam from his top lip and gave the bar a sour glance. 'Wish I could say the same. It hasn't changed much in twenty years.' He nodded to a couple of grizzled old boys propped up at the bar. 'I wouldn't mind betting they were in that very same spot when I was in here last.'

Laura waggled her fingers in a little wave when the two men looked curiously her way, and then turned her attention to the man opposite her.

'Tell me what's wrong,' she said.

'Want a bag of potato chips? Peanuts?' He started to rise. She put her hand on his arm.

'No, I don't want any chips or peanuts. Apart from what's happeneing with Jess, something's bothering you. Your father can tell. *I* can tell.'

He sat down, nursed his beer. He was probably deciding what to tell her.

'Jess is a total mess, and the boys are devastated. Not only did Darren, the prick, take the only decent vehicle they had, but he cleaned out what little they had in their joint bank account as well.'

'Oh, no. How awful for Jess. How will she manage? I can lend her some mon—'

'Laura,' he said, steel in his voice. 'Don't even go there. I have money.'

'The offer's there.'

He drained the schooner, sat back, closed his eyes. 'I'll never get out of this fucking place.'

She almost choked on the silly, dizzy bubble of hope that rose in her throat. 'You won't?'

He opened his eyes. She drew back at the fierceness of his glare.

'I'm hardly going to leave her to manage the farm on her own, am I? The boys are just boys, they're too young to be expected to work the way I was . . . Talk about history repeating itself.' He stopped, cleared his throat, and when he spoke again his voice was rough. 'Neill's dying and I'm here to help there. I don't know how I'm supposed to pick up the slack on the farm as well.'

Laura bit back a retort about it being his *father* who was dying. The anger, the guilt, the grief, she remembered them all so well. Taking a steadying breath, she bit back on all the things she wanted to say, said gently instead, 'You poor bugger, you've really been dropped in it this time,' and he looked away.

She reached out and gave his arm a squeeze, much like she had his father's only hours before. Only this time the arm was warm, almost hot. His muscles were thick, bunched with tension, and the springy dark hairs tickled her fingertips. He looked at her hand, then his gaze locked with hers and she slowly withdrew, wrapping her fingers around the cool glass in front of her.

'So,' she said at length. 'What are we going to do?'

'*We* are not going to do anything.' He shook his head slowly from side to side, his mouth a grim line. 'And as much as I appreciate the offer, Laura, this isn't your problem. Do you want another drink?'

'My shout,' she said and stood up, the chair grating across the wooden floor. She picked up both glasses. 'Same again?'

'Yep, thanks,' he said. She was halfway to the bar when he called out after her, 'And while you're there, I'll have a bag of chips or peanuts, not fussy.' She rolled her eyes and kept walking.

Half an hour later she dropped him off at Neill's front gate. 'That wasn't so hard, was it?' he said, his hand resting on the doorhandle.

'What do you mean?'

'All work and no play —'

She thumped him on the arm. 'I am not dull!'

'No, you're not. In fact you're very un-dull, and you're very —'

'Go, while you're still ahead,' she said and gave him a firm shove with one hand.

His fingers snaked around her wrist. The temperature in the car went up five degrees. He pulled her towards him. She licked her lips, and then he kissed her on the cheek, discombobulating her completely.

'Thank you, sweet Laura,' he said, and she felt the words against her cheek, felt them shiver right through her body. 'Thank you for the drink, and for being so loyal to Neill and persisting until I talked

to you.' He tilted his head to one side, expression wistful. He feath-
ered his fingertips across the cheek he'd just kissed. 'As much as I
hate to admit it, you're far too good and kind for a bitter bastard
like me.'

Chapter 20

Neill's forecast storm didn't arrive until Tuesday evening.

It was preceded by another hot, sticky day without a breath of breeze. Laura's morning run had been a chore that left her sweaty and drained. There'd been no sign of Jake or the dog first thing and the ute had been gone from the carport. The health centre had been hectic and she'd ended up seeing a man with chest pain at the hospital and missing lunch.

Later that afternoon, the Magpie Creek locum had rung about one of the patients Laura had admitted. He sounded about Milt Burns's vintage, and about as grumpy, and she had to wonder if she'd still be hanging in there when she was as old as they were. She seriously hoped not. Unless she was enjoying it as much as she was now, and could keep up with the ongoing changes in medicine.

Laura hadn't been home from work long when the rain came down in sheets, thunder rattling the windows, water overflowing the gutters. Standing at the kitchen window she watched with increasing dismay as water steamed down the back wall between the house and verandah roofs. Her dismay turned to horror when a trickle of water made its way down the inside wall above the window. The gutters would be choked with leaves and unable to cope with the downpour.

The rain stopped but Laura wasn't fooled into thinking the storm was over. In the distance lightning snapped and snaked across the eerie blue-grey sky. Thunder rumbled. There was only an hour or so until sunset. Making the most of the brief reprieve, she shoved a pair of pink rubber gloves into her pocket, grabbed a bucket and carried the light aluminium ladder she used for painting out onto the back verandah.

Propping the ladder against the verandah roof she swung up the rungs to peer over the edge and into the verandah gutter. Sure enough, it was clogged with twigs, rotting leaves and dirt. But she needed to get to the gutter on the back of the house; that was the one causing the water to leak in through the eaves and into the kitchen.

She glanced back over her shoulder. The lightning looked brighter, the thunder closer on its heels, gusts of wind swirled soggy leaves on the cement path below. There was no time to lose. She heaved herself up onto the verandah roof, crawled along on all fours to the house gutter. It was chock-a-block with rotting organic matter. In one spot blades of grass pushed through the slimy mess. Many moons had passed since these gutters had been cleaned. Gritting her teeth, she pulled on the rubber gloves and began scooping the muck into the bucket.

It would have been okay if a sudden squall hadn't sent the ladder clattering to the ground. She dropped onto her haunches, squeezed her eyes shut and cried out with dismay. The sky darkened, there was a snap of lightning, a crack of thunder. With a frightened yelp she flattened herself on the verandah roof. The last thing she wanted was to become a human lightning rod. Then, in one almighty burst, the rain came down again.

It only took a minute of sheeting rain until she was saturated, her hair plastered to her scalp. Laura crabbed across the verandah roof on her stomach and gripped the edge of the gutter, blinking water out of her eyes as she carefully looked down. Yes, there was the ladder, swamped on the cement path. She wanted to scream. She was getting colder by the second.

With the rain and the gloom of night falling, she could barely see into Neill's backyard but she was sure the carport was empty. Jake wasn't home and the chances Neill would come outside were slim to none. She wanted to cry out with frustration.

Instead, she cupped her trembling hands around her mouth and called out at the top of her voice, 'Help! Help! Someone – anyone – please help.'

Against the pounding rain and the deafening claps of thunder, her shouting was almost inaudible. Laura waited a few minutes, then felt the goose bumps erupt across her body and knew if the rain didn't stop, it wouldn't be long before she started to shiver. She called out again, called until she was hoarse, and her tears of fear and frustration mingled with the rain. She was afraid that if she wasn't frazzled by the lightning, she'd be drowned by the incessant rain. Imagine the headlines if she was struck by lightning. *Woman dies by lightning strike . . . two years after husband electrocuted.*

Soon the terror subsided and gave way to a different sort of fear. Now, as she hugged herself and curled into a ball as small as she could against the corrugated iron roof, she began to worry about hypothermia. Please, let her be rescued before her hands and feet went numb and she started to feel sleepy.

Eventually the rain eased to a light drizzle, and then stopped altogether. The storm had passed. It was nearly dark when a pair of headlights swung into Neill's driveway. Giddy with relief, she waited until the door slammed before shouting at the top of her voice.

Moments later she heard the gate being unlatched and the crunch of gravel.

'Laura?' said Jake. 'Where the hell are you?'

'I'm up here, on the verandah roof.'

'I'll just turn the verandah light on.'

'Don't!' she shrieked. 'Water's leaked in everywhere. You could get electrocuted.'

He looked around, saw the ladder on the ground and turned back the way he came.

'No!' she yelled. He was headed back towards the gate. 'Don't leave me up here any longer,' she pleaded. She scrambled on all fours to the edge and stared down at him.

He looked up at her. 'Laura, I won't leave you up there. But I need to go and get another ladder, that one doesn't look safe,' he said. He vanished next door.

Minutes later he was back with a larger, sturdier ladder. Setting it firmly against the edge of the verandah, he climbed up. 'What the hell are you doing up here?'

'Sunbathing. What do you think?' she snapped and flung the bucket of muddy sludge towards him. 'Here take this.'

'Pink rubber gloves, nice touch.'

She glared at him. 'Move,' she said her voice thick with tears of vexation and relief. When he'd disappeared from sight she man-oeuvred around, tentatively searching out the top rung of the ladder with her foot. She eased onto the ladder and, with wobbly knees and chattering teeth, slowly backed down. Warm, strong hands encircled her waist and Jake lifted her off the last rung.

'Are you okay?' he said gently.

'No, I'm not,' she said, sniffed, hiccoughed, and pushed past Jake. She toed off her sodden sneakers and rushed inside.

✶

The rain had stopped. Cool, fresh air drifted in through the open back door.

The bathroom door opened and Laura dashed through the kitchen wrapped in a towel, with another one wound turban-style around her head.

'I've made coffee,' Jake said. His mouth dropped open as she flashed past and disappeared up the passage, all legs and skimpy towel. He let out a low, appreciative whistle and chuckled when he heard the bedroom door click shut. He shook his head and carried the steaming mugs to the kitchen table.

'Thanks,' she murmured a few minutes later, as she slid into the chair opposite his, dressed in well-worn denim jeans and a t-shirt. She wasn't shivering anymore and her lips weren't blue.

'So tell me, Laura, what were you doing up on the roof in an electrical storm?'

She pointed to the wall above the kitchen window and he saw the watery tracts. 'The gutters just couldn't cope. It's probably years since they'd been cleared out. There was water running down the light bulb on the verandah.'

Her face had paled, she licked her lips, her eyes wide. He remembered her husband had been electrocuted. It must have been terrifying for her up there on the roof.

'How long were you up there? Why didn't you ring me?'

'I took my phone out of my pocket when I came home from

work and changed my clothes.' She glanced at the kitchen clock. 'I was up there for about half an hour, forty minutes. It felt like half a day.' She shook her head, wrapped her fingers around the coffee cup. 'I couldn't believe it when the wind blew the ladder over. It always looked so easy when Brett did it.'

'Brett?'

'My husband,' she said, glancing at him and then away. She scraped at a mark on the tabletop with her fingernail.

'Of course, Brett. Your husband.' Jake gulped his coffee and told himself the burning in his gut was from the hot drink. He couldn't be jealous of a dead man.

'What did he do, your husband?'

'He was a carpenter.'

'Ah.'

'Ah, what?'

'Explains your expertise and penchant for home renovations. I remember you said he was electrocuted.'

'Yes, at work. By an unearthed generator. It happened when no-one else was around. Apparently he wanted to finish what he was doing before he went to lunch.'

'Bloody hell,' he said. 'Must have been a shock.'

She made a strangled sound and his eyes widened in horror. 'Shit, Laura, I'm sorry, no pun intended.'

'I know that.'

'What was he like?' he said, the words tumbling out before he could think. What was the matter with him? Talk about picking at a scab until it bled. He held up his hand. 'Sorry, you don't have to answer that. It's none of my business.'

'It's okay,' she said, sitting forward in her chair. She tilted her head to one side, her expression pensive. 'He was gorgeous – tall, blond, everything I'd ever dreamed about. Kind, funny, handy.' She smiled. 'That's how we met – I hired him to help me with the reno-vations at my place in Adelaide.'

Brett sounded like Mr Perfect. 'It must have been hard,' he said.

'It was . . . It is. But it's true what they say, time does heal, slowly, but it heals, and then you can move on.'

'I suppose so.'

'If you let it. If you don't let it heal you'd probably end up bitter and twisted, always ranting at fate.'

'Like me, you mean.'

She didn't answer. She just looked at him with those beautiful blue eyes, brimming with life and hope, and he wished he could drown in them. He had a sudden, overwhelming urge to be whole again, to heal this gaping wound in his soul once and for all. He'd been alone for too long, his bitterness preventing him from really living.

'I'd better go,' he said. He felt like he was coming out of a trance. 'The old man will be wondering where I am.'

She stood up and followed him out into the porch.

'And Jake, thanks for coming to my rescue. I could have been up there for hours, all night even. That's if I didn't get struck by light-ning.'

'You're welcome. Don't use the light until it's dried out and I've had a chance to look at it. In fact, put some tape over the switch.' He reached out and tipped her chin up with his finger. 'And next time, before you go climbing about on the roof in an electrical storm, ring me.'

'Okay,' she whispered and it took every gram of strength he could muster to turn away from her, to not pull her to him and kiss her until their lips went numb. There were things he needed to do and conversations he needed to have before he'd be in a position to push Mr Perfect off his pedestal.

Laura went back into the house and it felt empty, as if Jake had sucked all the energy out with him when he'd left. She tipped the dregs of her coffee down the sink, went to the fridge and grabbed a bottle of white wine. Then she remembered she was on call until eight the next morning. She looked longingly at the bottle and slipped it back into the fridge door.

She threw her wet clothes into the washing machine and reflected on her conversation with Jake. The subject of Brett was becoming easier to discuss than she'd ever imagined it could. Now, when she thought about Brett, about them, about their life together, it almost felt as if it had been someone else's life, not her own.

This was her life now, the new life she was creating for herself, in the present day, in Potters Junction. Or, more truthfully, it was the life that was falling into place around her. And if Jake became part of that life, for however long, that would be okay. More than okay, actually. She shoved her dirty clothes into the washing machine, scooped in the detergent and turned the machine on.

After dinner, while Laura contemplated what she'd do the next day, Milt Burns rang.

'Hello, Milt.'

'I'll cut to the chase. I'd hoped you could work tomorrow. Something's come up and we're on our way to Adelaide.'

'All right, I'll go in,' she said as she scanned the unpainted walls, the ones she had been going to paint the following day. 'Do you want me to cover call until Thursday morning?'

'I'll be back by eight tomorrow night, I'll cover call from then.'

There was the sound of a displeased woman's protest in the background. His wife, Linda, she supposed. 'All right, eight a.m. Thursday,' he said, and disconnected.

Laura restacked the drop sheets and paint tins she'd laid out for the following morning. She found some gaffer tape and taped over the switch to the verandah light. After the storm, the humidity had dropped considerably and the air was now lighter, easier to breathe. When she went outside with a torch to inspect for water damage to the garden and vegetable patch, the twinkling stars were visible above.

Jess fed the dogs and shut them up for the night. The storm had broken just as she'd been about to do it earlier. All through the lightning and thunder, the two kelpies had cringed on the back verandah, squeezing in behind the wood box. Jess was glad Jake had taken Skip home with him – the wood box was huge but there wasn't room enough for three dogs behind it.

As she walked by the ancient gum trees behind the house, the roosting galahs squawked and squabbled, slow to settle after the electrical storm. The torch beam bounced along the ground in front of her; she sidestepped a puddle, glanced up at the open sky. On the distant horizon, a bank of clouds and intermittent flashes of lightning were the only remnants of the storm.

With the torch balanced in her armpit, Jess managed to empty the rain gauge on the back fence. Seventeen millimetres. Nice, but not all that welcome this time of year for those further south who'd be making hay or preparing for harvest.

No issues there for Jess. There was no hay – or anything, for that matter – to reap on this barren property. If they could just keep alive the few hundred head of stock they had left . . . Jess sighed and slid off her shoes, let herself in the back door. When she wasn't cursing Darren, hating him for what he'd done to the boys by leaving, tossing and turning in a lonely bed, she could sympathise with why he'd wanted out of the place.

Her husband had been gone a week. Through seven painful days she'd dragged herself, and for seven endless nights she'd lain awake until she couldn't bear it any longer and had downed the sleeping pills Jake had brought from Laura. She had to carry on for Sam and Mikey, she would give some semblance of normalcy to their upheaved lives.

She put the kettle on, thought about the wine in the pantry. The television blasted in the background and Sam's laughter rang out. She dropped a tea bag into a mug and spooned in sugar. Last night Darren had phoned, asking to speak to the boys. When she'd heard his voice, the chaos of her emotions had sent her dashing to the bathroom to be sick. Sam had watched her, and had then taken the telephone handset, his sweet, guileless face creased with concern.

She sat at the kitchen table, her tea cooling in front of her. Her anger towards Darren was threatening to paralyse her. Jake wouldn't be around forever and she couldn't manage the farm on her own. Decision made, she leaped to her feet, the sudden movement sending the chair skidding back across the linoleum. She swiped at the tears running down her cheeks, lifted the phone handset out of its cradle.

★

'Dad?'

The single syllable felt uncomfortable on Jake's tongue. Since that conversation he'd overheard twenty years ago, he had only ever thought of him as Neill or the old man.

Neill put the telephone down; his haggard face was leached of any colour.

'Are you all right?'

'Why didn't you tell me Darren had left her?'

'It wasn't my secret to tell.'

'I knew something wasn't right. I haven't seen Darren for a couple of weeks, and she never mentioned him, until now. She's upset.'

'Of course she's upset. Life as she knew it is over.'

Neill drew a shaky hand across his face, eyes glistening with unshed tears. 'Do you think he'll come back?'

Jake grabbed a beer from the fridge. 'No idea. And I don't know if she'd have him back if he came.'

'There's no way she'll be able to manage the place on her own.' Neill looked at him, expectantly.

Jake's fingers curled around the cold beer.

'Not going to happen,' he said quietly, calmly. 'I'll help her out while I'm here, but that's it.'

Neill sagged, but the recriminations Jake was expecting didn't come. The old man didn't say anything. No lecture, no nothing.

Jake slowly sipped his beer but there was no enjoyment in it, it left a sour taste in his mouth.

Chapter 21

Kaylene Curtis didn't hide her surprise when Laura walked through the automatic doors into the health centre the following morning.

'Milt rang me about nine last night,' Laura said. 'He was already on his way to Adelaide. Said something had come up.'

'Oh.' Kaylene looked miffed. She studied the computer screen and then the printed patient list she'd prepared for Doctor Burns. 'I guess he'd want you to see his scheduled patients.'

'I guess so. What would have happened if I hadn't been here to cover?'

'I don't know. I suppose I would have contacted all his patients and rescheduled them. It's never happened before.'

'What, he's never missed a day because he was sick or something?'

'Not in the twenty years I've been here.'

'Amazing. I'll ring the hospital later, ask if there's anyone up there I need to see.'

Kaylene nodded her perfectly coiffured head. 'I wonder what's going on?' she said, soft enough that Laura had to strain to hear her.

'I guess he'll tell us if he wants us to know.'

Kaylene didn't say anything more. She handed Laura the patient list and then busied herself at the desk, ignoring her, so Laura made her way to her consulting room to prepare for the day.

Laura stifled her grumbling stomach as she studied the pathology results again. A thin, nervous woman sat in the chair facing her.

How could Milt Burns have missed *that*?

The patient had come for repeat prescriptions. Because Laura had never seen her before she'd quickly scanned her most recent visits and pathology results. She re-read the clinical notes on the screen. When you put together that history with the ongoing signs and symptoms, it was plain as the nose on your face. But he'd missed it.

'Is everything all right?' the patient asked.

'Yes, all okay. I just wanted to double-check what blood tests Doctor Burns had done already before I ordered any more tests for you.'

The woman fidgeted with her lacy handkerchief. 'I didn't realise I'd need more tests. Doctor Burns said I was getting older and doing too much physical activity, that's why I feel so tired.'

'That might be part of it, but perhaps there is something else going on and another blood test will help confirm that.'

'You don't think it's cancer, do you?'

'No, I don't. However, we need to be sure and this test, and then maybe a referral to an endocrinologist, will give us the answers we need.'

The woman's expression clouded, her wrinkled brow furrowed

even more and she shifted in the chair. And then she slowly pushed up the sleeve of her blouse for Laura to take the blood.

After she'd shown the patient out, Laura went in search of coffee and something to eat. The lunch room was empty, the smell of something savoury lingered in the air and the kettle was still hot. She reheated her leftovers and thought about how Milt Burns would react to her provisional diagnosis, and the ongoing investigations she'd ordered.

In her city practice, Laura had had some patients who were officially 'hers' but, increasingly, the GPs she'd worked with had been happy to see anyone. This was becoming the norm and it had an upside and a downside. On the upside, the frequent flyers, those patients who were very dependent on the health system for one reason or another, were shared around. On the downside, after working to establish a rapport with a particular patient, there was a chance that you might not see them again. Laura's opinion was that with the appearance of more and more mega-practices and 24-hour clinics, the pressure was on, much to the detriment of the traditional role of the family doctor.

Milt Burns had been the go-to person, the family doctor, in this community for years. And here she was, much younger, not as experienced, and a woman to boot. Laura accepted it would take time for the community, and for him, to trust her. She looked up from the sink and caught her reflection in the window. She was thinking like someone who planned to be around long enough for them to do just that.

Laura's heart had given an extra thud when she'd knocked on Neill's back door later that evening and Jake had greeted her with obvious pleasure.

'You look beat,' he said, holding the door open.

'So do you.'

Now she stood in Neill's kitchen, watching Jake wash up dinner dishes. Up to his elbows in suds was a new and unexpected look; it suited him. His hair was still damp from the shower, his jeans and t-shirt freshly laundered. Reluctantly she shifted her focus, picked up a tea towel and began to dry the dishes.

'I've had a long, busy and sometimes frustrating day. What about you?'

He dunked the dirty frying pan into the water. 'Same. I've been out at the farm today. I'd forgotten how never-ending farm work was. There's not a time when you've done everything. And the place is pretty rundown.'

'How's Jess?'

'She told Dad last night.'

The tea towel stilled in her hands. 'How did he take it?'

Jake pulled the plug, wiped the frying pan over with the dish-cloth and set it on the stovetop. 'He didn't say much at all. He hardly ate anything tonight, went to bed straight after. Looks more like a skeleton every day. But we did agree I'd need to lend a hand out there. She can't manage on her own. It'll be up to us to juggle Neill's care and the farm work.'

'So how is she in herself?'

'So-so. Darren rang on Monday night and asked to speak to Sam and Mikey.'

'Wow. That would have been tough.'

'She seemed a bit brighter today, now that she's told the old man. Although I don't think she's sleeping much. The boys' grand-mother offered to come and stay, take some of the pressure off, but Jess knows everything she says or does will get back to Darren.' His expression darkened. 'Prick.' He went to the fridge. 'Do you want a beer?'

'No, thanks. I'm still on call,' she said, draping the tea towel over the oven doorhandle. 'Anyway, I'll leave you to it. I really just wanted to see how Neill was.'

'Oh,' he said. With a click and a fizz he opened a can and quickly raised it to his mouth before the froth ran down the side. He leaned against the sink, crossed his ankles, swiped his fingers through his hair, pushing it off his forehead. 'Any after effects?'

'What do you mean?'

'From your adventure on the roof.'

'It scared me. But I was counting on you coming along eventually.'

He lifted his eyebrows. 'Do you want me to clean the rest of the gutters?'

She tipped her head to one side. 'Thanks, Jake, but no, you've got enough of your own stuff to do. I'm not about to risk getting up there again. I'll ask Gav when he gets time.'

'Whatever,' he said. Judging by the way his lips tightened, she wondered if she should have accepted the offer.

'I'd better go,' she said but her feet felt as if they'd stuck to the floor. He took another swallow of beer and put the can on the sink.

'I'll see you out,' he said but made no move to do so.

Not game to look at him, she focussed on his chest, on the black cotton t-shirt stretched across its broad expanse. Her eyes travelled down over the faded denims, which clung to his lean hips and then, when she realised what she was doing, she snapped her eyes quickly back up to find him watching her, a faint glint of amusement and something else in his hazel gaze.

'So, what's Doctor Burns like to work for?' he said. He went to the fridge again, looked in, shut the door.

She settled back against the cupboard. 'Oh, I don't see that much of him. I shouldn't really see him at all, given he's meant to be having days off when I'm there.'

Jake filled the electric kettle and turned it on, then reached around her for a mug. 'Tea, coffee?'

'Tea,' she said and moved so he could get to the canisters on the bench. 'There are a few things I'm not comfortable with, but I'm sure that's more about my not understanding the right way of going about things. What's politically correct in any given circumstance seems to vary, which makes it difficult.'

'Like?'

She sighed, debated whether or not to say anything about the issues worrying her.

'Oh, I don't know. Sometimes the lines around whose patient is whose aren't clear, for instance, especially because I work part-time. And the after hours on-call, well, there's no formal protocol. The other night he was on call but didn't answer his phone, so they called me. When they finally raised him, he got all snippy.'

Jake poured water onto the tea bag and passed her the brew. 'Personally, I don't have much time for the bloke. He's probably a good doctor. I dunno, Dad says he's all right, and to give him his due, he's stayed here, looked after this community.'

'I agree, he has done the right thing by Potters Junction, and although I know he wants to cut back, I have a feeling he'll have trouble letting go.'

Jake took his beer and sat down at the kitchen table, pushing closed the passage door on his way past. She dunked the tea bag a few times and dropped it into the bin before pulling up a chair opposite Jake.

'It must be hard to let go, especially in a place where you've been so important for so long. The GP whose place I took at the Adelaide practice was seventy-six when he finally put down his stethoscope. He'd got quite a reputation for relying on Doctor Google. Every patient went away with a fistful of printed information and not much else, so the story goes. Then one of his longtime patients asked him if he'd retire when his printer ran out of ink.'

'Ha!' Jake leaned back in the chair, laced his fingers behind his head. 'Here's what I think – everyone, including him, realises he's getting past it, needs to cut back and transition into retirement. I appreciate how hard it would be to get a doctor to come out here and stay. And then you come along . . . ' He let the sentence hang and Laura chewed at her bottom lip as she considered his remarks.

'I'm not sure it'll be me that stays but just the same, it works for now.'

'You love it,' he said. 'You'll always be a GP. What do they say? *It's your calling.*'

She rested her elbows on the table, her chin on her hands. 'What about you, how does it feel to be back on the farm?'

His indulgent expression disappeared. He rocked forward in his chair, picked up his unfinished beer. 'I'm here, helping Neill, and Jess needs help. I can offer it. Like you, it works for now.'

'But do you like it?' she persisted.

'It's what I know. A bit like riding a bike. Some things have changed, although not as much as you'd think.'

'You were quite young when you went away.'

'Yeah, but how do you reckon I supported myself when I left home? I worked as a farmhand. Ironic, huh?'

'Life has one irony after another. How'd you get into what you do now?'

'I fell into it, in a way. When I left I headed to the west, I wanted to find Mum.' He took a sip of beer. 'I found her and you know how well that went. I haven't seen or heard from her since. Her choice, not necessarily mine.'

'Your mother must have been so very unhappy here, to give up you and Jess like she did.'

'You think she did the right thing?'

'No, I'm not saying that at all. What I've concluded from my years in general practice, and from my life experience is that does anyone ever really know what goes on between a man and a woman in a relationship like marriage? Except them, of course? There are times when even they don't understand what's going on. And often there aren't right decisions, there are only decisions that are less wrong.'

He didn't say anything but his eyes never left hers. He leaned forward again and picked up where he'd left off.

'I left Perth and headed north, picked up farm work wherever I could, did a bit of shearing and hated it. That went on for about three or four years, until an opportunity to work in the mines came up, which I took. At one point, a couple more years down the track, I was looking for work near Geraldton and they were making some film out in the bush, so a mate and I signed on as extras. That didn't come to anything but I met a few of the crew, helped out a bit, lugging gear about, and one of the blokes said if I was ever in Melbourne to look him up. So I did.'

'And one thing led to another and you ended up making documentaries?'

'Yeah, something like that. I always liked cameras, photography. Even as a kid. Dad gave me a camera when I was fourteen.'

'He knew you liked photography.'

'Yeah,' he said slowly. 'I suppose he did. Some of my early stuff is still out at the farm. Jess had a few shots framed, she said Neill had kept them.' His expression became pensive. 'Life's a funny thing, isn't it? Thank God for second chances.'

'It's good if you get them, you just have to make sure you don't muff them the second time around.'

He stifled a yawn and she stood up with a start, taking his empty can and her mug to the sink. 'I'd better head off.'

He didn't try to stop her. When she loitered on the back step he said, 'Goodnight, Laura. If you get caught up with work and want me to water your garden anytime, just let me know. You have my number.'

'Thanks. I'm off tomorrow. I'll drop in and see Neill, make sure he has some lunch.'

'That would be good. It'll save me driving in from the farm at lunchtime.'

'Goodnight,' she said, and he was already closing the door.

He closed the door. When he heard the gate clank shut he flicked off the back light.

'Shit,' he said to himself. Every time he saw Laura, or thought about her, his body ached from wanting. But he was exhausted and his muscles already ached from physical work. The ten-hour days at the farm plus the forty-minute return drive at lunch to check on Neill were taking their toll. And as tired as he was, his sleep was shallow, always alert in case he was needed in the night.

He snatched open the fridge door and grabbed another beer. It was still early, pointless going to bed when all he'd do was toss and turn.

Standing at the kitchen window he stared out into the dark shadows of the backyard and slowly drank the beer. What he'd said to Laura earlier had been the truth. Being back on the farm was all right. It was better than he'd imagined, in fact. Although tiring, there was a sense of satisfaction to be gained from a hard day's work and he could feel his muscles hardening, could see his skin darkening from the hours under the relentless sun.

Maybe, if he stayed the summer, until Neill . . . The can in his hand began to buckle as his fingers tightened around it. With a curse he threw it into the sink, wincing at the discordant sound. The last few mouthfuls of beer gurgled out and ran down the drain.

'Son?'

He spun around to find Neill standing in the doorway, leaning heavily on the frame.

'Dad?'

'I heard voices.'

'Laura came. You were asleep and we didn't want to wake you. Do you want a cup of tea?'

'No, just makes me want to piss. I'll go back to bed.'

'I'll help you,' Jake said and for the first time his father didn't protest, didn't push his hand away as he guided him back to bed, helping him into the toilet on the way.

Beneath the flannelette pyjamas there was nothing to him. When his father stopped to catch his breath and steady himself, grey and gaunt, against the edge of the bed, Jake easily scooped him up and onto the mattress.

'What did Laura want?'

'To say hello, to see how you were.'

'Oh,' he said. He closed his eyes but his face was pinched with pain.

Covering him with a sheet and blanket, Jake gazed down at the man who for all intents and purposes was his father. Was the only father he'd ever know. Where had the vital, self-possessed man he'd grown up alongside disappeared to? All that was left now was the husk of that man. As he stood beside the bed and watched the jagged rise and fall of his father's chest, he wondered if the decay had set in way before the cancer. Had it set in about the time his wife, Jake's mother, had left? During that time, Jake had begun to rebel against everything and everyone – and the one man who had no blood ties to him but had loved him all the same had taken the brunt.

Jake's gut clenched. He'd left without a backward glance, at a time when this man had probably needed him the most. He'd lost his wife and, in the self-centredness and single-mindedness of early adulthood, his only son had walked out as well. The anguish Jake felt at that moment almost winded him. Was it a lifetime of malignant grief that had slowly eaten away at his father, that finally manifested itself in the invasive, cancerous growths?

The air in the room was heavy, thick with the cloying stench of sickness. It pressed in on him and he felt as if he couldn't breathe. He lunged for the window and threw it open, sucked the night air in like an elixir.

His father moved in the bed, coughed. Out of the shadows rose his voice.

'Son, sit with me awhile, tell me about your day on the farm.'

As weary as he was Jake couldn't refuse, so he perched on the chair beside the bed and surprised himself when half an hour later he was still talking, and Neill had drifted into a fitful sleep.

Later, alone in his single bed, Jake wondered how, after losing so much, Laura had managed to pick herself up and make a new life. Was the grief different when the ones you loved the most were taken as cruelly as her husband and mother had been? When they were so irrevocably gone? Was it any different to the grief he'd felt when his mother had left him and Jess? Was it different to the grief Neill felt when his wife had left him for another man, and when the boy he'd generously, and lovingly, taken on as his own son had walked away? Could you ever come to terms with knowing the people you loved were out there, somewhere, and it was they who'd decided they didn't want to be with you anymore, didn't want your love anymore?

He rolled over in the bed, guilt, regret and grief swamping him. Why had it taken him so long to see things for how they really were? The dying man in the bed in the room across the passageway was a far better man than Jake would ever be. He'd taken on someone else's child and brought him up as his own, he'd remained stoic when that child had blamed him and rejected him. With a groan he shoved his fist against his mouth to stop from crying out. How, in the short time left before the cancer destroyed his father completely, could he ever make it up to him?

Somehow, forgiving and asking for forgiveness didn't seem like anywhere near enough.

Laura was dragged from a deep sleep by the raucous screech of her phone. She fumbled for it, blinking, dazzled by the bright white light of the screen. It was the Potters Junction hospital.

'A fight, after the pub closed,' the night duty RN said. 'I wouldn't bother you but I reckon he's concussed; he has vomited and the laceration on his head definitely needs stitches. Hard to tell what his GCS is with so much grog on board.'

'Give me fifteen minutes,' she said and hung up. It was a quarter after midnight. She threw back the bedclothes and dragged on a pair of cotton capris and a t-shirt.

An enrolled nurse let her in the front door when she buzzed. The corridor was dark except for pools of yellow where the night-lights shone; the A&E was a long way from the nurses' station.

The patient lay prone, snoring, on the narrow bed, the cot sides in place. He had a mullet haircut and a sleeve of tattoos. The sweet-and-sour smell of stale alcohol and vomit almost made her gag as she approached. A pad had been placed over the gash on his forehead, blood had congealed and dried in his eyebrows, and one eye had swollen shut. A thawing icepack lay discarded on the bed beside him.

With a sigh she looked at the latest blood pressure reading on the portable machine beside him before going to the bench and reading the notes handed to her by the RN.

'Obs are okay. GCS is thirteen. Probably drunk, not concussed. Pupils are equal and reacting,' the RN said. 'Never seen him here before so don't know his tetanus status, or allergies or anything. He just tells me to eff off when I ask him.'

'Was anyone with him when he came in?'

'Nope. The ambulance brought him in. Cops broke up the fight and said they'd ring again when the patient sobers up.'

'Was anyone else hurt?'

'The ambos said the other bloke disappeared. Wasn't as pissed as this one.'

'Was he glassed?'

'Don't think so. Nothing in the paperwork to indicate there were broken glasses or bottles involved. It happened in the pub car park.'

Laura gloved up, noting the name at the top of the chart before she returned to the bedside and laid her hand on the patient's arm. 'Carl,' she said. 'I'm Doctor O'Connor.'

He groaned, opened an eye.

'I need to examine you, suture the cut on your forehead. How long since you've had a tetanus injection? Are you allergic to anything?'

'Fuck off. Lemme sleep,' he said, the words slurred.

The RN grinned. 'And here I was thinking it was me.'

Undeterred, she examined the laceration, careful to duck out of the way of Carl's poorly aimed swipes.

'Why don't you leave it until the morning? Let him sober up,' the RN said, pushing the trolley with the suture tray out of the way of his flailing arms.

'I'm here now,' she said through gritted teeth. 'I have things to do in the morning.'

With the help of the enrolled nurse, they managed to restrain his arms while she injected the local anaesthetic. He eventually calmed down and stayed calm while she put eight stitches into the ragged laceration.

'You'll probably have a scar,' she said.

After the RN had given him a tetanus shot, she sat down at the desk to write up the notes. They'd admit him for the night, continue the head obs, and if there were any changes she'd order a CT scan in the morning. It was unavoidable – she'd have to visit him first thing tomorrow and brief Milt.

The nurses settled him into a room nearer the nurses' station and Laura checked on him before she left for home.

He was awake, balancing precariously on the edge of the bed while the stoic enrolled nurse helped him with a urinal. He seemed to have sobered up a bit.

'You'll have a headache in the morning,' Laura said. 'I'll write you up for some painkillers.'

'Nah, don't worry about that, Doc. I don't like taking that shit, it's bad for ya.'

She nearly choked and she could see the nurse making a mighty effort not to smirk.

'What about the half bottle of Bundy you drank earlier? You reckon that's not bad for you?'

He grimaced, eased back onto the white pillows. 'Nah, mother's milk,' he said. He closed his uninjured eye and was snoring in seconds.

Chapter 22

It was Thursday afternoon, another hot summery day in spring. At Neill's request, Laura had just finished reorganising his front sitting room so his recliner chair was closer to the window. It was the only room with an air conditioner and when he wasn't in bed, he now spent most of his time in there.

As promised to Jake, Laura had downed tools at lunchtime and visited her neighbour. Half a cup of yoghurt and a chopped banana was all he'd eaten but Laura knew if she hadn't prepared it, he wouldn't have eaten anything. Jake was right. Neill was beginning to look like a skeleton with paper-thin skin stretched over it.

Neill sighed as he sank back into the chair. 'It's good to see what's going on outside. Now, tell me what you've been up to – I heard you go out early this morning.'

Laura plumped the crotchet-covered cushions on the two-seater sofa and sat down. 'I thought I'd have a patient to see at the hospital first thing but he discharged himself, so I went for a run. I've been painting ever since. I finished the passageway and just have the woodwork left to do.' She scraped at the paint caked under her fingernails. 'In hindsight I probably should have left the passage until last, after I'd done the other rooms, but I was tired of looking at all the cracks.'

'Dorrie let the place go a bit. It got too much for her, and back then I was too busy on the farm to offer any help. And Milt was never a handyman.'

'Milt Burns?'

'Yep, he used to visit her at least once a week, right up until she died.'

'I didn't know that.'

'Not many people did.'

'To my knowledge she wasn't sick. It was quite a shock for everyone when she died.'

'No, as far as I knew she wasn't sick. I was as shocked as everyone else.'

'So they were friends, then?' Why else would the local GP be a regular visitor?

Neill quirked an eyebrow.

Laura pursed her lips. Milt Burns would have to have been fifteen or so years younger than her great-aunt. 'Oh well,' she said and levered herself to her feet. 'Many a secret has gone to the grave.'

Then she remembered what Jake had told her, and heat spread up her neck and into her cheeks. Neill didn't seem to notice and she hastily went back to tidying up the room. She moved the coffee table closer to Neill and flicked on the vacuum cleaner to suck up the dust bunnies from where his chair had been previously. While she was vacuuming, Laura remembered there were several boxes of Dorrie's papers stacked in the dining room, waiting to be sorted through.

Perhaps she'd make a start on them soon. Who knew what they'd reveal?

'What about the television?' she said when the room was quiet again. She eyed the monstrous screen and the solid cabinet it sat on. 'You won't be able to see it from there.'

'It's heavy. I'll ask Jake to move it,' Neill said from over his shoulder. Something caught his eye and he leaned forward in his chair and peered out the window. 'There's Jess.'

There was delight in his voice. Seconds later a key rattled in the front door and a voice rang out.

'Dad?'

'In here,' he said, a smile splitting his face.

Jess surveyed the sitting room. 'Bloody hell, Dad, what's been going on here?' And then she saw Laura and the vacuum cleaner by her feet. 'Did you do this?'

'He wanted to see out the window,' Laura said and winced at how defensive she sounded. Of course Jess would feel territorial about her father.

Jess seemed to deflate. 'Don't mind me, Laura. Thank you. I've been a bit preoccupied this past week.' She looked at her father. 'Sorry, Dad, I know I've neglected you.'

He waved away her apology with a bony hand, he appeared far too pleased to have his daughter with him then to mind her recent absence.

'I didn't mind doing it.' Laura turned to Neill. 'I'll put the vacuum cleaner away and leave you two to catch up.'

'You don't have to go,' Jess said.

'But I do. I have paint brushes to clean and a heap of other things to do. I'm still trying to find my routine where work's concerned.'

'Good luck with that,' Jess said and picked up the vacuum

cleaner. 'I can put this away. I'll be back in a minute, Dad. I'll just see Laura out.'

When they were out of Neill's earshot, and had manhandled the vacuum cleaner into the broom cupboard, Jess touched Laura's arm and said, 'Thank you for the sleeping tablets. I don't know how I would have made it through the week without them.'

'But —'

'I know you know Darren has left me, and Sam and Mikey,' Jess interjected. 'And I know you suspected something was going on that day I brought Mikey to the health centre. I'm just not ready to talk about it yet.'

'I'm glad the sleeping pills helped. And when you are ready to talk, I'd be more than happy to listen.'

Jess swallowed and quickly nodded her head. 'I better get back to Dad.'

Two hours later Laura was in the aisle of the Foodland supermarket shoving groceries into her trolley, when her phone vibrated in her pocket. She'd already given the passageway woodwork its first coat of paint and was shopping while it dried.

'Laura?'

'Julia?' Laura's eyes widened in surprise. Why was the Magpie Creek practice manager calling her?

'The locum hasn't come back from lunch. He left over two hours ago and I haven't seen or heard from him since.'

'Have you tried his mobile phone?'

'Of course I have! It goes straight to message bank. I've phoned the bakery and the hotel but they didn't see him there. I asked the maintenance man at the hospital to check their locum accommodation – the cottage is empty and there's no sign of his car.'

'What about his patients?'

'If he doesn't show up soon, I'll have to send them home. Some have already left. Should I call the police?'

'The police?'

A shopper gaped at Laura as she passed with her trolley. Laura moved the phone to her other ear, turned to face the rows of pet food.

'I'm sorry, but there's no-one *here* to call,' Julia said. 'They're all at a management meeting in Port Augusta.'

'But why the police?'

'What if he's keeled over somewhere? Had a heart attack or something? Dropped dead?'

'Unlikely, if his car's gone and the accommodation is empty, but . . .' Laura closed her eyes, pinched the bridge of her nose. 'I guess if there's no other option, and it's what you'd usually do, then it's the police.'

'I'll keep you posted,' Julia whispered and the phone went dead.

Barely fifteen minutes later Julia rang back. Laura was stacking the bulging bags of groceries into the car when the phone buzzed.

'Found him. Well, sort of,' Julia said. She didn't sound at all relieved.

'Sort of?' Laura prompted.

'He quit. He's probably halfway to Adelaide by now. The locum agency rang me after he'd rung them. They're in a state, too. They had him booked to go elsewhere for another three months after he completed his three weeks with us.'

'And the police?'

'The locum agency rang first, which saved me the call and the embarrassment. I sent all the patients home. What a debacle.'

Laura heard Julia inhale and she knew what was coming. 'I'll do tomorrow, Julia, and Thursdays and Fridays until the next locum arrives, but that's all. No weekend visits unless there's a genuine emergency. I'll check any inpatients at the hospital when I'm there.'

'Thank you. I'll see you Friday morning. First patient's at ten.'

Laura stashed her phone back in her pocket and felt a stab of sympathy for the absconding locum. Being the solo GP in a semi-remote community was a hell of a responsibility. She could understand why, at his age, he'd suddenly decided he didn't want that responsibility anymore, decided he didn't need the pressure anymore. It was just a *bit* irresponsible to up and walk out, though.

It was almost dark when Laura arrived home the following evening after a hectic day at Magpie Creek medical centre. Much to her dismay there were ants traipsing in military-like formation across the kitchen sink to the sugar bowl on the bench. The sugar inside the bowl was black with them. With a muttered curse at her absentmindedness, she dropped her bag on the table, grabbed the torch from the windowsill and took the bowl outside to throw the contents on the compost heap, swiping at the ants crawling over her hand as she went.

As she walked down the cement path she splashed the light over the vegetable patch, expecting to see the plants wilted after a hot day without water. But they looked lush and the ground damp. When she threw the sugar out there was a pile of rotting leaves and other debris on top of the compost heap.

Jake.

He'd watered her garden and cleaned the gutters. Her fatigue and the frustrations of the day lifted for a moment. As soon as she'd changed, she'd go next door to thank him.

Jake heard the car the moment it turned into the street. He didn't need Skip's yap to know it was Laura and though he wouldn't admit it, he'd taken to listening out for her whenever he was back from the farm before she was home from work, or when she was on call. He'd heard her leave on Wednesday night, had lain awake until she'd come back at about two a.m.

'Busy day,' he said, when he opened the door.

'And then some. Julia had crammed one and a half day's worth of patients into one day.' She brushed against him as she stepped into the house. At the sound of his sharply indrawn breath she glanced at him and, in the dim light of the back porch, their eyes met and held.

'And you?' she said softly. 'I see you've been busy cleaning my gutters and watering the vegies.'

'I took a day off from the farm, did a few things around here,' he said and hungrily scanned her face. He knew she'd kept an eye on the old man the day before, but he hadn't seen her for two days. 'I'll look at the verandah light tomorrow. It should have dried out by now.'

'How's Neill? It was good to see Jess here yesterday. I'm glad she's told him.' She followed him into the kitchen.

'Beer, tea, coffee?'

'No, thanks. Just a quick visit to thank you for being my odd-job man. And to say hello to Neill.'

'You look whacked.'

She rubbed her eyes, her shoulders drooped. 'I am *exhausted*.' She updated him on the locum at Magpie Creek and her new work hours. 'And it's my turn to do the on-call in Potters Junction this weekend.'

Jake took in her blood-shot eyes, the purple shadows underneath. 'Don't run yourself into the ground, Laura. You'll get no thanks for it. What would they do if you weren't here?'

'I know. But how can I refuse when I am right here, Jake?' she implored. 'Most of the people are genuinely unwell, and they do need to see a doctor. It wouldn't be fair to expect Meghan Kimble to go back to work before she should, and Milt would be stretched even further.'

'Laura, not that many weeks ago you were wondering about ever going back to work. What about your renovations? All the things you want to do?'

'They'll wait. I can put things on hold for a while. And it's only for a couple of weeks until the next locum comes.'

He studied her for a moment. 'I can keep watering the garden for you.'

'Thanks. That would be terrific.' Her whole face lit up. His mouth went dry. He had to look away, knowing his desire for her would be written all over his face.

After Laura had talked to Neill for a few minutes she turned to Jake on her way out.

'You seem different. Some of the anger has gone.'

'I guess I hit rock bottom. Down there I faced some of my demons and the only way out was up.' He shoved his hands into his pockets, bewildered by what he'd revealed. He hadn't even realised that that was what had happened until he said the words out loud. But that *was* what had happened in the long, lonely hours before dawn, when he'd lain awake in the lumpy single bed, staring into the darkness and thinking.

'Yep,' she said and shivered suddenly as a breeze puffed through the open door. 'You get to a point where the *what if*s and the *why me*s cease to have any meaning or purpose. You realise the only way forward is to accept things the way they are and try to make the most of it.'

'Is that how you did it, Laura?'

'Yes, I guess it is.' Her voice cracked. 'It took me a while to work my way through it all. At first I pushed everything to the back of my mind, pretended that if I kept working, stayed professional, then I could carry on. And I did carry on for a long time. Then a couple of things happened, minor in comparison to everything else, and I crashed and burned and couldn't pretend any longer. And I stubbornly clung on to the *why me* and the *what if* – probably for too long.'

'Christ, Laura, cut yourself some slack. You lost your husband and your mother in a matter of weeks. I don't know what happened with your job, but I gather something did or you wouldn't have come here. What you've been through would have tried anyone.'

'I suppose.'

They stood in silence, each lost in their own thoughts. She jumped when he said, 'What made you realise it was time to move on?'

'To be perfectly honest, I don't know. Nothing . . . everything.' She paused, looked bemused. 'If I had to identify one thing, I couldn't. It was a combination of a whole lot of things. And time itself. The old adage "time heals all wounds" rings true. I've learned that either you can let the scars around your heart harden, contract, disable you, or you can get back amongst it, back into the real world, and work the scars until they're supple and resilient.'

'And are they?' He held his breath, her answer important to him.

She glanced at him and then away. 'Yes, I think they are. Going back to work without going to pieces has been a real milestone for me. I know I'm not completely out of the woods but every day I feel my confidence returning. Being able to be there for Neill, well, that's been good for me as well.' She cleared her throat. 'I have a way to go yet but I know I'll get there.'

Her expression was gentle, introspective, and he felt relief tangle with frustration, and an overwhelming sense of hope.

She said goodnight for the second time and the gate clunked behind her. After she'd gone, he stood on the back step staring into the night. Unlike Laura, he'd let his scars harden, contract and disable him. Because of that, he'd distanced himself from any meaningful relationships with people; he'd lived on the edge, in more ways than one.

Jake knew what it would take to make his scars supple and resilient. Forgiveness. He needed to forgive his father for keeping the secret about his paternity so he, in turn, might be forgiven for walking away all those years ago. And he needed to forgive himself for his stubbornness, for carrying the emotional baggage for so long, and for being an unworthy son.

Jake scrubbed his hands down his face, his chest swelled. Because of Laura, he felt himself wanting to live again, to love again, but he couldn't until he'd limbered up the scars around his heart. It was true that admitting to and accepting a problem were the first steps to resolving it. What had once seemed impossible was beginning to feel possible – imperative even.

Chapter 23

The next two weeks passed quickly for Laura, each working day reminiscent of the one before. Up before the sun to get in a run; home again often after the sun had disappeared behind the horizon. And the road from Potters Junction to Magpie Creek became increasingly familiar. The timeless landscape slipped past her in the bright sunshine of early morning, in the golden hues of summer sunsets and under the shifting shadows of night-time.

As a GP she saw it all and dealt with it, frustrated when there wasn't the support or allied health services she'd had access to in the city. That said, her hospital work in Adelaide had been limited, and she felt as if she was on a steep learning curve. Never before had she managed clients in a residential aged-care facility, been accosted in the supermarket and expected to do an on-the-spot consult, or had patients bring her eggs from their chooks and lemons from their gardens. It could have been overwhelming but she took it in her stride, touched that some of the patients seemed to genuinely care about her wellbeing.

'It's in their best interests to look after you,' said Kaylene Curtis. 'They know Milt is getting on and those who've thought about it don't want to experience what Magpie Creek did. They didn't have a doctor at all.'

Laura hadn't said anything, just divided the lemons into several plastic bags she'd found in the lunch room.

On the home front, the renovations were put on hold. She didn't see as much of Neill as she would have liked, but often noticed Jess's car in the driveway when she passed. She rarely saw Jake, only the evidence of his having been there: her vegetables were watered, the verandah light and leaky washers were fixed, and on bin night she found her garbage bins out on the street when she arrived home.

The days were long and hot. School would break up in a couple of weeks and Christmas was bearing down like a freight train. The red-ribbon brigade had been out tying bows on the trees in the main street of Potters Junction, and posters around the town advertised the annual street party and carols by candlelight. Laura had been too busy to even think about it.

And then it was her last Friday at Magpie Creek medical centre. Laura flicked off the computer and tidied up, careful not to leave anything behind. Julia had turned off the air-conditioning when she'd left an hour before, after the last patient, and the room was getting stuffy. She closed the vertical blind at the window and scooped up her bag. One last stop at the hospital to see a patient she'd admitted, and she could go home.

The meal trolley was parked against the wall, no sign of a nurse. An elderly lady in a cotton dressing-gown wobbled her way down the corridor, leaning heavily on a walking frame. Laura made her way to the nurses' station, pulled the patient case notes she wanted and scanned what the nurses had written since the morning. The chest X-ray she'd ordered was waiting on the bench in a large, grey envelope. Sliding it out, she clipped it onto the light box. She beamed with satisfaction. The patient she'd admitted the day before was getting better. Her temperature was down, oxygen saturations improving and her chest certainly looked clearer. She returned the X-ray to the envelope, tucked the case notes under her arm and went to see the patient.

Laura headed to the dining room of the residential aged-care wing, in search of the nurses. They'd be cleaning up after dinner, taking the residents back to their rooms. But the dining room was empty except for a man in a specially designed reclining chair. He was almost skeletal, a Port Power beanie pulled low on his shrunken head. A soiled bib rested on his chest. His eyes were vacant, his lips slack and saliva glistened in the corners.

Laura turned at the sound of footsteps and was unable to hide her surprise when Julia came in with a wet facecloth in one hand and a towel draped over her arm. The older woman faltered when she saw Laura.

'Julia,' she said, looking from the competent practice manager to the man in the recliner.

Julia's mouth lifted at the corners, in a parody of a smile. 'Laura.' She went to the man and started gently wiping his mouth with the face washer. 'This is my husband, Harry.'

Stunned, Laura took a step towards the man. 'Hello, Harry,' she said softly.

'This is Doctor O'Connor, Harry. She's been helping out here while Meghan's off with her new baby.' There wasn't a flicker of acknowledgement. Julia went back to her job of cleaning him up and said with a sigh, 'Lights aren't even on anymore.' She rolled up the bib with the face washer and threw them into the dirty-linen hamper in the corner.

'I had no idea.'

'You couldn't have known,' Julia said almost flippantly.

'I know,' she said and put a staying hand on Julia's arm. 'I'm sorry I've never taken the time to ask more about your family, about your life.'

Julia blinked rapidly behind the lenses of her glasses. She covered Laura's hand with her own. 'It's all right, love. He's had Alzheimer's for a few years now. He came in here about eighteen months ago when I couldn't manage at home anymore.' She looked at her husband tenderly, then pushed the beanie up his forehead. 'I try to get here to feed him as many nights as I can.' Her expression became resigned. 'These days he hardly eats anything.'

'You should have said something,' Laura said, trying to keep the reproach out of her voice. When the nurses had run through the aged-care residents with her, she remembered a Harry Pritchard in the line-up, only she hadn't connected him with Julia. The residents were only seen by a GP if they were sick.

'What's there to say?'

'Julia,' the registered nurse said as she whizzed in. 'Shall I take Harry now? It's probably time to put him to bed.'

'Hello,' Laura said, and the nurse noticed her for the first time. 'I've been in to see Lottie Crawford.'

'Thanks,' the RN said.

'I've written up her notes. Keep the IV antibiotics going for another twenty-four hours and then switch to oral. I've done the medication chart.'

'Okay,' the RN said as she manoeuvred Harry's unwieldy chair through the door into the corridor.

'I'll see you soon, Laura,' Julia said as she followed the RN and Harry out. 'Thanks again for your help at the clinic. Have a nice weekend.'

'You too.' Laura watched them until they turned the corner, trying to imagine what Julia's weekends were *really* like – endless trips to the hospital interspersed with housework and preparation for the next working week, most likely.

It was after six when she reversed out of the Magpie Creek hospital car park and headed home. She was ravenous, and a headache was beginning to pound behind her eyes. The thermometer on the dashboard read thirty-five degrees. Dusty's roadhouse was open so she stopped and fuelled up. She bought a cold, sugary drink and a chocolate bar. She gobbled them down but it only made her feel nauseous.

About ten kilometres out from Potters Junction, Milt Burns rang. He asked if she could start her weekend on-call from that night. They usually changed over at eight on a Saturday morning but he was going to Adelaide for the weekend and wouldn't be back until the following Wednesday.

'Okay,' she said with only a second's hesitation. Knowing she'd be the only doctor for both towns was daunting, but not as daunting as it'd been a few weeks ago.

But when the phone rang at eleven-thirty that night, waking her from the deep sleep of exhaustion, her first thoughts weren't so altruistic. Then her heart sank. The RN on night duty said Jake Finlay hadn't been able to rouse his father. The ambulance was on its way.

She could feel tears clogging the back of her throat as she dragged on a skirt and shirt, forced her feet into sandals and grabbed her bag. Laura had dreaded this happening. She'd thought about it often and understood why the AMA was so against doctors having any kind of personal relationship with their patients. But how could you live in a small country community and not befriend people you might have to treat sometime? And what about situations like this, when you were the only doctor within cooee? You'd have to live like a hermit, she supposed.

When she dashed out the back door the red and blue lights of the ambulance strobed eerily against the side of the house. She recognised Jake's deep voice, urgent, but with no hint of panic. They were loading the stretcher into the back of the ambulance as she arrived.

'What's happened?' she said, and Jake spun around.

'Laura?'

'What's going on? Why didn't you phone me?'

'Laura, you're dead on your feet. Milt Burns can deal with this, he's dad's GP. The ambos reckon he probably got a bit dehydrated, a bit fuzzy, and gave himself one too many doses of the painkillers.' He scrubbed a hand across his unshaven jaw. 'Jess dropped in this morning, but I've been out at the farm all day. The bore pump shat itself and the sheep had no water. I got home late and he was already in bed. He's usually up and down to the toilet, but when I hadn't heard him at all —'

'Milt's away. I'm on call.' She pushed past him to the back of the ambulance. 'I'll ride with him,' she said to the ambulance volunteer, and then climbed in.

Jake peered into the back of the ambulance before they closed the doors. He said something that she didn't catch, she was too busy finding a vein to get an IV and some fluids into her unconscious patient.

Neill woke up after he'd had a litre and a half of intravenous fluid.

'Where the hell am I?' he croaked from behind the oxygen mask. He was groggy, disorientated, and surprised when she told him he was in hospital. When she was satisfied he'd be all right, the nurses admitted him for the night and Jake drove them home in the old ute. It was almost three a.m. Jake's face was drawn, shadowed with sadness.

He pulled into the carport, turned off the engine and looked at her in the glow cast by the front verandah light.

'Do you have to go back to Magpie Creek in the morning?'

She closed her eyes, rested her head on the back of the seat. 'I've finished there. I did enjoy it but the travel would get to me if I had to do it long-term.'

'I should have been here,' he said, his voice raw.

She opened her eyes. 'Mmm. I totally understand how you feel. What are you going to do when he can't manage at all on his own?'

'Jess talked about moving in and staying with him, but he wouldn't hear of it. There's no space for the boys, he said, and he's right. But he wants to die at home.'

'So you've discussed it? It's what he wants?'

'Discussed? No. He told me that's what he wants, and I'm not about to go against his wishes.'

'Is there someone else who could help out on the farm, so you could be here more?' She yawned and her jaw cracked. 'I can keep him in hospital for another day. If there's any more help available from the community nurses, or anyone else, I'll organise it. And now I've finished up at Magpie Creek, I'll be around more.'

'It's not your problem.'

She sat forward, bristling. 'I'm already involved therefore I am entitled to make it my problem, especially if I can be part of the solution. And I like Neill.'

Jake glanced at her, his eyes glittering in the gloom. 'You can't save everyone, Laura.'

'I know that,' she said quietly. 'Jake, we're both too tired to talk about this now. Go to bed, get some sleep. Your dad's in good hands and you'll be no use to anyone if you don't get some rest.'

'You okay to get home?'

'It's only next door.'

'You haven't locked yourself out again?'

'Not a chance! I've planted a key outside. And I left a light on.'

'That's a shame,' he said and he reached out and cupped her face with his hand.

His fingers were warm, strong, and Laura couldn't move – didn't want to move. With a sigh she let her face sink into his palm, and when he pressed his lips against hers in a brief, tender kiss, then drew away, she wanted to scream with frustration.

'Thank you for what you did for Dad,' he said. 'I watched you. You're a good doctor.'

'You're welcome,' she said, and groped for the doorhandle. Maybe he didn't want to kiss her properly. Maybe she didn't know how to read the signs anymore. Maybe this was how he said good-night. Maybe it was better this way. He'd leave after Neill died, and that wasn't a maybe. The door swung open and with a brisk goodnight she slammed it behind her and hurried home, had a cold shower and fell into bed.

The house was eerily quiet. He opened windows and doors to let in some fresh air. Standing under the shower, he let the cool water pound down on him until his fingers started to wrinkle like prunes.

He thought about Neill, his own panic when he couldn't rouse him, the distraught look on Laura's face when she'd burst through the carport. He thought about Laura some more. Her competent and efficient treatment of her patient, the respect the nurses gave her, the look in her eyes when Neill had opened his. The feel of her skin, her soft, wet lips against his . . . He closed his eyes, swallowed a groan. She'd wanted him to kiss her properly. He'd wanted to do just that, and more. But until he'd tried to sort out this mess with his father he didn't dare . . . He liked her too much to lead her on and then ride away.

Tired but too wired to sleep, he booted up his laptop and hot-spotted it to his phone. He checked emails and went through the photos he'd taken at the farm and around town until his eyelids drooped over gritty eyes. When he finally slept, pre-dawn light had started to soften the night sky, rubbing out the stars.

He was woken from a deep sleep by the ringing of the landline. The thought it might be the hospital had him stumbling out of bed to answer it.

'I checked the troughs like you asked and there's no water, again.'

Jess. *Shit.* He rubbed his eyes, yawned. 'You need a new pump on that bore. I have tried fixing it. It's buggered. I've done everything I can.'

'I can't afford a new pump. They won't give me any more credit until we pay off what we owe.'

'If you want water for the sheep, you need a new pump. Carting water indefinitely is not an option.'

'Yeah, well, thanks, Einstein. You sound terrible. Are you getting a cold or something?'

'Or something. Dad's in hospital again. I didn't get to bed until five.'

'Why didn't you ring me? What happened? Is he all right?'

'Well, no, he's not all right. He's dying, in case you hadn't noticed.' Jake closed his eyes, felt the twist of regret as soon as the words left his lips. 'Sorry,' he mumbled, 'I'm wrecked.' He recounted what had happened, how Neill had rallied after the IV fluid.

Silence thundered down the line until Jess said quietly, 'I'm glad he's okay. I don't think I'll get in to see him today. Mikey didn't go to school. He's miserable. I hope he's not getting tonsillitis again.'

'Dad'll be disappointed.'

'Yeah, well, while we're slinging shit at each other, where were you for the last twenty years?'

Jake had an almost blinding impulse to tell her to fuck off and slam down the phone, to pack his bags and go. But she was right.

'I'm sorry about that, Jess, I really am. One day I'll explain.'

'Oh God, Jake, everything is such a stuffed-up mess.' There was a wobble in her voice.

'I'll be out as soon as I can. I'm going to call in at the hospital on my way. I'll bring a new pump with me. See you then,' he said and hung up. She had two children, she was broke and her husband had just left her. He needed to cut her some slack. He put the kettle on, spooned three teaspoons of instant coffee into a mug, and wished he had time to beg a decent cup of coffee, and a kind word, from Laura.

'I really think you should stay in another twenty-four hours,' Laura said to her patient on Saturday morning.

'But I feel good,' Neill said. Laura knew he was lying, he looked terrible. Even with the extra fluid and oxygen, he was as white as the bedsheet.

'What about I organise another blood transfusion, perk you up a bit?'

Neill fiddled with the oxygen tubing. 'Save the blood for some-one who really needs it,' he said, and Laura sat down in the chair beside the bed.

'What about pain relief? Is it time to move on to the next step?'

'The needle?'

'Yes, a small needle under the skin there,' she said and pointed to the area just below Neill's collarbone. 'We connect it up to a syringe pump and you get a steady flow of a painkilling mixture, twenty-four hours a day.'

'No, but soon.' He coughed, spat and Laura winced. When he had his breath back he said, 'It's my birthday the week after next. Jess wants to have dinner out at the farm.'

'All the more reason for you to stay here for another day. You need rest.'

'All right, whatever you say, you're the doctor,' he said and closed his eyes.

It wasn't like Neill to give in so easily. She stood up, staring intently at the man before her. There was a tap on the door and with a silent apology one of the catering staff came in to retrieve his untouched breakfast tray.

Laura watched him sleep and felt the same sense of hopeless-ness she'd experienced as she'd watched her dying mother sleep. All she could do was help make him as comfortable as possible. She smoothed her fingers across the translucent skin on the back of his hand. He had deteriorated in the past two weeks, while she'd been busy working.

Chapter 24

On Sunday morning Laura woke early after ten hours of sleep. The weather forecast was for thirty-eight degrees, and she wanted to get a run in first thing. After pulling on shorts and a skimpy tank top, she laced her shoes and slathered sunscreen onto her face, neck and arms. The sun wasn't up yet but it would be before she was back and there'd be a real sting in it.

About fifteen minutes into the run, while Laura was congratulating herself on how well she was doing, Jake and Skip fell into step alongside her.

'Morning,' Jake said. Skip looked up, grinning, pink tongue lolling out of the side of his mouth.

'Hello. Are you collecting Neill from the hospital this morning?'

'Yep. About ten.'

Laura quickened her pace to match Jake's easy stride but it wasn't long before she had to drop back. She shook her head.

'You go ahead. I can't keep up,' she said, huffing the words out.

He grinned, gave a mock salute. 'I'll catch you on the way back.'
Sure enough, he fell into step with her again when they were about
five minutes from home. His t-shirt was dark with sweat. When they
reached Neill's gate they slowed and Jake and the dog peeled off.

'I'll have a quick shower and see you for coffee.'

'Okay,' Laura said without stopping, then she waved and headed
around the corner to her home.

She was towelling her hair dry after a quick shower when Jake
knocked on the back door.

'Come in,' she called. She flicked the comb through her hair
and, with one last glance in the mirror, she straightened the hastily
donned shorts and t-shirt and went out to make coffee.

'I rang Dad and he said he slept a bit better last night.'

'The extra fluid on board probably did him the world of good.
He would have needed it in this heat.' She dropped a pod into
the coffee machine and set it going. Jake took two mugs from the
dresser and put the sugar bowl onto the table. She was glad that the
ants hadn't returned.

'The hospital is delivering all this gear to the house on
Monday – a commode and some other stuff. And a nurse will come
and shower him every morning. The nurses said we can have a hospital bed at home too, if we want.' Jake leaned against the kitchen
bench, watching her make the coffee. 'Did you organise all that?'

She nodded. 'It's worth thinking about the hospital bed. He'll be
bedridden pretty soon, I'd say, and it will make it easier for you to
move him, and for him to move around the bed.'

'I suppose.'

She brushed against him as she reached into the cutlery drawer
for teaspoons. Her breath hitched. He smelled clean, of fabric
softener and toothpaste. She almost whimpered, aching with need.

He looked at her and she saw her own need reflected back. They stared at each other for a long moment, and then he moved out of the way. She grabbed the spoons and mentally doused herself with cold water. It was better this way. Saying goodbye to him was inevitable and at the rate Neill was deteriorating, it would be sooner rather than later.

'You could move his bed out and a hospital bed in. There's room in his bedroom, but you might have to rearrange some of the furniture.' She hoped her voice didn't sound as croaky as it felt. 'It'd be a much easier way to manage him when he can't do anything for himself any longer.'

He drew up a chair and sat down at the table, spooned sugar into his drink. She frothed milk for a cappuccino.

'I don't reckon it'd fit through the bedroom door.'

'True,' she said, lips pursed thoughtfully. 'But it would go through the double glass doors and into the sitting room. We could use that as his bedroom. And the TV is already in there.' She poured the milk into the coffee, stirred it, licked the spoon. 'Problem solved!'

'What about all the furniture?'

'Store it in his bedroom for the time being.'

He downed his long black in several mouthfuls and stood up to make another. 'Sounds like a plan – for when the time comes.' He started the machine going again and turned to face her. 'When do you reckon that time'll be?'

'Who knows, Jake? My best guess would be not long at all. It didn't take much for me to convince him to stay in hospital another day.' She took out two bowls and a packet of muesli. She poured herself a generous helping, then offered the packet to him.

'No, thanks, I'll have some toast later.'

She shrugged and spooned yoghurt and fruit onto the muesli.

Jake looked at it, looked at her and picked up the empty bowl. 'This is probably better for me than toast,' he said, helping himself to the breakfast on offer. They sat at the table and ate in silence.

'Are you going out to the farm later today?'

He passed her his empty mug. 'No, by the time I pick Dad up and settle him in, I'll have the rest of the day off. Unless Jess has a crisis of some kind.'

'Any word from her husband?'

'No, not since that phone call. Mikey and Sam really miss him.' He stretched his long legs out and laced his fingers behind his head. 'Do you need a hand with anything today?'

'I don't think so,' she said and observed him, so comfortable in her kitchen. 'I'm finally going to finish painting the woodwork if I can. I really pushed it this morning. I'm going to be as stiff as a post tomorrow morning.'

He got to his feet with the grace of a panther. 'Join the club,' he said, amusement dancing in his hazel eyes. It wasn't until he'd gone that she got it, and she did laugh out loud.

'Why didn't you come and ask me to help you? I offered this morning,' Jake snapped.

He was staring up a ladder at Laura, who was balanced precariously, a cordless drill in one hand and a matchstick blind in the other. She swung around at the sound of his voice, nearly losing her balance.

'Bloody hell, Laura, what is it with you and ladders?' He reached out to steady it.

'Well, you're here now so could you please give me a hand putting this blind up?' She was frustrated, by the sounds of things. He held out his hand and she passed him the blind and the cordless drill, and climbed down the ladder.

'The fascia board is old and the crappy screws that came with the blind aren't long enough. I've a good mind to take the damn thing back to the shop.'

He studied the screws and the blind and then laid them down on the verandah. 'Don't move,' he said. 'I'll see what Dad's got in his shed.'

He was back in minutes with a jam tin of assorted screws and nails. She held one end of the blind while he fixed the other and in about five minutes the job was done.

'Thanks,' she said as she rolled the blind down. 'This'll keep the afternoon sun off the kitchen window.'

'It'll flap about when the wind comes up.'

She grabbed a plastic shopping bag from one of the cane chairs. 'Ta-da,' she said and held up two occy straps.

Amazed, he took one of the elastic ties from her and fastened the bottom corner of the blind to a verandah post, while she did the other. Her shorts and tank top and her arms and legs were splattered with paint. She looked flushed and sweaty. She looked gorgeous. He tried to remember why he wasn't supposed to pull her into his arms and kiss her senseless.

She collected the plastic wrapping from around the blind while he scooped the screws and nails back into the tin. 'Did you want something?' she said. 'Is Neill okay?'

'He's good. I got back to him at about eleven. He had yoghurt for lunch, and a cup of tea —'

'What?' she said when he paused, his expression bemused.

He threw up his hands. 'I can't believe I'm talking about what he had for lunch, and how pleased I am about it.'

'He's dying, he's your dad, and no matter how much you fight against it, you love him.'

He looked away, couldn't believe he had tears collecting at the back of his eyes.

'Jake,' she said gently, and he picked up the cordless drill and snapped off the battery. He knew she understood but he couldn't talk about it. Not now.

'Where do you put this on charge?' he said. 'It's nearly flat.'

'Laundry.' She took it from him. 'Do you want a beer?'

'That's what I came to ask. I was heading down the pub and wondered if you wanted to come for a quick drink?'

She looked down at her clothes, lifted one arm and smelled her armpit. 'I'm filthy, I pong and I'm still on call. Sorry,' she said. 'You go right ahead, though.'

'Do you have beer?' He realised he didn't want to go to the pub at all if she wasn't coming. What he really wanted to do was to spend time with her.

She named the brand he drank – what were the chances? – and he raised his eyebrows. He was delighted when she started to blush.

'Works for me,' he said.

When she came back a few minutes later she handed him a can of beer in a stubby holder and opened a bottle of spring water for herself, pressing it to her forehead with a blissful sigh before gulping down half of it. She sank into the chair beside him and unlaced her sneakers.

'Did you finish painting the passage?'

'Yep. And I've booked to hire the sander again on Wednesday to do the floor in the front room. Then I'll seal it.'

'Why the rush?'

'Oh, no rush, really. I just thought Alice might come up sometime over the Christmas break and it'd be good to have a spare bedroom again. I don't fancy sharing my bed with her.'

He wondered if she'd mind sharing it with him. He took a long pull of ice-cold beer, hoping it'd work its way down to where things were beginning to heat up.

'So,' he said eventually. Her head whirled around and she cleared her throat, pressing the water bottle to her face again. Her thoughts had gone the same way his had, he'd put money on it. He up-ended the beer can and drained it, slipped it out of the stubby holder.

'Anther one?' she said. He was sorely tempted. It was pleasant sitting on her back verandah looking out over the vegetable patch as the heat of the day dissipated with the lowering sun. He put the empty on the cement beside him.

'I'll get it,' he said and rose. 'Do you want anything?'

'Nah . . .' She leaned back in the chair. 'I'm buggered.'

'You drive yourself too hard, Laura.'

'Life's short,' she said when he came back with another beer.

'But there's such a thing as a work-life balance, or so I'm told.' He sank down into the chair again.

'Hah,' she said, and nudged his leg with her knee. 'You're a fine one to talk.'

'Exceptional circumstances. But it won't be forever. When this is over —' He hesitated, flipped open the can, took a sip. 'When this is over and I get on with my life, you can rest assured it won't be all work and no play.'

She closed her eyes, swiped lazily at a fly. 'Whatever,' she said, and for some reason her response, or lack of it, irritated him.

'What do you do to relax? All I've seen you do is work. You don't have a social life.'

She opened her eyes and her lips pressed together and he knew he'd scored with that one. But then she closed her eyes again. 'You know, my sister always tells me that.'

He leaned forward, rested his elbows on his knees. Her eyes were still closed. She looked relaxed. Paint in her hair, a smudge on her chin.

'She's been telling me I need to get a social life for months now. What she's really telling me is I need to go out, meet men, start dating again.' She chuckled, and her merriment was catching, but the thought of her dating other men left him cold. She opened her eyes and they were still dancing with amusement. 'Really, she's been telling me that since I was eighteen. I think she was happier than I was when I started going out with Brett.'

Jake grunted, went back to finishing his beer, and imagined her as a medical student, nerdy, all study and no play. The diligent, committed doctor. She stood up and stretched leisurely.

'I reckon I'll take a shower and think about what I'm going to make for dinner.' She stood in front of him with her hands on her hips. 'You know what, Jake Finlay? This,' she said, and made a sweeping gesture with her hand to encompass the house and garden. 'This is my social life, and I think I'm quite happy with that for the moment. I spend all my working hours with people, hearing about their ailments, listening to their woes. I enjoy this.'

He stood up, reached out and swiped at a smudge of paint on her chin with his thumb. 'Go and have a shower. Don't worry about dinner. Let's go to the pub for a meal.'

Her jaw dropped and he grinned. 'Close your mouth, Laura. If you want to, you can tell your sister you've been on a date.'

'But what about Neill?'

'He'll be more than okay for a couple of hours. I'll set him up in front of the television with the phone close by.'

'Give me twenty minutes,' she said, and he almost danced back to his house.

★

Jess turned on the tap and it gurgled, coughed, spat out a few slugs of water and then there was nothing. The sink full of dirty dishes sat there, high and dry, green detergent dribbling down the side. She wanted to hurl them all against the wall. First the bore pump, now the house pump.

'Mum, the toilet won't flush.'

Jess squeezed her eyes shut, steadied herself before turning to her eldest son. 'I don't think the pump's working. Let's take a look. Will you hold the torch for me, please?'

Mikey raced into the kitchen. 'The pump's busted and Mum's going to fix it,' Sam said.

'Mum's going to *look* at it and *see* if she can fix it,' Jess corrected, and the two boys traipsed out after her.

They walked across the farmyard to where the tanks stood and collected rainwater from the shed roofs. The pump shifted the water from the tanks to the house. No pump, no running water. And the pump was old, way past its use-by date, like everything else in this place.

Sam held the torch steady while Jess gingerly lifted off the cover.

'Watch out for red-back spiders, Mum. Last time Dad took off the cover there was this *huge* one underneath, and some eggs.'

'Oh, good,' she muttered and kneeled down beside the pump. She was flummoxed, she didn't know where to start. Darren or her dad always did this sort of stuff. She turned the power switch on and off a couple of times, found a reset button and flicked it, but the pump remained mute, like the inanimate lump of metal it was.

Mikey peered over her shoulder. 'Any red-backs?'

'I dunno, mate. Sam, pass me the torch, will you.'

She shone the light all over the pump, hadn't a clue what she was looking for. Water dripped from the bottom. She didn't think it was supposed to.

'Dad would know how to fix it,' Mikey said, and Jess gritted her teeth.

'Yeah, but he's not here, is he, dumb arse?' Sam said.

'Sam, don't call your brother a dumb arse. In fact, don't call anyone a dumb arse.' Mikey giggled. She leaned on the pump and pushed herself to her feet. 'I'll ask Uncle Jake in the morning. Tonight we'll have to fill buckets from the tank by the back door. It's school again tomorrow so we'll heat water in the kettle for your baths.'

Mikey ran off towards the house. 'I'll get buckets,' he yelled.

'Slow down or you'll trip over,' Jess shouted after him.

'Mum,' Sam said as they walked side by side, the torchlight a narrow beam in front of them. 'Do you think Dad will ever come back? On the phone the other night, when I asked him, he said he didn't know. If he doesn't come back, will Uncle Jake come and live here so he can look after the farm?'

Jess put her arm around her son's shoulders. 'I don't know, mate. I didn't know he was going to go, so I have no idea if he'll come back.' She cursed Darren for the millionth time. 'I know he loves you. You and Mikey. Remember that.'

'What about Uncle Jake?'

'He has his own life, Sam. He left the farm twenty years ago because he didn't want to be a farmer. We're lucky he's here now, helping out because Poppa's sick.'

Sam fell silent and Jess wondered what was going through his head. It broke her heart that he'd been forced to think about these things, things no ten-year-old should have to consider. When her mother had left, she'd only been a year older, and she remembered the pain and confusion.

'I love you, Sam,' she said. 'I promise we'll manage, one way or another, whether your dad comes back or not.'

He nodded and the torch beam wavered.

'I reckon the batteries are getting flat, Mum,' he said.

Another thing to replace and no money to do it with. She'd have to ring Centrelink again, first thing in the morning. She felt sick at the thought.

Chapter 25

Laura's last patient for the day reminded her of her mother.

There was something about the way the woman tilted her head and said hello. When she did, Laura's heart constricted and her mouth went dry. She sat down and reached for the glass of water on the desk, glancing at the computer screen for the patient's details. *Claudia Samuels*. Born the same year as Amelia O'Connor, Laura's mother.

'Mrs Samuels, what can I do for you today?'

'Please call me Claudia,' she said. Claudia crossed slim, tanned legs and moved her handbag from her lap to the floor.

Laura took a sip of water and it was like she knew, before the patient spoke again, what Claudia was going to tell her.

'I'm not sure you can do anything. It's probably just old age catching up with me, but my daughter's been on my back to see a doctor because I haven't been feeling myself lately.'

'In what way, and for how long?' Laura's lips felt clumsy as she formed the simple words. Trying not to gulp the water, she concentrated on the feel of the cool liquid as it slid across her tongue and down her throat.

'I've felt off over the last couple of months, I'd say. Hot flushes, and I have this dragging, nagging, lower back pain. I've lost a few kilos and I feel *so* tired all the time.'

'Have you been trying to lose weight?'

'Not at all! For once in my life.'

Laura looked at Claudia and saw her mother. Spinning back through time she shifted in the chair and tried to breathe into the band of anxiety tightening around her chest. It was over two years ago but it seemed like only yesterday her mother had been saying the same things to her . . .

Claudia coughed politely. 'Are you all right, Doctor O'Connor?' she said with genuine concern.

Laura snapped back to the present. She blinked. This woman wasn't her mother. She was her patient. There was no reason it should be the same in any way.

'Yes, I'm fine. It's been a busy day. Mondays always are. Now, you said you hadn't been trying to lose weight but you had lost weight regardless, and you feel tired.'

'Yes, that's right.'

'Well, Claudia, we'll start with the obvious and work our way through.' Laura reached for the blood pressure cuff. The tightness in her chest had eased. 'If there is something wrong, we'll find it. I won't leave one stone unturned until we do.'

Claudia's expression lightened. 'I was hoping you'd say that.'

Laura had promised Claudia Samuels she'd contact her when the results for the tests came in. The health centre was deserted, everyone had left except her, and the only sounds were the hum of the air conditioner and the rattle of the drug fridge in the treatment room. She tapped her fingers on the desk as she waited for the file to open on the computer.

Then her eyes were scanning rapidly. Blood rushed in her ears. As she scrolled down the columns, she saw the asterisks and notations against several of the figures indicating they were outside the normal range. A lot outside the normal range. Laura's head pounded. She looked at the results again, at the notes that went with them, and the report from the emergency pelvic ultrasound. Then she rang her patient.

Forty-five minutes later Laura lifted her arms above her head and stretched. The air-conditioning, on a timer, had turned itself off and the room was stifling. She needed to go home. A specialist's referral letter for Claudia Samuels, with a Post-it note saying the patient would pick it up tomorrow, sat on the desk in front of her.

A door slammed. She jumped up, then stood stock-still, listening, heart about to burst out of her chest. Kaylene should have locked the doors on her way out. Footsteps. Laura swallowed, her throat as dry as sandpaper. There were drugs on the premises. Her consulting door was three-quarters shut. She opened her mouth, about to call out and ask who was there, when the door burst open and her knees buckled.

Milt Burns stalked into her consulting room. Where the hell had he come from?

'How dare you!' he spat, a piece of paper flapping in his hand.

'Excuse me?' she said, bracing herself on the edge of the desk. 'How dare I what?'

'How dare you go behind my back ordering unnecessary tests for one of *my* patients,' he snarled, his face an unhealthy shade of purple. He threw the slip of paper and it fluttered across her desk and onto the floor.

Bending to retrieve it she quickly scanned the pathology report, a picture coming to mind of the thin, unwell woman, reluctant to have another blood test. Laura had seen her the day Milt had been away. She tapped the paper with her finger and let the anger swell inside her. She'd had a crap day, she was tired, heartsore and she had just given a patient some not-so-good news.

'I'm not surprised,' she said. 'There was certainly something going on with her. All that weight loss. At least we know now and can start treatment. She'll need a referral to an endocrinologist.'

'I've been seeing that woman most of her adult life,' he blustered. 'I've delivered her babies, taken her husband's gallbladder out, buried her father and, to this very day, I take care of her demented mother in the nursing home.'

Laura drew herself up to her full height, stabbed a finger at him and said, 'And your point is?' She launched in. 'I saw the patient. She was unwell. I assessed her. I read her case notes and path reports and in my professional opinion she needed more tests, so I took blood and sent it off.'

He swore and told her to bloody well butt out of his patients' business.

'And just how do I determine which patients are yours and which are mine, Milt? To my mind, if I see them here or at the hospital, they are in my care. That makes them *my* patients for the duration and I'll treat them accordingly. I treated Jason Coombes accordingly, but you put your ego ahead of good practice and subsequently threatened his life.'

Milt's face went from puce to pale in a matter of seconds and he shrank before her very eyes.

'Forgive me,' she gasped, her hand going to her mouth. 'I should never have said that.'

But her words were out there. They seemed to hang in the airless room.

'No, no, I'm the one who should apologise. I did exactly that. I put my ego ahead of good practice.'

Laura's eyes widened. Milt's shoulders slumped and he looked like a defeated old man. Her mouth opened but no sound came out. She rasped her tongue over dry lips and tried again. 'Why are you at the health centre, anyway?'

'We got back from the city a while ago. I wanted to go through a few things before tomorrow. It seems to take me twice as long to get half as much done these days.' He made a hollow, joyless sound.

'I suppose you'll be moving on soon, returning to your practice in Adelaide,' he said.

Laura was taken aback by Milt's adroit shift from a patient's pathology results to her practice in Adelaide. She hadn't given the place a serious thought for weeks. Was he building up to giving her the sack because she'd interfered with his patients? She reached for the glass on the desk but it was empty, not even a sip of water left to moisten her dry mouth.

'I have no immediate plans to leave,' she said. 'Unless . . .' she added when the silence began to echo.

'Right.' And with that he turned and left her room, leaving her more bewildered than before.

She sank into her chair. She dropped her head into her hands, and tried to make sense of what had just happened.

When she walked out to the car park fifteen minutes later, the streetlights were on and there was no sign of Milt's Holden Statesman. Laura felt like she'd been run over by a truck. She'd seen

patients nonstop since arriving at the health centre that morning
and the day before had been the same. She'd missed lunch today
to stitch a lacerated arm at the hospital, and then, to top it all off,
had copped Milt Burns's tirade. And of course she couldn't forget
Claudia Samuels.

★

Jake looked up from his laptop to find Laura silhouetted in the
kitchen doorway. It was Tuesday night, late, the kitchen was cast in
shadows and there was not a breath of breeze through the open window. The smell of garlic, tomatoes and melted cheese lingered from
the frozen dinner he'd zapped earlier.

'Laura?' Her name came out as a question. His chair scraped
across the vinyl as he rose. She didn't budge from the doorway.
'What's the matter?'

'Oh, nothing. Everything. I knew I wouldn't be able to sleep.
I had a shit of a day. And just when I thought it couldn't get any
worse, Milt Burns showed up and tore a strip off me for correctly
diagnosing one of his patients.' She frowned. 'I, um, well, I said
some not too complimentary things about him. I thought he was
going to give me the sack, but then he just walked out.'

'You need a hug?'

'Yep.'

In three strides he crossed the room and gently pulled her into his
arms. She sank into him, her arms slid around his waist as she bur-
rowed her head against his shoulder, and it felt so right. He rested
his cheek against her hair, absorbing the smell and feel of her and
willing his body not to rise to the occasion and disgrace him.

He smoothed his hand up and down her back. Slowly she eased
herself away from him with a flicker of a smile.

'Thanks,' she said.

She went to the sink, filled the kettle and began the tea-making ritual. He leaned against the kitchen bench and watched her, not having the heart to tell her the last thing he felt like was tea. A good single malt, or two, might go some way to hitting the spot, numb the ache that got worse every time he looked at her, touched her.

'So,' he said. 'What if he had sacked you?'

He couldn't see her expression but he saw her hands tremble as she poured boiling water into the pot. 'I've never been sacked before. Just given leave —' She paused but not before Jake heard the self-recrimination in her tone. When she finally turned towards him her eyes were glassy with tears.

'Hey,' he said and reached for her. He pulled her close again, wrapping his arms around her, but she stood rigid against him. When she didn't relax he let her go again and it left him feeling frustrated, useless in the face of her distress.

'Wanna talk about it?' he said gently.

Indecision flitted across her face.

'I thought I was going to have another anxiety attack yesterday. I haven't had one for months.' He raised his eyebrows and her focus flicked to a spot somewhere over his shoulder. 'It's why I'm on leave, I had a serious meltdown at work,' she said, and he could hear how hard it was for her to talk about it. 'And then the patient yesterday, she was so much like my mother,' she whispered. 'This evening her blood results came —' She gave a choked sob. 'I'm not sure I can do this, Jake. I thought I could. I thought I was ready, but now I don't know.'

Jake itched to reach out to her but she was lost in her own private hell. Like an automaton she poured tea, added milk to hers, then picked up the mug and cradled it with both hands, staring into the steaming brew.

'Maybe he should have sacked me.'

'Will you listen to yourself, Laura? I've never heard such crap in my whole life. So he tore a strip off you? It sounds like you gave back as good as you got.'

She gave a tired lift of her shoulders. His tea cooled on the kitchen bench as he watched her absently drink hers. When she'd finished, she rinsed the cup and reached for his, and noticed he hadn't touched it.

'Sorry,' she said with a twist of her lips as she tipped the tea down the sink. 'I just assumed you'd want tea.'

'I've made the old man so many cups of tea I'm about over the bloody stuff.'

'How is he?'

He heaved a heavy sigh, let her change the subject. 'In a lot of pain, I think, but he keeps it to himself. I hope he's well enough to make the trip out to the farm for his birthday. Jess has her heart set on it. It'll be the last time and all that, and I don't think he'll make Christmas. Oh, yeah, she asked me to invite you to the birthday bash, if you're free.'

'I'd like that very much. As long as I'm not intruding.'

Jake rolled his eyes. 'I won't even dignify that with a response, Laura.'

'Okay,' she said, 'I'll come. Do you want me to ring Jess, or will you tell her?'

'I'll tell her.'

Laura glanced at his laptop on the kitchen table. 'How come you're still up at this hour? Couldn't you sleep either?'

'No.'

She tipped her head to one side and gave him a professional once-over. Her blue eyes had lost some of their bleakness.

'If you're having trouble sleeping, why don't you see Milt Burns and get a script for some sleeping pills? Something mild that doesn't knock you out, that way you can hear your dad if he calls out. It might help get you through.'

'Don't worry about me,' he said, uncomfortable now under her steady scrutiny. She was one of the reasons he couldn't sleep. 'We were talking about you, remember?'

She reached across the space between them and put her hand on his arm. 'Jake, you can't work all day at the farm *and* care for your dying father without eventually falling in a heap yourself. You'll be no good to anyone.'

He got it. She wasn't going to say any more about why she couldn't sleep. He went to the kitchen table, stabbed at the computer keyboard to shut it down. And damnit, he knew she was right. He closed the lid on the laptop. He was wrecked. Darren the loser had left Jess to manage the farm and the finances, both of which were in chaos, on her own. The farm was on the verge of bankruptcy. Plus she had the kids to think about. He was trying to work out how she'd manage when he wasn't there, and he was trying to look after the old man but he was dying before his very eyes. He shoved the laptop into its bag, while Laura stood across the table from him, watching him.

'Have you talked to him yet, sorted out your differences? Time's running out.'

'You think I don't know that?'

'Jake,' she started. 'You need to sleep. Do you want me to ask Milt to write you a script? I could write you one, but I'd rather not, seeing as you're not my patient.'

Emotion roiled around inside him. Anger, guilt, frustration, fear.

'Laura,' he said, 'I'm not Doctor Burns's patient either and

I don't need any fucking sleeping pills.' He saw her recoil, but he ploughed on. 'If I wanted pills, the old man has a whole fucking pharmacy I could choose from. What I need right now is —' He stopped.

Just in time.

'What?' she said.

He bit down until his teeth ached.

'Jake?'

Her voice was soft, insistent and oh so sexy.

'You.' He looked straight at her. 'You. You must have realised by now, I want you so much it hurts.'

She took a step towards him.

He laughed with self-derision, then softened it with a small smile. 'But I wouldn't do that to you, Laura. I won't inflict my screwed-up self on you.'

The silence roared.

'But what if I wanted you to?'

Jake groaned. 'Don't say that, Laura. It's difficult enough as it is.'

'What is so difficult?'

He stared into her luminous blue eyes. 'I have nothing to offer you, Laura. I'm forty, of no fixed address. The U-Store in Melbourne where I leave my bike and other crap is the closest thing I have to a home base. I spend most of my time overseas in some of the world's most troubled spots.'.

'I don't remember asking you for anything.'

He blew out a frustrated breath. 'Laura, I know you're smarter than that. I've got more baggage than the Indian Pacific, and you know it. I've never had a relationship that lasted more than a few months, I don't know how. I haven't even got the balls to talk to the dying man who was brave enough and generous enough to take on

someone else's unborn child, then bring him up as his own son.' Jake
could hear the bitterness in his own voice. Something compelled him
to go on. 'And what did that *son* do?' He swallowed hard. 'He's a far
better man than I'll ever be.'

'Jake, you're a better man than you think,' Laura said firmly,
bringing him back to the room, back to her.

She looked as wrecked as he felt, her eyes red-rimmed and shadowed. He threw back his head. 'Listen to me. You've had a mongrel
of a day, and here's me dumping on you, preoccupied with what I
need.'

She went to him, pressed her cool fingers to his lips. 'Enough,
Jake,' she said. 'It's late. You're right, I'm so tired and drained I can't
think straight.'

He didn't trust himself to speak as he followed her to the back
door.

'Goodnight,' she said. 'We'll finish this conversation when we've
both had some sleep.'

Before he realised what was happening she'd brushed her lips
across his, tender, sweet, but with the hint of heat, of promise.
Seconds later there was the clang of the side gate, the crunch of her
footsteps on the gravel and her backlight flicked off, plunging the
yards into darkness. He stood on the back step facing the house next
door. Then, for his own sanity, he put all thoughts on hold and went
inside to check on his dad, and to try to get some sleep.

Laura lay in bed covered only by the sheet. She was wide awake.
She visualised the cracks on the walls and the peeling paint on the
ceiling, memorised from other times. She rubbed at the knot of anxiety lodged just below her diaphragm and tried not to think about

Milt Burns, about the health centre, about Claudia Samuel's blood results and what they might mean.

But then thinking about Jake had her shifting restlessly in the bed. He wanted her as badly as she wanted him. It had been a revelation. A revelation that made her ache with wanting. Damn him for being so noble, but she had to respect him for being so honourable, so honest.

She folded the pillow around her head and tried to block out her thoughts. Sleep. She desperately needed the oblivion of sleep. Her phone rang, a muffled sound. She swore, threw back the pillow and fumbled for it on the bedside cupboard. The caller ID read *Jake*, not *Potters Junction hospital*, as expected.

'I knew you wouldn't be asleep,' he said.

'You're not either.'   .

'Wanna talk some more?'

'I don't know. I just keep thinking about – well, everything.'

'It must be hard having to give patients the bad news. Easy for you to get bogged down in everyone else's misery.'

'There are good things too.'

'Like?' He sounded doubtful.

'Telling someone they're pregnant when they really want to be, that the tumour is benign and simple surgery will remove it. Or the person who's been trying so hard to lose weight and does then gets their blood sugar and cholesterol down.'

He laughed and the sound vibrated through her, right to the soles of her feet.

'What are you laughing at?'

'You, and the ridiculous notion that anyone in their right mind would give you the sack.'

She rolled onto her side, curled her knees up towards her chest, the phone wedged between the pillow and her ear. 'How come you're not asleep?'

'Neill needed help. I made him a cup of tea.'

'Not more tea!'

There was a shuffling sound on the line, like he'd moved his phone to the other ear, then she heard him smother a yawn.

'Hang up, if you're sleepy,' she said.

'Wide awake. You?'

'Same.' She shifted onto her back and swapped the phone to her other ear. 'Hey, I've got an idea. I could sleep there and you could sleep here for a couple of nights. I could listen out for your dad. Give you a chance to get some real sleep. I could do it when I'm not working or on call.'

When he didn't answer she said, 'Well, what do you think?'

'Laura, listen carefully,' he said. 'Here's what I think: thanks for the offer, it's very generous, but if I ever sleep in your bed, you'll be in there with me. And trust me, we won't be doing much sleeping.'

'Oh.' She fanned herself with the edge of the sheet, the cotton whispering across her bare nipples. She could hear him breathing at the other end of the phone, imagined him lying in his chaste single bed. She pushed the sheet back and sat up. 'We need to get some sleep.'

'I only rang to convince myself you were all right.'

'I am. Thanks for distracting me.'

'Happy to distract you anytime. And Laura, I promise I'll talk to the old man – to Dad, real soon.'

They disconnected and Laura pulled on her robe and padded to the kitchen to get a cold drink.

Chapter 26

It was barely seven on Thursday morning when Laura stripped off her sweaty running clothes and slid under a cool shower. Christmas was just around the corner and she hadn't done any shopping, sent any cards, or planned any food. It didn't even seem like Christmas. But all that could wait – she had other plans for today.

The run, followed by painting the first coat of sealant on the freshly sanded floor, would work out the stiffness caused by yesterday's sanding. First coat today, the second one on tomorrow. In this dry heat it'd have plenty of time to harden. Then the furniture could be moved back in, and if Alice did drive up, the room would be available.

She put on a load of washing and made tea and raisin toast when the phone rang. She picked it up, glanced at the display before answering. Milt Burns.

'Could you work for me today?' he said. He didn't greet her.

She glanced at the time, at her cooling toast, at the four-litre tin of flooring paint on the table. 'I guess so,' she said. 'Pretty short notice, though.' *And this is the second time in as many weeks.*

'I know,' he rumbled. 'Something's come up. I can't leave the patients in the lurch.'

'No, of course not. Are there any patients at the hospital I need to know about?'

'Sybill O'Grady is in with lower back pain, but there's nothing that can't wait until tomorrow. Unless you admit anyone.'

'Are you all right?' she said.

'Fine,' he snapped.

'Okay, I'll cover until eight tomorrow morning.'

He disconnected.

She gave the phone a disgruntled glare. He *was* a grumpy old sod, and getting grumpier. And what was it with all these things that were suddenly coming up? Any wonder Kaylene's radar was pinging. Laura had yet to meet Linda, his wife, which in itself was a little strange. She stood at the kitchen window and ate the cold raisin toast.

It took twenty minutes to water the herb pots on the back verandah and to hose the thirsty vegetable garden. At eight-thirty she called the health centre to ask Kaylene what time she was wanted, and then the hospital to ensure she didn't need to detour there on her way to the health centre.

The first appointment was at nine-thirty and all was well at the hospital.

A white station wagon with government number plates was parked in Neill's driveway when she swung around the corner on her way to work. It was the outreach nurse, there to shower him and sort out his medication for the day. She had time, just, so Laura pulled in behind the car. She'd promised Jake she'd look in on Neill mid-morning, so it was best she checked in now. Jess was going to be there for lunch.

'I've put him back to bed,' said the nurse, Gayle. 'He wanted to go back straight away. He's getting frailer by the day. And then there's the pain relief.' She looked flushed, her fine blonde hair stuck to her sweaty forehead. 'That bathroom is a nightmare,' she added, swiping at her brow with the back of her hand.

'I know,' Laura said with sympathy, remembering the time he'd hit his head on the handbasin.

Neill, who was fast asleep, was ashen, and even in sleep his face was screwed up with pain. Laura backed out of the room. 'I won't disturb him. I can't stay anyway. Can you please tell him I can't drop in later this morning like I promised? I have to work. I'll ring his son. His daughter will be here at lunchtime.'

'He shouldn't be here on his own for that long.'

Laura glanced back into the bedroom and for a moment it was her mother lying there, a mere bump under the bedclothes, and she was saying the same thing to her. *I can't stay long, I have to work.* She blinked, pushed the lump back down her throat.

'You're right. I'll see what I can do,' she said and was scrolling through her contacts to Jake's number as Gayle closed the front door behind her.

Frustrated when the call went straight to voicemail, her message was a terse 'Ring me.'

Laura outlined her dilemma to Kaylene at the health centre.

'Not a problem, Laura. Slip out between patients. If you hadn't agreed to fill in they wouldn't be seeing a doctor here at all today. I'm sure they'll be happy —' She stopped, gave a gurgle of laughter. 'Well, perhaps not happy, but they'll wait. I only wish I knew what was going on with Milt.'

Jake didn't ring back until lunchtime. She'd been out to see Neill at eleven, between a patient with bleeding haemorrhoids and a toddler who'd poked a pea into her ear. Neill had looked as if he hadn't moved since the outreach nurse had left.

'What's up?' Jake said. He sounded irritated and over it.

'I'm at work.'

'Yeah, Dad said when I phoned.' She pictured him raking his fingers through his hair. 'I'm stuck out here. A burst pipe now. First it was buggered pumps and now it's burst pipes. Gotta fix it. Dry troughs mean dead sheep. I spent all morning looking for the leak. That's why I didn't get your call, I was out of range.'

'Don't worry. I'll look in on him between patients this afternoon. Tell Jess.'

'Laura, it's not your prob—'

'Jake, stop right there. I'll pop in about three-thirty.'

Silence hummed down the line.

'All right,' he said eventually. 'Thanks. I'll get back as early as I can. Jess should be there now for the next hour or so.'

'I'll be free tomorrow and over the weekend.'

'We can talk about that later.'

'We can,' she said and they disconnected.

Laura sat on her own in the lunch room and forced the sandwich down her throat. Her heart ached for Jake. She remembered too well what it was like to watch a parent die before your eyes, to feel helpless, powerless to do anything to change it. And she'd had a good, loving relationship with her mother; she hadn't been burdened with the tangle of blame, shame and regrets that Jake was. Plus he had the farm and Jess's mess to deal with. Laura believed Jake was doing the right thing being here, but she wouldn't hold it against him if right about now he was wishing he'd stayed in Turkey.

✦

'Jess?'

'Darren. What do you want?' Jess's fingers tightened around the phone as she fought the urge to hang up.

'How're Sam and Mikey? I miss them.'

'They're fine. No-one forced you to go.'

'You know I had to do something. The way we were living —'

'How do you think we're living now? After you took what cash we had, and our only decent vehicle?'

'I know you're angry, Jess, and you probably hate me —'

'You have *no* idea, Darren. Why are you calling now? The boys are at school.'

'I wanted to talk to you.'

'Why would I want to listen? You had eleven years to talk to me. I had no idea you hated this place so much.'

'I didn't at first, Jess, you have to believe that.'

Jess stared out the kitchen window. Her dad's ancient Toyota ute drove through the gate by the implement shed and Skip was standing proud on the back. Jess's heart leaped and then she recognised her brother at the wheel. Not her father. Tears blurred her vision.

'Jake's back, I have to go.'

'Before you do, how's your dad?'

'Dying.' She disconnected. She didn't know if she wanted to laugh hysterically, cry or be sick. Or all three at once.

The back door slammed and Jake appeared in the doorway looking hot and bothered, a battered old Akubra in his hand.

'You're back. How was Dad?'

He went to the fridge and poured himself a glass of cold water, downed it in a couple of swallows. He looked at Jess, frowned, his gaze moving from her face to the telephone handset she was trying to crush.

'Darren?'

She nodded.

'What the hell did he want?'

Jess put the handset back in its cradle. 'He wanted to talk.'

Jake snorted, refilled the empty glass.

'The boys miss him, Jake. We both know what it's like to have a parent walk out. At least he rings. Mum never did. She turned her back on both of us and on Dad. It's like she never really cared about us at all.'

'I don't think she did.'

'She must have been very unhappy. I don't know how else she could have done what she did. And I knew there was something wrong here, but I had no idea Darren was that unhappy. Have you eaten?'

'Nope.'

Jake pulled out one of the kitchen chairs and sat down. Jess went to the pantry for the bread and began making sandwiches. 'Cheese and tomato okay? There's no cold meat.'

'Anything,' he said.

She paused, knife loaded with margarine. 'Was she happy when you went to see her? You know, after you left here.'

'She couldn't wait to see the back of me. I reminded her too much of what she'd run away from.'

She arranged sliced cheese and tomato onto the bread, halved the sandwiches and passed them to Jake.

'You're not eating? Or did you eat with the old man?'

'I don't feel hungry.'

'So how was he?'

'He only wanted ice-cream for lunch.'

'At least he wanted something.' Jake took one of his sandwiches, put it on another plate and plonked it on the table in front of her. 'Eat,' he said. He went to the sink and put the kettle on. 'No more problems with the house pump?'

'No, thanks for fixing it.'

'It's only temporary. It needs replacing.'

Jess picked at the food, forced it down. The bread tasted like cardboard. Jake put a coffee in front of her with milk and two sugars.

'This farm is in need of a huge injection of money, you know that? Everything is just hanging together. What are you going to do with the place when Dad dies?'

She looked up at him. 'It won't just be my decision what happens. Part of the property is yours. I've seen Dad's will.'

'You are joking, aren't you?'

'No, I'm not. We're to sell his house, invest the money for Sam and Mikey, but the farm is ours. Yours and mine. I get a slightly bigger share because of Darren. For what that's worth.'

'Fuck,' was all Jake said.

Jess noticed the way his expression hardened, and knew there was no point asking him again what had happened between him and his father. He threw back the rest of his coffee and carried the crockery to the sink.

'I'll be out near Werner's, fixing that section of fence. If your sheep get in with theirs, you'll never hear the end of it.'

'They're your sheep as well. Do you want a hand?'

'No. You'll need to be here when the boys get home.'

She watched him go. Jess had imagined he'd be glad to know he was getting something out of the place, after all the years he'd spent missing out because he was helping on the farm. He'd missed out on many things that teenagers did because of his responsibilities.

Jess dropped her head into her hands. Could her life get any more complicated than it already was?

Until he turned onto the main road, the late-afternoon sun almost blinded him. Jake still couldn't believe what Jess had told him – part of the farm would go to him when Neill died. Talk about twisting the knife in the wound. He slammed the heel of his hand on the steering wheel.

'Dad?' he called as he walked through the kitchen and up the passage. He would discuss this with the old man now. Now he knew about the will he had to sort everything out, before it was too late.

The front door was open and he could see through the screen out onto the street. Why wasn't the air conditioner on? He went into the sitting room expecting to find Neill propped up in his recliner by the window, the radio on low. But the room was silent, the pillows and folded knee rug stacked neatly where his father usually sat. Jake's heart skipped a beat. What if he'd already left it too late?

He spun around, the anger he'd been holding on to since Jess's gone, all sorts of scenarios fast-forwarding through his brain. He rushed to the bathroom, expecting to find Neill on the floor, broken, bleeding, unconscious . . . But it was empty. Christ. He had left it too late.

'Dad?' Louder this time, the word echoing in the house. The passage floorboards creaked as Jake rushed towards the bedroom. He pushed open the door, he took in the pile of pillows, the bed, and was sick with relief when his eyes fell on the mound in the bed.

'Dad. Bloody hell, you gave me a scare. I expected you to be in your recliner chair. Have you been in bed all day?'

'I'm buggered,' Neill said.

'Did you have a shower this morning?'

'Yes, but I asked her to put me back in bed.'

Jake scratched his head. This was the first time he'd stayed in bed all day.

'I'm so tired, boy.' He coughed, his face crumpling up with pain. 'I'll get up tomorrow.'

'Do you need anything? Do you want me to bring in the radio, the paper?'

'No.' His eyes fluttered shut.

A lifetime of tears burned at the back of Jake's throat. If someone had asked him what emotion he was feeling right then, he couldn't have named it. There were so many. He moved Neill's phone closer on the bedside cupboard, made sure the cup was full of water, the tissues in easy reach.

'I'll go and have a shower,' he said. 'Get us some dinner.'

His bedroom was stifling. He pushed up the window, to replace the stale hot air with fresh hot air. When he emptied his pockets he held his phone for a moment and then sat down on the bed and rang Laura. She picked up on the second ring.

'Why didn't you tell me Dad stayed in bed all day?'

'I thought Jess would have mentioned it.'

'What does it mean?'

'It means he's getting weaker, and I know he has more pain, but he doesn't want the next level of pain relief, not until after his final visit to the farm on Sunday for his birthday.'

Jake unbuttoned the dusty khaki shirt with one hand. The work clothes he was wearing were a mix of Darren's and Neill's. His wardrobe had had to fit into the gear pack on his bike. He eyed the empty black pack shoved into the corner by the wardrobe, a reminder of a life put on hold.

'Bloody hell, Laura, this is all getting too hard.'

'It'll get a lot harder before it gets easier, Jake.'

Chapter 27

'Laura.'

Jake hadn't meant to startle her. He hadn't sneaked in: he'd knocked, found the door open, as usual, and now here he was, standing in the doorway.

She swiped at the tears running down her face. 'Jake. I didn't hear you.' She rested the paintbrush on the tin and pushed herself to her feet. 'I was just remembering the last time I sanded and painted a floor. Brett and I did it together. It was fun.' She hiccoughed, squeezed her eyes shut.

'Come here,' he said, and she came, and he folded his arms around her. Laura settled against him, resting her face against his shoulder.

'It just comes out of nowhere,' she said. 'I'm fine, and then . . .' Jake tensed when she slid her arms around his waist and nestled closer.

'Laura,' he said and gently but firmly removed her arms and stepped back.

'Sorry.' She pulled out a tissue and blew her nose. 'This is getting to be a habit, me upset, you there for me to cry all over. What'll I do when you've gone?'

Jake cleared his throat. He couldn't answer that, didn't know what the answer was. But he knew he was changing, that what had once seemed important no longer did, that his old life belonged to the old him. And the new him? Well, that was a work in progress and the outcome was uncertain.

He dragged his hand across his mouth.

'You won't believe it but the maintenance bloke from the hospital just delivered a hospital bed. Dad reckons he doesn't need it, and I'm inclined to agree. But he said the outreach nurse insisted, said they don't want to do their backs in moving him in and out of the bed.' He shook his head. 'I reckon he just sees it as another nail in his coffin.'

'I can see the nurse's point, but I do also understand your reticence.'

'Now that it's there we may as well set it up. Will you help me move furniture so we can at least fit it in properly? Jess had to pick up the boys from school and get on home.'

'Of course I'll come and help. I'll just clean up, wash my hands.'

Laura ducked out and Jake took the opportunity to gather himself. He tapped the lid back onto the paint and dropped the brush in to soak, then wiped his hands on the rag she'd dropped. He scanned the floor. She'd done a good job of the sanding and the clear seal brought out the golden hues of the floorboards.

He waited for her on the back verandah, hands shoved into his pockets, gazing out onto the backyard, squinting into the sun.

'What's with all the stuff on the kitchen table?' he said when she came and stood beside him.

'They're boxes of Dorrie's old stuff: papers, photos, recipe books. They were in the wardrobe in the spare bedroom. I'm gradually sorting through, putting aside anything I want or anything I think might appeal to Alice.'

'Amazing, the stuff people collect,' he said. He'd have Neill's papers to sort through soon. Hopefully Jess would know what to do with it all. He couldn't think of anything he'd want. A bonfire would be the best thing.

'Vegies look good,' he said as they stepped off the verandah.

'They do, thanks to the joint watering effort. A couple of the tomatoes are colouring up nicely, should be ripe by Christmas. I'm already picking lettuce, and I've had one zucchini.'

He unlatched the gate, stood back to let her through. 'You know, I've never worked out why this gate's here,' he said. 'Have you?'

She flicked him a quizzical look. He was beginning to sound morose, but he couldn't seem to help it. Right at this moment everything seemed hopeless.

'When I first came here,' she said, 'I was about twelve, and the block Neill's house is on was an orchard that belonged to my great-aunt. There were almond trees, a fig tree, apricot trees – you name it, Dorrie grew it.'

She stopped and took in the deserted dog kennel and the forlorn Hills Hoist.

'Dorrie used to make jam, preserves. I remember sitting on the back verandah with Alice and pulling husks off the almonds.' She shuddered. 'We hated it. Broke our fingernails. Then she sold the land and someone put this house on it. It came from Woomera, on a truck. But the gate always stayed, for some reason.'

'The next owners will probably block it off,' he said. Laura didn't comment but followed him to the house and into the sitting room where Neill was propped up in his recliner chair. Jake had dragged the two-seater sofa and the coffee table into the passageway temporarily to make room for the new bed.

Neill opened his eyes, mouthed her name and she laid her hand on his arm.

'A lot of fuss for nothing,' he said, tipping his chin towards the bed.

'It'll be easier,' she said and picked up the bed's hand-held electric control. 'When we plug it in I'll show you what it can do, put it through its paces.' Her enthusiasm raised the semblance of a smile from Neill, but Jake couldn't even dredge up a flicker of interest.

Together they moved as much of the remaining furniture as they could into the other rooms to clear a workable space around the hospital bed. Neill would be able see the TV when he was propped up in bed and, if he wanted to sit out, the recliner was still by the window. Laura plugged the bed into a power socket and showed Neill how it worked.

'Anything else?' she said, looking around at their efforts with satisfaction. 'Do you want me to help make the bed?'

'No, thanks. I won't use it until I have to,' he said and Jake raised his eyebrows.

'I'm going to shower, Dad. I'll see you, Laura. Thanks for your help today.' He turned to go, swinging back to her to add, 'I'll be home tomorrow. You can have the day off.'

'Oh, okay then,' she said, nonplussed by his sudden abruptness.

Moments later they heard a door close, firmly. 'Hard for him,' Neill said between breaths. 'Fancy-free one minute, bogged down with all this the next. He's doing well, considering.'

'He is.' Her respect for Neill increased. After all Jake had or hadn't done, his father still defended him. With a sigh she'd lifted her hair off her sweaty forehead.

'Another storm's brewing. We never used to get as many storms.'

'Yeah, it's as hot and humid as a sauna. My floor's not going to dry enough for another coat by tomorrow.' She touched his arm and winked at him. 'I'll see you in the morning. I don't need a day off.'

As she walked down the passage to the kitchen she slowed at the bathroom, heard the shower running, tried not to think past the closed door.

Home again she sat outside to drink a bottle of cold water and eat an orange, enjoying the juicy sweet tingle over her tongue. The heat pressed down like a hot, wet blanket. As much as she tried, she couldn't dredge up the energy to go take a shower, or to rustle up some food and keep going through Dorrie's papers.

Settling deeper into the cane chair, she let her mind wander though she tried to guide it away from all things Jake. She spent enough time dwelling on him, worrying about him, lusting after him. Her body had well and truly woken up after a long, grief-induced sleep.

Milt Burns. She'd think about him. That would be enough to strangle anyone's libido. He hadn't bothered to call. It wasn't that there was any particular need for him to check in, and the practice staff hadn't phoned either, so she assumed he was back at work this morning and everything at the health centre was the status quo.

But Kaylene was right. There was something a bit off. He was grumpier than usual, and whenever she'd spoken to him about patients lately, he'd been preoccupied. She'd talk to Kaylene on Monday morning.

When the sun sat like a golden orb on the horizon, dusting the backyard with gold, Laura stood up and stretched. The cane chair had left ridges across the backs of her legs, and her arms ached from painting the floor and moving furniture. Mozzies whined. There were no sounds from next door, no screech and clank of the gate. The yard was melting into the night.

With a shrug she threw the water bottle into the milk crate and walked down the path to toss the orange peel onto the compost pile. With a final glance at the silent gate she went inside to have a shower.

She was naked except for her knickers, the ceiling fan barely stirring the air, creaking with every turn. The bedsheet beneath her already felt damp. The bedroom window was up as far as it would go and thunder sounded in the distance. For about the third time in the last half-hour she swiped open her phone to check the time and almost jumped out of her skin when it vibrated in her hand and then rang.

'Sorry for being such a moody prick and then disappearing earlier,' Jake said.

'That's okay. You've got a lot on your mind, so has Jess. Everything is changing.' She heard him take a breath, as if he were going to say something, but then he didn't.

'It's hot,' she said, and he laughed, a low rumble that mimicked the thunder and sent a tremor right through her.

'Did I wake you?'

'Nah, too hot to sleep.'

'The storm's coming, you can see lightning over towards the west.'

'Are you outside?'

'Yep. Coolest place to be. Mozzies are a bastard, though, it must be all the pot plants.'

She sat up, swung her legs off the bed and felt about for her robe. 'Where are you exactly?' Neill didn't have any pot plants.

A shadow moved past her window. 'Come out the back and watch the lightning,' he said, his face close to the flyscreen, then the phone went dead and he disappeared.

'What are you, some kind of a pervert?' she said a few minutes later and tossed him one of the bottles of cold water she'd grabbed out of the fridge. 'Peeping in women's windows.'

'Only your window,' he said, catching the bottle with one hand. 'Only ever your window, Laura.' He unscrewed the cap and took a long swallow.

Lightning flashed across the sky, white-hot forks. A growl of thunder followed. She unscrewed the bottle in her hand, splashed cold water into her palm and pressed it to her face. It dribbled down the front of her robe. He cleared his throat, took another long swallow, recapped his bottle.

Without a word they sat down in the cane chairs. He'd already pulled up the matchstick blind and they had a clear view of the western sky and the awesome light show.

'Fires,' he said. 'Lightning like this will start fires. The hills are already tinder dry.'

'What, out here? Nothing to burn except scrub and saltbush.'

'It all burns,' he said and waved his hand to the south-west. 'The Southern Flinders Ranges, Wirrabara Forest, Beetaloo Valley, the Clare Valley, there's plenty to burn there.'

They sat for an hour or more, not talking much, just watching the sky, waiting for the first swirl of breeze, and swatting at mosquitos.

'Mozzie coils,' he said. 'Put them on your shopping list.' He stood up and yawned. 'I'd better go, check the old man and try to get some sleep.' He went to the edge of the verandah, craned his

neck to peer up at the sky above. It had got darker, the clouds oblit-
erating the moon and the stars. 'I reckon it'll hit us in the next hour.'

She came up beside him, felt his heat, took in the faint smell
of soap on his skin. A puff of breeze rustled through the vegetable garden and stirred the shreds of pea straw on the cement path.
She shivered. Lightning flashed. He looked down at her, rubbed his
shoulder up and down against hers and she leaned in to him.

'Go get some sleep,' he said. His voice was rough. 'And lock all
your doors and windows.'

The gate clanged shut before Laura realised what he'd meant,
and she blushed all over.

Mikey and Sam were in bed after they'd watched the lightning from
the approaching storm. A short, sharp wind squall had made the
windows rattle, a few fat raindrops had peppered the roof, and now
the storm was gone, disappearing off to the east. Jess had let them
stay up. Tomorrow was Saturday, there wasn't a school bus to catch.
In her insomnia, she sat out on the back step. Although the urge to
finish the bottle of red was strong, she stopped after two generous
glasses. A few hours of alcohol-induced sleep would have been bliss,
but there were the boys.

Darren had called again earlier that night. Jess knew he wanted
to talk, could tell by his tentative questions. She was in no mood to
answer him, hadn't got over his call from the day before, so she'd
quickly passed the phone to Sam.

*When would this constant feeling of sick anxiety ease? When
would it disappear?* Darren's phone calls didn't help. He'd broken
her heart, but she missed him like she'd miss one of her limbs if it
were suddenly lopped off.

As grim as things had been in the months before he'd left, Jess had always felt certain they'd sort it out. They'd been together since high school, she'd never imagined being with anyone else. In the long wakeful hours before dawn, her thoughts had taken her many places and she felt a new and deep empathy with her dad. How it must have been for him when his wife, the mother of his children, had turned her back on them all and walked away. *Had he experienced the same feelings she was having?* Worthlessness, loss, the anger that came with grief. *How long did it take to pass? How long before she felt better?* She returned the half-drunk bottle of wine to the pantry, rinsed the wine glass. She didn't feel the slightest bit mellow.

The forecast change came in the night and Saturday morning dawned clear and fresh, the air sweet. After breakfast Sam and Mikey went outside to play and chase the dogs around the yard. There were three dogs now, Skip a more permanent fixture. Jess made herself another coffee and settled at the kitchen table to peruse her cookbooks, hoping to find something special that would tempt her dad tomorrow, on his birthday. It would be the last time so she needed to make the effort. Her head thumped from too little sleep and the late-night wine. The pictures in the recipe books had her feeling more nauseous than she already had been.

Chapter 28

The paint on the spare room floor was still tacky. Laura threw open the windows and doors to let the gentle breeze blow through in the hope it would speed things along. She pulled on a t-shirt and a short denim skirt and drove to the supermarket to buy strawberries and cream for tomorrow's promised pavlova.

There was a flashy white Mercedes SUV parked in front of her house when she returned and a short, roly-poly woman dressed in white capris and a candy pink blouse with a perky collar was walking up the path. Laura suspected the woman's lipstick would match her blouse perfectly, and when she opened the front door minutes later, she wasn't disappointed.

'Doctor O'Connor?'

'Yes, that's me.'

'I hope you don't mind, but Kaylene Curtis told me where you lived,' the woman said. She extended her hand. 'Linda Burns,' she said. 'Milt's wife.'

Laura swallowed her surprise and accepted the proffered hand. 'Please, call me Laura,' she said. 'Would you like to come in?'

'I won't keep you long,' Linda said, twisting her plump fingers together as she followed Laura into the house.

When they reached the kitchen and Linda refused her offer of tea or coffee, Laura said, 'What can I do for you, Linda?'

The older woman licked her lips and nervously plucked at the hem of her blouse.

'I'm worried about Milt. He —' She closed her eyes and Laura was shocked to discover the woman was on the verge of tears.

She gently shepherded Linda into a chair and brought her a glass of water, then pulled up the chair opposite and leaned towards her. 'Now, start from the beginning.'

'I'm sorry, but I didn't know who else to talk to and Kaylene said you were lovely.'

'So, what's been happening with your husband?'

Linda sniffed then searched in her pocket for a tissue. 'He's got no energy, drags himself about, and he's grumpy all the time. He's up to the toilet nine or ten times a night and I hear him grumbling and cursing, but he refuses to talk to me about it, or to go and see anyone, as far as I know.'

'Has he got his own GP?'

'What do you think?' Linda snorted. 'I don't remember him ever going to *a* doctor, let alone his *own GP*. I've been on his back for the last twenty or thirty years to find someone he trusts, to get himself checked out regularly. But with Milt it's "do as I say, not as I do". He thinks he's bulletproof.'

'Yes, I can imagine,' she said.

'It's his prostate, isn't it? I bet it's riddled with cancer. I bet he's got secondaries everywhere.' She blew her nose and Laura retrieved the box of tissues from the dresser.

'He'd need to have some tests before a diagnosis could be made but given his age and the symptoms you describe, there could be something going on with his prostate.'

'It'd be just like him to up and die of cancer before we got to actually enjoy our lives.'

Linda sounded angry now and Laura took a mental deep breath.

'How do you think I can help?'

'I don't know,' Linda said, anger evaporating as fast as it had come. 'I just thought that you might be able to talk to him . . .' She trailed off, a hopeful expression on her face.

'I would talk to him, but I'm not sure he'd listen to me.'

Linda reached out, put a hand on Laura's arm. 'Of course he would. He's said what a skilled GP you are. How you've picked up things he's missed.' As soon as she'd said it Linda put her hand to her mouth. 'Oh my goodness! Now look what I've said. Don't you ever, ever, let on I told you that. I'd never hear the end of it.'

'Of course not,' she murmured. It was news to her that Milt Burns thought she was a good GP.

Linda stood up and began pacing around the kitchen. She came to a sudden halt and peered out the kitchen window, her back to Laura. When she spoke, Laura had to strain to hear.

'I know he wants to cut back,' Linda said, 'but what he needs is to retire. But he just can't seem to let go. This place, the people, his practice, they've been his life. I don't know what to say to him anymore. If I raise the subject, he either ignores me or it ends in an argument.' She turned to face Laura. 'I keep telling him, with you here it's a golden opportunity for him to step back. I don't mean to presume anything, Laura, and I have no idea what your long-term plans are, but I just wish Milt would do something proactive about his health and his retirement – not just talk about it – before it's too late.'

Laura opened her mouth to speak and then closed it again. What was there to say?

'Perhaps we could have that coffee now. I know I need one,' said Linda.

Laura jumped to her feet and busied herself with the coffee machine.

'I hope I haven't scared you off completely,' Linda said, when they were settled with coffees in front of them.

'No, you haven't,' Laura said slowly. 'And as far as long-term plans go —' An image of Jake popped into her head and something swelled deep inside. 'Well, I haven't made any long-term plans.' With Jake, well, if anything did happen there, it'd only ever end in goodbye. 'But I am fond of my neighbour, Neill Finlay, and I'm helping with his terminal care.'

Since coming to Potters Junction she'd been living her life a day at a time and then, as things got better, a week at a time. When she'd agreed to work part-time at the health centre, all she'd thought about was the immediate future, how it would help her get back to work, rebuild her confidence. Maybe the time had come for her to sit down and really think about what she was doing here, where she was going with her medical career. No point giving everyone false hope if she was going back to Adelaide to pick up where she'd left off.

'Laura, I apologise for coming to you with all this. I did try to talk myself out of it, but I'm worried about Milt. He can be such a stubborn old so-and-so.'

'It's all right. And if it's any consolation, Kaylene and I had noticed that Milt is grumpier than usual. I'll say something to him, but I can't promise he'll listen.'

Linda finished her coffee. 'Thank you, Laura, that would be wonderful. I'm sure he will listen, even if he pretends otherwise.'

There was no sign of the apprehensive woman who'd knocked on Laura's door forty-five minutes earlier. Linda collected their cups and took them to the sink. She looked out the kitchen window into Laura's backyard and said, 'I guess you won't be going anywhere until you've harvested that lovely crop of tomatoes.'

'No, I guess I won't be.'

The conversation with Linda left Laura feeling edgy. She had no idea how she was going to talk to Milt Burns about his health. The man didn't exactly invite conversation or confidences. And if he was as sick as his wife suspected, what would that mean for Potters Junction and the health centre? There was the nub of Laura's disquiet. If she decided Adelaide was where her future lay, and Milt Burns was sick and had to retire, it would leave Potters Junction without a GP. Meghan Kimble's workload, which was big enough already, would be unmanageable. When she had this conversation with Milt, Laura needed to be clear in her own mind what she was prepared to offer Potters Junction in the way of an ongoing commitment. The last thing she wanted was to be pressured into making a long-term career decision she'd later regret.

Laura took the eggs out of the fridge and put them on the bench so they'd be ready to use for the pavlova base later. She quartered and cored an apple, brewed a cup of tea and sat down at the kitchen table to sort through more of Dorrie's boxes.

An hour later Laura held up a slim bundle of letters tied together with a red ribbon. She pulled off the ribbon and opened the first yellowing envelope, quickly scanning the single page it contained.

Her eyes widened. The letter wasn't signed but she recognised the handwriting immediately. It was a lot scratchier these days but there was no mistaking the distinctive scrawl.

Oh. My. God.

Her eyes skimmed over the clever prose, pulse banging in her ears. Her fingers trembled as she opened another envelope. She felt herself blush, felt like a voyeur, remembered the recent conversation she'd had with Neill. She pushed the pages back into their envelopes and quickly squared the stack of correspondence. Retying them with the faded ribbon, she slid them between a pile of old knitting patterns. She'd think about what to do with them while she was painting the floor.

Chapter 29

'Dad, hold still, will ya?'

Jake was fast finding out that dressing someone else was nothing like dressing yourself. And when had Neill stopped being able to dress himself? When Jake had been out at the farm working and the outreach nurses had started doing everything for the old man, he supposed. Jake's gut clenched. It had been a matter of weeks. It was all moving too fast.

'I'll need to put another notch in your belt,' he said and slipped it out from the loops around the waist of the trousers. 'Sit down while I do it, or your strides will fall down.'

'This shirt needs ironing,' Neill said and held up the offending item. 'I can't wear it like this.' He tossed it back onto the bed.

'Jeez, when did you get so particular?' Jake went to the wardrobe to rummage through the musty smelling rack of shirts. 'What about this one?'

'Too thick, it's a winter shirt.'

'This one?'

'Buttons missing.'

'This?'

'Doesn't go with the trousers.'

'Bloody hell, fashion conscious as well! I suppose I'll have to iron this one then.' Jake plucked the shirt up off the bed.

'Thanks, boy, and we'd better get a move on. Laura will be here at eleven to drive us out. Wouldn't want to be late for my last birthday party.'

Jake examined the belt in his hand, smoothing a thumb across the worn leather. 'Have you still got that leather punch?'

'It should be in those drawers on the bench. That's if you didn't throw it out.'

Jake looked at Neill, perched on the edge of the unmade bed. His emaciated arms protruded from a sagging singlet and his bony fingers clutched at the waist of baggy trousers, his chest seesawing like a pair of old bellows. The stone that had taken up residence in Jake's chest got heavier.

'You look lovely, lass,' Neill said.

Laura wore a summery dress of swirling blues and greens, and strappy sandals on her feet. She looked gorgeous. Jake felt his dark mood lift a little. Her skin was golden from the hours she spent working outside; there were sun-burnished highlights in her glossy dark hair. Although he hadn't liked it at first, the short hairstyle she wore did look good on her.

'You scrub up pretty well yourself,' she said to Neill and then turned her blue gaze to Jake. 'You both do.'

He'd worn his best pair of jeans and a sage-coloured cotton

shirt – the only one he'd brought with him. Because he'd had to get the ironing board and iron out to do Neill's shirt, he'd ironed his own as well. The first time it'd ever been in contact with the hot side of an iron.

Neill was huffing and puffing by the time they settled him into the car and Jake wondered for the hundredth time if this was such a good idea.

'He'll be okay once he gets his breath again,' Laura said quietly, as if reading his thoughts. 'I've got my bag and I've borrowed a small oxygen cylinder from the hospital, just in case.' He kept forgetting they had a doctor at the wheel.

During the drive out to the farm, Jake watched his father take in the familiar countryside. From the way Neill's head moved from side to side, like a spectator at the tennis, Jake suspected the old man didn't want to miss anything. They all knew it would be his last trip out to the place he'd lived at and worked on for most of his life. Jake caught Laura's eyes in the rear-view mirror and he knew she was thinking along similar lines.

'Country's pretty dry and it's barely summer,' Neill said.

'Dad, the country's always dry out here.'

'Dryer now than it used to be. It's the effects of global warming, I'd say.'

'Now there's something we both agree on,' Jake said.

Jess and the boys came out to greet them when they arrived and to help Neill. 'Happy birthday,' they chorused.

'Maybe we should have borrowed a wheelchair,' Jess said, but Jake shook his head and gently lifted Neill out of the car and carried him the short distance into the house. Neill didn't try to stop him.

The sitting room looked bright and festive. Christmas bunting decorated the mantelpiece, streamers and tinsel had been strung across the windows.

'We put up the decorations yesterday,' Sam said proudly. 'And the Christmas tree. Dad usually does it but he's not here.'

There was a tense moment, Sam looked uncomfortable and then Jess put her arm around his shoulders and pulled him against her.

'But we managed, didn't we, mate?' she said and he nodded vigorously.

'Seeing as it's nearly Christmas, Dad, I thought we'd combine it with your birthday, so it's turkey with all the trimmings.'

Jake could see behind his sister's cheerfulness. She still looked hollowed out with hurt and he felt a new twist of anger towards her absent husband.

'Yeah, Mum said you wouldn't be here on Christmas Day, Poppa, so we're having it now,' said Mikey. Everyone in the room froze and Mikey pushed on, oblivious. 'But we can't have our presents yet and we didn't get you anything because Mum said you wouldn't be needing anything where you were going.'

'Mikey, shut up.' Sam cuffed his younger brother.

'Shall I put the pavlova in the fridge?' Laura asked, proffering a Tupperware container and a basket of garden produce.

'Of course,' Jess said, the words like a sigh of relief. 'And Dad, we're just glad you could make it. It makes today very special. Do you want a drink? Sam, get Poppa a drink if he wants one. Laura, follow me. We'll eat in about fifteen minutes.'

Jess lifted the turkey roast onto the board to carve. They'd be eating bread and Vegemite if it weren't for Jake's generosity. The overdraft was maxed to the limit and navigating to the moon would be easier than navigating Centrelink. The woman on the phone had promised her everything would be sorted out before Christmas, but Jess wasn't holding her breath.

'What can I do to help?' Laura asked.

'A winning lottery ticket?' Jess said, swatting a blowfly away from the meat.

'That bad, huh?'

Jess forced a smile. 'We'll survive.'

'Jess —'

'Ignore me, please. I'm trying hard, but sometimes it's hard trying.' Jess began slicing the meat. 'Maybe you could do the gravy. Everything's on the bench by the stove, it just needs making. There's an apron hanging on the back of the door, I'd hate to see your lovely dress get splattered.'

'Have you been sleeping?' Laura said a few minutes later as she stirred the thickening gravy.

Jess transferred the sliced meat onto the serving plate. 'Not much. I either can't sleep or I get to sleep and wake up an hour later and that's it.'

'Appetite?'

'None. I just feel sick all the time. I feel like the carpet's been ripped out from under me and any minute the ceiling is going to crash down on top of my head.'

'Ring the health centre first thing in the morning. I'll fit you in.'

Laura turned off the gas stove, rested the wooden spoon on the side of the pan. She walked around the table and put her hands on Jess's shoulders, turning her to face her.

'If you don't ring, I'll ring you. And I'll keep ringing you until you come and see me. I'll stalk you if I have to.'

At first Jess resisted the display of support but she eventually relented and let Laura put her arms around her. Before she knew what she was doing, Jess found herself clinging to Laura, tears of relief coursing down her cheeks.

Chapter 30

Lunch was over, the pavlova history. Neill was having a rest, Sam and Mikey were watching a DVD and the dishes were done.

'Jake, why don't you take Laura for a drive out to the bluff? I'm going to put my feet up for a while.'

Laura glanced from one sibling to the other. 'The bluff?'

'It's a hill really, with a bit of scrub. It's on the northern boundary of the property, the highest point,' said Jake. 'Pretty good views north to the Flinders Ranges. We used to camp out there when we were kids.'

'Yeah, we did, lots of times.' Jess nudged Jake with her knee. 'Until you discovered *girls* and didn't have time for your sister. After that you just wanted to take them out there to make out.'

Jake flicked her with the tea towel. 'Careful, or I might just start spilling some of your secrets.'

'Yeah, right,' Jess said and then zeroed in on Laura's sandals. 'You might need something different on your feet. And a hat, if you've got one.'

'No hat but I do have sneakers in the car.'

'You continue to amaze me, Laura. You're always prepared. You could have been a boy scout,' Jake said and draped the tea towel over a cupboard door to dry. 'We'll have to take your car. The track's in reasonable nick.'

Ten minutes later they were bouncing along a rough track, with Jake at the wheel. If this was reasonable Laura would hate to know what unreasonable was. They hit an extra deep pothole and Laura glanced sideways. Her heart gave a lurch at the sight of him, jaw shadowed, hair flopping across his forehead. Over lunch, she'd observed the way he interacted with his family, and the way they almost worshipped the ground he stood on.

He threw her a sideways look and she returned his grin.

'I feel like I'm one of those girls Jess was talking about,' she said, and he wiggled his eyebrows. Hazel eyes darkened and Laura's stomach fluttered.

'This is the western boundary of the property,' Jake said, focussing his attention back on the track. 'The only really arable land is along here. It's dry but if Dad was still at the helm he probably would have had a crop in this paddock. Although, these days, with what it costs to get it in the ground, you'd be lucky if you broke even so maybe Darren made the right decision.'

'Must be tough. What'll Jess do?'

His fingers flexed on the steering wheel. 'I don't think she knows yet. It's too soon.'

Laura took in the barren landscape, the clumps of native vegetation in the distance, the sheep relentlessly grazing on nothing much at all. They passed what must have been a dam, already an empty crater this early in summer. Dust billowed out behind the vehicle and, although it wasn't outrageously hot, heat shimmered across the landscape.

'Generally, the fences are pretty good, but the property doesn't have much else going for it. The machinery is old, the sheds are falling down.'

'What would you do, if you were making the decisions?'

'Maybe run more head of sheep.' He squinted towards the horizon. 'But the smartest thing would be to lease it all out, because you'd be lucky to sell it the way the market is. And there's better land for sale in the vicinity if you had the money to buy.'

'Sounds like you've been doing some research.'

'I've had a bit of a look on the internet.'

They drove for several more minutes before Jake stopped the car to open a gate. Off from the side of the track a windmill creaked and clanked. Green grass sprouted around the base of a leaking tank and the muddy ground by the trough was pockmarked by sheep's hooves.

'Tank needs replacing,' Jake said as he swung back into the car. 'Underground water is hard as nails so nothing lasts.'

'Is this it?' Laura asked as Jake dropped the car down to a lower gear and they slowly climbed towards a rocky outcrop with a smattering of low trees.

'Yep, this is it, the highest point of the place. When I was a kid I'd come up here and pretend I was on top of the world.' He parked the car in the shade of a solitary gum tree. 'On foot from here.'

Laura tied on her sneakers and they headed up the short, steep slope.

'Wow,' she breathed, when they arrived at the top. 'What a view! All the way to the Flinders Ranges.' She flapped her hands in front of her face. 'Are the flies always this friendly?'

'They've always been friendly from what I can remember.'

Laura perched her backside on one of the boulders. Jake handed her the water bottle. She had a drink and passed it back.

'It is very beautiful,' she said, shading her eyes with her hand as she took in the timeless landscape. 'Dry, harsh but gentle. The colours are unique . . . blues and mauves. They're soft, haunting.'

She turned to Jake, who was leaning on the rock beside her, the breeze ruffling his hair. A crow, perched in a nearby silver mulga tree, stared at them with a beady eye.

'Didn't you miss it?'

'Obviously not enough to make me want to come back,' he said.

Laura swatted some more at the flies. The crow swore and flew off.

'But now that you're here?' she persisted, not sure what she wanted him to say but knowing it was more than what he was saying.

'Laura,' he said, and then sighed. 'Over the last few years the place has been let go. I'm not blaming Darren and Jess. It's been tough for a lot of people on the land. So much so there's probably never been a spare dollar to put back into it, and from what Jess says, Darren lost the urge to do it.'

'The farmhouse is in such a lovely spot with those majestic gum trees as a backdrop. It has real character. All that gorgeous timber! It's a renovator's dream.'

'More likely a renovator's nightmare. It's riddled with salt damp, there's wood rot in some of that gorgeous timber and I wouldn't be surprised if there were white ants as well. It needs a new roof, new wiring and new plumbing.'

'You make it sound as if it's about to fall down. Don't tell Jess.'

'Jess has lived there all her life. I'm sure she knows exactly what's going on with that house.' He bumped his shoulder with hers. 'Come on, we'd better get back. Take the old man home.'

'It's so peaceful up here. I feel like I'm out in the middle of nowhere.'

'You are,' he said and they slowly made their way down to the car.

When she'd buckled her seatbelt she turned to him and said innocently, 'Thanks for bringing me out here, Jake. But you know, I'd be really disappointed if I was the only girl, besides your sister, who you'd brought out here and hadn't made out with.'

His head jerked around so fast she heard the tendons creak. She grinned but the hungry look in his eyes quickly wiped the merriment from her mouth. A ribbon of heat curled through her.

'I wouldn't want to disappoint you, would I,' he said, his voice shivering across her skin, swamping her in sensation.

She popped the catch on her seatbelt and met him halfway. Warm, strong fingers framed her face and a callused thumb pulled across her bottom lip. She made a sound, low in her throat, when he replaced his thumb with his mouth, nipping and sucking lightly up to her top lip. Then his tongue gently pushed open her lips, and he was upon her. He kissed her deeply, hungrily. Everything in her body snapped to attention. His fingers pushed into her hair, held her head steady while he all but devoured her mouth. Her arms snaked around his neck and she kissed him back, giving in to her body's desire, surrendering to the moment. She couldn't get any closer to him without climbing onto his lap.

When they let go of each other, their chests were heaving, their breath heavy.

'Disappointed?' he whispered and she shook her head. Her lips felt swollen, bruised, and her body electrified.

'I am,' he said and lifted himself up, shifting in the seat. 'I'm disappointed we're not somewhere other than a damn car, out in the middle of nowhere.'

He started the vehicle, rammed his seatbelt home. Laura felt the burn of his gaze when he flicked it sideways and said, 'But then again we're not kids. If we'd been somewhere else we wouldn't have stopped at a kiss, would we?'

Laura licked her tender lips and stared at his hands on the steering wheel as he reversed the car back onto the rough track.

'No,' she said on a breath, imagining those clever hands undressing her slowly, plundering her body, continuing on from where his mouth had left off. But as they moved further away from their kiss Laura's lust morphed into a dragging feeling of despair. Neill would die soon and Jake would go. She swallowed hard, and focussed on the passing landscape. She would have to trust her newly healed heart not to break again.

Neill was grey with fatigue and his face twisted with pain when Jake carried him to the car before their journey home.

Jess embraced her father, tears glistening in her eyes. 'I'm so glad you came, Dad. I love you. I'll see you tomorrow.'

He nodded weakly and squeezed her hand.

Laura hugged Jess. 'Thank you. It was a lovely meal. And I'll be seeing you tomorrow, too.'

'You will,' Jess said. 'And thank you. Jake, don't forget to email those photos you took at lunchtime of Dad and the boys.'

The drive home was quiet. Jake drove, Neill sat up the front with his eyes tightly shut, bracing himself for each bump, and Laura sat in the back. When she was through convincing herself Neill was all right, she let herself relive every second of Jake's passionate kiss. When she came to, she caught him watching her in the rear-view mirror. His eyes were dark and knowing and she felt her cheeks heat.

After they'd arrived home and she'd helped settle Neill, made sure he took his pain relief, Jake gently grasped her shoulders.

'I need to stay with him, you know that, don't you?' His voice was thick with desire and regret.

'Yes, I understand,' she said, though she wished it were otherwise.

Jake's hands dropped from her shoulders. 'And maybe it's better this way, Laura. You and I —'

She stopped his words with her fingertips. 'Don't say anything more,' she said. When she lifted her fingers from his mouth he grabbed her wrist, stilled her hand, crushed his lips against her palm, then let her go. She curled her fingers around the kiss.

Jake eased back.

'He needs more pain relief,' Laura said. 'He's really suffering.'

He looked away and with a sinking feeling Laura realised that things between father and son had yet to be resolved.

'I'll go,' she said quietly. 'Leave you to it.'

Tired, both physically and emotionally, Laura drove around the corner home. The first thing she did when she'd unpacked the car was ring her sister. Laura desperately needed someone to talk to. Her life was suddenly getting complicated.

After their big lunchtime meal, Sam and Mikey were happy with baked beans on toast for tea. It was just as well, because Jess felt like a wrung-out dishrag and pulling the lid off a tin of beans was about as much as she could handle. What she wouldn't give to have a break from the constant loop of her thoughts: *Dad's dying, Darren's gone, the farm's bankrupt, as soon as Dad dies Jake will go* . . . It didn't matter how hard she tried she couldn't get past the problems to start thinking about solutions. Perhaps she'd come away from tomorrow's appointment with Laura with the embryo of at least one solution for her mounting pile of problems.

Jess contemplated the cracked skin on her hands, the split fingernails, then caught her reflection in the kitchen window. Her normally lustrous brown hair was dull and lifeless and it wouldn't be long before her eyes were swallowed by the bags underneath.

'Mum?'

'Sam?'

'Would Dad come back if we asked him to? He said on the phone that he missed us.'

'Do you want to ask him to come back?'

'Maybe,' he said. 'Poppa said we could always give it a try.'

'Did he?' Jess answered, surprised her father had said that. He'd never been Darren's biggest fan. 'What else did Poppa say?'

'He said sometimes adults do things that kids don't understand until they become adults.'

'And sometimes, Sam, adults do things that other adults don't understand.'

Darren had phoned earlier, while Jake and Laura had been at the bluff. He'd wanted to wish his father-in-law a happy birthday. The boys must have told him Neill would be there. After he'd talked to Sam and Mikey and then Neill, he'd asked to speak to Jess.

'I've put some money back into the account,' he'd said. 'For the boys' Christmas presents.'

'What about food, Darren, electricity, gas? Let's not forget Sam needs new sneakers and Mikey needs to see an ENT specialist for his tonsillitis. And that's before I get to tyres for the car, a new house pump so we can have running water. You get my drift?'

'Jess, there wouldn't be any more money if I was there. There'd be *less* with another mouth to feed. I'm looking for a job. As soon as I get one I'll send money. You get my drift?'

'Okay,' she'd said and it was the first time she hadn't felt like throwing up after he'd disconnected.

'Mum,' Sam said, snapping her back to her son and his question. 'If you don't want him to come home, we don't have to ask him. I can do more stuff around here. I can help Uncle Jake.'

Jess nearly choked on the guilt she felt for the role she'd unwittingly played in the situation they now found themselves in.

'You already do more than enough, mate,' she said, blinking back bitter tears. She pulled her eldest son into a fierce hug. 'Is it okay if I think a bit more about asking your dad to come home? With Poppa being so sick, maybe we can decide after Christmas?'

Sam nodded; he looked so serious. 'I'll tell Mikey,' he said.

'Okay, you do that. And Sam, remember you can ask me anything, anything at all, anytime.'

When he'd gone Jess sat for a moment to collect her scattered thoughts. Their children were blameless in all this and they were suffering because of it. Her fingers clenched into fists as she made a promise to herself that whatever happened she would do her best to give Sam and Mikey the home they deserved, just like their father had for her and Jake all those years ago. Smothering a yawn she went and put on a load of washing.

That night Jess slept for six solid hours and on waking felt more refreshed than she had since Darren had left. She rang the Potters Junction health centre first thing and made an appointment with Laura. As the day progressed, she nurtured the kernel of hope she'd felt for the first time that morning – that things would work out in the future.

Chapter 31

When Jake turned the ute into Neill's street late Monday afternoon, Milt Burns's Statesman was parked out the front, halfway onto the footpath. Heart racing, Jake punched the accelerator and then the brakes, bringing the ute to a shuddering halt in the carport. Not stopping to close the door he jogged across the front verandah and tugged open the front door.

'Dad?' he called and Milt Burns's mournful visage appeared around the bedroom door.

'It's all right, boy, he's in here. I came to see him on my day off and we've had a chat and decided it is time for the needle. The palliative-care nurse will be here shortly with all the gear. Someone will need to be around all the time from now on, or we can put Neill into the hospital.'

'No hospital.' Jake stopped at the bedroom door, a loud roaring noise in his head. 'What happened, Dad?'

'Nothing, I just can't put up with it any longer.'

Panic and anger shot a red-hot bolt through him. He wasn't
ready to lose his father to a drug-induced fugue. He hadn't talked to
his dad yet. He turned to Milt. 'Did Laura contact you?'

'Nope. Should she have?'

Jake's eyes narrowed. The old bastard wouldn't tell him if she
had. He looked through the door to where his father lay.

'It wasn't Laura. I talked to the nurse this morning. And Jess was
here earlier.' The room was hot and sick smelling. Jake went to his
bedside.

'Dad, why haven't you got the fan on? Do you want me to open
the window?'

Milt plonked himself back in the chair by the bed. 'It's not too
bad in here. Wouldn't mind a beer, though. What about you, mate?'

Jake glared at Milt.

'Do you want a beer, Dad?'

'Tea. Half a cup.'

Once, just once, Jake would like to punch Milt Burns. All he ever
did was cause upset in this family. He went to the kitchen to make
tea and to get the good doctor a beer. It was while he was waiting for the kettle to boil, pacing the kitchen trying to tamp down
his emotions, that he remembered he'd left Skip on the tray of the
ute. He went around the side of the house into the carport only to
find Laura walking down the driveway towards him, her car parked
behind the Statesman.

'What's Milt doing here?'

His heart did a somersault at the sight of her. He avoided her
gaze and unclipped Skip's chain. The dog bounded off the side of the
ute. He felt a moment's remorse – he'd just suspected her of interfering.

'Jake? What's happened?' she said.

He slammed the driver's side door.

'You were right. Milt's sorting out more pain relief for Dad. The palliative-care nurse is coming.'

'Oh, I see.'

'It's his decision.'

They stood there, sweltering under the carport's thin tin roof, looking everywhere but at each other. This was it, the beginning of the end. He wanted to cry out, to hit something. There were so many things he needed to say to the old man, to Laura, but the words wouldn't come.

'I'll go in and say hello,' she said and the moment was lost, and all he could come up with was, 'The kettle will have boiled if you want a cup of tea.'

★

The bleak look on Jake's face brought tears to Laura's eyes. He turned his back. She so wanted to hold him but he was angry, hurting, had closed himself off.

As she moved away he muttered something about tea. Laura knew exactly what he was going through, remembered how she'd felt when they'd started her mother on the morphine pump. It was the final slide downhill to oblivion, and then death. From here, life could be measured in days, not weeks. Laura had just spent the last hour of her working day listening to Jake's sister talk about how frightened she was, how angry she was that all the men she loved had left, or would in the near future. Jess had kept asking what she'd done wrong and Laura couldn't answer her. There was no answer.

'Jake,' she said, pausing in the carport entrance. He didn't turn around.

'What?'

'If you want to talk, I'll listen.' He acknowledged with an up-and-down jerk of his head and then he disappeared around the back.

Laura followed the murmur of voices to Neill's bedroom. Milt was sitting in a chair beside the bed, talking softly to Neill. It took a moment before they realised she was there. When they did Neill lifted his hand from the bed in greeting. 'Ah, another doctor calling.'

'Hello, and what are you two blokes plotting? Nothing good, I'd bet.'

Milt pushed himself to his feet. He did look guilty.

There was a knock on the front door. 'That'll be Angela, the pal-care nurse,' Milt said, as he plodded past Laura to answer the door.

Laura went to Neill's bedside and took his hand in hers. 'You've made the right decision. There's a point when the pain becomes too much. No-one expects you to put up with it.' Neill clung to her, his grip surprisingly firm.

'Thank you.' He tugged at her, urging her towards him. 'I have had enough, Laura. After yesterday . . .' He sighed, seemed to sink further into the pillows. 'I know Jess'll be fine, she has Sam and Mikey, and Darren, he'll be back. He's no farmer but he loves his family and they'll sort things out.'

Neill pulled on her hand again, urged her closer. She could hear each tortured breath struggle from his chest.

'It's Jake who I worry about, he's made it so he has no-one. It breaks my heart. I'd hoped —' He paused, eyes glassy with tears. 'Look out for him, Laura. I see that you care for him.'

She folded her other hand around his, gave his fingers a gentle press while blinking back her own tears. 'I promise, Neill. I'll look out for him. As much as he'll let me.'

Neill withdrew his hand. 'I knew I could count on you.' He closed his eyes, a satisfied expression settling on his face.

Laura straightened up, swiped at her eyes with the back of her hand just as Milt came into the room with the palliative-care nurse and Jake, hot on their heels.

'It's getting pretty crowded in here, so I'll go,' she said.

When she left, Laura felt Jake's intense gaze follow her out.

The sun had set, the brightest stars appearing in the encroaching darkness. The cane chair creaked as Laura moved. Her empty glass scraped on the cement verandah. Zephyrs of air, with just a hint of night-time coolness, lifted the hairs on her bare arms. The air was laced with the smell of herbs and damp soil. She leaned her head against the back of the chair and closed her eyes.

Alice was coming to visit soon. It would be good to see her sister. Someone familiar. On the phone the previous evening she'd asked her to come for Christmas, or at least to visit sometime over the break.

'Only if you come here for new year,' her sister had replied.

'Agreed.'

The bed and other furniture would need to be moved back into the spare room and the new sheets and quilt cover washed. Laura made a mental list of the things she had to do at home and at work. *Talk to Milt Burns* kept popping up and she kept pushing it aside.

Her lids felt heavy. She heard vehicles come and go next door, the sound of people talking, and tried to ignore the stab of hurt when she recognised Jake's voice amongst the others. She must have slept because when Laura opened her eyes it was completely dark and she sensed rather than saw him sitting beside her in the other cane chair.

'You snore.'

'Do I?' She sat forward, massaged the crick in her neck.

'Jess brought Sam and Mikey to see Dad. She wanted them to see him while he was still with it.'

'I'm going to get a glass of water. Do you want anything?'

'Laura,' he said and reached out, took her hand. 'I need to apologise.'

'What for?'

'For my earlier rudeness. For not being who and what you need me to be. You deserve the best.'

'What I need is up to me to decide.'

'I care about you, and I don't want to hurt you.'

'Well, you are hurting me. You're a much better man than you give yourself credit for.'

He expelled a frustrated breath, let go of her hand. 'Like I've said before, I have nothing to offer you, Laura.'

'You have yourself.'

'I'm hopeless with relationships, I've ignored my family, hurt them, been the biggest disappointment to them.' His voice cracked and he shifted in the chair restlessly. 'Time's running out and I don't even know how to make amends, how to say sorry.'

'And like *I* said before, Jake, you say sorry, just like that, and you mean it.'

'It's too little, too late.' The words were muffled behind his hands.

'It is how it is. You can't go back, so make the most of the present.' She meant the advice for herself as much as for him. 'Do you want a drink, coffee?'

She flicked on the verandah light, bathing them in its buttery glow. Moths appeared instantly out of the darkness.

'No, thanks. Jess will want to go home soon. The boys have school tomorrow.'

'I'll come over in the morning and take Skip for a run.'

'If you like. I brought him in because I know Dad likes to see him.' He stood up, raked at his hair with his hand, almost like he wanted to pull it out. 'The palliative-care nurse helped us move Dad into the hospital bed. He didn't protest like I'd imagined he would.'

'It'll make it easier for him, and for you.'

'The nurse showed me how to check the syringe pump with the morphine in it. Either Jess or I will be here from now on.'

'If you have any problems with the pump, give me a call. And I can help out when I'm not working.'

'Thanks. I'll see you tomorrow.'

'Goodnight, Jake.'

They stood there awkwardly for a few moments, and when he'd made it to the edge of the verandah he swung around and said, 'What about that bed you wanted me to help you shift? Do you want help to move it now?'

'I'd love you to help me move it now, but you need to get back. We'll make it another time, okay?'

'How about Wednesday afternoon? Jess'll be here and you won't be working, will you?'

'Not that I know of. Wednesday would be great. I'll call you if anything changes. Thanks,' she said.

His face was shadowed and she sensed his longing, and his regret. It matched her own. Moments later the gate screeched on its hinges.

'Milt?' Laura tapped on the door. It crept open a few more centimetres and she peered around the edge.

Kaylene said he'd arrived about an hour earlier, while Laura was consulting. Catching up with him now would save her dropping in the next day: the conversation she'd promised to have with him wasn't one for the telephone.

'Can I come in?'

'You're practically in, you might as well come the rest of the way.'

She hovered in the doorway until Milt waved towards the chair opposite his desk. She pushed the door closed behind her. Unlike Laura, he kept the desk between him and his patients.

'You know you really are very much like your great-aunt Dorothy. She was tall and was always looking for the best in everyone. I hadn't thought about her for years.' He sat back and appeared as if he'd drifted off to someplace else. 'What can I do for you?' he said at length.

'Linda, your wife, came to see me. At home.'

Milt sat up straighter in the chair, his eyes narrowing. 'And?'

'She's worried about you, Milt. She suspects you're not well but you won't talk to her and that worries her even more.'

'And this is your business, how?'

'You're right, it isn't any of my business, and I'd rather stick bamboo slivers under my fingernails than have this conversation, but she was very upset and I agreed to talk to you.'

He picked up his pen and tapped it on the desk blotter.

'I'll make a deal with you,' he said and Laura found herself instantly on guard. 'You tell me why you took a break from medicine, and I'll fill you in on what's probably worrying Linda.'

'I'm not sure that's fair,' she said.

'It's not, but then what about life is? Ask Claudia Samuels. Ask Neill Finlay.'

'True.'

Laura heard muffled voices, laughter, and then a door slammed. The staff had left. Milt tilted his head and she knew he'd heard them leave, too.

'Well?' he said.

Laura fiddled with one of her diamond-stud earrings and then folded her hands tightly on her lap.

'I had a breakdown,' she said matter-of-factly. 'Anxiety attacks. It happened while I was seeing patients.'

In a few blunt sentences she went on to recount the life events that had culminated in her breakdown.

'I had no idea. And Neill Finlay wouldn't give anything away.'

'Good for him, and I'm all right now. I was concerned when I came back to work, and there have been moments when I've wondered if I came back too soon. But generally, it's all good. Now, it's your turn.'

He dragged at his jowls and then reached into the bottom drawer of his desk, handed her an envelope. She took it, opened it and slid out the sheets of paper. The further she read, the dryer her mouth became. When she'd finished reading she carefully returned the reports to the envelope and handed it back to him.

'Milt, why have you kept this from your wife?'

'I suppose I wanted to be sure about the diagnosis. And Linda's been caught up with the new grandkids. Twins, you know. I didn't want to put a damper on all that.'

'Yes, but . . .'

Milt shook his head slowly and Laura shut up. 'It's done. It was my choice, all right? Now I have all the information, I'll tell her.'

'What are you going to do?'

'I haven't decided. Not keen on the surgery. They're making breakthroughs with radiotherapy, though. And I need to have the

MRI to see if there're any metastases before I make any decisions.'

'You need to tell Linda, Milt. She's your wife, she deserves to know, and she should be part of the decision-making process.'

'Yes, ma'am,' he said with a mock salute.

She smiled. 'I suppose you'll need some time off work.'

'I'll need time off work for more investigations, and then treatment. If all else fails, I'll need time off to die. It's certainly not how I envisaged my retirement.'

'No,' Laura said softly, thinking this wasn't at all how she'd envisaged this conversation. 'What can I say, Milt? I know your plan was to cut down and then retire, and I can appreciate that you'd want to do that in your own time, not be forced out by illness.'

'God knows I've broken bad news to enough patients over the years. It's another thing entirely when the bad news is all about you.'

Resignation chased despair across his craggy features.

'Milt,' she said. 'When Linda visited she asked me what my long-term plans were. I said I didn't really have any but there's still heaps of work to do on Dorothy's house.' She looked directly at him. 'What I'm trying to say is, I can stay here for the short term, if that's what you want. I like working here, I like the community and I think they might like me. And I have several months of leave left before I have to make a decision about my job in Adelaide.'

He sat for a few minutes and Laura waited. Then he looked at his watch, pushed himself to his feet. 'That's a generous offer, Laura. I need to think about everything, digest it all, talk to Linda and the kids.' He rubbed the small of his back as he ushered Laura towards the door. 'I'll let you know as soon as I've worked out what I'm going to do,' he said.

'Is there anything I can do now?'

Milt paused. 'Yes, there is one thing. My specialist has pulled some strings and I can have the MRI Thursday. I was going to say no —'

'Of course I'll work for you on Thursday. I'd offer to do Friday as well but Neill is going downhill fast, and I want to be available for the family as much as I can.'

'Life is full of cruel ironies, is it not?' He closed the door behind her.

Laura mechanically tidied her desk, shoved the stethoscope into her doctor's bag and the lunch box into her shoulder bag, her mind going at one hundred miles an hour. Prostate cancer. *Advanced* prostate cancer. What was Milt's prognosis? Had it metastasised already? And had she just offered to stay in Potters Junction while Milt Burns had more investigations and whatever treatment he needed?

She dropped into the chair. Staying in Potters Junction for a while was okay. It was feeling more like home every day. The health-centre staff were lovely and the hospital staff were gradually accepting her. And she was enjoying the medicine. It was much more challenging and unpredictable – you never knew what you might have to deal with from one day to the next. At first it had been daunting but with a few successes under her belt she could feel her confidence building. Laura wondered if subconsciously she'd already made the decision to stay. It's not like she was locking herself in forever. She would stay while it worked for her.

What would Jake say about her decision? Did it matter? Heat and longing coursed through her. With a moan she propped her head on her hands. Their relationship . . . Her breath came out of her nose with a rush. Relationship! You could hardly call what they had a *relationship*. They'd been on one date, if dinner at the pub on a Sunday night was a date. And they'd kissed, once. But wow, the chemistry of that kiss!

Over the weeks they had become friends. Reluctantly, tentatively. And now, with a flash of insight, she realised her feelings for Jake ran far deeper than friendship. Her pulse leaped and a surge of adrenaline tightened her stomach. She sat up straight in the chair. She'd fallen in love with him. Of course what Jake thought about her decision to stay on in Potters Junction mattered. The sad part was it probably wouldn't matter to him. The phone on the desk beeped and Laura jumped.

'Kaylene? I thought you'd gone.'

'No, I'm still here. I just saw Doctor Burns leave. He walked right past reception, didn't even speak to me. He looked —' She paused. 'Strange. He looked strange. Is everything all right?'

'Kaylene, you'd need to ask him that.'

'Right,' Kaylene said, drawing the word out into a whole sentence loaded with meaning.

'Now, did you want me for anything?'

'Yes. Please ring the hospital.'

Chapter 32

It was one hell of a day for Laura, and it ended late after the RFDS had retrieved a farmhand who'd fallen backwards off the tray of a semitrailer and fractured his skull, and maybe some of his vertebra. When she'd first spoken to the RN, her heart had missed a beat. For a moment she'd imagined it was Jake and then with overwhelming relief she remembered he was home with Neill. She drove straight from the health centre to the hospital.

Laura didn't let herself relax for a moment until, after several hours with the patient, the retrieval team walked through the doors of A&E and took over. Spinal boards and Stifneck collars were way out of her comfort zone, and she was the first to admit it.

She came home, went straight to the bathroom and stripped off her clothes to take a much-needed shower. The phone vibrated on the bathroom cabinet as she stepped onto the bath mat. She swore, quickly dried her hands and picked it up.

'You're home.'

'Jake. I just stepped out of the shower.'

'Don't tell me things like that. It's better for me if I don't know that you're naked.'

She laughed, tried to dry herself with one hand, nearly dropped the phone, then gave up and sat on the edge of the bath.

'It's after ten. How come you're so late?'

'We had an emergency at the hospital. The retrieval team came.'

'Are you okay?'

'Yes.'

'I watered the vegies and the pots on the back verandah earlier and helped myself to coffee. You know you really should hide your spare key in a better place.'

'Thanks for doing the watering. I didn't get to see Neill today. Please tell him I'll come tomorrow.'

'I'll do that. I'll talk to you tomorrow. And put some clothes on, Laura.'

'Night, Jake,' she murmured and disconnected. Her skin was flushed and hypersensitive as she finished drying off.

It was lunchtime on Wednesday when Jess pulled into her father's driveway. School broke up for the summer holidays on Friday and Jess was driving Sam and Mikey to Port Augusta on Saturday to do Christmas shopping, if all was well. That is, if her dad was still alive and it was okay for her to leave for a few hours.

Darren had been phoning every night and they had actually started to talk, really talk. Last night he'd asked if he could visit on Christmas Day. Jess had said that she needed to think about it a bit more. And she had. It was all she'd thought about, listing the pros and cons in mental columns. It unnerved her that at the top of the 'against' list was the fact that she didn't know how she'd feel when she saw him again. Darren was the person she'd loved since they were teenagers. They'd grown up with each other, learned how to be adults, how to be parents. All of this they'd done together. Now they were apart and it hurt.

She opened the car door. It was stinking hot already and what was left of Neill's garden wilted under the relentless sun. Jess grabbed Laura's basket off the front seat – the one Laura had brought out to lunch filled with garden produce. Now it bore a carton of home-grown eggs, which was nowhere near enough to begin to repay Laura for what she'd done for Jess and her family. Potters Junction had been big-time lucky when Laura O'Connor had chosen it as the place to come to do whatever it was she'd needed to do. Jess hoped she'd stay and wondered if the way she'd seen her brother look at Laura would make him want to stick around, too. Jess sighed as she stepped up onto the front verandah. No point getting her hopes up, given Jake's track record.

She let herself in the front door. The double glass doors to the sitting room were closed and she could hear the whir of the air conditioner. When she entered and took in the room, its transformation into a virtual hospital ward, the reality of the situation hit her like a vicious punch. He father was dying.

She gave him a peck on the head. 'How are you, Dad?'

'So-so, love. You?'

Jess had to strain to hear him. She nodded, forced a smile. There'd be time enough for tears later.

'I'm okay. Sam and Mikey are counting down the days to school holidays and Christmas. Where's Jake?'

'Jake's right here,' her brother said from behind her. 'Dad doesn't want any lunch. He's had a drink. I'm going next door to help Laura move furniture.'

Jess quirked an eyebrow. 'I brought her basket back, and some eggs. Can you take them to her?'

He picked up the basket. 'How long have I got?'

'How long do you need?' Jess winked.

He held up his phone. 'I shouldn't be long. Ring me if you need me.' He gave Neill's shoulder a squeeze. 'Be back in a while.'

The heat was fierce. The lemon tree had succumbed, no matter how much water he'd poured onto it. The few wizened lemons had fallen to the ground and were turning brown.

Laura was waiting for him, the shed unlocked and the tools ready. She'd even dusted off the bedstead where it leaned against a rusting corrugated-iron wall. And in shorts and a tank top, she looked good enough to eat. She'd blushed when he'd come through the door and he'd been about to make a comment about her being overdressed, when reality had slammed into him. No point wanting what you shouldn't have.

'Who helped you move the bed out here?' he asked as they carried the brass bedhead into the house.

'Neill did, believe it or not. Clearing out that room was one of the first things I did, and at that stage he was still up to helping me.'

With an old towel for protection, they carefully leaned the bedhead against a freshly painted bedroom wall.

'Is the old man deteriorating faster than normal?'

Laura dusted her hands together and looked at him. 'What's normal? How it happens for one person is different from how it happens for someone else. Some people go kicking and screaming, others gently and accepting.'

'Hmm, I'll probably be one of the kicking and screaming variety.'

'You never know, Jake,' she said. 'Come on, let's get the rest of the bed inside so we can put it together. You'll need to get back.'

They hauled the remaining parts inside and together they assembled it. When they'd finished and Laura stepped back, her face suffused with pure delight, Jake's heart wedged in his throat.

'Wow! It does look *so* good. I knew it would. I can't wait to get the new bed linen onto it.' She turned to him, her blue eyes dancing with anticipation. 'What do you think?'

Jake tilted his head to the side, hands on hips. 'Yeah, it does look good. I'm not a fan of brass beds but it suits the room. The floorboards came up well. You've done an amazing job, Laura. I'm impressed.'

'Thanks. The mattress. It's next door in the dining room.'

They went and manhandled the double mattress into the refurbished room and onto the vintage bed frame. When the mattress was in place Laura sat down on the edge of the bed and looked around.

'It's slowly coming together. One room at a time.'

'What happens when you finish? What then?'

Laura flopped back on the bed, spread her arms wide, legs dangling over the edge, feet still on the ground. 'Mmm, there's still heaps to do, and with being back at work it'll all go slower now.' She pursed her lips, gazed at the pressed tin ceiling. 'And I haven't decided what I'll do in the kitchen and wet areas.'

'Bathrooms and kitchens cost a shitload to renovate. Don't overcapitalise and risk not getting your money back.' Jake perched on the windowsill opposite her. Only centimetres separated his jean-clad knees from her bare ones.

'Oh, I doubt we'll ever sell the place. I'll stay here for a bit. At least until my leave finishes. But whatever I decide to do long-term, Alice and I will still use it as a weekender.' She lifted her head and peered at him. 'And just how much do you know about renovating kitchens and bathrooms?'

'Not that much. I did a bit of labouring for a builder way back, and I've helped a couple of mates with home renovations – enough to know it was a career I didn't want to pursue.'

'Oh.' Her head dropped back onto the mattress, eyes closed. 'I thought you might be good for the job. Gavin O'Driscoll seems to be stuck in Roxby Downs. Don't think I'll ever get the salt damp fixed. Would you help me shift the wardrobe while you're here?'

'Okay. Where is it?'

'In the dining room.'

Laura didn't move and Jake let his gaze, and his imagination, wander. Her arms were above her head now. Long, lightly tanned, nicely muscled. Soft chestnut curls framed her face. A strip of paler, bare skin was visible between the bottom of her pale-blue tank top and snugly fitting shorts. Her face was relaxed and long lashes brushing the shadows under her eyes were the only sign of how hard she worked. Need pounded through him and blood rushed south. He ran his fingers around the neck of his t-shirt, watched the slow rise and fall of her chest under the thin cotton of her top.

'Guess I'd better get up so we can move this wardrobe,' she murmured but stayed where she was.

Jake shifted uncomfortably then stood up.

'Not yet,' he said.

He could not resist her any longer. He would not. He had principles, but he was no saint. Plenty of time for regret later. He lowered himself down onto the bed beside her. Her eyes flicked open and their gazes met and held and he watched, mesmerised, as colour warmed her cheeks and her blue eyes darkened to indigo. Her tongue darted out to lick at her bottom lip and before he could stop it a low groan came from way down deep.

Jake felt as if he was going to burst. Then she answered the unspoken question that hovered in the air between them by parting her lips, reaching up to slide her hands around his neck and pulling his mouth down onto hers. He pushed aside the nagging thought that he was about to make it even harder for both of them when the time came for him to leave, and did what he'd been imagining moments, hours, weeks before.

When the mattress dipped Laura opened her eyes. She tried to swallow but her throat wouldn't cooperate. Desire rippled through her. She reached for him, sure fingers gliding through his hair to the back of his neck, guiding his lips down to hers. His mouth was hot, his lips hungry and she revelled in the taste of him, the way his hair curled on his nape, the sandpaper feel of his whiskers, the hard press of his body.

As he eased down onto her and into their kiss, Laura knew that this time they wouldn't stop at a kiss. This time they weren't making out in her car. Jake's large hand pushed up and under her tank top. Her nipples hardened in anticipation.

'Protection,' she whispered. 'I don't have any.'

He lifted his head, withdrew his hand, balanced on one elbow and reached into the back pocket of his jeans for his wallet. 'In there,' he said. She plucked out a single condom, the packet slightly frayed around the edges.

'Now who's the boy scout?' she said.

'And aren't you the grateful one,' Jake gloated. He rolled over onto his back and took her with him. Her laughter was swallowed by their next kiss, and her feet were no longer on the ground.

Sweat glistened on Jake's chest. Resting her head on his outstretched arm, Laura shifted, the bare mattress hot and prickly under her skin. With her fingertips she reached for a discarded piece of clothing, swiped it between her breasts.

'Overhead fans,' she murmured and Jake's eyelids flickered. She rolled onto her side so her head was resting on his shoulder. Sticking out her tongue she rasped it across his salty skin. His eyes opened.

'Overhead fans. I need one in here.'

'Mmm,' he said and closed his eyes again, his arm wrapping around her. 'I should go. I told Jess I wouldn't be long.'

'You weren't that long,' Laura taunted, and his eyebrows arched and he opened one eye.

'Ungrateful woman,' he growled and in one powerful move he'd flipped her onto her back.

'Still not a fan of brass beds?'

He laughed and she felt it vibrate through his chest as he pinned her to the bed, swooping in for another kiss. His mouth moved over hers, devouring its softness, and desire thrummed through her.

'Your phone. It's ringing,' Laura said against his lips, minutes later, their bodies slick with sweat and need.

'Shit,' he mumbled. Laura felt him tense and then the mattress bounced as he moved away.

She propped herself on her elbows and watched him rifle in the pocket of his discarded jeans.

'Jess,' he said, more like an expletive than a greeting. 'Ten minutes.'

He threw the phone onto the bed and started pulling on his jocks, looking back over his shoulder at Laura.

'Sorry, but Jess needs to get going, something about the supermarket and collecting the boys from school.'

'That's okay.'

He stood, picked up his jeans. 'No, Laura, it's not okay. But it's how it is.'

Laura shimmied to the edge of the bed, gathered up her clothes and got dressed, trying not to feel like she was being abandoned. She understood how it was. And how it would be. None of it was okay but it was how it was, and she'd gone in with her eyes open. She tried not to let her disappointment show.

He shoved his phone into his pocket. His sigh was deep. Laura tried to smile but her mouth wouldn't cooperate. He cupped her face with his hand and she wanted to throw herself at him, beg him not to go. Not now, not ever.

'I am sorry. I wish circumstances were different.' He brushed his lips across hers and when he spoke again his tone was light, almost teasing. 'But I'll have to come back tomorrow . . . We still have the wardrobe to shift, and then there're all those other jobs you'll need help with.'

'Yeah, you're right. I'll start making a list. I can see myself needing help most days.'

Jake's phone beeped and with a muttered curse he dropped a kiss full of promise onto Laura's still tingling lips. 'That'll be Jess again. I'll see you,' he said.

The house felt empty but Laura's body hummed. Her thoughts were saturated by all things Jake. She wandered from one unfinished task to the next, finally settling at the kitchen table to sort through more of Dorrie's papers. She told herself over and over to make the most of every moment she had with Jake because she'd only have him for a while. And that would have to do, as much as she might wish it were different. At least this time she could prepare herself – she *knew* he was going to leave her. It wouldn't be at all like Brett.

Chapter 33

The only sounds were of the kitchen clock, the intermittent grumble of the refrigerator, the whir of the fan in his laptop. It was late. He'd thrown open the doors and windows, an invitation to the cooler night time air.

Jake sat at the kitchen table and stared at the screen, scrolling through the photos he'd taken at Neill's birthday lunch. When he came to the one he'd surreptitiously taken of Laura on her own, he stopped scrolling. He remembered the moment. She'd been smiling at something Mikey had said, her blue eyes dancing with amusement. Looking at her made him ache to be with her. He wanted to go to her now, to pick up where they'd left off twelve hours earlier.

There was a crash and Jake was on his feet and at the door to the sitting room in seconds.

'Dad?' He flicked on the overhead light, blinking in the sudden brightness.

'I wanted a drink,' his father wheezed. 'Mouth's dry.'

The water had been tipped over, the glass knocked to the floor. Jake picked it up, surprised it hadn't broken. He topped it up from the jug nearby and held it while Neill took tiny sips between laboured gasps. When he'd had enough Jake set the glass on the cupboard beside the bed.

'Do you need to use the bottle?'

'No. But sit with me for a while.'

'All right,' Jake said and turned off the overhead light, the lamp on the cupboard casting the room back into shadows. He dragged a chair close to the bed and made himself comfortable.

'Was Laura here earlier?'

'She was, around teatime. You were asleep. She sat with you for half an hour. She's working again tomorrow.' They'd stolen a hungry kiss in the kitchen on her way out. The memory quickened his pulse.

'Tell me what's bothering you, boy. I know there's something.'

Neill's speech was remarkably lucid, his eyes gleamed in the low light. Jake's heart rate kicked up even further, but now for an entirely different reason. He swiped at his lips with his tongue, leaned forward in the chair. Time was running out. It was now or never.

'Jess told me what's in your will, and I won't take it.' He hadn't meant for his voice to sound harsh, but it did.

Silence, and then the scrape of Neill's head on the pillow. 'Why not?'

'I don't deserve it. I know I'm not your biological son.'

'Oh, son. I wondered if you'd found out somehow, and that's why you'd left.'

'I overheard a conversation between you and Milt Burns, it was back when Jess had tonsillitis and he did a home visit out to the farm.'

'I remember the time. Milt wanted to put Jess into hospital, she was that crook. So it wasn't your mother who told you.'

'No. I asked her who it was. She wouldn't say.'

Neill frowned. 'You looked her up then, after you left?'

'Tracked her down, more like it. She wasn't exactly thrilled to see me.'

Jake sensed the old man's scrutiny. When he finally spoke, his words were measured.

'You were hours old the first time I held you, and you were my son. I was there when you cut your first tooth, took your first step. I picked you up when you fell, taught you what I knew. It never mattered that I wasn't your biological father.'

Jake felt as if someone was standing on his chest. He had to fight to suck in enough air to speak.

'I'm sorry now that it mattered so much to me,' he said. 'I'm sorry it took me so many years to open my eyes and see.' *And without Laura, I probably never would have.* 'I'm so sorry, Dad.'

Neill had closed his eyes. The room was hot, the air felt too thick to breathe. Jake lurched to his feet, went to the window, threw it open, dragged hungrily at the freshness that billowed in. Why had he put this conversation off for so many years? They'd missed out on so much because of his obstinacy.

When he'd given himself time enough to garner a semblance of control, he sat down beside the bed again and Neill opened his eyes.

'We all make mistakes, son. It's what we do about them that counts.'

Awed by his father's capacity and willingness to forgive him for his twenty years of absences and rejection, all Jake could do was stare at his hands, a knot in his lap.

But there was something he needed to know.

'About Mum,' Jake started, not sure how to go on.

'She was never happy, Jake. She was eighteen, pregnant, I was thirty and thought I'd end up a crusty old bachelor. I won't say I shouldn't have married her because I wouldn't have you or Jess.'

'Did you love her?'

Neill took a while to collect his thoughts and when he spoke, Jake was taken aback by his candour.

'I thought I could, that I would, but I don't think that I ever did. I've never hated her, though. Even when she left. For myself, I was relieved more than anything.'

Jake leaned closer; his father's voice was fading fast. Neill coughed, squeezed his eyes shut, his face a paroxysm of pain.

'Dad.' Jake moved out of the chair and perched on the side of the hospital bed. The coughing shook his father's frail body. Jake found the morphine pump, pushed the button like the nurse had shown him. The light flashed and he pushed the button again.

As the coughing subsided Neill sank back into the pillows. 'About the farm, it's been in the family for three generations,' he said, his lips barely moving, each word pushed out on a shallow exhalation. 'Take twelve months to try and turn it around, that's all I ask. Jess needs help, even if Darren comes back. If it's not working by then, you two do whatever you want with it.'

Neill's words winded him like a sucker punch to the gut. He felt light-headed. He thought about Laura, he thought about the life he'd put on hold. He stared at the man in the bed, eyes shut, mouth slack. His father. Grief and regret swelled in his throat: grief for all the things that never would be, regret that he'd been too small-minded and stubborn to realise how small-minded and stubborn he'd been. It would always be his loss.

He lifted his father's hand, the translucent skin scarred and sun-spotted. Tears burned behind his eyes.

'Have you said anything to Jess?'

'No.'

'All right,' he said, his voice raw. 'Twelve months.' It wasn't long but it felt like a life sentence. Nothing more or less than he deserved.

Neill's fingers tightened around his. He looked the most peaceful he had in days.

✦

'Kaylene, you need to ask him,' Laura repeated for at least the sixth time in response to the practice manager's barrage of questions.

'He won't tell me anything. I'll ring Linda,' Kaylene said with a determined gleam in her eyes.

Laura sighed. 'Probably the best thing to give them is their privacy. I'm sure when they're ready to talk about whatever it is that's going on, you'll be one of the first to know.'

Kaylene's lips thinned, but she gave a Laura a curt nod before she turned back to her work.

Laura heard her mumble, 'Bloody doctors are all the same,' and she smothered a laugh as she walked the short distance to her consulting room.

The day passed with a steady flow of minor ailments, repeat prescriptions, follow-up blood tests, a Pap smear and, Laura's highlight, an elderly woman who wanted to know what to do about her husband's snoring.

'I'd really need to see your husband, to determine what's causing the snoring and then what we can do about it. But I think you're right: if the earplugs don't work anymore, best if you sleep in another room for the time being.'

The woman left promising to make an appointment for her

husband. 'Whether the old bugger will come is another question,' she said on her way out.

When the final patient had gone Laura ducked out the health centre's back door and hurried home. Another interrogation by Kaylene was more than she could deal with, and Jake hadn't answered her lunchtime phone call or either of her text messages. Jess's car was parked in the driveway behind Neill's ute when she drove past. Perhaps Jake would be able to get away for an hour? Even half an hour?

It was overcast but the clouds were thin and wispy, not plump with rain. As Laura walked up the path from the shed to the house, she passed the vegetable patch. The air around it was heavy with the fragrance of the basil planted between the tomato bushes. There was a splash of water on the cement path – Jake must have watered the garden again.

Dumping her bag on the kitchen table, she opened windows, decided against changing her clothes and went next door. Skip's kennel was empty, the chain in a tangle on the ground. His water bucket had been tipped over.

'I took him back to the farm,' a voice said. 'Dad's past it now, and it wasn't fair, Skip being chained up all day.'

'Hello, Jess. How are you?'

Jess blotted her eyes with the back of her hand. 'I'm not sure. You know how it is. Sam and Mikey are at a friend's place and I've been here since nine this morning. I had to get out of there for a few minutes. Dad hasn't moved all day. Jake said he woke up about two a.m. last night, they talked, and then he closed his eyes and he hasn't opened them since. He's coughed a couple of times, and I think his breathing has changed, almost like he's run out of puff.'

'That's how it happens.'

'I know. It's slow but quick, if you know what I mean.'

'I do. How's Jake?'

She shook her head. 'I dunno. He doesn't say much. I hope they got to sort things out. If they didn't, I'd say it's too late now.'

Laura murmured her agreement and went into the house to find Jake. She couldn't wait to see him. He was in the sitting room, next to his father. The room was cool, the air conditioner humming away quietly. Jake's eyes crinkled at the corners when he saw her.

'You're home.'

'It was a busy day as usual, and I sneaked out the back door so no-one could bail me up to chat.'

'Sorry I missed your call. Phone was on charge and I forgot all about it.'

'Never mind.' She went to the bedside, picked up one of Neill's hands, shocked to see it was mottled, the nail beds blue. It was only twenty-four hours since she'd seen him.

'Hello, Neill,' she said softly, watching his face for any sign of recognition. Nothing. Jess was right, his breathing was slower, more irregular, gurgling through the pooled secretions. She laid his hand back on the bed and glanced at the syringe pump pinned to the sheet. There was a portable suction unit on the floor beside the bed.

'The nurse left that today. Not sure either of us is game to use it.'

'I can if we need to. Are you okay?'

He pushed his hand through his tousled hair, stared at his father. 'Dad and I got to talk a bit in the early hours.'

'That's good, isn't it?'

'I'm not sure yet.'

Laura waited. He didn't elaborate. She masked her disappointment. 'Thanks for doing the watering,' she said.

'Anytime. It got me out in the fresh air for a while.'

Anytime. As long as it was in the next week or so. Laura scanned his face, committing every line and shadow to memory. She didn't offer her heart indiscriminately and Jake was the second man she'd ever fallen in love with. The first she'd married and he'd left her – not his choice but he was just as gone. And now Jake would walk out of her life as well. He had warned her, yes, but the unfairness of it all sent indignation vibrating through her.

'What's wrong?' Sitting within arm's reach of where she stood, Jake was watching her intently. 'You look like someone stole your favourite toy.'

'I was just thinking how unfair life could be.'

'You and me both, sweetheart,' he said, a moment before the sitting room door swung open and Jess came in. Anything more he might have said was lost. She wanted to stamp her foot in frustration.

Laura stayed, prepared food that nobody ate, made tea that sat and cooled. Jake sat opposite her at the kitchen table for half an hour and didn't say a word, his head in his hands. She left to see an outpatient at the hospital with a tooth abscess, returned to find Jess and Jake sitting either side of their father, the only sound Neill's stertorous breathing.

'Laura, you look dead on your feet. Go home,' Jake said.

He was right, she should go home. She ignored the selfish pang of hurt. Now was the time for the Finlay family to be together.

'Call me if you need anything, I'm only next door,' she said but didn't think either of them heard her.

Laura kept her phone close, expecting, maybe even hoping, for a call from Jake, but when midnight came and there was nothing, she put away the packet of Christmas cards she'd been staring at for the last hour and went to bed. The cards she'd use next year. Emails to friends and family would have to suffice for this Christmas.

She woke at four, her heart pounding. Without thinking she threw back the sheet, dragged on a t-shirt and a pair of cotton track-pants and went next door. The back light was on, the door open and the ute the only vehicle in the carport. Jake stood stiffly in the middle of the kitchen, staring at nothing, his eyes red-rimmed. He didn't seem at all surprised when Laura rushed past him, only to return minutes later.

'He's gone,' she said.

'About half an hour ago.' His voice was thick with grief and he didn't look her way.

'Where's Jess?'

'The boys wouldn't settle at her friend's place tonight so she picked them up and took them home. She said goodbye before she went.'

Laura felt the well of tears, felt the weight of his sorrow, the unequivocal memory of her own. 'Oh, Jake,' she said and went to him, slid her arms around him.

He was standing so rigidly and she tensed, prepared herself for rejection but then, on a sigh, she felt him relax and his arms went around her and she rested her cheek on his shoulder and held him.

Chapter 34

Jake sat with his father's body and remembered all the best things about him, all the good times they'd had, and he felt a void inside because there weren't more. He let the tears run unheeded down his cheeks when he thought of how his father had suffered. And not only because of the cancer.

Because he was Neill's GP, Milt Burns made the last Finlay home visit he'd ever make early on Friday morning. Laura had gone home to shower and change and Jess wasn't back from the farm.

Milt Burns stood uncomfortably beside the bed of his friend and former patient.

'Wonder who'll be the lucky son of a bitch to write my death certificate,' he said.

'I wouldn't be surprised if it was Laura,' Jake said and Milt looked up in surprise. Jake shrugged. 'Play your cards right . . . She looks pretty settled to me.'

'And what about you? Staying around to help out on the farm,

I dare say,' Milt said, and didn't try to hide the sarcasm.

'Be careful what you wish for.'

Jake followed him out to his car and caught the doctor completely off guard when he extended his hand.

'Thanks for everything you did for Dad, not just now but over the years. I know he had a lot of respect for you.'

With an astonished look on his face Milt took the proffered hand and shook it.

'It was my pleasure,' he said, stumbling over the words. He cleared his throat, tugged at his jowls. 'We were mates,' he said, 'your old man and I. Mates look out for each other. I couldn't just stand back and watch her make a fool out of him any more than you could have. Everyone knew she was carrying on with that bloke, everyone but him. Or he chose to ignore it.'

Jake folded his arms and Milt lifted his shoulders in a tired shrug.

'She was unhappy, your mother. She came to hate her life out there. If she hadn't left with that bloke, she would have left on her own or with some other bloke.' He looked at Jake squarely. 'I know that for a fact, and I'm sorry if you thought I interfered too much.'

'What about the other little secret, the one about my paternity? A pity no-one thought to mention the fact to me. I had to overhear it.'

Milt's face drained of all colour. 'Neill said he thought you knew, that's why you'd upped and left.'

'I did know. I heard you talking to Dad about it. And I was too young and stupid and headstrong to see past my anger, to see who my *real* father was. I wasted all those years, half of my life, ignoring him. I broke Dad's heart.'

Milt gaped at him. 'I did what I thought was right at the time. Don't think badly of your father. Neill wanted to tell you. I told him not to, primarily because *she* would never say who your father was, even Neill had no idea.'

Jake was gobsmacked. Not only was Neill not his biological father, but nobody except his mother knew who was. And she wasn't telling. Too stunned to speak, he nodded once and then turned on his heel and walked back into the house, slamming the front door after him. If Doctor Burns had hoped for absolution for the advice he'd given years ago, advice that had been the catalyst in the break-up of Jake's family, it wouldn't come from Jake. With that last little pearl of information the old bastard should be grateful Jake hadn't punched him.

Heartsick, he went and sat by his father's bed until Jess came, put her hand on his shoulder. 'Laura rang the local undertaker for us and someone should be here soon. In this heat . . .' She trailed off. 'Do you want some breakfast?'

He shook his head. He could feel Jess watching him.

'Will you be all right?' she said.

He wearily wiped his face with his hands. 'Yeah, I'll be all right.'

'Jake, don't punish yourself.' She looped her arm around his shoulders and hugged him. 'I'll wait for the undertaker if you like. You were going to check the stock for feed and water. It's been days now.'

'You're right.'

'Do you want to grab some gear, stay out at the farm?'

'No. Thanks. I'll stay here. Start clearing up, take more junk to the dump.' He needed some time on his own to try to sort through everything.

They discussed the farm, Neill's house and his will. Jake didn't mention the deathbed promise he'd made to his father. He would, he just needed time to get used to the idea himself. And there was the life he'd left on hold. There were decisions to be made about his job, his lifestyle. And there was Laura. Right at that moment he felt as if his head might explode.

He left, Jess promising to let him know if they could get an appointment with the funeral home later in the day. On the drive out to the farm he rang Laura. He needed to talk to her even though he didn't quite know what he wanted to say.

'I'm on my way out to the farm to feed and water stock. I'll be back by one. I'll take you out for lunch,' he said.

'That sounds lovely,' she said. 'I'll look forward it.'

It was either the hotel or the Potters Junction Cafe and Laura chose the latter, where the coffee was passable. They ate fish and chips in one of the booths at the back and Jake told Laura about his conversation with Milt Burns.

'I'm not defending him, Jake, but it would have been a hard call, in both instances. Remember we're talking a lot of years ago. I'm beginning to appreciate how blurry the lines can get when your patients become your friends, and vice versa. And what *do* you do when there is no choice but to see the GP everyone else sees, unless you want to leave town?'

Jake pushed his plate away, the chips only half-eaten.

All these years he'd been seeing what happened through the eyes of a teenager. He'd been a man for a long time now, it was high time he grew up. Perhaps if he'd had a family of his own, he might have understood his father and the reasons he did what he did. Perhaps he would have found forgiveness easier. He didn't tell Laura that Neill had asked him to stay. The words wouldn't come.

The greasy meal sat heavy in his stomach. They finished their coffee in silence. Laura dropped him off at the funeral home – a modest cream brick building two streets back from the main drag and separated from the road by a strip of manicured lawn and a border of standard roses. Jess's car was already parked along the kerb.

'Thank you for everything you did for Dad, and what you did for Jess, and for me.'

She stared at him across the narrow space. He wouldn't look at her because he couldn't bear to see the hurt and confusion in her blue eyes.

'Thanks for lunch,' she said coolly. 'I'll see you later.' Almost arctic.

Jess's black shoes were killing her and a plastic bag would have been more breathable than her synthetic frock. Sweat trickled between her breasts, down to her belly, and she prayed it would finish soon so she could go home and soak in a cold bath. And begin to get used to life without her dad.

The minister droned on. A funeral only days before Christmas was unfortunate enough, but the afternoon heat made it unbearable. Jess already knew what a good man Neill Finlay had been.

Mikey tugged on her hand. 'How much longer, Mum? I'm hot.'

'Go and stand in the shade,' Jess whispered. 'There's more water in the car.'

Mikey mumbled something but resolutely remained standing beside his brother. Jess smoothed his hair and he shook her hand off. Sam rolled his eyes.

The gleaming coffin was finally being lowered into the ground by Jake, Milt and two other beetroot-faced pallbearers, fellow farmers and long-time friends of Neill, when Mikey piped up and said, 'Look, Mum, there's Dad!'

The bottom dropped out of Jess's stomach. She caught the joy that spread across Sam's face as he turned in the direction Mikey was pointing – Mikey, who was now jumping up and down and yanking on her hand. The people on both sides of her were staring, most she knew, some she didn't. In a community this size word travelled fast and news of her and Darren's split would have reached most ears. Between the heat and the perspiration at least no-one would know she was embarrassed as well as hot, that there were tears of humiliation mixed with the grief. She wished the ground would swallow her along with the coffin.

The minister finally finished and she was filing past the coffin, walking in Jake's shadow and dropping limp rose petals onto the pristine varnish. Laura hugged her and she wondered how the woman could look so elegant in a simple navy blue linen shift on such a stinking hot day.

People embraced Jess, shook her hand, kissed her cheek and offered their condolences. She pinned on a mannequin-like smile, carried on through the blur of tears, when all the while she was thinking, *Darren's here, Darren's here.* The same thought looped, over and over, and she was surprised to realise how much she'd hoped he would come.

Then he was standing beside her, one son hanging off each arm.

'Jess,' he said. 'I am so sorry. I know how much you loved your dad, and how much he loved you.'

He looked different. His hair was shorter, he'd lost a few kilos. He looked more like the man she'd married, not the angry, bitter husband who'd walked out on her six weeks before.

'Thanks for coming,' she said, her voice wobbly.

'I would never have missed it, Jess,' he said, and when he smiled, Jess let the tiny kernel of hope she'd been nurturing grow a little more.

★

Laura had noticed the handsome, blond man in black trousers and an open-necked shirt. He'd been standing at the very back of the church. At the cemetery, when Sam and Mikey launched themselves at him, she realised it was Jess's husband, Darren. Riveted, she watched as Darren approached Jess, and held her breath when Jess turned to greet him. Jake strode over to his sister and her estranged husband and Laura gaped as he put a protective arm around Jess. Then he reached out and shook Darren's hand.

All through the church service and here at the graveside Laura had hardly taken her eyes off Jake. In a fashionable black suit bought for the occasion, clean shaven and with his hair trimmed, he could have stepped straight out of *Men's Style* magazine. Laura's first thought when she saw him was, *Who is this man?* And from the looks thrown his way by women young and old, they were all think-ing along the same lines.

At the graveside he'd stood a few steps from Jess, far enough away to appear alone, his expression remote. Laura ached to go up to him and link her fingers with his, reassure him that he wasn't by himself in all this. But his body language screamed *keep your distance*, so she did. He was grieving and she knew how that was.

But it was more than that. In the days since Neill's death, Jake had subtly, but unquestionably, begun to distance himself from her. First there was that dreadful lunch at the cafe where he'd thanked her for all she'd done. Then there were her invitations for coffee that he'd rebuffed, the offer to help pack up things at Neill's that was brushed off, the vegie patch untouched the two days she'd worked. And there'd been no repeat of their impromptu and, for her, unfor-gettable lovemaking.

He'd never given her any reason to expect otherwise, but know-ing that didn't ease the gnawing sadness and hurt. Telling herself it was better this way didn't make one iota of difference.

The crowd was beginning to disperse, everyone invited back to the Anglican Church hall for light refreshments, when Laura felt a firm hand on her arm and a waft of summery perfume.

'Laura, how are you? I hear from a reliable source that you've taken Potters Junction by storm!'

'Meghan, hello, lovely to see you. You look well.'

The two women embraced, Laura shook Sean's hand then, with a grin, reached up on tiptoes and pecked him on the cheek. He looked embarrassed, but pleased.

'Too hot to bring the kids,' Meghan said in answer to her unspoken query. 'We're not staying for the afters, we just wanted to support Jess, to say goodbye to Neill. Is that the son?'

Laura turned to where Meghan was looking. A solitary Jake was standing by his father's grave, anonymous behind mirrored sunglasses. 'Yes, that's Jake Finlay.'

Meghan nudged her. 'Easy on the eye,' she said, but then her eyes narrowed. 'He's tall, not much like his father to look at.'

Trust Meghan to notice. Laura didn't comment.

'Come on, Meghan, let's go,' said Sean. 'I've got stock to feed.'

They started walking towards the few remaining parked cars. A scorching wind rushed through the native pine trees. Heat radiated off the polished granite headstones.

'Milt and Linda came to dinner on Saturday night. Milt told us his news. Linda was so pissed off with him for not telling her sooner.' Meghan glanced sideways at Laura. 'She said you knew before she did.'

'She was worried about him, she asked me to talk to him. I did. He told me about the prostate cancer.'

'Milt and I talked until Linda went to sleep in the chair and Sean went to bed. I don't think he'll retire yet. Linda thinks he will. He'll have treatment and he'll need time off for that, but he can't let go. It's what keeps him alive. Even if he only does a day or two a week, he'll come back.'

'He said he'd talk to me after he'd told Linda and they'd worked things out. I offered to stay around as long as he needed while he was having the remaining investigations and any preliminary treatment.'

'He will talk to you.'

They'd reached Meghan's car and Sean was opening doors to let out the super-heated air.

'You've been fantastic, Laura, and Milt and I are both hugely grateful for what you've done. Milt doesn't expect you to exile yourself out here unless you want to, and then only for as long as it works for you. We'll manage, we'll keep trying to recruit.'

'I do like it out here, I didn't think I would, but I do. Needless to say I have the remnants of another life back in Adelaide. I'm not certain I want to give that life up. Before I say exactly how long I'll stay I need to talk with my colleagues back there.'

'I think that's very fair. We couldn't ask for more and I'm glad you like it here. From what I hear, everyone likes you, especially one dark, mysterious man, who reminds me of a rock star in that suit and those sunglasses.' Meghan looked to where Jake was, still standing beside the grave in the shade cast by a bank of gum trees.

'How did you know . . .' The penny dropped and Laura rolled her eyes. 'Jess.'

'Uh-huh. The grapevine around here, you gotta love it. Like I told you once before, nothing's sacred. But you can trust Jess, she won't breathe a word to anyone else.'

'There's nothing to breathe.'

One of Meghan's eyebrows arched upwards. 'Are you sure?'

Pain and longing squeezed at Laura's heart. 'Positive.'

'Come on, Meghan,' Sean said, sounding impatient. 'I've got stock to feed.' Meghan pulled a face at him. He shook his head and climbed into their 4WD.

'Better go,' Meghan said. 'He's slow to the boil, but wow, when he boils! And never get between a farmer and his stock.' She winked at Laura and the women embraced. Meghan and Sean drove away and Laura looked longingly to where Jake stood, but then she trudged to her car and drove to the church hall.

The first person Jake recognised when he walked into the crowded hall was Milt Burns, and his mournful visage was bobbing through the crowd towards him.

'Accept my condolences, son,' the old doctor said. 'He was a fine man, your father.'

Their gazes clashed. Jake nodded. 'He was, and thank you,' he said, and Milt Burns tipped his head in acknowledgement before heading towards the door.

Jess beckoned him to where she was standing beside a trestle table strewn with the remains of the afternoon tea. With a pang he realised she looked wrung out. Hard enough she'd buried her father, then Darren had shown up. Plus Jake had left her to manage the masses.

'Where're Mikey and Sam?'

'Darren took them home.' Jess folded her arms.

'Really. And you're okay with that?'

'Yes, I am. They were hot and tired, and he's their father. And where the hell have you been? I've been looking all over for you. It would have been nice if you'd been around to share some of the load.'

'Sorry.'

He'd been at the graveside, staring at the mound of earth where his father lay, trying to get his head around the promise he'd made him. He still hadn't. And his mind kept playing tricks on him, whispering that no-one else knew what he'd promised a dying man, a dead man. He could ride off into the sunset and no-one would ever know. Except him, and his father, wherever he was. Jake almost couldn't believe he was having this conversation with himself.

'Earth to Jake,' Jess snapped. 'Do you reckon you could take your head out of your backside long enough to mingle? These people were good enough to spare the time to see Dad off, so the least you can do is help me thank them.'

'All right, you've made your point.' He turned towards two elderly ladies standing in the corner gawking at him. 'I'll go mingle, press the flesh.'

'Oh, yeah,' she said and caught hold of his arm as he moved off. 'Laura went home. She said she'd got a touch too much sun at the cemetery and didn't feel well. She looked upset.' Jess's eyes glistened, she dabbed at them with a tissue. 'She was very fond of Dad. And you've been such an arse.' She dropped his arm and strode off.

Jake swore under his breath. The thing that pissed him off the most was that his sister was 100 per cent right.

The main street was next to deserted when Laura drove home from Neill's send-off. Heat rippled off the bitumen and litter swirled in the gutters. Christmas decorations put up by the local district council flapped and flashed from the straggly bushes and the Stobie poles. When she passed Neill's place and saw Jake's bike crouched in the carport, it was as if someone had struck her.

She parked the car in the shed, rested her forehead on the steering wheel and closed her eyes. He was going; she'd foolishly let herself fall in love with him. The moment of truth was here and it hurt way more than she'd prepared for. She'd let herself indulge in a pity-fest today, tomorrow she'd get on with it again. She'd picked herself up and moved on after far worse.

When the heat inside the car became unbearable Laura climbed out. Even with the shade-cloth canopy, the tomato bushes were limp, the leaves on the zucchini plants wilting. She dropped her handbag onto one of the cane chairs, kicked off her shoes and turned on the hose. Water gushed out hot enough to scald. When it had cooled to lukewarm she let it wash over her bare feet and legs before giving the vegetable garden another good soaking. Silence echoed loudly from the house next door.

Laura was unpegging washing hung out before the funeral when the gate rattled, followed by the crunch of footsteps on gravel. She forced herself not to look up, kept methodically folding tea towels and pillowcases.

The stacked basket was whisked out of her hands the second she picked it up.

'Let me carry that for you,' he said, and she flicked him a quick sideways glance. He'd changed into jeans and t-shirt. Her heart leaped at the sight of him.

'Thanks, but I can manage.'

'I know you can.'

She held the back door for him and he put the basket on the washing machine and followed her into the kitchen.

'I missed you at the hall. Jess said you weren't feeling well.'

She shrugged. 'The heat, and I haven't been sleeping that well.'

'I don't think any of us have.'

She folded her arms, leaned against the sink. 'Was there something you wanted?'

'Why so fractious, Laura?'

'Why so fractious? You can ask *me* that? You kissed me. We made love. We shared something. I sat with you after your father had died.' She paused, her heart in a vice, the burn of tears in her throat. 'Then, you took me to lunch and you *thanked* me. And since then you've all but ignored me.'

'I never made any promises, Laura.'

'No, you didn't.'

She went to the fridge, took out a bottle of water, offered him one. He shook his head. She cracked the screw top, gulped down several mouthfuls, her back to him.

'You're leaving, aren't you?'

'Yes.'

That one affirming syllable sucked the breath right out of her.

'Laura,' he said but she wouldn't look at him until he gave her no choice. He gripped her arms and turned her around to face him.

'Laura, I have a life, a job that I walked out on to come here and look after Dad. I need to go back and sort it all out. I called in a lot of favours so I could leave when I did.'

'When?'

She wanted to pummel his chest with her fists, demand that he not leave her, that her heart was too freshly healed to be broken again.

'The weekend.'

Chapter 35

'Why wait until then?' she said and shrugged out of his grip.

His expression hardened. 'Don't do this, Laura.'

She threw her hands into the air, the tears creeping closer.

'I know I'm not being fair. I always knew you'd go. You never made a secret of the fact. I just hadn't expected to like you so much. I didn't think I was ready to fall in love again.'

His Adam's apple bobbed up and down, he closed his eyes. Laura held her breath. When he opened his eyes they bored into her with searing intensity.

'Tell me how it feels to be in love, Laura.'

Her expression softened. She let her gaze glide over him from head to toe, and back up again before she answered.

'I think about you all the time. When I'm not with you I can't wait until I'm with you again. I miss you if you just go into another room. I want to touch you all the time. I want you to touch me. It feels scary, but somehow wonderful.' She sniffed the tears back. 'But you can't, or won't, stay or love me back, and that hurts like hell.'

He turned away and she watched him withdraw.

'I never meant to hurt you,' he said, and Laura braced herself for the slap of the screen door as it closed behind him.

At least she knew now, at least she could get on with getting over him. All the while he stayed she'd let her foolish heart hope. But she would be okay, she would push on. With grim determination Laura set out the ingredients to bake fruit mince pies to take to the staff at the health centre and hospital. *Keep busy, keep focussed*, was her mantra from days gone by. And it worked, for that afternoon at least. Exhausted, Laura fell into bed at midnight, six dozen pies cooling on racks on the kitchen table.

The moment the bedroom light was switched off, her mind switched on. She lay staring, dry-eyed, into the dark, reliving every minute since Jake had burst into her life. At two a.m. she relented and took a sleeping pill and fell into a fitful slumber, only to be woken with a start several hours later.

A bike roared to life.

Grey light was edging around the blind, the first hint of the day ahead, and in the carport next door, Jake was getting ready to leave. Laura sat up in the bed, eyes wide, heart pounding. He wasn't waiting for the weekend after all. She squeezed her eyes shut, listened as the motor revved, then held her breath until the guttural growl of the motorbike was absorbed by what was left of the night.

Jake stopped by the farm to say goodbye to Jess, Sam and Mikey. He'd half expected Darren's ute to be parked by the house, but it wasn't.

'Change of plans?' Jess asked, yawning as she put on the kettle.

'Something like that,' he said, peeling off his leather jacket and draping it over a kitchen chair.

'It's barely six, the boys are still in bed.'

'I've got a long ride ahead of me. The roads will be packed with Christmas traffic.'

'I can't understand why you won't stay for Christmas. It's only days away.'

He didn't answer her. Jake had put any real thinking on hold until he could put some distance between himself and this place. While he was here nothing was clear, the past and the present mixed up in a murky concoction.

She made him toast and coffee and leaned against the sink, both hands wrapped around her mug, watching him while he ate.

'Did you say goodbye to Laura?'

He stopped chewing. 'After a fashion,' he said and took a sip of the coffee. The toast felt as if it'd got stuck halfway down his throat.

'Jake, you really are an arse.'

'So you said.'

'What do I do about Dad's will? And God knows how I'll manage the farm, the stock and everything else on my own. I can't believe you're just riding off and leaving me in this mess, with Dad not even cold in his grave.'

'I'll keep in touch, and I'll come back and help you sort it all out, I promise, I'm just not sure when.'

He drained his coffee mug, stood up and took the crockery to the sink, couldn't meet his sister's eye.

'What's happening with Darren?'

'He's coming back for Christmas Day. Sam and Mikey are that excited. And we're talking. He's got a job up north, starts in the new year. And then he'll start sending money.'

'Maybe he can see to the sheep.'

'He'll only be here for the *day*, Jake.'

'What about Bob Tomlinson next door?'

'I'll ask him,' Jess said after a moment's hesitation.

'Tell him we'll pay, you let me know how much and I'll transfer it into your account.'

'What happens when you run out of money to buy your way out of your responsibilities, Jake?' Jess's cheeks flushed the moment the words were out of her mouth.

He glared at her. 'I'll pretend you didn't say that.' He hated it when she was right. 'We've both been under a lot of pressure lately.'

He went to the boys' bedroom to say goodbye. Mikey sat up in bed, yawning, rubbing sleepy eyes. 'When are you coming back, Uncle Jake? Will you be back in time for my birthday in February? I'll be seven.'

'Dunno, mate,' Jake said. 'I'll do my best.'

Jake tried to ignore Jess standing in the bedroom doorway, arms folded. Sam sat on the edge of the bed and gave him a solemn hug.

'I gotta get on the road,' he said, kissed both his nephews. They scrambled out of bed and looked on in awe as he pulled on his leather jacket. They followed him out to the bike. Before he slipped on the helmet he embraced his sister.

'Jess, I have to do this. Please try to understand. Ring me or email me anytime.'

'I love you,' she said, 'believe it or not. Keep safe.'

Jake's gut twisted when he glanced in the rear-view mirror to see Jess and the boys standing forlornly in the driveway, just as the sun crested the horizon. Three days before Christmas, their father had left them, they were about to have the first Christmas without their Poppa, and Jake was leaving them as well. There was no doubt about it, he really *was* a bastard.

As the kilometres grew between him and Potters Junction, the relief he'd imagined he'd feel eluded him completely. He felt empty. As he rode the long stretch between Tailem Bend and Bordertown, he finally admitted to himself that again he was turning his back on all the people who loved him – Jess, Sam, Mikey and Laura. But that hadn't stopped any of them loving him.

For fuck's sake, what was the matter with him? He'd been so focussed on getting away that he couldn't see what he was leaving behind. He'd done the same damned thing twenty years ago. Had he learned nothing in all that time?

Chapter 36

Alice arrived on Christmas morning, looking fresh and stylish, and laden with food and wine. She took one look at Laura and said, 'What's happened?'

'My neighbour died.'

'Yes, but you knew that was going to happen. He was terminally ill when you met him. What else has happened? You look as if you haven't slept for a week.'

'I fell in love with his son.'

'And?'

'He didn't fall in love with me. He's gone: back to his job, to his life.' She pressed her fingertips to her lips to hold back a sob. She'd cried buckets in the three days since Jake's departure.

Alice opened her arms and gathered Laura close. 'Oh, Laura. And your poor heart had only just healed after losing Brett.'

'I know,' Laura said against her sister's shoulder, enveloped in a cloud of White Linen, her sister's favourite perfume.

'Will you be all right?' Alice asked, holding Laura at arm's length to study her face.

'Of course I will. And anyway, it's for the best,' she said, sure her nose was growing as she formed the words. 'He wasn't the easiest man to know, and between the two of us there was a huge pile of baggage.' *But I would have done my damnedest to make it work.*

Alice snorted. 'Tell me one person in their late thirties who doesn't have any baggage?'

'Speaking of baggage, grab your overnight bag and I'll show you what I've done with the spare room.'

Alice picked up her Louis Vuitton overnight and followed her sister to the front of the house.

'Laura! This is gorgeous!' Alice said when she stepped over the threshold of the refurbished bedroom. 'The floor looks fabulous. You clever thing.' Alice sat down on the edge of the bed, bounced up and down a couple of times and smoothed her hand across the broderie anglaise doona cover. 'This sets it all off perfectly.'

Laura quickly averted her eyes, swamped by a wave of fierce longing. She couldn't look at the old brass bed without thinking of Jake.

'Tea or coffee?' Laura said when they went back to the kitchen. She started unpacking the food Alice had brought.

'Too early for bubbly?' Alice lovingly held up a chilled bottle of sparkling wine.

'Just a tad. It's not even midday.'

'But it's Christmas.'

'Oh, all right, you win. But only pour me half a glass. I'm on call. Milt promised to cover new year if I did Christmas. All his kids are home.'

'That man ought to be bloody grateful you came along when you did,' Alice said.

Her sister was right, and unfortunately Alice didn't know the half of it.

They piled prawns and salad onto a platter, plonked the bubbly into a bucket of ice and sat on the cane chairs outside in the shade. They wiled away the warm afternoon chatting or just sitting in companionable silence.

'It's a pity you can't stay longer than a night,' Laura said.

'I promised friends I'd babysit their dog. He's a sweet old thing. They leave tomorrow to visit interstate rellies. They're back in a week.'

'Why didn't you bring him with you?'

Alice nearly choked on her wine. 'A Golden Retriever? In my car? All that hair and slobber? Not bloody likely.'

'So he's not that sweet an old thing?'

'He's fine, just not in my car. And don't worry, we'll party when you come down for the new year.'

Alice went inside and came back with a basket of assorted sweets and chocolates. 'Eat up,' she said, putting the basket on Laura's lap. 'Don't think I haven't noticed how little you've eaten. I'll be leaving all the leftover food with you. It was expensive. Don't waste it. You can't afford to lose any weight.'

On Boxing Day, Laura received a phone call out of the blue. Now that Neill was gone and Jake had left, she hadn't expected to hear from Jess.

'We're having a BBQ tonight, would you like to come? It won't be anything fancy, just a few chops and snags. Darren and his mum are here. And I thought you might be lonely.'

'Thanks, Jess, that would be lovely. Shall I bring a salad? I have a load of homemade mince pies going begging, too.'

'Perfect. We'll see you about five.'

The invitation was touching, but Laura wondered if it was wise to spend more time with Jake's family. Jess reminded her of Jake, and of what she'd lost.

But Jake's sister or not, Jess had also become a friend. A friend to be admired and respected. After all, look at everything *she* had lost, Laura told herself in silent rebuke.

At lunchtime she helped Alice pack up and load her car. Laura gave her a pot of herbs from the garden and a box of Dorrie's ephemera she thought Alice might like to go through.

Alice gave her sister a peck on the cheek. 'I'll see you New Year's Eve, then. Come as early as you can. We've been invited to a heap of things. We'll party! Let's bring the new year in in style.' Alice pulled the car door shut, started the motor and with a whir the window went down. 'And Laura, next year will be heaps better than this one's been. I guarantee it.'

'I seem to remember you said the same thing last year, and the year before,' Laura said.

'Third time lucky!'

Laura walked to the gate and watched until Alice's car had disappeared from sight. She glanced at the empty house next door and was enveloped with sorrow and loneliness.

Laura was pooped. The BBQ at Jess's had been pleasant; Jess had seemed bright enough given her circumstances. Darren came across as a reasonable sort of a bloke, and his mother was friendly.

Darren had been attentive to Jess and spent a chunk of time with Sam and Mikey, and it had been obvious to Laura that he loved his two sons.

Laura had given Kaylene the go-ahead to load her up with consultations on Tuesday and Wednesday, because of the Boxing Day public holiday. She wanted to stay busy, she was sticking to her mantra, but, between the workload and the emotional couple of days, she felt wrung out.

Early on Wednesday evening Laura was packing up and looking forward to going home and having an early night when Milt came into her consulting room and sat down.

'I ran into Claudia Samuels at the hotel on Monday night,' Milt said. 'She goes in for surgery on the second of January. Would have been earlier if not for Christmas. She said the surgeon is optimistic, that he praised her diligent GP for getting onto things straight away.'

'That's wonderful news. Thank you for the feedback. Ringing her was one of the things I had on my to-do list.'

Milt cleared his throat. 'Linda and I have talked and I've given your offer some thought, and I'd like to accept any help you can give.'

'I can stay for three months,' she said. 'That'll give you time to finish the investigations and get a start on the treatment.'

'What if I don't want treatment? What if it's already got out of hand?'

'What did the MRI show?'

'I have a specialist appointment next Thursday. If you can cover for me again I'd appreciate it.'

'Of course I will.'

'I'm not giving up work until I have to.'

'That's up to you, Milt. You might change your mind when you know what you are up against.'

He shifted in his seat. 'Is three months your limit?'

Laura sighed, leaned back in the chair. 'By then I will have used all my leave. I can't expect the practice in Adelaide to carry me indefinitely. I'd have to resign if I decided to stay here longer, and I'm not sure yet if I want to do that.'

Milt nodded slowly and then stood up. 'Fair enough,' he said. 'Can't ask for more than that.'

'If I change my mind I'll tell you. But the hospital board should continue trying to recruit, don't you think?'

'Yes, they should.'

He was almost to the door when she remembered. 'I almost forgot, I have something here that you might want.' She reached into her shoulder bag.

He turned back as she withdrew the letters tied with the faded ribbon. She handed them to him.

He took the slim sheaf of envelopes, slipped one from its binding and opened it, and promptly turned an unhealthy shade of pale. 'Where did you get these?' he said, his voice hoarse.

'I found them when I was sorting through some of Dorrie's stuff. I recognised the handwriting.'

He folded the letter and put it back in the envelope, slipped it in with the others. 'What are you going to do?'

'Do? Nothing. It's your business, not mine. I almost burned them but then I thought you might want them back.'

'You've read them?'

'Only the first one. I loved my great-aunt. At first I couldn't decide whether to be horrified that she'd had an affair with a married man, or happy her life wasn't without passion.'

'And did you decide?'

'Yes, I think I did. I was happy.'

'Dorothy was a decent and a passionate woman, and she helped me through a difficult time in my life, in our lives. Linda and I —'

'Please don't tell me.' She cut him off. 'I already know more than I want to. I'm still not convinced I shouldn't have burned them.'

'Thank you, and I'm glad you didn't,' he said slowly, tiredly, and slipped them into the pocket of his trousers. 'I know you were close to Neill Finlay, and his son, so no doubt you know something of my involvement with the family.'

'A little,' she said.

'You must think I'm the biggest hypocrite ever.'

What Laura saw was a tired, unwell old man who'd been the custodian of the community's secrets for a very long time. It was no surprise that he had secrets of his own. Was he a hypocrite? She wasn't about to judge him. And his secret was safe with her.

Milt left and Laura finished packing up and went home.

Laura found the hours in between work and the mind-numbing renovation jobs the hardest. Sitting on the back verandah watching a sunset, running in the mornings as the sun crept over the horizon, lying awake in the lonely hours before dawn. She missed Jake. She missed what they might have had if he'd been able to put the past behind him and accept that he was a good man, worthy of being loved.

Rising early on Saturday morning, New Year's Eve, Laura went for a run. She'd changed her route now to avoid passing Neill's place. The roads were lonely without Skip, without a cup of tea and chat to look forward to, without Jake. But she made good time and she found some satisfaction in that.

The hot weather had been unrelenting, with no relief forecast for another week. Back from the run, Laura gave the vegetable garden and the herb pots on the verandah a good soaking. She picked the few ripe tomatoes and zucchinis to take to Alice, showered and packed an overnight bag, and then she was on the road to her sister's place by nine.

Chapter 37

'Mum, wake up!'

Jess opened her eyes.

'Mikey. What's wrong? Where's Sam?' she said, wide-awake now as she pushed back the doona and swung her legs over the side of the bed.

'Uncle Jake's back.'

'What?' she said and rubbed her eyes, sure she must be dreaming.

'I saw him first. I heard his bike. Sam slept on the lounge. Uncle Jake's in the kitchen and Sam's making his breakfast. Weet-Bix,' he added as an afterthought.

Jess reached for her robe, pulled it on over the t-shirt she wore to bed. 'What's he doing back here?' she said, more to herself than to Mikey, who'd raced off down the passage. 'He's only been gone ten days.' She counted them off on her fingers.

She glanced at the clock radio on the bedside cupboard.

Six-thirty a.m. The year had slipped in silently while they were asleep. Sam had tried to sit up so he could see the new year in, but he'd only lasted until eleven before falling asleep on the lounge. The minute he'd dropped off, Jess had covered him with the doona from his bed, turned off the lights and gone to bed herself.

The floorboards creaked when Jess walked down the passage towards the kitchen. Sure enough, she made out Jake's gravelly baritone amongst the boys' excited chatter.

'Jake?' she said from the kitchen doorway and he turned sideways in his chair. His eyes were bloodshot, his jaw thick with stubble. He looked like someone who'd been on a long ride, and back.

'Jess,' he said. 'We need to talk.'

'Okay,' she said. She went to the cupboard for a mug, topped up the kettle and flicked it on. 'Wouldn't it have been easier to phone?'

'No,' he said, and Jess raised her eyebrows as she spooned coffee and sugar into the mug.

'Sam, why don't you and Mikey take your breakfast and go watch a DVD while Uncle Jake and I talk?'

Sam looked from one adult to the other and then nodded. 'Come on, Mikey,' he said and they picked up their cereal bowls and took them through to the lounge.

'So, start talking,' Jess said, sitting down at the kitchen table opposite her brother.

'First, where's Laura? I went to her house. Her car wasn't there, the place is all locked up.'

Jess frowned. 'Oh, yeah, she went to her sister's in Adelaide. They were going to a New Year's Eve party somewhere.' She grinned, kicked Jake under the table. 'Obviously not pining for you, bro.'

Jake rolled his eyes, rose stiffly to his feet and made himself another coffee. 'Obviously not,' he muttered under his breath.

'Seriously, though,' Jess said. 'She came here for a BBQ on Boxing Day and I thought she was pretty flat, not her usual cheery self, although she hid it well. Darren and his mum really liked her.'

He sat down, the steaming brew in front of him. 'Do you know when she gets back?'

'No. But I have an appointment with her on Tuesday at the health centre, so I guess she'll be back by then. So, what is it you couldn't tell me over the phone? Not that I'm not pleased to see you.'

'I'm glad, because you'll be seeing a lot more of me.'

Jess's eyes widened. 'Tell me more.'

Jake rubbed at his lips with his fingertips, his eyes trained on his sister. 'Just before he died, I promised Dad I'd stay around for twelve months to help out here on the farm. If the place is still going down the toilet after a year, we can do whatever we want with it. Sell it, lease it, whatever.'

Jess sat back in the chair. 'I didn't see that coming. He didn't say anything about it to me.' She tried not to sound hurt, but she was.

'No, he thought you had enough on your plate, what with Darren and all that. And we had a few things to settle, he and I. Like the fact that he wasn't my biological father.'

'What?' Jess said, her jaw dropping. 'Who told you that? You and I are obviously related! We have the same colour eyes, the same shaped nose —'

'We are related, Jess, we have the same mother, but I have a different biological father. I don't have a clue who he is, Mum wouldn't tell me, and Dad and Milt Burns didn't know either.'

'How did you find out?'

'I overheard a conversation between Milt Burns and Dad. Dad wanted to tell me but Milt Burns advised him not to. He didn't think there was any point because no-one knew who my father was.' Jake cleared his throat, took a sip of coffee. 'You were sick. Milt had made a house call. I heard them talking in the kitchen. I was so fuck-ing angry I left as soon as shearing was over, remember?'

'Bloody hell, Jake, of course I remember. Dad was devastated. I thought good riddance because you'd been such a moody pig. But then when you didn't come back . . .' She scratched her head. 'Why didn't you tell me all this when you were here last time? After Dad died?'

Jake shifted in his seat, sighed deeply. 'Because I was an arse, as you've so accurately observed on previous occasions.'

Jess folded her arms. 'You weren't going to tell me, were you? That's why you left.'

Jake didn't break eye contact. 'I was going to tell you, Jess, I just wasn't sure when. I needed to put some distance between me and this place so I could think. There was a lot to get my head around.'

They sat for several minutes while Jess tried to digest everything Jake had told her.

'You saw Mum. When?'

'Not long after I left here. She was living in WA and she wasn't exactly pleased to see me. When I asked her who my real father was, she said for all intents and purposes Neill was my real father, and I should be bloody grateful. I haven't had any contact with her since.'

Jess just nodded. A long time ago she'd come to terms with her mother leaving, wasn't interested in raking over old memories and old hurts. There was no purpose to it.

'So, you're here for twelve months. I suppose we'll all get used to having you around, and then you'll go again.'

'Let's not get ahead of ourselves, Jess. A lot can happen in twelve months, and whatever that might be, I promise I will never again just walk away from the people I care about, and who care about me.'

'It took you long enough to realise that.'

'I know, and I'm truly sorry about that. I regret that I spent twenty years caught up in so much righteous anger and angst, thinking I'd been lied to, that I'd never know who my father was, when he was here all the time.'

'What about your biological father? Don't you want to know?'

'Perhaps. Maybe one day. I'm sure there are ways if you have the means. But I find it doesn't matter as much as I once thought it did.'

Jess's mind was spinning. She had her brother back, well, her half-brother, really, but she wasn't one to quibble. And she was optimistic that she and Darren would be able to work things out eventually and they'd be a family again. No better way to start a new year. She couldn't hold back the joy bubbling up inside her.

'What about Laura?' she said and watched Jake's face cloud.

'I probably don't deserve it, but I hope and pray she gives me a second chance.'

Laura couldn't remember leaving the kitchen light on. She slammed the car door. Alice had determinedly filled their time with doing things. They'd been somewhere posh for lunch, where they'd quaffed champagne cocktails and pigged out on seafood. And as Alice had people dropping in whenever they were home, Laura hadn't had a chance to mope. The sun had set on another day and now she was home in Potters Junction again, and Laura was caught unawares by how happy and relieved she felt to be there. But the kitchen light?

In the semi-darkness she unloaded the car, wheeled her small suitcase onto the cement path, past the fragrant vegetable patch, through the puddles on the path. She stopped in her tracks. Why were there puddles on the path? It had been another hot day and there wasn't a cloud in sight. Oh no, she thought, shoulders sagging, a leaking pipe would be impossible to get fixed at this time of year. The water would have to be turned off at the meter and she'd have to call a plumber in the morning. But, damnit, the puddles reminded her of Jake.

Laura tightened her grip on the suitcase handle and trudged towards the house.

She sensed him before she saw him. Heat chased the shivers across her skin.

'Jake?' she whispered into the gloom.

He was on his feet. 'I was beginning to think you were never coming home.'

Home.

She tried to swallow but her throat wouldn't cooperate. Jake was here, on her back verandah. Her instinct was to launch herself into his arms, but common sense prevailed. His leaving was too fresh in her mind, and in her heart.

'Why are you here? How did you get in? I locked the house. Oh God, are Jess and the boys all right?'

'Jess and the boys are fine, I remembered where you hid the spare key, and I'm here because you are, Laura.'

He stood stock-still, poised for her response. Without a word she walked around him, onto the verandah and into the house. He followed her inside, blinking in the brightness.

'How long for this time, Jake?' she said with her back to him. 'Until the house is sold? The farm on the market? A job comes up in Uzbekistan, or somewhere else as faraway and unreachable?' She dumped her bag on the dresser and started when she felt his hand on her shoulder.

'At least look at me while you bawl me out,' he said. She shook him off but turned to face him, her expression intractable.

'I don't blame you for being angry with me, Laura. I've been angry with myself. I've felt anger, regret, remorse, sorrow.' His voice was gentle, the pain on his face apparent. 'Take your pick. But then it hit me what I needed to do, and I let hope creep into the mix.' He tilted his head to the side. 'Was I right to hope, Laura?'

She crossed her arms tightly, wouldn't look him in the eye. 'I'm not just a thing, Jake, that you can toss aside when you get bored or something better comes up. None of us are. And you didn't answer my question, how long this time?'

'Twelve months to start with. I promised Dad I'd stick around and help Jess for a year. I don't know what'll happen after that, but I'd like to think whatever it was, it would be with you.'

Her arms dropped to her sides. She studied his face, perplexed. 'Why did you leave the way you did, if you knew you were coming back? Why didn't you tell me you were coming back? You just walked out. You didn't really even say goodbye.'

He moved away from her, pushed his fingers through his hair. And then it hit her.

'You weren't going to come back, were you?' Her heart felt as if it had been plunged into icy water. 'But then your conscience got the better of you, didn't it? And you thought, if I have to be here for a year to fulfil a deathbed promise, then why not have someone to keep my bed warm while I am.'

'No, Laura, that is not what I thought,' he said. 'You, more than anyone, knew how screwed up I was when I came back that first time.'

Laura's jaw began to ache. She tried to relax. He pulled out a chair from the table. 'Please can we sit down? Hear me out, that's all I ask. Then if you want me to go, I will.'

She sat down reluctantly, mentally braced herself. Could she bear any more disappointment? He pulled out another chair, turned it so he was facing her and sat down. He reached for her hands and she let him take them in his, told herself the feel of his skin against hers wouldn't make any difference to how she felt about what he said.

'I love you, Laura,' he said and she closed her eyes, wanted to curse him for not playing this fair. 'That day, when you described how it felt to be in love – I felt the same way about you. It nearly killed me to leave.' He squeezed her hands and she opened her eyes.

'I won't lie to you, not now or not ever, but the thought of leaving and not coming back did cross my mind. No-one else knew what Neill had asked me to do. He was dead. And when it comes to my family, I've been shirking my responsibilities for a long time.'

Laura could see a vein pounding in his neck and she appreciated how hard this was for him.

'This might sound weird, but it was like I had to go, so I could come back because I wanted to, not stay because I had to.'

'You needed for the choice to be yours,' she said softy, and he nodded.

He lifted his hand, caressed her cheek with his fingertips. 'When it came to you, Laura, there was never a choice to be made. It was you from the get-go, but I didn't think I was worthy of you. In hindsight, I think I started falling in love with you out there on the road that day.' His features softened. 'There you were, standing in the middle of nowhere, all legs and righteous indignation. Deep down I knew then I was lost.'

'You could have killed us both,' she said.

'I know. And I gave myself one hell of a fright. You woke me up, Laura. To coin a phrase of Jess's, you forced me to take my head out of my arse long enough to see what was really happening around me. And seeing how you'd picked yourself up, dusted yourself off and got on with it after what had happened, it left me speechless.'

'I still have my moments, but I know I'm all right.'

The fridge rattled to life. It was stuffy in the house after being shut up for three days. Laura licked her lips.

'I need a drink of water,' she said. He tightened his grip on her hands, stopping her from getting up.

'I need to know, Laura. Where does this leave us? Was I right to hope?'

She glanced down to where their hands were intertwined, just how she'd wanted them to be. She looked into his eyes. 'I love you, Jake, but you hurt me when you walked out like you did.'

She stood up and this time he let her fingers slip out of his.

'Laura, please forgive me. I know how much you've already lost,' he said, his voice ragged. 'You were the last person I ever wanted to hurt.'

She took two bottles of water out of the fridge, handed him one, cracked the lid on hers.

'Tell me, what exactly were you hoping for? For us?'

He fiddled with the bottle in his hand. 'You and me, here,' he said and gave the house an encompassing scan. 'I'd help Jess with the farm, you'd work, and if you wanted me to I could help you finish the renovations. I want to make it work, Laura.'

'I'm not sure how long I'll stay in Potters Junction. Milt Burns isn't well and I've promised him I'll stay for three months. I don't know what I'll do after that. There's my job in Adelaide, my house.'

'Laura, I love you. I know we'll be able to make this work, no matter what happens. And I promise, no more secrets.'

She regarded him for several long moments.

'Please don't ever stop talking to me, Jake. I do love you, and I want what's between us to work, more than anything. But now? Well, I'm hot, thirsty and so tired.' She swallowed down half the bottle of water, wiped her mouth with the back of her hand. Then she studied him through narrowed eyes.

'Do you think it's too early to go to bed?' she said and raised her eyebrows. A slow grin spread over his face.

'No, not at all, I'm feeling a bit tired myself,' he said and faked a yawn. He carefully placed his bottle of water on the table, took hers and put it down beside his. He opened his arms and she willingly went into them.

Acknowledgements

Thank you again, Ali Watts and Clementine Edwards at Penguin Random House, for your ongoing guidance and advice. A special thank you to Dr Alison Edwards for taking time out of your busy schedule to read and provide feedback. To my family for believing in me, especially my sister, Sandra Watson, who's been there beside me every step of the way. To my friends and writing colleagues, life is far richer because of you. And to my readers, thank you all from the bottom of my heart!

ALSO BY MEREDITH APPLEYARD

Meghan Kimble is finally following her dream of working as a country GP. Her first stop is remote Magpie Creek, and as the new girl in town she's attracting more than her fair share of attention.

The whole community has been waiting for someone like Meghan, but no one is more interested than forthright farmer Sean Ashby, who's not shy about making his intentions known.

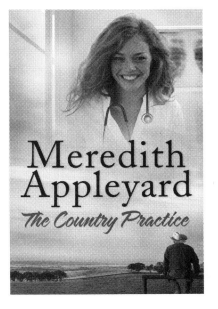

Meghan is determined to keep her mind on the job, but in such a tiny town it proves impossible to separate business from pleasure . . . and from pain.

'A page-turning romance with a medical flavour capturing the essence of rural Australia. Meredith Appleyard is a fresh new country voice.' TRICIA STRINGER

'A beautiful and intriguing tale about country life.' WEEKLY TIMES

'This sweet tale puts a twist on the rural-romance formula . . . An author to watch in the genre.' HOBART MERCURY